TANGLE OF RUIN

TANGLE OF MAGIC
BOOK SIX

J.E. NEAL

To all of my readers—
Thank you for coming on this adventure with me. There's so much more
to come

CHAPTER 1
HELP
~DAN VINDICO~

Still feeling vile and trying desperately to both figure out what to do and how to calm Fionna down, Dan flung the front door open.

Jeff looked absolutely exhausted.

"Thank you for coming. I'm sorry," Dan apologized.

Jeff had been to school, then gone to work, then gone to Georgetown to have dinner with Becca, before he'd gone back to work. When Dan had phoned him, he'd gotten permission from Portwood to come over to the Vindicos.

"It's fine, sir. I'm sorry this happened. I racked my brain all the way over here. You're sure you never put one of those drives in your personal laptop?" Jeff asked again as he hung his coat on the rack and entered the living room. Fionna was sipping tea. Her breaths were still shuddering through her. She'd been crying for the past half hour.

"Baby, I swear to you no one will ever see those. I will figure this out," Dan vowed to her again. He prayed he wasn't lying. Fionna managed a slight nod.

"And no, I'm not certain I never put one of those damn drives in my personal laptop. Sometimes I didn't want to carry both around with me, but I swear I don't remember when I might've done it. I've certainly never backed my phone up to my Venton laptop." Dan wrapped Fionna back up in his arms as he answered Jeff's questions.

Jeff nodded his understanding and offered Fionna a hesitant smile. He looked rather uncomfortable.

"Can you think of anytime when you handed your phone to anyone, or sometime that you weren't with your phone? Could you have set it down in a class or something?"

"It's possible, but I can't think of when I would've done that either."

"I was thinking since neither of us wants me to see what's in that email, maybe I could cast your laptop first and delete all of the graphics from your emails. Then I can try to trace it back."

Fionna's energy eased slightly.

"That's perfect. Thank you." Dan allowed himself to breathe by reminding himself that he had to be alive to choke the motherfucking son of a bitch who had seen pictures of his baby and was threatening to flood the Internet and media sources with them if Dan didn't cough up two hundred and fifty thousand dollars by the end of January.

"I'm okay. Go help him," Fionna whispered with her chin trembling again.

"No one else will ever see those. I will figure this out, and then we are getting the hell out of Arlington. You never have to leave the farm if you don't want to."

Jeff's jaw clenched as he casted Dan's personal laptop along with the one assigned him from Venton.

Dan began to allow himself to treat this as a case that wasn't so personal. They'd emailed the photos to his personal laptop, but they'd called him Mentor Vindico. That had been their first mistake. He began his tally.

Jeff shook his head in disbelief. "Whoever is doing this has some balls, I'll say that. This is yet another digital crime. I think the same hackers are behind it. But to mess with you…."

"Yeah, well, trust me. I plan to live up to my reputation."

"See, here's the thing." Jeff gestured to a diagnostic page he'd pulled up on Dan's Mac and then something similar on the Venton PC. "I've been going over those drives from the paper your dad assigned, and I eventually found the well-hidden program that's been copying your hard drive and sending the information back. I can see it working here on your Venton laptop. That's what I've been working on every night at the hospital with Bec. But I don't see it running on your Mac. Whoever programmed this is a genius. It must detect which operating system is running and embed itself differently. All of the Venton computers are PCs, so that's the only one I've identified."

Dan glanced back at Fionna. He couldn't believe he'd allowed this to happen. Those images were for his eyes only, and the vile vengeance he'd carried in his soul for so many years came surging back through his veins. This would not happen. He would not allow it.

"I need to know who's doing this. I need every copy of those pictures destroyed. She will always be Fionna Styler, the most beloved Receiver to ever challenge for the Arlington Angels, America's sweetheart. I cannot let people see her like that."

"I know, sir. I'm sorry. I've been so busy with work and so worried about Becca I must've missed something."

"No, it's not you." Dan sighed out his regret. "I was a disaster when I took this fucking job." He threw his hand vengefully toward the laptop. Jeff's expression softened. "She was pregnant, and you know everything that had happened. Everyone knows everything that had happened." Dan couldn't seem to stop talking.

Everything he'd done wrong and everything it stood to cost the only woman in the world he cared about filtered through his mind and out of his mouth. "I knew I was going to hate it from the moment I signed the papers. I was trying to keep her safe, and instead..." He shook his head. "This all got dumped in my lap on the first fucking day. I wasn't ready. I tried to play mentor and detective, and I'm really only good at one of those full-time jobs, not to mention that the only thing I really wanted to do was be here with her."

He glanced back at Fionna. She'd curled up in her ball in the corner of the sofa with her quilt and her phone. When a hint of a grin played on her lips, he knew she was texting Garrett. He was the only human alive who could've made her smile right then.

Dan wanted desperately to hold her. She normally curled up in that ball in his lap and in his shield, but instead, he was the one that stood to hurt her yet again.

Harrowed memories choked him. Her swollen, exhausted eyes dark from the depths of her depression. Her being sick every morning but insisting it was the flu. She'd looked him right in the eye and lied to him day after endless day. She was terrified to tell him the truth. She grew more and more despondent with each passing hour, and it had all started one afternoon when he'd come home from the office to find her curled up in her ball on that sofa.

Jeff gave Dan a sorrowful nod. "Let's get this figured out."

"Oh, trust me, I'm going to figure this out, and then we're getting the hell out of Arlington." A sudden thought occurred to Dan. "Are you and Becca looking to move anytime soon? You'll be making Elite pay as soon as Ramier leaves for Boston, right?"

"Honestly, with Bec in the hospital, I hadn't really thought about it. We talked about it some after Portwood offered me the job, but I don't know. It's gonna be tough in our place with a newborn. If we make it that far." Jeff let his own terror fall from his lips as well.

"She's gonna be okay."

"Yeah, she is better in the hospital. She's getting pretty big. He's growing. She just can't really move or do much."

"I'll gladly cut the cost of this house if you want it. You'd be less than ten minutes to work. You could come home for lunch and see Becca and the baby."

Jeff's mouth hung open. "Mentor Vindico, we can't afford this house. I mean, it's kind of big, and I'd have to talk to Becca."

"Talk to her. I'll cut you a deal. I have to get Fionna out of here. No ties back. She doesn't belong here, and I'm not sure how well she's going to handle dozens of strangers coming through here while she's trying to take care of Halia. Receivers need a safe space that's all their own." He stated one of the many things Tutu had taught him about loving an Empathic Receiver. "On top of all of this, I cannot take that away from her."

"I'll ask Becca." Jeff looked simultaneously thrilled and overwhelmed as he turned back to the laptop screens. He seemed to see things Dan had no hope of ever seeing. He casted both laptops and leaned in. He lifted the screened projections up inside of his shield and studied them. It was phenomenal to watch.

"This email links me straight back to the Venton servers just like all the others. Whoever is doing this, they've harnessed one of the Venton servers, and all of the emails come from there. I need to get in there and cast those machines."

"Done. Let's go." Dan stood. He was finished. He wasn't going to allow his wife's body to be gawked at all over the Internet. This was personal, and they'd fucked with the wrong guy this time.

"I'm not sure how much I can get done by tomorrow morning. I may have to be up there for a few nights," Jeff explained.

"I'll call my dad on the way. We're getting this done. Whatever you need, name it."

Dan moved to Fionna on the couch. "I don't know when I'll be home. Are you okay for a little while?"

"I'm fine," Fionna assured him, but it was one of the biggest lies she'd ever told. Dan couldn't leave her there grappling with the what-ifs. He grabbed his phone. He started to call Garrett but then remembered Kaimi hadn't been feeling well. Garrett had left work before their last class to go check on her. Dan went with option number two.

"When you call me now, do I answer Officer Lawson, or hey man, how's it going?" Rainer chuckled.

"Either is fine. Do you think you and Emily or just Emily could come hang out with Fionna tonight? Jeff and I are heading up to Venton. He's gonna cast his way into the Venton servers."

"Uh, well," Rainer considered. "Logan and Adeline are here hanging out. Would you like a little help on both sides? Ad and Em could come see Fionna, and we could go as your Iodex escorts."

"That'd be great. I'll take all the help I can get this time."

"We'll meet you at Venton. Emily and Adeline are heading to your house now."

CHAPTER 2

RIGHT IN FRONT OF HIM

J eff fell into the Ferrari beside Dan. "If I can't figure this out by the end of the month, are you gonna pay?"

"You never pay a ransom. Portwood should've taught you that." Dan floored the Ferrari. The car jolted forward. The speed equated to his anger.

"He did. I just didn't know if you were thinking about it. I'd go nuts if someone had pictures of Becca like that. Not that I even have pictures of Becca like that," Jeff stammered uncomfortably.

"No," Dan huffed. "I could sell this or empty some of our bank accounts, but all I would have done is given this prick more resources, and they still have pictures of my wife. All that happens in a blackmail case when the money is paid is that you've delayed the threat. I'm not buying a few more weeks. I will end this long before January thirty-first if I have to break into every Venton student's home until I find what I'm looking for."

"Could we do that?" Jeff seemed terrified that if he couldn't break the case that it would be his fault if pictures of Fionna went viral.

"Don't tempt me."

"Okay, but this is a little different." Jeff seemed to muster courage as they drove.

"Different how?"

"Whoever is doing this has gone after you and Mrs. Vindico this time, not just kids. All the other emails we've traced have been to students who are afraid of what might happen if their parents find out that they've been buying tests or using or whatever it is, but this is different. This is a crime against you, and you're an adult. Selling or even distributing photographs of someone is illegal unless they've signed away their rights to the images. It isn't highly prosecuted, but it is a law. You can take legal action where everyone else won't because they've also done something wrong. It just seems like an insane move to make."

"Like whoever's behind this thinks they can't be caught," Dan concluded for him.

Jeff nodded as Dan phoned his father.

❧

Chief of Elite Iodex Landon Portwood

"Hey, John, you didn't have to work late. I know you and Kendra are trying to get everything packed for the big move." Landon was exhausted himself. He needed to get home to Julie. He missed her and missed feeling their little girl roll and kick in her severely protruding belly. He reminded himself that he'd come in several hours late after taking Julie for her appointment with Adeline and then out to breakfast and shopping for their little one.

He was also worried. He hadn't expected Ramier to be moving quite so soon. Jeff still hadn't tested out of school, and Elite had to have a technology officer.

Jeff's frantic explanation that someone at Venton had photographs stolen from Dan's phone of Fionna in extremely compromising positions swam through his psyche again. He couldn't imagine how Dan must be reacting. The guy never seemed to catch a break. Landon had known Dan would hate being a mentor, but even he'd thought at least Fionna and the girls would be out of harm's way.

"Yeah, I need to head on. I can't believe it's my last week. I'm ready to get moved in though. Little tired of eating takeout." Ramier chuckled. "Can I talk to you for just a second before I go?" He handed Landon a rather mundane looking manilla folder.

"I thought I'd let you decide how you want to handle this."

"What is this?" Landon flipped open the folder. His eyes landed on the many varied screen names of their white hat hacker.

"I thought it was odd the whiz kid couldn't figure this guy out. Strenton's outrunning me at barely twenty-one. I was never that good. I'll never be that good. So, I thought I'd take a look. I'm pretty sure he doesn't want to see what's right in front of him."

Landon flipped through the couple of pages in the folder until he landed on the last document. His eyes goggled. "Are you certain?"

"Yeah. The way they work is even basically the same. Jeff's much better than his sperm donor, but...he's your white hat. Maybe he knows it's Jeff he's helping. Maybe he's trying to make amends the only way he knows how." John shrugged.

"He never even stuck around to see him be born." Landon tossed the file folder on his desk.

"Are you going to tell him?"

"I don't know. He's already a disaster. Becca's not doing well. Logan told me Adeline is worried the baby isn't going to survive. He still hasn't taken his final exams. Now, Dan's got him out trying to figure out this disaster at Venton. I'm not sure how much more the kid can take."

John nodded his agreement. "I can't believe this is happening to Dan again. Listen, I think I'm gonna stay on until we get this figured out. I owe that much to Dan. If I can help him some way, I want to."

"I wish he'd call me," Landon huffed. "He doesn't have to take down a gang of vigilante kids on his own. None of the students being blackmailed will come forward and ask Iodex to help. They're all terrified because they've all either broken school rules or actual Realm laws. Threatening Dan is just as illegal, but he's the only person who hasn't done anything wrong in the eyes of the law. All he has to do is ask me, and Iodex can blow the case wide open."

"Yeah, but you know Dan. He's not gonna risk anyone else seeing Fionna like that. Not even you. The fewer people he's got in on this the more of her sanity and privacy he saves. You'd be out ripping people's heads off if this was Julie. Plus, you know he's got Lawson and Haydenshire out there, and he already has Garrett up at the school with him. He'll call you when he needs you."

Suddenly, Landon's cell rang in his pocket.

John stood. "I'll see you tomorrow."

Landon gave him a nod as he answered his cell. He was unable to believe who was calling. "Hey, Dan, are you okay?"

"No. I need some help."

CHAPTER 3

STRATEGIC SAFETY
~DAN VINDICO~

Dan blinked constantly as he pulled the Ferrari into the garage.

"I'll figure it out. I swear," Jeff pledged yet again.

"I know you will. It's four in the morning. Just crash here." Dan wasn't really in the mood for company nor was he in any shape to argue. Jeff seemed to sense this.

"Are you sure, sir?"

"Absolutely." Dan eased open the door and gestured Jeff inside. He pointed to the guest bedroom as he moved past.

"Whatever you want in the fridge, it's yours. I'm gonna get a few hours' sleep before I go back to that hell hole."

"I'm just gonna crash, but thank you, sir. I swear I will not let these morons do this to you and Mrs. Vindico. I'll figure this out."

"I know. Sleep and eat and then we'll go back to work." Dan slipped in the door to his and Fionna's bedroom. Pain seared through his chest as he took in his precious baby surrounded by their beautiful girls. He momentarily debated sleeping on the couch, but he wanted to be in the middle of it all.

Aida was curled up right beside Fionna, and Halia was sleeping soundly on her mother's chest. Swallowing down the terror that had taken up residence in the marrow of his bones, Dan undressed and pulled on a pair of sweat-shorts. He slid in beside Aida and tried not to take up too much room.

"Hey," Fionna's timid whisper had his heart thundering.

"Hey, baby. I'm sorry. I didn't mean to wake you. I'll go sleep downstairs." He forced himself to sit back up.

"No." Fionna shook her head. "I only meant for us to lie down together, but we all fell asleep."

He edged closer to her. She leaned around Aida and managed to wind herself to the side so she could lay her head on his shoulder. A smile formed on his lips as all of his girls were now against him. "I can never tell you how sorry I am." The need to tell her suddenly had sleep far from his mind.

"Dan, this isn't your fault. It was my idea to make that video, and I know you. You'll catch these guys. I can feel it this time. I called Tutu and…."

"What did Tutu say?" He cradled her closer. Aida turned to her side and wound herself around his muscular thigh. She nuzzled her head in his lap and fell back into a deep sleep. Dan chuckled as he kept Fionna and Halia embraced on his chest and began tenderly running his fingers through Aida's hair.

"That you weren't going to shut me out this time." Fionna's eyes were still swollen as they begged for her grandmother's prediction to be true. The moonlight shone through their windows and reflected her anguish. Dan nodded. As he'd paced the halls at Venton and Rainer and Logan had tried their best to cheer him up, he'd tallied his past mistakes.

As she'd seen it, her choices had been to get rid of a child she wanted or keep it and lose her career and all of her income without so much as an engagement ring on her finger or any kind of commitment from Dan. She also knew that if Wretchkinsides found out the child was Dan's, he would hunt her down and kill her and the baby.

Dan had realized what was wrong, and he'd convinced himself she would be fine as long as he ended Wretchkinsides. He'd let her sit day after day in agony all alone, while he worked harder and longer and accomplished nothing but making her more miserable.

This time would be different. He didn't have to fight this battle alone. He couldn't. He needed his friends, and more importantly, he needed his wife to stand by him, and she needed to fight with him instead of feeling like she had to fight *for* him when she had nothing left to give.

"She's right," Dan vowed. "Do you feel like talking for a few minutes?"

"Of course."

"I need you," he began, and tears of relief began leaking from her eyes. She gave a hopeful nod. "I need you to help me do this. I have to figure this out before some moron takes something from you that I will not allow. Something from us. That isn't an option."

"I want to help you. Just tell me how."

Halia shifted slightly on Fionna's chest, and Dan slid his hand from Aida's hair to Halia's back. He patted her gently until she curled up in the safety of her mother's arms and located her fingers with her mouth.

"This is going to be a rough few weeks. So, I was wondering…" Dan hated this part of his plan. It made him sick, but he couldn't see a reasonable alternative. He needed to know that his children were not going to get caught up in this sick game.

"What?" Fionna urged. "Anything, just tell me."

Dan kissed the side of her head and drew a deep breath. "I need you up at Venton as much as you can possibly be there. You're the strongest Receiver in this Realm or any other. These fuckers are walking around that school with pieces of us they have no right to have or to see, and they sure as hell have no right to sell. I don't know what else they'll do. I don't know how far they might be willing to go, and I know I always said that people who have nothing left to lose are the most dangerous, and that's true. But, people who think they can't be caught might be even more volatile.

"I think they sent that threat because Garrett has been up at the school with me. It was along the same lines as how they set up the test vault surge when my father took over Venton. Whoever this is, they have traps set anytime they think I've gotten too close. They're scared. I don't know what they'll do when Iodex shows up there tomorrow. If you're with me, or Garrett, or all of Iodex, we can keep you safe, but sweetheart…" Dan shook his head. He was both furious that he was having to make this plea and relieved that he could.

"What?"

"I think we need to send the girls on to Kauai with Garrett and Kaimi. They're leaving Friday after lunch. I want our babies to stay there where they're safe and healthy and happy. Where no one can get to them. You know they'll be safe on the farm with Tutu and Papa. They can go ahead and enroll Aida in school, or we can do that when we get out there. We need to get out of here as soon as I end this. It isn't safe for any of us here anymore."

"As soon as *we* end this," Fionna corrected him. Then her body folded in around Halia as she broke down over their baby girl.

"Mommy!" Aida awoke in a panic and wrapped her arms around Fionna. Her mother's despair was so great in that moment it had awoken her.

"You can fly out there whenever you want. You can go with them if you want to. I understand, and I swear I will work day in and day out until I find these…people," he amended his original wording since Aida was awake.

"What about the house and everything?" Fionna managed after several long minutes of wrapping herself up in her precious girls.

"I'll pay someone to pack everything up while we're working. We can stay in a hotel room if we need to." The plans formed in Dan's mind as he spoke.

"Jeff and Becca are going to buy our house," she informed him in a reconciled sigh.

"Did you talk to Becca?"

"No," Fionna whispered, and Dan understood. Her grandmother had allowed her to briefly tap into the rhythms of her island, and she'd gained insight into their future. "So, if you want, we could leave most of the furniture for them. Shipping it is crazy." She shuddered as she fought back another onslaught of tears. Her rhythms were frantic momentarily and then they ran low into the depths of despondency. Her body couldn't seem to regulate them. It vacillated between determined strength and hopeless terror.

"Fi, stop planning for a minute and look at me." Her terror-filled eyes sought his. "Can you do this? Can you send them on, or do you need to go with them?"

"I can do it. I need to help you. I need to be with you. I can feel that. But I can't stand it." She broke down again, and Dan wasn't certain his heart would survive this time. It had been broken and repaired so many times before. He wasn't sure he could do it again. He managed to nod as he kept his precious family wrapped up in his arms.

CHAPTER 4
TIME GOES ON

Two hours later, Dan was downing a third cup of Fionna's outstanding coffee. She seemed to need to batten down the hatches. She'd cooked a full breakfast and heaped it onto Dan, Jeff, Aida, Garrett, and Kaimi's plates. Dan noted that Kaimi looked pale and sickly.

"Fi." Dan heard Garrett corner her in the kitchen.

"What?" She bristled.

"Come here to me."

Dan stayed in the breakfast area though he could see her fold herself into Garrett's tender embrace. This had happened many times throughout Dan and Fionna's relationship, but this was the first time Dan hadn't had to quell his own jealousy. Garrett was her best friend, and though he was nothing more, he was also nothing less. "I'm not gonna let some prick do this to you. Okay? Never. I will not let this happen."

Fionna nodded against his chest as he swayed her in the kitchen for several long minutes. Kaimi offered Dan a weary smile.

"They're really important to each other. At first, that freaked me out, but she really is a part of him, and he's a part of her. I think they make each other better people. If you'd moved without Garrett, I don't think she would have been okay," she whispered.

"Yeah." Dan nodded. "And you figured that out a hell of a lot quicker than I did." Kaimi chuckled, but it turned into a cough immediately.

"I promise we will end this." Garrett released Fionna and kissed the top of her head.

"I know. I'm just kind of crazy right now."

"I will take care of my girls. Dan and I will find this shitbag, and we will end this before anybody sees anything."

"Thank you."

Dan slipped into the kitchen and smiled as she slid from Garrett's embrace into his.

Kaimi whisked to Garrett's side. His face lit in an instant.

"It's okay. You know Dan and Garrett would never let this happen to you, and we'll get you packed up, and then as soon as it's all over we can move." Her body didn't seem to have the strength to give enthusiasm to her vow. Fionna grinned and nodded though she was still clinging fiercely to Dan.

"Let's go. We need to get everything ready. Let's go scare the shit out of several students and see who needs a shovel to get out," Garrett huffed.

Jeff was telling Aida about all of the times he'd moved from one apartment to another growing up. Dan appreciated him spinning the tale to sound as if he'd gone from one thrilling adventure to another instead of being repeatedly evicted. Aida was enthralled.

"But did you ever have to move without your mommy?" she asked, and Dan's heart fissured.

Garrett stepped in. "Hey, Aida Mae, do you want me to take you to school?" He knew precisely how to bring a grin back to her timid face.

"Okay." She downed her orange juice before she raced to his side.

"I'll see you at Venton in an hour." Garrett took Aida's hand and led her out the door.

"Dan." Portwood raced to Dan's side as he headed into the admin building. The bile that flooded Dan's throat as he stepped on the campus grounds tasted of vengeance and wrath.

"Hey, thanks for doing this." Dan shook Portwood's hand.

"Last time I checked, this was my job, and it was also my understanding that commanders of state Iodex branches were to be treated as National Iodex officers in any jurisdiction outside of their own. Therefore, we've received a threat against a National Iodex Officer, and as you well know, my friend, we will not stand for that."

Dan gave a genuine chuckle. He certainly had known all of that. It just hadn't quite occurred to him yet. Dan threw his office door open and longed to pack up the photos of Fionna and the girls. He wanted anything that meant something to him out of that space. He wanted to move on.

"I should just hand in my resignation and let Mentor Jackson take over. I'm not doing any good here. I don't even want to be here." He collapsed the framed photo of Fionna in the white gauzy shirt that hung open over her pregnancy-swollen belly. The one with Dan on his knees kissing Halia's swell. He couldn't stand to think of the people that had seen even that level of intimacy between them. The need to shut everyone out of their lives reverberated in the very cells of his body.

He grabbed a box that had contained three car batteries Dan had used to show his senior lab classes how to harness the contained energy when involved in an urban assault. He frantically dumped out the remaining order slips and packing material and began placing every photograph of Fionna or the girls inside the box.

Deep concern etched Portwood's face as he watched Dan work. With a shrug, he eased Dan's many commendations and framed medals from the wall and helped him.

He hesitantly grasped Dan's massive bicep. "I wondered something."

"What?" Dan began pulling books off his bookshelves. With an eye roll, he tossed *Oral Boards for Elite Iodex* on the floor and picked up the next book.

"I talked to Governor Haydenshire this morning, and he thought maybe you and I could run this one together, for old times' sake. He wanted me to bring you this." Portwood gently laid Dan's former Elite Chief Badge on the desk. "And as long as I'm running this case, could you not quit? You're the linchpin here. You're the guy being threatened, and you have more access to these kids than any of us."

Dan picked up the badge. The weight of it in his hand held everything he'd gained and everything he'd lost in his relatively short life span.

"Landon, you're a hell of a Chief. You don't have to do this."

"I know." Portwood chuckled. "But I'd be honored to solve this last one with you, Chief Vindico. Maybe we'll get to work together once you take over Hawaii, but I doubt we'll cross paths too often, so let's make this one count."

"I'd be happy to swear you back in, son." Governor Vindico appeared at the door. Governor Haydenshire was standing behind him.

Dan drew a deep breath and considered the offer. He'd learned a great deal in the past year. He'd learned who he was, who he needed, and who he couldn't live without. He was meant to be an Iodex officer. It was the only thing he was really any good at, but moving back onto the National Battalion wasn't what he wanted. He wanted nothing at all to do with Arlington or DC ever again. His heart resided on a tiny island in a home with his beautiful island girls.

"If you happen to be the one to find these extremely misguided children, Daniel, you have no jurisdiction to arrest anyone outside of the state of Hawaii," the Crown Governor reminded him gently.

"Okay." He nodded. "Thank you."

Dan was quickly sworn back in by Portwood and his father, who stood in for Governor Willow. Dan stowed his old badge on his belt. He wasn't certain what he should feel. He was too angry and too terrified to feel anything at all.

He couldn't fathom shipping his baby girls off for the next few weeks, not hearing all about Aida's days at school. Not being there to take her to her first day at a new school. Not snuggling Halia between him and Fionna when she awoke for her evening bottle. Not hearing her sweet coos of delight when he came in the room. It was too much. He had to push the thoughts away. He reconciled their safety and his ability to focus solely on the case. The justifications quelled the ache in his heart.

Governor Vindico smiled at Portwood. "I've been thinking about what you asked me this morning about Jeff. Stephen, Mason, and I have decided that perhaps in light of everything else, we might could offer Mr. Strenton a little help as well. He's certainly more than proven his smarts here at the academy."

"I really appreciate that, sir. I wasn't sure what to do. We have to have a technology officer. In the past five months, he's helped take down eleven Internet scam companies that were stealing credit card information. And so far, he's prevented three cyberterrorist attacks on the Senate."

Governor Vindico nodded his agreement. "I know, so we think that should count for something. We told him we'd let him graduate with the grades he currently has in each of his remaining classes. No more exams. His grades stand, and he's a full-fledged Elite Iodex Officer. We discussed it with him a few minutes ago, and he seemed pretty excited."

"I'm sure." Dan couldn't halt the broad grin that spread across his face. Governor Haydenshire stepped to the side and eased Jeff forward into Dan's office. Jeff was visibly thrilled. The relief broadcast from his entire body. His shield spun in waves of elation.

"But he had a special request." Governor Haydenshire smiled.

"What's that?" Dan slapped Jeff on the shoulder. He couldn't have been more proud.

"Uh, my mom's gonna be up here in a few minutes." Jeff's eyes rolled though Dan knew he was actually pleased. "I was just kind of wondering if you'd swear me in, sir?"

The emotional roller coaster Dan had been riding since the night before was catching up with him. Emotion clogged his throat.

"I'd be honored."

As soon as Jeff's mom raced into the office, the rest of Elite followed after her. Dan made Jeff Strenton the newest member of the Elite Iodex Squadron. Portwood, Logan, Rainer, Tuttle, Ramier, Ericcson, McCoy, and Barron all whistled and applauded as Dan pinned the badge on Jeff's Iodex polo.

He hugged his mother, eliciting chuckles from his fellow officers.

"I wish Bec could have been here."

"She was." Ms. Harrickson held up Jeff's cell phone.

"Hey, baby, I'm so proud of you." Becca, who'd been watching via camera on her own cell, was sitting in a hospital bed with tears of pride leaking down her face.

Jeff was ecstatic though he tried very hard to play it cool. He quickly switched Becca off video and talked to her in private.

"All right, if I may." Dan chuckled as Portwood held his hands out for him to continue. "I want officers at every single entrance. Look frightening. Intimidate just for the hell of being intimidating. Search bags. Let's see if we can catch a few snakes that get scared and start slithering in the grass. Then we'll see if we can burn out the viper's den."

"Yes, sir," rang from *his* squadron.

CHAPTER 5

THE SQUADRON
~ELITE TECHNOLOGY SPECIALIST OFFICER JEFF STRENTON~

Since Ramier had vowed to stay on until the Venton cases were solved, he took post with Tuttle, who would effectively become Jeff's new partner. Jeff was relieved to have been stationed with Rainer and Logan.

He wasn't particularly looking forward to having Tuttle as his partner. The guy talked about nothing but sex, and Jeff was sick of hearing about Tuttle and Dan's sister, Lindley. Jeff hadn't had sex in months, and listening to Tuttle's stories tended to make his longing to be with Becca grow even stronger. He wanted nothing to do with the things that Tuttle and Lindley claimed they were into. He just wanted to be with his wife, to feel the sweet, timid tremble of her body as he eased inside of her. To feel her energy pour into him and consume his own rhythms as they fused together. Jeff choked back a whimper and shook himself.

It was still a few minutes before students would be arriving, so he joined Logan and Rainer by the vending machines. He was exhausted from the past few weeks and then only sleeping for a little while the night before. Logan and Rainer had stayed with him and Dan the entire time, so they were exhausted as well.

"How's Becca and the baby?" Rainer quizzed before he downed a Dr Pepper.

"Becca is okay as long as she doesn't move much, and Aaron's readings are strong. Adeline says his rhythms are the way they're supposed to be and everything, but Bec has to stay in the bed most of the day. She gets up every few hours to walk around, but she can't do much. She's completely miserable," Jeff admitted.

"That's rough, man." Rainer shook his head.

"I feel terrible for her. They keep her sedated a lot, and she gets casted a bunch. They're trying to get Aaron to develop faster because the sooner she can safely deliver him the better."

"Yeah, but Ad said if she can go another couple weeks, they can take the baby," Logan added hopefully as they took position at the main entrance doors.

"Yeah, but he'd have to stay in the hospital for a long time because he'd be so early, and there's a lot of complications with that."

As he discussed Becca and the baby this morning with two of his closest friends, there was still a lightness in his heart. It seemed possible now that school was officially behind him that maybe, just maybe, he really could get Becca and Aaron through this and really take care of them. He almost allowed himself to feel like an adult discussing his wife and child with his coworkers. *I'm really done with school. As soon as I get this case solved, I never have to come back here*, he had to keep reminding himself.

Students began trickling through the doors, and Jeff followed Logan and Rainer's moves. He sported a fierce scowl and let his newly acquired badge and gun show from every angle.

"What's your name?" Logan jerked a guy he'd picked at random to the side. He patted him down and went through his bag. Rainer waited another minute and repeated the action with two girls who Jeff recalled had always made snide remarks about Emily when she and Rainer had been in school.

Jeff scanned the students as they wandered inside. It was odd to try and intimidate people he'd been in class with the day before.

"What the hell?" Ben Cobson approached Jeff. "You look all official and all." He tapped Jeff's badge and grinned.

"Yeah, finally." Jeff nodded. "Just this morning actually. They took my current grades and waived my second-semester exams, so I'm here on business not for class anymore." He couldn't help but brag just a little.

"Wow. What brought all that on?" Ben sounded thrilled for Jeff.

"I can't discuss the case, but we're going to be up here for a few weeks anyway."

Ben's brow furrowed. "Oh, yeah? How come?" He gestured to Rainer and Logan and then to Portwood and Vindico who'd positioned themselves in the middle of the corridors so they could see every student that moved through the building.

Garrett Haydenshire and Chase Barron were stationed very nearby. The scowl on Garrett's face frightened Jeff, but he never would've admitted that out loud.

"I can't say." Jeff wasn't breaking any Iodex protocols. He'd worked too hard to be where he was currently standing, and he wasn't going to screw this up.

"Come on, you can tell me. I could help make you look good."

"Nah, man. I'm sorry. I really can't." Jeff refused the guilt that plagued his humanity by turning and grabbing a pre-freshman prick and forcing him to empty his backpack.

Dan Vindico

"Well, we caught three freshmen who bought and split one test." Garrett sighed as he followed Dan into the house late that afternoon.

"Yeah, I figured it would start small but not that small."

"Lots of nerves. Lots of kids heading out of classes. Your dad said by afternoon classes, half the school had left. We just need to squeeze a little tighter."

"Believe me, I plan to." Dan inhaled deeply. The house smelled amazing.

"Fi," he called as he eased in the door. He offered Kaimi a smile. She appeared even weaker than she had that morning. Panic armored in Garrett's shield as he moved to her. Halia was sound asleep in her bouncy seat on the counter, and Aida was on her stool at the counter stirring something.

Kaimi smiled as Dan approached, and it did ease the dark circles under her eyes.

"Daddy!" Aida leapt off the stool and into Dan's arms.

"Hey, baby girl. Did you have a good day?" Aida nodded solemnly and then nuzzled her head between Dan's neck and shoulder blade.

Kaimi glanced at Fionna with a great deal of concern. "She's been cooking all day. I tried to get her to pack, but she just kept making all of your and Aida's favorite things to eat. She went to the grocery store three times."

"Yeah, she does that," he and Garrett commented simultaneously.

"Hey, baby doll, that smells phenomenal." Dan wrapped his arms around Fionna from behind her. No matter what might be threatening them, he would always be her Shield. He ordered himself to act as if nothing at all was wrong. If she was coping with having to send their children away by cooking enough food to feed the Gifted army, he'd do his part to eat it and tell her how amazing it was.

"Did you find out anything today?" Fionna spun. Her eyes were frantic as she slid to the side and checked a batch of Hawaiian sweet rolls that were rising in their oven. Dan's mouth watered.

"Uh, yeah, kind of," he hemmed. "I have a few ideas I'm planning to implement as soon as we get the girls settled."

"You're supposed to let me help you."

"Baby, you are, but we have to get the girls packed, and I have to know that you're okay with all of this."

Fionna nodded and seemed to slowly climb her way back to their terrifying reality. "Okay, I made most of your favorites. It was a little too cold to grill steaks, but I made meatloaf and crab cakes and huli huli chicken and fried chicken and four kinds of potatoes. I also fixed that sausage and potato soup you like. Oh, and jambalaya, and tom kha gai soup. And I made sweet rolls for tomorrow morning."

Dan forced a smile. "It looks amazing. I can't wait to dig in, and we can eat on it for the next few days. Then when the groceries are gone, we'll just go out, okay?"

"Okay." Fionna managed a smile and then lifted Halia from her seat though she was still asleep. Fionna kept the baby cradled on her shoulder the entire time they ate. Garrett and Dan shared concerned expressions. Kaimi picked at her food and seemed to pale with each bite she managed to consume.

"Sweetheart, are you okay? Do you want me to call Adeline?" Garrett finally blurted out.

"Oh, yeah. I'm just a little tired. I think I may be coming down with something," Kaimi confessed.

Garrett nodded. "I think Adeline's at Georgetown tonight. Let's go by there on the way home."

Dan noted that it sounded much more like a command than a request, but he didn't disagree.

"Do you want me to make you some more tea?" Fionna offered.

"It's okay. You have so much going on."

"Well, here, at least let me give you some to take back to your apartment." Fionna retrieved a tin of tea bags from Tutu's that she placed beside Kaimi.

"Thank you. I could bring you back some from the farm if you want."

Aida's head shot up from her plate. "Aren't you and Uncle Garrett moving with me and Halia?"

Dan lifted her into his lap. "Uncle Garrett and Aunt Kaimi are going to stay with you for a few days on the farm, but then they're going to come back. And in just a few weeks, Mommy and me and Uncle Garrett and Aunt Kaimi will be there with you all the time, okay?"

Aida nodded though her chin began to tremble. "I need to take care of Nanea and Sophie and Davi." She raced from the table and into her room. Dan felt like he was being stabbed brutally. How could he have allowed this to happen?

"I'll talk to her." Fionna handed Halia to Dan.

He took the baby but stood with her. "We'll talk to her," he corrected.

"I'll clean up, and we'll get out of here. I want you to go see Adeline anyway." Garrett began clearing away dishes and the copious amounts of food still left on the table.

Aida was on her bed with Nanea. She was brushing her long hair and telling the doll about the farm. She was trying so hard to be brave it crushed Dan. Halia awoke with a big yawn that contorted her entire little face. She grinned when she saw Aida. Dan laid her on the bed beside her big sister.

"I talked to Mrs. Powell today," Fionna soothed.

"You did?"

"Yes, and she said that I can bring Halia to meet your class tomorrow since you're going to be moving to the farm on Friday." Fionna's hand laced through Dan's, and she drew from him deeply. Dan's eyes closed as he concentrated and sent soothing rhythmic pulses of strength through to his wife.

Aida nodded but wouldn't raise her head.

Dan took Aida's hand. "Baby, please tell me what's wrong. You love the farm, and Mommy and I will be there as soon as we can, okay?"

"I think Halia is afraid to move without Daddy," Aida explained to Fionna as if Dan hadn't spoken at all.

Fionna nodded. "I know it's hard to move without Daddy. I'm sure Halia is afraid and that's normal, but she knows that you'll be with her and Tutu and Papa. She loves the farm so much. Almost as much as you and I love the farm. I can't wait to move." Dan felt Fionna allow herself a moment to pretend they weren't being driven from their home by fear and to embrace the fact that they were going home.

"But Halia's never lived on the farm without you and Daddy. And who will take care of her and throw her up in the ocean when we swim and play in the waterfall? And who will hold her if she has a nightmare? And who will keep her safe?"

Dan and Aida had always had a very close bond, but he hadn't realized fully until that moment that he wasn't just Fionna's Shield, he was also his precious baby girl's. Dan scooped her up into his arms. Her legs wound around his waist as he held her tightly.

"Papa and Kai and Uncle Garrett will keep you and Halia safe for me until I get there. You know Papa would never let anything happen to his girls." Dan squeezed his eyes shut to the emotion that threatened to overwhelm him. Aida nodded against him as she tightened her death grip around his chest.

CHAPTER 6

RISOTTO RAISES

~JEFF STRENTON~

"Hey there." Jeff eased into the hospital room. He hated going there every night. He hated seeing Becca in a hospital bed. It wounded him. His shield abhorred it.

Becca stood and threw her arms around his neck. "Congratulations."

Jeff tried not to panic as he hugged her tighter. "Careful," he warned.

"I'm okay. I'll just take my long journey to the rocker." Becca sighed as he held her hand as she took the ten steps from the bed to the rocking chair. "Why aren't you way more excited? One of us should be jumping up and down, and I can't."

He was always astonished at how upbeat she stayed in that horrible room.

"I'm sorry. If I could be here instead of you, I would." He made the same vow night after night after night. She rolled her eyes.

"Stop it. Aaron and I are fine. He's growing, and Adeline says his scans improve every day. Just a few more weeks and they can deliver him, and he'll be safer, and I can be me again. Please just be happy. You became a full-fledged Elite Iodex officer today, and Dan Vindico swore you in. You should be over the moon."

"I am. I just miss you, and it's my fault you're both in here."

"If you say that one more time, I'm going to scream and then hit you with one of the pillows on that bed," Becca sassed defiantly.

"Is that so, Mrs. Strenton?" Jeff finally allowed himself just a minute to relax and engage his wife in a little playful banter. He was certain very few marriages began with as much tension and drama as theirs had, but there was no one else he would ever want to share his life with.

"Yes, it is." Becca beamed as her hand flew to her belly. She stayed swollen due to her body's not handling the pregnancy well, and she looked much farther along than she actually was. The light in her eyes beckoned Jeff as he moved to her. She placed his hand over the spot where Aaron was moving either a little foot or hand. Jeff couldn't quite tell.

"Hey, little guy." Jeff had grown quite accustomed to speaking to his son through Becca's stomach. He was overwhelmed as he felt Aaron respond. Becca laughed and blinked back tears.

"Do you hear Daddy?" She rubbed her hands over her swell.

A knock on the door stopped Jeff from tapping in to Aaron's rhythms. He lowered the hospital gown Becca was wearing and answered the door.

"Oh, hey Jeff. Are you staying here tonight? I'll bring you an extra pillow," Adeline offered sweetly. She'd even arranged for an extended bed since Becca was going to be staying for so long so that Jeff could sleep beside her when he stayed over. He hated going home alone. He'd stayed at his mom's when he didn't stay over at the hospital or at work. The sleepless nights were catching up with him though.

"Yeah, I'll be here. Mentor Vindico didn't want anyone over at his house tonight. They're trying to get Aida and Halia ready to move without them. He's going crazy not working the case though."

Becca's broad, beaming grin had him even more thankful he could spend the whole night with her, even if trying to hold her in an extended hospital bed meant he wouldn't sleep well there either.

"Do you want something from the cafeteria?" Adeline continued.

Jeff thought for a moment and then grinned at Becca. "Actually, I just got a huge pay raise. The biggest of my whole life, I'm sure. Let me go get us something for dinner tonight. Anything you want, and we'll hang out and watch TV."

"Okay." Becca nodded.

Adeline guided Becca back to the bed and began checking the monitors that were constantly hooked around her midsection.

Jeff kissed Becca's forehead. "Passaggios good?"

"That would be amazing."

"I'll be right back." Jeff tried to think of something else he could do for her while she was stuck in a hospital room trying desperately to grow his baby boy. He'd already juiced a speaker system for her phone. He'd linked her laptop into the hospital staff Wi-Fi and casted the television in the room so that she could watch her favorite movies or shows on repeat. He'd gone by the video game store and talked one of the owners into letting him have a broken handheld console they couldn't repair. After he quickly casted and repaired it, he'd purchased several games he knew she'd like. He'd done everything he could think of to make her more comfortable and less bored, while he juggled school and work and bills on a house neither of them were ever in. Every few days, he went by the used bookstore and library and brought her all of the books she requested or that he thought she might like.

After a quick ride on the Metro, Jeff hooked his new badge over his belt and threw on his Elite jacket before he went in Passaggios, Becca's favorite Italian restaurant. They were typically very kind to Iodex officers. He explained where his wife was and that they were celebrating. The hostess fixed Jeff and Becca several large portions of baked ziti, mushroom risotto, and some of their phenomenal meatballs. She added in two salads and an entire loaf of bread. Then gave him two pieces of tiramisu for free.

"Thanks," Jeff called as he headed back to the Metro station.

A few minutes later, he eased back in Becca's room and halted as he took in Adeline and another medio talking. They were both staring at one of the Georgetown iPads.

Fear played heavily in Becca's rhythms, and Jeff's heart seized. He set the food on a nearby rolling table and moved to her. He wondered what could possibly have gone wrong in the last half hour.

"What's wrong?" Jeff demanded.

"I don't know." Becca's lip trembled.

"Oh, nothing's wrong! I'm sorry. I didn't mean to scare you. The treatments we've been doing are working better than we could've hoped." Adeline showed the iPad to Jeff and Becca. "See, his lungs are developing ahead of schedule, and he's gaining weight rapidly. If we keep them up and keep you on the IVs, I feel like we can deliver him safely in two to three weeks." Air returned to Jeff's lungs with a gasp. Becca was still clinging to Jeff's hand as she allowed that information to settle on her as well.

She'd been undergoing a relatively new form of treatment for her condition. Jeff knew she would never have been a candidate for the intense casting that was forcing the energy in Aaron's body to help him develop more rapidly if Becca were not a governor's daughter, but he certainly wasn't going to argue.

"Oh, I'm sorry, Jeff. This is Medio Winston Ellington. He's the head of the lab. He's been running all of the tests on Becca and Aaron for me," Adeline introduced Jeff.

Jeff extended his hand. "It's nice to meet you, sir."

"You too. I've heard a lot about you. Listening to your lovely wife talk, I'd had you casted as some kind of superhero," Medio Ellington offered with a kind chuckle. Heat immediately formed in Jeff's face as he tried to think of some way to respond.

"He's Libby's dad," Becca offered him a change of subject.

"Oh, right." Jeff nodded. But suddenly Medio Ellington's face turned dour. He had to force his next smile.

"Are you friends with Libby?" He began studying the iPad again.

"I see her around some. I've been so busy with school and work and being up here as much as I can, I really don't have a lot of friends."

"It sounds like you have all of your priorities in order then, so I'd say keep up the good work." Medio Ellington gave Jeff a slight nod and then headed out of the room.

A thought struck Jeff. The last time he'd seen Libby was the last day of school the year before. Her mom had posed with her for campaign photographs in front of Venton. Libby had been furious and let everyone on campus grounds know it.

CHAPTER 7

HALL PASS

"Okay, how about kind of a night off if you promise to be good?" Adeline asked.

Jeff forced his mind back to his wife and wondered what a night off might entail. "Aaron looks great, so how about if we go off the monitors for the night, and I leave you two alone. You are still on pelvic rest!" she reminded them vehemently.

Becca and Jeff both laughed. "But I think with the intense casting we did this morning and all you two have to celebrate tonight, maybe Aaron could do with a little more of his daddy's rhythms than mine. Keep it maybe PG-15, and I'll leave you alone until morning. Then it's back on the monitors, but I know this has been a rough few months. I'm going to go ahead and tentatively schedule the C-section for two and half weeks from today as long as the castings continues to work as well as they have been."

A million thoughts vied for Jeff's attention. Two and a half weeks. He tried to imagine what needed to happen between now and then. They didn't even have a crib yet, but Aaron would likely have to stay in the hospital for weeks.

He moved on to what a monitor night off meant. Jeff tried to formulate some plan that incorporated everything he'd longed to feel with his wife over the last few months. *She's still in a hospital with people everywhere.*

Becca couldn't seem to keep her eyes off Jeff's for any length of time. Deep yearning swam in their heavenly blue hue and in her rhythms though she tried to hide it from Adeline.

"The baby needs to be casted for about an hour now and then again at midnight. Are you up to that after you two eat that food that smells out of this world?" Adeline was politely ignoring the longing that permeated the air around Jeff and Becca.

"Yeah, however long they need. I'll keep them in my shield." He was unable to look anywhere but into the hungry pools of Becca's eyes.

"Eat first," Adeline reminded them as she unhooked all of the monitors from Becca's stomach. "And I'll see you in the morning." She lowered the lights in the room to a somewhat romantic glow, considering they were in a hospital room. She closed the door softly as she left.

"I know this isn't our bedroom, but we could pretend we're all alone in some romantic place." Becca's hopeful plea seared through Jeff.

"Okay." He kicked off his boots. He would do anything in the world to keep her smiling like that. He slid into the bed beside her. "Where are we?" He turned and cradled her body to his. Aaron's bump prevented him from being as close as he would've liked, but Jeff let his hands massage down her arms and then caress his son's swell.

"We're at the beach. Remember two summers ago when Dad let you come with us to Hilton Head?"

"I remember. You liked that room upstairs that had the deck off it. We hung out up there while your parents played golf all day and your brothers were off being pricks."

Becca nodded against his chest. "Yeah, and we opened the doors out to the water and just stayed up there and told Mom and Dad we were watching movies."

"I really can't believe they bought that." Jeff chuckled.

"Let's just pretend we're there all alone."

"Okay, hang on a sec." He retrieved his phone and after casting it for a split second had it playing the sounds of crashing waves endlessly. "Do you want to eat or do you want to make out in the bed some more?"

Becca's energy rolled in trilling waves of elation. Jeff wanted to get drunk on the heady energy flowing out of his wife.

"Let's eat. It smells so good, and we're on the beach celebrating the fact that you are officially Elite Technology Officer Jeff Strenton and my incredibly sexy husband."

"And what shall we do after we eat?" Jeff urged. His voice was low and raspy in his need.

"Whatever you want, Officer Strenton," she cooed, and a shuddering groan echoed from his chest.

"If you keep calling me Officer Strenton, I'm not gonna be able to keep it PG-15." He forced himself to move to the table and bring her their meal. Becca looked delighted with his predicament.

"You should tell your wife all about your day, Officer Strenton."

Jeff gave her another hungry growl as they dug into the food together. Two forks among the three large dishes was perfectly fine with both of them. He told her about their assignment to intimidate the students and then how he'd spent the day casting computer after computer. Something occurred to Jeff as his eyes fell back on the monitors that had been pushed off to the side of Becca's bed.

"BEC!" he gasped. He nearly flung the food onto the table. "Libby Ellington's father is the head of the lab here!"

"Uh…yes." Becca gave him a bewildered gaze.

"And his wife is the Senteon representative from Maryland!"

"Yes." Becca was growing more and more concerned.

"Holy shit!" Jeff frantically flipped through the contact list on his phone. He shut down the wave sounds and touched Logan's cell number.

"Libby Ellington!" he nearly shouted as soon as Logan answered.

"Jeff," Logan mocked. "My wife just gave Becca a monitor night hall pass, so if you're getting your groove thing on with your wife and calling out some other woman's name, that is marriage suicide, my friend."

Jeff rolled his eyes. "Just shut up a minute and let me tell you this and then I'm turning off my phone and…well, never mind, just listen." Becca began giggling, and Jeff winked at her as he talked rapidly. "Libby Ellington is one of the girls that Fionna identified as being high back before Thanksgiving. Her father is the head of the lab at Georgetown, and her mom is a Senteon representative! That was the evidence I hadn't thought of yet. She's definitely someone who would not want it getting out that her daughter is using. It could cost her the Maryland seat."

"And you figured all of that out during a monitor night pass? I'm impressed."

"So, you'll run all of that by Vindico and Portwood?" Jeff was getting impatient.

"Actually, Garrett and Dan did that off-the-books thing when Kaimi was in the hospital. They copied all of the Venton files out of the lab. Garrett and Kaimi are up at the hospital with Adeline now. Kaimi's sick again or something, so I'll call Garrett. I'll let him call Dan," Logan explained. "Dan won't rip his head off, and as you saw today, he is not in a good mood, not that I blame him."

"Okay, I'll see you tomorrow." Jeff ended the call. "I'm sorry, but I think I may have just broken the drug test part of these cases."

"It's okay. I mean, you're the greatest Iodex officer ever, right?" Becca stated as if that were even a remote possibility.

"Uh no, not even a little."

"Can we go back to the beach now?"

"Absolutely. No more interruptions. I promise." Jeff casted the phone again. He turned off all calls and texts and returned the beach sounds to the room as they continued to eat.

"I'm so full of baby and fluids I can't eat, and I look like a whale." Becca pushed the plates toward Jeff.

"I think you're beautiful." Her statement wounded him. She was always so upbeat. It hurt him that she couldn't see how amazing she was. "I know this pregnancy has been really rough, but I think you're so beautiful pregnant with my baby. That's probably really stupid and macho though, right?"

"No," Becca whispered. Her energy was craving to the point of desperate as she touched his hand with her fingertips. Their rhythms tried to fuse from the touch alone.

"It's the truth." Jeff shoved the rolling tray away from the bed and eased his body beside hers. "You'll probably never want to have another one, so I keep trying to memorize the way you look now with our little boy inside of you, so I'll always remember. It's incredible."

Becca's breaths came in the familiar pants that always made him ache. It had been so long since he'd watched her eyes darken and her cheeks and lips flush from desire. He let his eyes close for a moment as he tried to will composure and control.

She had the most beautiful lips he'd ever seen. He remembered thinking that just before he'd kissed her on her parents' front porch after the fall ball freshman year. That was long before he'd seen the luscious set she kept hidden from everyone but him. *My God, how did I ever get so lucky?*

"I do want to have another one." Becca's soft plea shook Jeff from his reverie. "I want to have two more at least. Adeline says it probably won't be like this again, and I do want to have more babies with you." The knowledge and confidence that he'd just earned his way into being the youngest member of Elite Iodex ever and making Elite pay filled his soul. They could afford more children if that's what she wanted. It didn't matter what she asked for, he'd find a way to give it to her.

"We'll have as many as you want." He let his thumb hesitantly brush over her full lips. If all he ever got to do in this life was to kiss those soft, sweet, hungry lips, he would die a happy man. Becca's chest was rising and falling rapidly as she let her eyes close to revel in his tender touch.

"I love you." He dipped his head to hers. He kissed her softly and let the feeling of her energy craving his wash through him. He brushed those lips with lush voracity, keeping her head cradled in his hand. Jeff felt her right hand lace through his hair as she pulled him close. With a shuddered moan, he thrust his tongue inside of her mouth and let her need drive him. He feasted on her.

He began slowly, but a moment later he pulled her tongue into his mouth and sucked, then he slipped his teeth over her bottom lip. He devoured her with every arsenal available to him at that moment. If they weren't going to have sex, he saw no reason why each kiss couldn't last a lifetime.

CHAPTER 8

CELEBRATIONS AND CONSIDERATIONS

Without thought, he unsnapped the hospital gown and pulled it over her head. Her breath caught and then her body gave the delicious tremble that always had Jeff reeling.

The first time he'd kissed her, the first time he'd run his hands over her breasts and then up her shirt and bra, the first time he'd eased her zipper down and had tenderly let his hands and fingers explore the heated silk between her legs, and every single time he'd eased himself inside of that heavenly perfection of her, Becca's breath would catch and her body would quiver in anticipation. That perfect, delicate, tremble of her love and her trust in him drove him to absolute distraction each and every time he felt it.

"God, I missed you." He panted as he helped her remove his shirt so their energy could pass between their bare skin. Unable to help himself, Jeff tried to remember that her breasts were sensitive due to their nearly doubling in size in the last few months as he cupped them tenderly. Becca's heady groan had him massaging with more force.

He eased his mouth to her swollen nipples. Her back arched. With a lust-filled growl, Jeff sucked her and let the erotic energy pour from the storehouse and into his mouth. He pulled his head away and fought a loud groan of ecstasy.

Becca had the button on his trousers undone and his zipper down in a second flat. Her hand slipped through the slit in his boxers, and his body thrust upward of its own accord. He was strung so tightly he hurt with a pain only she could soothe. A ravenous moan echoed from her as she felt how hard he was and the fevered need that spilled from his cock into her hand.

"I want you inside me so bad. I need you inside me. Nothing will ever feel as good as you. I miss that so much," she whimpered as she continued to grope him. She pulled and spun her index finger around his throbbing head before going back for more.

"Not too much longer, baby. Okay? After we get Aaron here safe and healthy, then I promise you, whenever you're ready I'm gonna let you feel me as often as you want." Jeff prayed she wouldn't beg him again. He wasn't sure how much he could take, and she most certainly could not have sex. He couldn't halt the thunderous groan that rumbled from his gut as she drew his erotic energy into her body straight from the source.

Before he could stop her, Becca managed to ease her body downward.

"Bec, no... You don't..." Jeff's eyes rolled back in his head, and his plea was drowned in a gasped moan as her tongue lapped at his head.

"I want it." She urged him on.

"No, baby...not until...." He tried to argue, but he was just too weak. He intended to stop her. He didn't want reprieve until he could provide her release as well. His body shuddered from the heavenly sensations.

Unable to formulate words, he groaned as she began to suck him in earnest. Her tongue licked like consuming fire. Her mouth drowned him as she pulled in heavenly syncopation. The room spun. Her heaving, fevered breasts surrounded him and moved with her body against his thighs. Her long, blonde hair teased at his abdomen and cut lines as she worked. It was utter perfection.

"Bec," he managed to gasp as his body gave hungry, aching thrusts. He tried to guide her mouth away, but she pulled harder. It was too much. It had been so long. His vision clouded. With a convulsive shudder and a moan of replete satisfaction, he lost it all. His body quaked in ecstasy. He stared down at his beautiful wife as she drank him dry. She released him a moment later and sported a smirk that was quickly replaced with a deep blush.

"You're absolutely incredible." Jeff managed to speak as soon as he regained the ability to breathe.

Becca giggled, and Jeff's heart sped once again. "I think you're just about the most incredible man in the world. You work so hard for us. I'm so proud of you, and I love you so much. And when I do that, I still get all of your yummy energy inside of me so Aaron can feel it," she explained as she buried her face against his chest. Jeff kissed the top of Becca's head and cradled her to him.

"I'm not sure that was PG-15," he couldn't help but tease her. He missed her so much. He missed being at school with her. He missed hearing her laugh at something stupid he said. He missed having her in his arms.

"Let me eat a little more and then I'll cast you, okay, sweetheart. Then we'll get some sleep." Jeff was absolutely exhausted after that all-encompassing release, but he would take care of his little boy and his wife before he allowed himself any rest.

She eased the sheets and blanket back around them, wearing nothing but a pair of cotton panties. Jeff tried to pretend they weren't in a hospital room. He tried to relax and lie in bed with his wife, in nothing but a pair of boxers with their little guy between them. As he began inhaling the rest of the meatballs, he wondered how many men could honestly say they'd been given a blow job in a hospital room.

He cleaned up the remnants of dinner and set his phone alarm to wake him up at midnight so he could cast her again. He decided that since this was their one night of uninterrupted bliss, he'd just force himself to pretend they were at home. He laid his clothes on the rocking chair and slid under the covers with Becca. She sighed contentedly and clamored up onto his chest. His shield formed around her, and he felt Aaron move against his own stomach.

"Hey, Bec." Jeff lowered the lights in the room completely.

"Yeah?" She began tracing over his abs and pecs with her index finger. She spelled out "I love you" with her finger, making him chuckle.

"What do you think about us buying the Vindicos' house? He really wants to sell it, and it's so much bigger than where we're renting. I'd only be seven minutes from work. I'd save a lot on gas, and I could come home and see you and Aaron for lunch, which would save me from having to eat out." Jeff hadn't realized until he was trying to talk his wife into buying the house how much he wanted to live there.

"Can we seriously afford that? It's a beautiful house and in such a good school district for Aaron." Becca seemed overwhelmed.

"He hasn't given me a price yet, but I think he'll cut us a deal just not to have to make Fionna go through with showing the house to strangers and everything."

"Wow."

~

Garrett Haydenshire

"You're having an autoimmune response to menstruation." Adeline looked extremely concerned.

Garrett was pacing in the exam room. "What does that mean?"

"Her immune system is confused. It thinks she's sick, but she really isn't. So, she's running a low grade fever. It's causing inflammation in most of her joints and making her nauseous. Her rhythms are running erratically trying to heal her, but there's really nothing to fight off. You've been through a lot in the past few weeks, and I think the piercings and the new tattoo irritated your immune system. Being back on Kauai should re-regulate your body, but you're probably going to feel pretty miserable until you get there. It may take a day or two for you to feel healthy again after you arrive."

"I had this a few times in New York. They always just gave me steroid shots." Kaimi sighed.

"I would do that as well, but I think with you leaving Friday for Kauai the steroids are unnecessary, and they really aren't good for you."

"Does she need to go now? I can put her on a plane tonight and then I can just bring the girls with me Friday." Garrett started to call his father.

"I don't want to go without you," Kaimi fussed.

Garrett moved back to her and laced his fingers in hers. "I don't want you to be sick, sweetheart."

"I'll be okay. It's really just two more days."

Garrett turned on Adeline. "Can't we cast her or something?"

"There's nothing to treat, Garrett," Adeline stated firmly. "There's nothing to heal. Her cycle threw off her rhythms, and she's been off the island for too long. And quite frankly, you cannot have any more tattoo work or piercing done off Kauai. Your body doesn't know how to handle them here."

"Okay." Kaimi nodded. Garrett ran his hands through his hair to keep from shouting at Adeline. Kaimi didn't need to be scolded. She certainly hadn't known her body wouldn't heal.

"Just take a little ibuprofen. That will keep the fever at bay. Try to rest and then probably spend some time in the waters as soon as you get to Kauai, or as soon as you can."

"Tutu probably has stuff for this," Kaimi offered hopefully.

Adeline smiled. "Kauaian healthcare is her thing. I'd say do what she says. I'm not one of those medios who believes we have it all figured out. Fionna's grandmother's remedies do work, and I would feel better if you'd let her check you out once you arrive."

"I will."

CHAPTER 9

DIFFERENTIAL PRESSURE

~DAN VINDICO~

Friday evening, Dan was throwing baby toys into one of the diaper bags that was sitting by the door for Halia. He'd been trying not to bark at Fionna all evening, but the entire thing finally set his temper loose. "Fionna, this is ridiculous!"

"Do not yell at me! *Your* mother insisted," Fionna sneered.

Dan shuddered slightly. His blood ran cold, and he had to force himself to draw a deep breath. It didn't happen often, but occasionally, Fionna would say something that reminded him of the way he and Amelia used to fight. The flashbacks were harrowing and always rendered him terrified for a split second.

"Hey." He took the tiny shoes out of Fionna's hands. "I'm sorry. I didn't mean to snap at you. I know how my mom is. I'm just as sick about the girls leaving tonight as you are. I really am sorry." He wrapped his arms around her and inhaled her heavenly island scent. He let his nostrils pull in the warm vanilla coconut and the scent of sunshine deep into his soul.

"I know." Fionna squeezed him and then stepped back. "I'm just a little chaotic. I didn't mean to be mean." Dan shook his head. She'd been so far from mean the statement was genuinely humorous, but to his sweet baby, she'd bad-mouthed his mother and shouted at him.

"Let's just finish this up and then we'll head to Mom and Dad's. Then we'll go to the Senate, okay?"

Fionna nodded and willed away more tears. Tutu had instructed her to see this as a way to better understand Dan's work and as a little vacation from the girls.

Dan thought it was a noble effort on her grandmother's part, but getting Fionna to see the weeks without their children due to the fact that nude or partially nude photos and videos of her stood to be posted all over the Internet as a vacation was highly unlikely.

"I really am looking forward to being your partner for real. I know the girls will be fine and happy on the farm. I'm just going to miss them so much." She sighed as they completed the boxes of things from Halia's nursery. Dan loaded them up in the Mercedes.

He scowled at the for sale sign on the back of his Ferrari. He had every intention of selling it. He even had Sam looking for a buyer, but to put a sign on a Ferrari seemed blasphemous. The criminals they were dealing with were young and without worldly sense. They were playing Pendergrath's favorite game without all of his vast worldly power and knowledge.

Dan had been driving to work in the Ferrari as a sign that he was trying to acquire the money needed to pay off his blackmailer. Fionna would be spending hours up at Venton trying to get readings off as many teachers and students as she was able. Several of the governors and banking officials were coming to the school tomorrow, along with Elite, to try to figure out what was going on and how deep it ran while no students were there.

Brodie Quentin hadn't been in school for the last two days. Dan wondered what that meant. The attendance secretary had phoned his parents but hadn't gotten a response.

Dan loaded his family up into the car and begrudgingly drove to his parents' home. His mother had insisted that if Dan and Fionna were shipping the girls off, as she'd phrased it, they at least got to see them before they left. Dan knew that it would probably be several months before either his parents made a trip to Kauai or he and Fionna brought the girls back to Arlington, but he hated that his mother had guilted Fionna into agreeing.

Aida extended her arms up to Dan when he parked the car and opened her door. He wasn't certain how much more he could take. Her trying not to cry was killing him. He lifted her from her pink flower seat and cradled her to him as she laid her head on his shoulder. Fionna carried Halia to the porch, trying to soothe Aida all the way.

"You can call Daddy and me as soon as you wake up tomorrow, and Aunt Malani and Tutu are going to take you to see your new school and get you anything you might need that we didn't get today, okay?" Fionna reminded her.

Aida was due to start at Koloa Elementary School Monday morning. Fionna had been given her choice of teacher for Aida. The reason given had been that Dan was going to be the highest ranking Iodex official on the islands, and that Papa was one of the Kauaian counsel magistrates. Tutu had ultimately chosen Aida's teacher. She was friends with all of the teachers at the same school Fionna had attended and chose a teacher she knew Aida would thrive under.

Dan wondered if he should give his parents his copy of the key to their home. He certainly wouldn't be needing it any time soon. His mother met them at the door wearing her customary weary disposition.

"Daniel, she is much too big for you to be carrying that way. You're going to injure your back. She isn't a baby," Mrs. Vindico huffed as she nearly closed the door on Fionna's heel.

"Mother, on a light day, I curl three times her weight with one arm. If she wants me to carry her, that's what I'm going to do."

"Do you two think you could can it for one night?" The governor looked rough. Dan's brow furrowed.

"Are you okay, Dad?"

"No, I am not okay. I am exhausted. Where are those antacids, Marion?"

"Here, Arthur." Mrs. Vindico thrust a bottle of Tums into the governor's hands and then removed a pie pan with some bizarre concoction of melted butter and some kind of cream with large purple things positioned throughout it from the refrigerator.

Dan scowled. "What is that?"

"Fionna said Aida liked grapes. I found this recipe in *Women of the Realm* for best burnt grapes. I just haven't burned them yet. This might help with your stomachache, Arthur."

"Highly doubt that," Dan whispered to Fionna. The odd mixture appeared to have black eyeballs positioned throughout it.

Fionna's giggle delighted him. It was the first he'd heard in several days.

Mrs. Vindico was serving her well-known ham burned to a rubberized crisp with slimy green peas. To everyone's delight, she'd purchased premade potato salad from the grocery store.

Fionna had taken the girls to her father's bakery that afternoon to let them tell their other grandparents goodbye. Gretta had doted on them and spent a pleasant afternoon with Fionna. Samuel had refused to speak but had then broken down in tears just before Fionna had taken the girls home. It had been a very trying afternoon, but Fionna had acquired a delectable chocolate cake she'd brought to the Vindicos' for dessert.

Dan decided to attempt to chew a little of his mother's ham, since he wouldn't have to endure any more Vindico family dinners for a while.

"Arthur, what is wrong with you now? You haven't played golf in months," Mrs. Vindico sniped.

Dan studied his father. He looked a little gray. Trying to work two full-time, high-powered jobs along with all of the flak for what was going on at Venton, and Wilshire still running his mouth, was taking its toll. The governor was rubbing his shoulders.

"When I tore my rotator cuff last spring, the medio said it wouldn't ever be as good as it once was. I'm not getting any younger."

"I could have Garrett and Kaimi bring you back a few of Tutu's oils and compresses. They worked last summer, remember?" Fionna offered sweetly.

"Thank you, sweetheart. That would be great. Finally, someone with an offer to help." The governor was in a vicious mood.

"Oh, Dan, I saved something for you and Fionna that came in the mail." Mrs. Vindico placed her linen napkin beside her plate and moved into the living room.

Dan and Fionna shared an ominous expression. When she returned, she handed Fionna several clipped pages from *Women of the Realm*. Fionna discreetly rolled her eyes as she laid the articles close enough for Dan to see the headlines.

How to behave when your husband is an important public figure.

How to lose the last fifteen pounds in two weeks.

Cheap and Easy is for your dinner not your husband.

The Latest Hairdos for the New Mom, and Reestablishing the Family Unit after a traumatic move.

Dan pointed to the article on mom hairdos. They all were short bobs that he found highly unattractive.

"No," he commanded.

Fionna bit her lips together to keep from laughing. "Uh, don't worry, honey," she assured him. "Thank you, Mrs. Vindico, but you gave me a subscription to this magazine."

"Yes, dear, but those were articles I really thought you should re-read. Here, Dan, I saw this and thought of you."

Dan opened the newsletter from a stringently conservative speaker in the Realm. "DD Digler on Dignity and Demeanor." Dan rolled his eyes dramatically.

"Yes, isn't that a cute little catchphrase? Maybe you should come up with a little catchphrase for your new job."

"How about—you break the law, I'll kick your ass," Dan quipped.

"Daddy," Aida sighed and shook her head.

"Sorry."

Dan glanced over the newsletter whose position it seemed was to throw yourself into your work and to make a name for yourself and your family, thereby finding the real meaning of life because of the perks.

"Mother, I'm moving my family to Kauai to spend more time with them, not less. Iodex officers work shifts. I'll be off by three or four every day. Aida gets out of school at one on Wednesdays and Fridays to spend time with us as a family." Dan tossed the newsletter aside.

"I don't know how you intend to be recognized with that lack of work ethic."

"I don't need to be recognized. I need to create a safe environment for the people who live on or visit the islands. After that, I need to be with my wife and my daughters." Dan had been in the mood to fight for days. It didn't take much to ignite him.

"Oh, so you're moving my granddaughters five thousand miles away so that no one will know who you are?"

"Yes!" Dan shouted back.

"Shut up, both of you!" the governor bellowed. "I am not in the mood for this tonight." He stood, dumped his still full plate in the trash, and cut himself a large hunk of chocolate cake. He poured a shot of brandy and sank back into his chair. The brandy was gone long before the cake.

"Arthur, your cholesterol," Mrs. Vindico huffed.

The governor's answer to that was to plunge his fork in the cake with a vengeance and inhale more of the delicious chocolate layers.

An hour later, the girls were getting many hugs from Dan's parents.

CHAPTER 10

DEFLAGRATION

With his heart in his throat, Dan made the drive out to the Senate where they were meeting Garrett and Kaimi on the Crown Governor's jet.

Slow tears leaked steadily down Fionna's face.

"You can go with them if you want," was Dan's constant reassurance. She shook her head and drew from him heavily.

Governor and Mrs. Haydenshire met them along with Garrett and Kaimi.

"Fionna, sweetheart, come here." Mrs. Haydenshire had her in her warm embrace in under half a second. Aida refused to let Dan set her on the ground, and Fionna was clinging to Halia as Mrs. Haydenshire tried to soothe her.

"We're going to get this figured out, Daniel. Then we'll get you back to your girls," Governor Haydenshire vowed.

"I know, sir. Right now, I just need to know they're safe, and I'm not certain how far these kids are willing to go."

"I agree with your reasoning, son. I think you're making the right decision." Governor Haydenshire and Garrett helped Dan unload all of the girl's things onto the plane.

"How's Kaimi doing?" Dan recalled that she'd been back to see Adeline.

"Not well. I need to get her to Kauai. Adeline says that will reset her rhythms. I know this is shitty, man, but we need to get going."

"No, it's fine. This is better. The girls should sleep most of the flight. Standing out here for another hour isn't going to make this any easier on any of us." Dan was sick as he guided Fionna up onto the plane and helped her strap Halia's car seat into one of the large seats.

Kaimi and Garrett constantly vowed to watch over them like their own. Aida began sobbing, and Fionna was done for. It took Dan a half hour to get them off the plane. He was an emotional wreck as he eased his sobbing wife back toward the car, after the plane taxied down the runway.

"Call us if you need us, sweetheart." Mrs. Haydenshire kissed his cheek.

Suddenly, Dan's cell rang. Hopeful that Jeff or Portwood had found something, Dan answered without checking to see who was calling.

"Dan," Kara sounded panicked.

"Hey, Care Bear, what's wrong?" He was certain he couldn't handle anything else.

"It's Dad. He's on his way to Georgetown. He had a heart attack. They don't know if he's going to make it." With that, Kara promptly began sobbing.

Zach got on the phone. "Hey, we'll meet you at the hospital, okay?"

"Okay," Dan managed.

"What's wrong now?" Fionna had instantly picked up on the panic in Dan's rhythms. She didn't look like she could withstand much more.

"Daniel?!" Governor Haydenshire reached to steady him. "Son, look at me." Dan could hear the governor saying his name, but he sounded tunneled and far away. "Daniel!" Dan stumbled forward, but Governor Haydenshire held him upright.

"Okay, let's sit down." Mrs. Haydenshire guided Dan down on the concrete. "Deep breaths."

"Dad's being taken to Georgetown. He had a heart attack."

Stunned silence echoed through the people surrounding him.

"All right. Can you drive, or do you want to ride with us?" The governor began making plans.

"I'm fine." Dan was aware that Governor Haydenshire and Fionna carried on an unspoken conversation.

"We'll meet you there."

Fionna helped Dan up. He settled in the driver's seat automatically. As he drove, he stared at the DC skyline and tried to make sense of his life as of late. His father would be fifty-six in March. He'd never eaten particularly healthy, given the fact that Dan's mother preferred to cook the life out of anything she prepared. He'd always been relatively active though. He jogged daily and had always played golf numerous times a week, until he'd taken on Venton. Dan knew the governor had smoked some in his teenage years and his early twenties, but he'd given it up altogether when Dan had been born.

"Dan, listen to me. He's going to be okay. I can feel it." Fionna touched Dan's forearm and sent her intoxicating, soothing rhythms through his skin. They mingled with his own energies and quelled his fears. "I should have realized that's what I was feeling when we were there. I got confused because I thought it was just me being upset about everything. But when I only focus on your dad's rhythms, I know he's going to be okay."

Dan found it odd that his only thought about his wife's sentiment was that she'd just confirmed Dinkerton's entire report about why Receivers can't be used to convict criminals. Their own energy strands and emotions could alter and confuse what they felt from others.

"I'm okay." Dan wasn't certain that was the truth, but it seemed like he should be. He tried to think if he'd ever seen the governor in the hospital at any point in the last thirty years. His father had always seemed to be some kind of impenetrable force. Dan parked the car beside the Crown Governor's minivan. Meredith leapt out of her car nearby, and they ran inside through the gathering press.

"Dan, can you give us a statement on your father's condition?"

"Meredith, have you been in contact with your mother?"

"Fionna, where are the girls this evening?"

"Crown Governor, have you heard from the cardiac medio team attending Governor Vindico?"

They ran on, ignoring the questions being screeched at them from each direction. Dan's eyes narrowed. Two cameramen ahead of them leapt in front of Meredith, blocking her path.

"Get away from my sister." Dan wrapped his arm around Meredith and guided her inside. He let her hide her swollen, tear-stained face in his chest.

"Tim's with the kids," Meredith managed as they all raced onto the elevator.

"He's going to be okay," Fionna promised. "I can feel his energy now."

Meredith paced in the three feet of available space between Governor Haydenshire and Dan. "He just can't keep doing this. I mean Venton and being a governor and dealing with Mom. Just that's a full-time job."

"No, he can't, and he shouldn't have to. I've had just about enough of this insanity at Venton. I'm taking over Venton Monday morning, and we're going to get some things figured out," Governor Haydenshire decreed.

Kara and Zach were already in the cardiac waiting room as was Ryan Tuttle.

Ryan stood and squeezed Dan's arm reassuringly. "Hey, they're still casting him. Lindley's on her way. She had to find someone to cover for her at the shop."

"Where's Marion, Ryan?" Mrs. Haydenshire asked.

"She's been in there with him the whole time, Mrs. Haydenshire."

"All right then, why don't we sit down." Mrs. Haydenshire and the governor kept close watch on Dan, Kara, and Meredith. Governor Haydenshire stopped his pacing after a few moments. Resolution etched the beginnings of the wrinkles on his face.

"Daniel, what needs to happen?" He sank down beside Dan in the waiting room. "This insanity has gone on long enough. We've been playing the ends against the middle trying to get Dean to retire to save his pension for Ellen. We've got children with severely lacking morals, and parents more interested in writing checks to get them out of their hair than in parenting. What needs to happen so that we can restore Venton to the academy it was when you and Will graduated? We need a plan, and you need something to do."

Fionna grinned and ran her hand tenderly up and down Dan's arm. She knew the governor was right. "He's going to be okay. I can see it now," she continued to assure them.

Dan wouldn't have survived sitting there endlessly waiting on word on his father's condition. He began talking, calculating, and planning his way out of that hospital, out of DC, and out of Venton Academy.

CHAPTER II

RESTORATION

~GARRETT HAYDENSHIRE~

"She just keeps crying." Kaimi was pacing the wide aisle and bouncing Halia in her arms. Garrett had better luck with her earlier, but Aida wouldn't sleep unless he held her, and he couldn't do both.

"She wants Fionna, and the plane is probably bothering her ears."

"She'll be okay as soon as Tutu has her. Her rhythms are Kauaian, and Tutu is so much like Maylea maybe she won't notice much."

Garrett doubted that. Until that moment, he hadn't realized how little Kaimi really knew about babies.

"We should be landing in just a few minutes, sweetheart. Maybe try another bottle." Garrett shifted slightly. Aida's entire little body was languid in his arms. She'd cried herself to exhaustion, and as soon as Garrett had casted her, she'd fallen into a deep sleep. The plane began its descent, and he allowed himself to breathe. Halia cried harder though, so the relaxation was short-lived.

Ten minutes later, he walked down the jetway carrying Aida. Kaimi thrust Halia into her great-grandmother's arm. Tutu chuckled as she cradled Halia and began whispering to her in Hawaiian. A moment later, Halia was yawning and drifting off to sleep.

"Thank you." Kaimi's body wilted in her own illness and exhaustion.

"I believe the Haydenshires and my little Vindicos need some tender care. Let's go get everyone settled."

Garrett helped Papa and Kai carry all of the girls' things and load them in Papa's truck. He fastened Halia's car seat in Malani's Jeep and remembered to help Kaimi up before he fell in the seat beside her.

Aida was in and out of consciousness as they rode. She would awaken, reach frantically for Garrett's hand, and then as soon as she was assured he was still right beside her, she would be out once again.

It broke his heart, and this was going to be the worst honeymoon in the history of honeymoons if his goddaughter refused to be out of his presence, but he would never deny her anything ever.

"We'll settle her down. She's a little lost without Dan and Maylea. She'll be better when they can give her a definite day they'll be here, but we'll see to it that you and our sweet Kaimi have a few nights to let the island seal you," Tutu assured him.

Kaimi grinned as Garrett's eyes goggled. Fionna's grandmother was going to take some getting used to. He supposed she'd picked up on his concern and then frustration and then lust though he was so worried and exhausted even he hadn't discerned his own need.

"I have just what you need, my precious Kaimi. We'll have you up and around and back to full health in no time. And you, Deputy Haydenshire—you're going to be a tough one, I can tell. I'm going to remind you that you agreed to let me treat you in exchange for living on the farm," Tutu urged with her customary knowing smirk.

"Hey, I'm fine, and I'm good with whatever makes Kaimi better and lets us get some sleep." Garrett didn't have it in him to argue.

"Yes, well, smart man that you are, our beautiful Kaimi is quite sleep-deprived. That is something I will tolerate only if the nights have been given to love, but that doesn't seem to be the case either."

Kaimi was beaming. Something about Tutu seemed to fully relieve the stress that had robbed his beautiful baby of vitality for the past week.

She nodded. "No, ma'am. I haven't felt up to anything. Garrett took excellent care of me though."

"Yes, well, I think Garrett might need a little help." Tutu didn't seem at all concerned that she wouldn't be up to the task of healing

Kaimi. "I think it would be best if perhaps you put off your beach campout for a night and sleep in your new home. Then the waters and the shore will be able to offer you their rhythms of peace, but you're not quite ready for them just yet."

"Yeah, I don't really feel up to camping right now," Kaimi admitted. She seemed afraid she was disappointing Garrett. He laced his fingers through hers.

"Sleeping in a real bed sounds good to me." He turned back to Tutu.

"Should we tell Aida about…"

"Not yet, and our sweet girl is homed in on you alone, so speak very carefully."

Garrett decided to just let Aida's grandparents tell her about Governor Vindico whenever they thought the time was right.

Aida roused a little when Kai parked the Jeep. Garrett lifted her back into his arms and carried her in Tutu and Papa's house. He saw a small grin form on her lips, and utter relief flooded through him.

"Are we home?" She yawned deeply.

"You are home, baby girl." Papa was delighted when Aida leaned out of Garrett's arms and into his.

"Tutu made you Aida tea before bed." Tutu poured Aida a small cup of tea, and Papa sat at the table with Aida in his lap so she could sip it. "All right, Miss Kaimi, this is for you." She handed Kaimi a large mug of tea, which she began sipping immediately. "I put several oils and salts in your new hale. The salt mixtures go in her bath tonight, Garrett, and the oils in her morning bath." Tutu began giving instructions as if them taking a bath that evening was a foregone conclusion.

Kaimi looked so much better and so relieved to be cared for Garrett didn't have the heart to argue. He considered balking at the bath. He was bone-weary exhausted. It was after two o'clock in the morning in DC. He'd been up most of the night before casting Kaimi in an effort to keep her fever down. It had worked, but they were both thoroughly drained.

"Three cups a day, and you already know my rules for healing, right, my sweet Kaimi?" Tutu ordered.

Kaimi nodded. "Yes, ma'am. Most anything can be cured if you eat lots of island food, take long walks in the waters of Kauai, take long baths with your prescriptions, take long naps, and have long lovemaking sessions." She spoke this information timidly.

"Yes, you are going to fit right in our little ohana. I can tell. In your case, we're going to start you off in the spring water here on the farm, until we've gotten rid of that fever, and then we'll let the ocean's salt waters heal your rhythms and restore your body."

"I didn't know you had a spring here." Kaimi's color was returning before Garrett's eyes. The more tea she sipped—and it seemed, the more air she breathed—the better she became.

Papa was sneaking Aida pineapple coconut cookies that smelled delicious. Aida smiled and handed one up to Garrett. He winked at her and accepted the gift.

"I use the spring waters in many of my tinctures. It's out under the waterfalls. Maylea spent half the summer under that fall with Daniel, and as you see, my sweet Halia is just as healthy as she can be." Tutu was preparing teas and cradling Halia on her shoulder as if she carried a baby around with her while she worked most of her life. He wondered just how many families on the island she helped.

Kaimi tried not to giggle as Garrett shook his head. He didn't have to guess what Fionna had been doing with Daniel out under the waterfall for most of the summer.

"Tonight, a nice long bath and another cup of what I believe I'll call Kaimi's tea. Then tomorrow, we'll let you and Garrett play in the waterfalls and spend the day eating island foods, then you'll be ready for your beach honeymoon."

Aida's blinks were growing heavier as she managed the last of the tea that Garrett suspected had chamomile in it.

"All right, Miss Aida, why don't you let Papa read you a story and tuck you in while I take Uncle Garrett and Auntie Kaimi to their new hale?"

"I want Uncle Garrett to take me to bed, please." Aida's chin trembled once again. Garrett scooped her up out of her grandfather's arms and let him lead the way to the room she slept in when she stayed overnight.

CHAPTER 12

THOUGHTS AND EMOTIONS

After lying down with Aida until she fell asleep for the night, Garrett yawned as he moved back down the hallway.

"All right, you two, this way." Tutu carried two large baskets on her arms as she guided Garrett and Kaimi to the guest home that Garrett had chosen.

"Can I get those for you, Tutu?" Garrett offered to relieve her of her burden.

"I'll be fine. You take care of your beautiful bride."

Garrett watched Kaimi take in the tropical hues of her island bathed in shades of blue by the glowing moon.

"I've packed you soaps, oils, massage oils, several jars of ʻŌhiʻa lehua, and several candles." Tutu gestured to one of the large baskets slung on her arm. "In here, I have you some coffee, fresh coconut milk, honey, sweet rolls, fruits, fresh eggs, a few things you might want for breakfast. I want you two to relax and let the island heal you and make you whole. I'm sorry you're going to have to share your bonding time with our sweet Aida, but this time away from Dan and Maylea is going to be so difficult for her."

Tutu opened the door to the guesthouse. Garrett was shocked to find it cleaned and prepared for them to move into. As Tutu set about unloading the food from her baskets, he noted that there was even beer in the refrigerator and candles lit around the huge outdoor bathtub.

"Is Aida going to be okay, Tutu? How can we help her?" Kaimi was so worried about Aida it made Garrett somehow love her even more, which he hadn't known was possible until that moment.

"She will ultimately be fine. She could feel Dan and Maylea's distress over what has happened with Dan's work, though they certainly didn't discuss it with her. She knows how much they miss her. She doesn't understand why they've sent her here without them. She desperately wants her daddy. She needs her Shield. Garrett is always her very next choice if she can't have Dan, so right now she is clinging to him fiercely. I'm hoping once we get her a little distracted she'll loosen her grip, but until Daniel and Maylea arrive, she will struggle." Garrett let that tidal wave of guilt wash over him as he thought about him leaving as well. "And things are not going well for Dan and Maylea. I worry over them so." She shook her head.

"Now, your bath. Tonight, we will rid your body of the toxins you've acquired while you were off your island. The problem with toxins is that the more they build the worse their effect is compacted until you have no energy with which to fight them off. We must get rid of them and that will take some time. Tomorrow, after a good night's sleep, we will begin to restore. So..." Tutu beckoned Kaimi to follow her out on the screened-in porch with the tub.

"Run the water as hot as you can stand it. Dump in these salts, this soda, and this vinegar. Add three droppers of lavender and two of magnesium oil. Then ten slices of this island ginger." She pointed to three different lidded jars she'd set on the side of the tub. "Let Garrett hold you and relax together. Breathe deeply and feel the sickness leaving your body. Stay in for at least an hour, so Garrett will need to reheat the water for you. After you get out..." She lifted up a clear bottle that contained an opaque golden oil mixture.

"Rub her down with this and fix her another mug of tea. You, Deputy, I want you to drink a half gallon of water for me tonight. Then leave your windows open out onto your deck. If you'd like to sleep on the outdoor bed, that would be excellent as well, but I highly recommend sleeping in the nude. No one will be out this way to bother you except perhaps the morning sun and the roosters. Let your body continue to release its toxins throughout the night. By morning, you'll be astonished at how much better you feel, and I've put four pairs of fresh sheets in your bedroom. Put on a new pair in the morning." Garrett could hardly believe he was actually going to follow Tutu's instructions for Kaimi.

If it hadn't involved so many things he'd been longing to do for weeks with his wife, he probably would've argued, but soaking in the biggest tub he'd ever seen, then rubbing oil all over Kaimi's luscious body, then sleeping with her completely in the buff sounded like heaven, so he decided it couldn't hurt.

Kaimi, however, seemed overjoyed that Tutu was caring for her so thoroughly. Garrett wondered if she'd felt guilty about Tutu's help with her grandmother's illness, so she'd never asked for any help for herself.

"Maylea made me some of your raspberry tea when I…uh, needed that. It really did work, and we've been using the ʻŌhiʻa lehua. I'm not hurting anymore," she vowed to Tutu.

"I don't make things that don't do what I say they will, and Maylea is a genius. She gets that from me." Tutu laughed as Kaimi and Garrett joined in. Kaimi threw her arms around Tutu and was embraced thoroughly.

"A bath, Kaimi, very, very soon," Tutu commanded as soon as Kaimi released her.

"Yes, ma'am."

"Garrett, dear, try not to doubt me so. It's insulting, and I just told you to strip her down and bathe with her before you rub oil all over her. So I can't be that bad, right?"

"I'm good with it all. Just tell me what to do." Garrett was frustrated that his own thoughts weren't even his own when Fionna's grandmother was around. He wondered if Fionna could read him that easily, but just didn't comment.

Dan Vindico

Several hours later, the cardiac medio team left the governor's room. Dan beat his sisters to them by two large steps.

"Your father is going to be all right. It was a stress-induced heart attack. He's going to be in here for a while, so we can make certain the repairs I made on his heart muscle hold. I highly recommend a long vacation for the governor after that. His blood pressure was through the roof. He's got to relax and get some rest. His rhythms need to be completely reset. We'll work on that for the next several days, and then I'll be better able to give him a full prognosis. If you'd like to see him one or two at a time, that would be fine, but then he needs to sleep. You can come back and see him later tomorrow if you'd like," Medio Urqkins instructed. "If it hadn't been for your mother's quick thinking, I'm certain his heart muscle would have sustained more damage."

All Dan could think in that moment as relief flooded through his rhythms was that now his mother would be absolutely incorrigible. Dan and Fionna were universally nominated by all of his sisters to be the first to go in and see the governor.

"Try not to argue with your mom. That stresses him out," Fionna reminded him. Dan tried to remember that as he eased the door open. *You're a grown man. You have kids of your own. You are the best trained officer in the Realm.* These thoughts became Dan's mantra as he tried to determine why he was terrified to enter his father's hospital room.

Fionna laced her fingers through his, and her energy wound through his terror. She'd always been and would always be the answers to his prayers, the perfect antidote to his every fear, his perfection, his other half.

Mrs. Vindico was seated in a chair near the governor's bed. Forced determination was her shield as she tried to conceal her own worry.

"Dad." Dan shook his head. The governor looked weak and pale. Relief played in his eyes when he saw Dan, and a slightly abashed grin formed on his face.

"Daniel."

"You like scaring the shit out of me? 'Cause I gotta tell you, old man, I can't take much more."

"I'm sorry, son." The governor chuckled, but it turned into a cough.

Dan bowed his head as Governor Vindico reached for his wife's hand. She supplied it with a tender smile. It wasn't something Dan often saw from his parents. It was distinctly intimate, and he wasn't certain he should be there to view it. Fionna kept her hand in his and constantly supplied him with her soothing life force. She leaned into Dan, and he wrapped his arm around her, drawing her closer.

"Did the girls get to Lihue?" Governor Vindico seemed to be piecing his evening back together.

"Yes, sir." Fionna smiled. "Garrett texted a few minutes ago. They'd just touched down."

A knock sounded on the door just before Governor Haydenshire poked his head in. "Would you mind if I broke the two-person limit and came in? I swear I won't bring up work."

Governor Vindico smiled again. "As I recall, the last time I was in this place I was about nineteen, and you brought me here after I wrecked my dad's Chevy Impala."

Governor Haydenshire laughed as he eased into the room. "I'd nearly forgotten that." He smiled at Dan's mother. "Marion, I hear your medical expertise came in rather handy." He leaned down to kiss Mrs. Vindico's cheek.

"I'd just read an article in *Women of the Realm* that said if you or someone you care for is having a heart attack that you should have them cough until the ambulance arrives and administer a large dose of children's aspirin, so that's what I did."

Dan wondered momentarily if his mother hadn't cared for the person having a heart attack if she would have offered assistance, but he didn't comment.

Governor Haydenshire settled in the other chair in the room. "Where are you two going to vacation when they let you out of here, Governor?"

Dan understood that the vacation would be mandatory per orders of the Crown.

"After I get Venton figured out."

Dan shook his head but stopped short of commenting when Fionna shot him a look that said they were cut from the same cloth.

"I'll be stepping in on your behalf at Venton, and unfortunately for

Dean Wilshire, I'm not nearly as kind as you are. I blame him whether directly or indirectly for everything that has happened, and quite frankly, for the fact that one of my dearest friends is lying in a hospital bed in the Cardiac Intensive Care Unit so..." Governor Haydenshire commanded, "I'll ask you again. Where are you and your lovely bride going to be spending the next few weeks?"

Governor Vindico sighed his defeat. "All right, well, I wish you luck with Venton. I'd be relieved for that to be over with. I don't suppose I'd mind visiting my son and daughter-in-law and my beautiful granddaughters out in Kauai if they wouldn't mind putting up with us for a week or two?"

Fionna smiled. "I don't know when we'll be out there, but we'd love to have you. Tutu will take excellent care of you. All of the omegas in the seafood would be good for your heart."

Dan tried to decide how he would feel about his parents being on the farm so soon after they moved. He and Fionna weren't even certain when they'd be arriving.

"Don't you think you should go somewhere sooner, Dad? I don't know when we'll be out there."

"Yes, Arthur, I'm just not sure about that farm." Mrs. Vindico seemed to be trying not to be argumentative. Dan was certain it was a mighty task.

"I think we're going to let Arthur decide this one, Marion." Governor Haydenshire turned back to Dan. "Is there some reason you and Fionna have to be on the farm for your parents to be there?" His mandate left no room for rebuttal.

CHAPTER 13

SWEET SATISFACTION

~GARRETT HAYDENSHIRE~

"I thought you liked Tutu?" Kaimi was visibly trying not to be irritated. She was exhausted, and her rhythms were tensing and contentious.

"It's just been a lot lately." Garrett willed himself to be in a better mood.

"I want to do what she says. I'm tired of always being sick and tired. I was better here, but I want to be me again. I want to dance and go camping and…be fun, and…" She couldn't quite seem to decide what else she wanted exactly, but what she didn't want was Garrett balking at Tutu's remedies. He closed his eyes and willed repose. If it was what she wanted, then that was what he would do.

"I'm sorry, honey." He pulled her closer. She tensed and considered jerking away, but Garrett kept her from moving. "I'm worried about everything going on. I'm freaked about whatever Dan had pictures of that might land my best friend all over the Internet, and I'm mad that we can't figure this shit out at Venton. I've been crazy worried about you, and now, I'm crazy worried about Aida."

Kaimi softened and allowed Garrett to really embrace her. "I think everything Tutu wants us to do might help you too. I mean, with being so stressed out and all. It's supposed to be our honeymoon, and most of the stuff sounded fun."

Garrett leaned his head down until their foreheads were touching. He drew from her. He needed a better reading of her energy strains, and truthfully, it had just been so long since he'd felt her rhythms inside of his own. The intoxicating, heavenly, erratic waves of his baby filled him. Garrett knew they made no sense to anyone but him. He also knew he could never live without them. He wanted to drown in them. They were the only things that *did* make sense to him. Kaimi gave him his beautiful, curious grin.

"Then let's get this honeymoon off the ground, Mrs. Haydenshire."

She shivered and then leaned up on her tiptoes to brush a kiss along his jaw as she slipped out of her jeans. Garrett's hands sought her hips. He massaged and pulled her back to him as she unbuckled his belt. His jeans hit the ground, as he edged her shirt up and off her.

"Come here to me. I've missed you." He wrapped his arms around her back and neck. His tongue was parched for hers. His wildfire began its blaze in her eyes. It had been too many days since he'd seen that hungry desire inside of her. He jerked her forward so she could feel the effect she was having. The hardened steel length of him slammed against her abdomen.

A slightly shocked moan was all she managed to verbalize before he dipped his tongue to hers, thrusted it into her mouth, and began guiding her body in rhythmic circles around his hungry strain.

"You make me so damn hard. I hurt so fucking bad to be inside of you. So tight and wet. Always such a sweet girl for me. I want you now. I need you." His growl was low and reverent in his intonation.

Kaimi's entire body swam in his desperate desire for her. She shook violently in his arms as her body quivered in voracious anticipation.

"Did you want that bath right now, sweetheart, or can I take care of a few things first and then give my baby her bath?" Defiance and desire mixed in a heady cocktail inside of him. His blood ran hot and thick with need.

"You promise we'll still take the bath?" Kaimi had to close her eyes and shut out her desire to make her request.

"Let me fill you full, or hell, let me come all over you, and then I'll clean you up. You're not even dirty yet, sweet girl, but I'll take care of that." He traced his fingers down her neck, over the swollen curve of her right breast. He circled her areolas, watching them darken until her nipples throbbed in their need to be cared for. He refused them as he let his fingers glide lower. He traced down the butterfly wings that led him to the tender heart of her.

He wanted the devil she kept hidden away. She was his sweet, sweet girl, with that virgin sweet body, but he wanted his sexy vixen in training. The one that let him do pretty much what he wanted as long as he gave her everything she needed, which was always his only goal.

She was stronger here. So much more than she'd ever been in DC. The beautiful girl with an impish grin and a dreamer's heart. His baby with the insatiable curiosity about anything at all. The one with the sense of humor that kept him laughing when nothing was going his way. The one with a heart of gold who wouldn't put up with his shit. The one he'd fallen hard for just talking to her over the phone. She existed here. She should never have come there. He should never have allowed it. He realized this instantly as his fingers eased her swollen lips apart, and she cried out for him.

The air around them was so thick and humid with her floral island scent and the delectable flavors of her arousal that Garrett's body quaked and shook in its desperation for her. He half laid and half threw her on the bed.

"I need to taste you," he demanded in a low guttural grunt.

"Yes, now," she urged him on. Her hungry plea only drove him harder. He let the tip of his tongue tease her opening. She spread her legs farther in a physical command.

"Are you wet for me? Are you wet like I need my sweet girl to be? You gonna give me what I want to drink? I need to taste you. I need you in my mouth." Her entire body trembled from his commands. His thumbs eased her apart again, and he found exactly what he wanted.

"Such a sweet girl. Watch me," he ordered. She lifted her head, as he licked between her folds, consuming the liquid form of her. He sucked her inner lips, and her breath caught in an instant. She came harder here as well, he realized instantly.

His mind momentarily went back to their time at the hidden-away chalet right after her grandmother had passed. How could he not have noticed the difference between her there and her in DC? He'd been too consumed with them and getting her down the aisle. No more. From then on, he would focus on her alone. He would help Dan and Fionna, and he would be the godfather that his baby girls needed, but Kaimi would always reign supreme in his heart.

He dipped his tongue deep within her while his fingers teased and slowly brushed her clit. The energy of her body pulsed there as she neared climax. Her legs began shaking, her temperature spiked hard, her clit retracted, and a hungry growl filled the air from Garrett's lungs as she spilled out in his mouth.

He sucked her dry, and fire lit from his groin as he climbed over her while wiping his hand across his mouth. He kept her legs apart with his knee as he lapped his tongue over her left nipple and then moved to suck her right. He dragged his teeth over the throbbing tips of her then sucked the exquisite pain he'd brought her. He leaned and grabbed the lube she needed and handed it to her.

She dipped her fingers in the jar and began massaging and caressing his hardened length. A rapacious groan echoed from him. It reverberated off the thickened air that surrounded them. She handed the jar back to him, but Garrett shook his head.

"You're not finished. Show me." He grabbed her hand and laid it on her mound. Fear flashed in her eyes as her mind fought with her body. "Sexiest damn thing I have ever seen. I may blow all over you from just watching. Show me. I want to see. You're not the only one who likes to watch. Show me, baby, like my sweet girl." With his adamant assurances, she began, and Garrett was woefully unable to look anywhere but at her fingers as she ran the lube over her lips and then inside of her. When he knew she'd had enough to take him, he pulled her hand away.

"Do you trust me?"

"What?" she panted heavily.

"Do you trust me, Kaimi? I'm your husband, and I love you more than life itself. Do you trust me?"

"Yes." She seemed to have no doubt.

"Close your eyes and don't open them until I tell you to. I'm gonna hold you down, and I don't want you to think about anything but what you feel between your legs. Be a sweet girl and do what I say." Her body contorted as an echoing moan seared through her lungs. Her eyes closed, and Garrett grasped her wrists. He pinned them to the bed above her head and dropped low to penetrate her fully.

"That's my sweet girl." He groaned in her ear as he began to thrust slowly. "Open up for me and take a little more. That's it. My tight, wet, sweet girl. Feels good, doesn't it? Feels so good when you're full of me." Garrett's eyes rolled back in his head as he transitioned from his slow, rhythmic thrusts to pounding into her and owning her fully.

"Harder," she begged and a ragged growl spilled from him. When she thought only of the feeling of him filling her hollow spaces and making her all his, her demands drove him wild.

"My baby likes it rough, and nobody knows that but me. You're all mine." His voice turned rasping and thick as his release throbbed fiercely in his groin.

Her head shook back and forth. Her body belonged solely to him. He refused to let her move as he continued to pound. Her temperature spiked again as her body gave a fevered climbing blush. She trembled around him as her muscles cinched so tightly he could hardly move. It was exquisite perfection.

"Open your eyes and look at me when I bring you," Garrett commanded. Her eyes flew open as her body released her energy, and he filled her full.

His body shook from the intensity of his release. He stared intently into her eyes. The love and the trust in them filled his heart as he spilled himself inside of her. He couldn't hold it back. It had been building for too long. He convulsed as she broke in heated waves of ecstasy.

When she stilled, he eased from her and fell beside her on the bed. He pulled her to his chest as he tried to catch his breath.

"Uh, wow." She buried her face in his chest. He could feel the heat still coursing through her body and her grin beside his pecs.

"I believe I promised you a bath, Mrs. Haydenshire. I should probably clean up my mess." He kissed the top of her head and listened to her sweet giggle of replete satisfaction.

CHAPTER 14

REST FOR THE WEARY

"My legs are all wobbly. We can never do that before I have to dance," she informed him with another luscious giggle. Garrett laughed as he slid from the bed and headed back to the porch.

"You stay right there." He began running the water again and heated it with his hand. He dumped in Tutu's prescribed remedy with a shrug. The island rhythms were certainly different from the ones in DC, and they absolutely affected and lit through his beautiful wife, so what the hell?

He scooped Kaimi up in his arms and carried her out to the porch. He lowered her into the water and then stepped in behind her. She reclined between his outstretched legs and let her head fall languidly beside his neck.

"Thank you," he whispered. He glided his hands up and down her arms and shoulders, using the water and oils as a lubricant against her heated skin. He began massaging out what tension still resided in her muscles.

"For what? I'm pretty sure I should be thanking you."

A cocky smirk Garrett couldn't hide formed on his features. He chuckled and let everything he'd done to her replay in his mind.

"I'm glad you had a good time, but thank you for trusting me like that. I know that's hard for you. I never want you to do anything you don't want to do, but thank you for trusting me enough to let me give you that."

"I told you. I have to make the jump because it's part of this dance, and I don't ever want this dance to end because I know you'll always catch me." Her whispered vow soothed the worn wounds of Garrett's heart.

Two and a half hours on her island and she was already so much better than she'd been for the last several weeks.

Garrett was astonished as his own muscles relaxed in the hot water. The tension he'd been carrying seemed to drain from him. Kaimi's rhythms still swam in their customary erratic waves, but they were less tense and less fraught with nerves. She seemed to really relax against him. They sat in peaceful silence for a long while. They watched their rhythms coil together and then dissipate in the humid evening air.

"I love you," he whispered. She was almost asleep. "Let's go to bed, sweetheart."

"I love you too." Kaimi seemed to force herself to slide forward, and Garrett helped her stand. He grabbed and quickly heated two towels that Fionna's grandmother had left out for them. He tenderly dried her off and then wrapped the towel around her.

She moved back to the tiny kitchen and heated a mug of water with her hand to prepare her prescribed tea.

"You're supposed to drink water," she reminded him with a deep yawn. Garrett tried to hide his eye roll. She moved to him and wound her arms around his chest. The towel fell away from her.

"I like this." Garrett tried to distract her.

She stared up at him with those innocent, beautiful copper eyes. "You know how you want me to trust you and kind of let you show me stuff?"

"Yeah, baby." He brushed a kiss across her forehead.

"Okay, well, I really want you to trust Tutu, and I want to do what she says. I don't want to be sick all the time anymore. Kauai makes me healthier, but I still don't have as much energy as I should and stuff like that."

Garrett's initial thought was that obviously she'd been exhausted the entire time she'd lived on Kauai. She'd either been teaching dance ten hours a day to try and make enough money to pay her grandmother's medical bills or actually at an endless number of medio appointments with her grandmother. She'd had no time to do anything but survive.

"You don't know what Nana was like before I managed to get the job here at Miss Leialanie's so Tutu could help her. She gave her two years she wouldn't have had, and they were good years of the chemo not making her so sick she could hardly survive."

"Okay, whatever you want, but I mean, I don't think Kauai is going to do the same thing for me, and there's not really much that I think I need help with." Garrett tried not to be offensive in his explanation. Kaimi's brow furrowed as she considered that. She was too exhausted, and her rhythms were flowing in too many directions for her to have put up much of an argument.

"Please just try what she says."

"I'll do anything for you." Garrett began drinking the water directly from the half gallon container.

"Thank you." Kaimi leaned against him as she sipped her tea.

"I'm gonna be up pissing all freaking night, just so you know."

She grinned and brushed a sweet kiss along his collarbone. "Just don't wake me up."

Garrett huffed audibly as he shook his head at her. When they'd finished their remedies, Kaimi grabbed his hand and the oil he was to rub on her and pulled him toward their bed.

"It's our first night in our bed where we're gonna live for real."

"Have you ever slept here on the farm?" Garrett recalled how absolutely incredible the beds and mattresses that Fionna's grandfather handcrafted were. Kaimi shook her head. "Yeah, well, I may never get you to actually go camping with me ever again after you sleep on this." He climbed in the incredibly soft sheets and guided her in beside him. He began rubbing the oils into her shoulders.

"I love to camp, and I can't wait to camp with you. But I'm pretty excited about sleeping with you here too, especially since you're buck naked." She giggled.

"That was my favorite prescribed remedy of Tutu's. Trust me." Garrett slid his hands from Kaimi's shoulder down her side. He massaged the rest of the oil into her thighs.

When he was finished, she laid her head on his chest. "We have to go to sleep. We have to make Aida feel better tomorrow."

Garrett smiled at her ever changing thoughts. "We're in paradise, and she loves this farm. Hopefully, we can ease her into everything before I head back to DC." He wondered if she would catch his slight change of phrase. "I'm gonna fly out late Monday. I'll take her to school her first day and then pick her up. I know Dan and Fi would do that if they were here." A yawn overtook Garrett.

"Why do you keep saying *you're* flying back Monday? *We're* flying back Monday." Kaimi immediately focused on his slip.

"Let's talk about it tomorrow. See how you're feeling. If you're not up to coming back to DC, I don't want you to feel like you have to. Let me go back and clean up this shit at Venton. You stay here and get well." Garrett could hardly keep his eyes open after his explosive release and the deeply relaxing bath.

"I don't want to stay here without you." Kaimi's stubborn adamance seemed to be at war with her body's desperation to relax.

"Hey." Garrett cradled her closer. "Let's just see how this weekend goes, okay? Let's get some sleep. Please, baby. I know you're exhausted after the week we've had."

"Tutu will make me better, and then I'm going back with you."

"Okay," he sighed. He knew better than to argue with her in her current state, and truthfully, he was too tired to come up with much.

"I am!"

"Kaimi." Garrett lifted his head and kissed her with a great deal of force, mostly to shut her up. "Okay. I'm going to sleep. I love you. I wasn't trying to start anything."

"I love you too." She seemed to decide to let it go for the moment at least, but her rhythms tensed toward frustration. He certainly hadn't meant to upset her. He wanted her to relax as much as Tutu did. He'd thought maybe she'd be relieved she didn't have to go back to the freezing cold temperatures, the disasters at Venton, and to packing up the apartment.

76

He'd grown rather accustomed to sleeping with a small golden retriever at his feet, and he missed Duke. *Duke*—he realized there was definitely something Kaimi would want to go back to DC for. She loved Duke almost as much as she loved Garrett.

Feeling even worse for bringing it up when she'd been so relaxed and they'd had such an amazing and desperately needed reconnection, Garrett let his shield spill from his pores.

"I love you so much. I'd miss you like crazy if you stayed here. It was a stupid idea. I just thought you might be happier here, and I always want you to be happy and healthy." He told the truth and reinforced it with his rhythms. The truth of his soul formed in the green haze around her.

She melted into him as the tension dissipated. "I love you too. I don't want to be without you. I didn't mean to get mad at you."

"Let's just get some sleep." Garrett brushed a kiss in her hair and tenderly caressed her again. He could barely keep his eyes open.

CHAPTER 15
NIGHTCAP NIGHTMARES

~DAN VINDICO~

Dan eased from the bed. He couldn't sleep. His mind offered him no reprieve. His father, the pictures of Fionna, his girls five thousand miles away, his new job, his old job, the house, the farm—it all swirled violently in his gut.

He heated the sheets as he covered Fionna. He whispered a kiss on her cheek and a prayer that somehow he wouldn't have to disappoint her yet again. This time by the entire world seeing things meant only for his eyes.

He slipped quickly down the hallway. He didn't want to look into the girls' empty bedrooms. It destroyed him. It was his fault they weren't there.

With a slight shudder, he headed to the dining room. He pulled a tumbler from the hutch and poured himself a small glass of Talisker, his favorite, and settled down at the evidence-covered table.

With a sigh, he opened his personal laptop. He couldn't bring himself to delete the email from the fake IP address with pictures of Fionna. It drove him. It fueled the wrath-filled fire that burned in him. He wouldn't allow it to happen.

Think, Vindico, just think. He glanced down at the evidence he'd recovered from Georgetown the night Kaimi had been admitted. The blackmail threat colored everything before his eyes.

Jeff was certainly onto something with the fact that Libby Ellington's father was one of the heads of the Georgetown lab, and she was most definitely using drugs recreationally, but why wouldn't he just cover her tests? Why would he change all the others? How had these students been emboldened enough not to just blackmail other students but to blackmail Dan?

What if it's not just me? His heart raced as he flung papers from the folders until he came across the thirty tests that had been positive originally but were then reported as negative for usage. He grabbed his phone. *Dammit!* It was almost five in the morning. They hadn't gotten home from the hospital until two. He'd been lying awake for hours, but now it was too late to call Jeff.

Hey, call me when you wake up. I may have figured something out. I need your help

he texted and then moved back to the laptop. He casted it and pulled up the Iodex records that Portwood had allowed him access to when he'd been reinstated as joint Chief of Elite. He quickly typed— Sandra Ellington.

Sandra Ellington is in her fourth term as Senteon representative from Maryland. Ms. Ellington is well-known for her staunchly conservative viewpoints on everything from criminal sentences to her stand against sexual education before marriage, and has repeatedly voted to keep drug users in Felsink for extended terms instead of being sent to Auxiliary rehab.

"Has she now?" Dan continued his search. His cell rang and he answered immediately.

"Hey, I'm awake. I don't sleep too well in a hospital bed with my very pregnant wife. What's up?"

"I slept that way a few times with Fi. You're a good guy."

"Oh, hey, Mentor Vindico, I talked to Becca, and we would really like to maybe buy your house…if we can afford it."

"Okay, couple of things. One, I'm not your mentor anymore. I'm hoping you count me as a close friend, so call me Dan. If not, then let's go with Commander Vindico. This mentor thing makes me want to vomit. Second, you and Becca call Patrick Haydenshire. I'll pay his fees and have him take it off the market. Get him to run a loan approval you're happy with. The only thing that has made my wife smile in the last week is knowing you and Becca are going to live here after we move. I know Becca can't leave the hospital, so maybe come over here one night and take some pictures. We can't move this furniture. It would cost me more to get it there than to just buy whatever she wants when we arrive. Whatever you want, just tell us."

"Wow. Thank you. Bec will flip, but what did you figure out?"

"Dan, are you okay?" Fionna's sleepy question startled him. "I promise your dad is going to be all right," she assured him again. "I can feel it."

He spun in his chair and pulled her to him. She was dressed in nothing but her favorite terrycloth robe that hung off her curves. Dan swallowed as she moved to him. He caught tempting glimpses of her left nipple and her lower lips as she walked. After momentarily forgetting that he was on the phone, he cleared his throat and wrapped his available arm under the robe.

"Jeff, I'm gonna take Fi back to bed. We need to talk about Representative Sandra Ellington. You're on to something about her husband working at the lab. I have a hunch we've been missing a big piece of this puzzle. We've been approaching this whole thing wrong. What if I'm not the only one being blackmailed? What if Medio Ellington is being blackmailed because of his wife?"

"Is she the one who wanted to change the laws so that people arrested for drugs went to prison instead of rehab?"

"Yes, and she's got a fair amount of approval from voters under her ridiculous premise."

"I'll look into it."

"Thanks."

"Who was that?" Fionna yawned as Dan stood and wrapped his arms around her.

"That was Jeff. I had a few thoughts about all of our situations at Venton."

"I thought once the girls were at Tutu's, I got to be your partner."

"You are, baby, but I want you to sleep too."

Dan eased the robe from her shoulders once they'd returned to their bedroom. It fell into a soft pile at her feet.

"I kind of forgot the girls aren't here. I don't know why I put that on." Her eyes were tender with fear hidden in their depths. She leaned into him as if she needed to cover herself. Dan cradled her close. His shield spilled rapidly from his pores.

He couldn't stand that she was so wary. Her confidence was so shaken. She was terrified of what other people had seen and what the entire world might see if Dan didn't stop it. How could he have let someone else see his baby like that? He was the only person who should ever see her so vulnerable and on display. She'd trusted him implicitly, and he'd let her down again. No. He still had time to keep the world from seeing her. He would not fail her again.

"Let's go back to bed. I'll tell you everything when you wake up." His harrowing fear filled his shield.

She squeezed him tighter. "I'm okay. I just had a nightmare."

"Come here." He crawled back in the bed and cradled her on his chest. "I'm sorry you had a bad dream. Do you want to tell me what happened?"

Receivers often had very vivid dreams. When Fionna had been pregnant with Halia, she'd had intense dreams, some oddly hilarious and some where she would recall being shot or losing her mother or even the attack on the Fitzroys' home. She would awaken sobbing. Dan would cast her the entire night to calm her and reassure her that he would keep her safe.

She shook her head against him. Her body shivered convulsively.

"I've got you, baby. I swear, I won't let anyone else see those pictures."

"I know. It was just a stupid nightmare. I just miss the girls. I'll be all right."

CHAPTER 16

ANXIOUS EMAILS
~GARRETT HAYDENSHIRE~

Garrett's eyes flew open. He gasped for breath as he sat up and then immediately slid back down in the bed. Aida was in their bedroom crying, and neither he nor Kaimi had anything on.

"Aida, baby, what's wrong?" He tried to lean up and keep Kaimi's top half covered.

"I was bad. I'm so sorry." Tears poured from her huge brown eyes. She cradled Davi the bunny tight in her hands and used his ears to wipe her eyes. It broke Garrett's heart.

"You weren't bad. You're never bad. Tell me what happened?" Garrett tried to listen to her while he determined the best way to get dressed. Kaimi rubbed her eyes. She blinked confusedly for a moment.

"I wasn't supposed to come down here. Tutu said not to, but I got scared, and Tutu is with Halia, and Auntie Malani isn't here yet, and I wanted you. Papa is working on my new house. I'm sorry. I didn't mean to be bad." The only time Garrett had ever seen Aida cry that hard had been right after her parents' murder. He couldn't stand it.

Kaimi nodded and eased upward in the bed. She kept her chest covered with the sheets.

"It's okay. You weren't bad. You were just scared. I'll talk to Tutu. You aren't in trouble, sweetheart. It's been a rough few days. Hey, I have an idea. Why don't you run back up to Tutu's house and get your doll you got for Christmas? Remember, you were going to show her to me? Bring her back down here, and we'll play."

Aida gave a solemn nod and turned to do as she was told. Garrett and Kaimi scrambled from the bed as soon as the screen door slammed on its hinges.

"Poor thing." Kaimi frantically threw on a short sundress.

"That is the only time my goddaughter has ever just defied what someone told her to do. I can't believe she did that. She's not all right. I think Tutu is wrong. She may not be okay, and I'm not going back to DC until I know that she is."

"Okay, but I know Tutu and Papa aren't going to punish her. She can stay with us all day. Tutu was right. She needs you because Dan isn't here, and you're her Shield. I'll share. How can you stand it when she cries? It's horrible."

"I can't stand it. It kills me. All I see is that sweet baby girl sobbing in my arms in Brazil. It physically destroys me." Garrett's own confession wounded his soul.

Kaimi wrapped her arms around his waist. "It's okay. You saved her, and we're going to take care of her. I promise. We won't go anywhere at all if she's not okay."

"I have to call Dan. I'm telling you this isn't like her."

"Okay, you call them, and I'll go meet her. I'll probably run into Tutu. You don't put much by her, trust me." Kaimi slipped into a pair of flip-flops and headed out the front door.

"Don't you want coffee, babe?" Garrett called after her.

"Later. Right now our girl needs us." Kaimi headed off down the path toward Tutu and Papa's small house in the center of the farm.

With a sigh, Garrett located his cell phone in the pants he'd been wearing the night before.

Dan Vindico

"Hey, is everything okay?" Dan answered Garrett's call and rubbed his eyes as he tried to focus on the numbers scrolling on the screen that Jeff was casting. It was after lunch, and they'd been at it all morning.

"Kind of. How's your dad?"

"He's all right. He wants to work from his hospital bed, which will not be happening. Your dad ordered him to take a vacation. They're thinking of coming to Kauai after we move, so that should be interesting."

Garrett chuckled uncomfortably, and Dan's Visium Predilection kicked into overdrive. "What's wrong?"

"Nothing really. I just thought I should probably tell you. It was no big deal, but I'm kind of worried about her," Garrett began his hemmed confession.

"Who? Aida?"

"Yeah. She showed up in our bedroom this morning, which is not a big deal except we weren't really dressed for company, but Tutu told her not to come down here. I'm worried about her."

Dan sighed. Although it was the first time he could recall Aida ever defying anything or anyone, he wasn't surprised. "Fi usually tells her she forgot to put on pajamas if she comes in our room before she's put on clothes. I'm sorry. I knew she wasn't going to handle this well." Dan had spoken without thinking.

He watched Jeff try to pretend that he hadn't just figured out that Fionna slept in the buff. Adding another layer to the *exposing his wife's deepest secrets* cake of horrible guilt, Dan rubbed his temples. He couldn't go on like this much longer. He was losing it.

"But Fi's grandmother's not gonna, like, spank her or anything? It's not a big deal, like I said," Garrett urged fervently.

Dan had to grin. He should have known that would be Garrett's concern. It would physically injure Garrett for Aida to be punished for anything.

"Tutu is pretty much the best there is when it comes to grandmothers, and she lets Aida do anything she's curious about within reason. She'll probably talk to Aida and help her figure out why she did that, but no, she won't punish her."

"Do you think she'll be okay 'til you and Fi get out here? Is there something I should do? Should Kaimi and I stay out here?" Garrett sounded more frantic than Dan had ever heard him.

"I think she'll be fine in a few days. Fi's a disaster as well. Remember, I told you they do not handle being apart well. Just let me get this shit cleaned up. Your dad's taking over Venton Monday morning, so that should be interesting."

"Dad's had his fill of it. He'll get something done. He won't be as diplomatic as your old man, but something will happen."

"That's what I'm hoping at this point. I'm sorry Aida intruded this morning. I'll call and talk to her." Dan suddenly remembered that this was supposed to be Garrett and Kaimi's honeymoon.

"Nah, it's fine. I'm just worried about her."

"Yeah, me too."

"Hey, Mentor Vindico. I may have something here," Jeff interrupted.

"Let me go look at this, Garrett. I'll call and talk to Aida in a few minutes."

Dan moved closer to the computer Jeff was working on at Venton. Fionna came out of the women's room. Governor Haydenshire was on his way up to the school along with the school governors. Portwood and Ericcson were already there. Everyone leaned closer to Jeff.

"Based on the idea that either Medio Ellington or Representative Ellington are somehow involved in the drug test swaps, I'm going to cast the firewalls to look for emails about them. We don't know if they're on the take or if Medio Ellington is swapping them under duress, but it seems like a fairly safe bet that voters finding out Libby is using when her mom's the big 'don't do drugs' representative would be a good place to start. It would take us all forever to dig through every single email that goes in and out of this place. Every student has an email address, every faculty member, even some past students can keep their address for a little while until they change it themselves. So, every clue we get, I can add words to the cast I put into the firewall that will flag the emails relating to those things or those people."

"But you'd already done that with Brodie Quentin?" Portwood pointed out.

"Yeah, but we weren't getting much. I don't really know anything more than he's gotten a few cryptic emails with a few addresses downtown."

Dan turned to Portwood.

"We checked them out. Nothing there. Mostly restaurants. We can stake them if you want, but remember, until you came forward with the threats against you and Fionna, I didn't have a dog in this fight."

"Let's see what we find out here first," Dan decided.

"I guess bad guys don't make the subject lines of their emails 'blackmail' huh?" Fionna leaned against Dan, and he wrapped his arm around her with a grin.

"Not unless they're really bad at what they do," Portwood lamented with her. Her abashed chuckle had Dan's heart swelling at a moment's notice.

"I'll cast the email servers and send all of the emails with any reference to Medio Ellington to all of our personal laptops. It'll take some digging, but for now it's the best lead we have," Jeff offered humbly.

"No, it's a great lead, and we'll dig as much as we need to." Portwood slapped Jeff on the back. Governor Haydenshire and Will arrived just in time to hear Jeff's instructions.

"I'm aware that I am not an Iodex officer, but I think I'm probably capable of reading emails. Let's see if we can't get something figured out today." Governor Haydenshire didn't appear to be joking. He was more than willing to lend his hands when something needed to be done.

"Yeah, I'm in. Let's get this done." Will pulled his Senate Bank-issued Mac from a bag slung on his shoulder.

"The more names or words we can come up with to feed through my casting, the more information we'll have, but remember that's also going to be more to be sorted and discarded. It won't all have to do with what we're looking for," Jeff continued.

Dan was impressed with Jeff's growing self-confidence. He was thriving under Portwood. He was clearly coming into his own.

"I have several plans for Monday morning. We'll go over them all later, but for now, let's start digging," Governor Haydenshire urged everyone on.

"The paychecks have all been tagged. We'll trace the extra and see where it lands. That should get us somewhere on that end, but let's read emails," Will added.

CHAPTER 17

PREDICTIONS
~GARRETT HAYDENSHIRE~

"I love you too, so much!" Aida exclaimed. Just talking to Fionna on the phone seemed to soothe her. "Yes, and Uncle Garrett and Auntie Kaimi and Tutu and Uncle Kai and Auntie Malani are all going to take me and Halia on a walk to our new house because I said I didn't know how to get there and that I know how to get everywhere else from when I'm at Tutu's house."

Garrett and Kaimi shared a delighted grin. Tutu had handed Halia off to Kaimi and Garrett and had spent the entire day devoted to Aida, after the episode that morning, and Aida had settled in.

"And Papa said that him and Tutu and Uncle Garrett are all going to school with me on Monday, and Tutu said that Sarah is in my class." Aida's eyes were beginning to hold the light Garrett had seen the last time they'd been to Kauai.

Whatever Fionna was telling her, she was nodding and biting her lip. Garrett had laid Halia in her crib after she'd fallen asleep on his chest an hour before, and he was beginning to feel like the girls might be able to handle being without Dan and Fi for a few weeks.

As Dan had pointed out that he didn't know how far these pricks at Venton were willing to go, the girls were certainly safer five thousand miles away from the insanity that seemed to breed without thought in DC.

"Hi, Daddy, are you and Mommy kissing?"

Garrett chuckled as Aida talked with Dan. Garrett determined that they must've had a pretty good day figuring stuff out at Venton.

A few minutes later, Aida handed Garrett the phone.

"Everything is set for Monday. I just hope this works," Dan sighed.

"It'll work. We'll fly out as soon as we pick Aida up from school," Garrett assured him. "Maybe take Fi out and try to forget about all of this shit. Go have a little fun. She's gonna go nuts if she doesn't get her mind off those pictures for a while."

"Yeah, I know. We're going to go see Dad. Then I'll see if I can't get her mind off everything."

Garrett chuckled. "I'm sure you could come up with something."

"Yeah, I got it, Haydenshire. Thanks."

"No problem. Tell Fi to chill. The girls are fine."

"I will and thank you." Dan's derision melted instantly.

Garrett ended the call and set the phone down as Aida grabbed his hands. She swayed herself back and forth, and he kept her balanced. "You're going out on a date with Auntie Kaimi and to go get the rest of the stuff from where she used to live. And me and Halia are going to go to the beach with Tutu and Papa and Auntie Malani and Uncle Kai, and Uncle Kai is going to take me on the paddleboard. Are you and Auntie Kaimi gonna kiss on your date?" Aida restated the plan as it had been explained to her a few minutes before.

Garrett wondered about Aida's sudden fascination with kissing. He tried to recall Emily at eight years old and decided maybe kissing was a normal thing to be curious about at that age.

"I don't know. Do you think I should?"

"Yes!" Aida's eyes lit, and her sweet grin spread across her precious face.

"You do, huh?" Garrett continued his inquiry.

"Yes, and you should kiss her now and then later because then you won't be mad."

"I'm not mad, baby girl."

"I know, but you're going to be mad, and that makes my tummy hurt." Aida's momentary thrill over kissing seemed to dissolve into worry.

90

"Why am I going to be mad?"

Dan and Fionna had both told Garrett about Aida's exceptional Receiver abilities. He wondered if somehow Kauai made her stronger as well.

"I'm not sure. Please don't yell." Aida extended her arms up to Garrett. His heart faltered as he lifted her upward.

"Aida, baby, I would never ever yell at you," he vowed adamantly.

Aida leaned her head down and nuzzled it in Garrett's neck. "I know because you love me so much, and I love you so much, but Auntie Kaimi loves you so much too. She didn't mean to."

Tutu stepped in. She startled Garrett.

"My precious Aida, Tutu had those same thoughts, and I know everything is going to be just fine. Let's let Uncle Garrett go enjoy an evening with Auntie Kaimi, and you and I will play at the beach. Tutu can teach you what to do with those tummy troubles just like I taught your mommy."

"Okay." Aida wiggled down from Garrett's arms. He was thoroughly confused. He had no idea how much stock to put in an eight-year-old's predictions.

"Go on. She'll be fine. She's just a little out of sorts with Maylea so far away. She misses her daddy terribly. She'll be all right." Tutu didn't speak until Malani had distracted Aida with Lanie.

CHAPTER 18
ALL THE WAY BACK HOME

Garrett couldn't keep Aida's plea out of his mind as he drove his new Iodex Hummer to Kaimi's old apartment complex.

"Tell me if any of these are lame." He glanced down at the list he'd made on his phone as he drove. "Leilands, Gertrudes, or The Bay Shore?"

Kaimi gave him the intoxicating look that said she thought she was incredibly lucky to have him. Garrett's heart soared every time she looked at him like that. "Well…" She wrinkled her nose adorably and Garrett chuckled.

"So, they're all lame. All right, I'll let you show me all the hot spots in our new town then, sweetheart." He tried not to feel defeated, but truthfully, he was used to being the one impressing her.

"It's not that they're lame. It's more like there are places locals don't really go very often because there are so many tourists. Whenever Nana was sick and had to be in the hospital, I hated being in the apartment all alone, so I would just go and hang out at these really cool coffee bars and little out-of-the-way places. I would get as lost as you can get on an island with barely one highway and then find somewhere and go in. I can show you some of those places if you want."

Kaimi's tender plea meant to share a piece of her precious soul with her husband touched the deepest wells of Garrett's heart. He'd thought he should find some expensive restaurants to take her to for dinner on their honeymoon, but he should have known that would never appeal to her.

"You're sure you want to head up to Anini tomorrow?" He wondered if she would feel up to their camping trip.

"I wish we could go tonight, not that I don't love our new house. I can't wait to make money again, so I can get stuff and make it our own. I have so many ideas. I don't know where to start. But we're not going anywhere until we're sure Aida is going to be okay with us leaving." She stared out at the brilliant pinks, oranges, and lush greens that surrounded the road.

Garrett slowed at a traffic light and gave himself a moment to admire his beautiful bride dressed in a teal, ruffled dress. It was made of some kind of gauzy material. It should have been see-through, but the gathered fabric made it frustratingly opaque. It skimmed and scalloped the tops of her thighs, and the spaghetti-string straps did nothing to hide the fact that his sweet girl rarely wore a bra.

"I'm so glad to be back here, I can't even stand it. I'm not made for jeans and sweaters." She continued to gush out her exuberance to be back in seventy-five-degree sunshine.

Garrett nodded. "I know. I hate we have to go back." A plaguing restlessness continued to needle Garrett. He didn't want to go back without her, but he couldn't help but think she'd be better off if she stayed there.

"It won't be for very long, and then we get to live here."

Garrett laced his fingers through hers as he drove. "I can't wait to get here and be here and start our life. I feel like I've been waiting years to actually want to have a life, and now I do and I'm still stuck in DC."

Her delight in that moment was so potent he felt her rhythms all trill together. She rarely felt only one emotion, and the sweet happiness his vow had brought on delighted him.

He pulled into the apartment complex. He assumed she had

dozens of boxes of clothes and things from her life there to load up, so he parked in the loading zone.

"Thank you for loving me and being the most amazing guy in the whole world."

Garrett leaned and kissed the side of her head. He inhaled deeply of her island scent mixed in with her cheap, mango-scented shampoo. He loved it all, and he didn't want to do anything but spend time in her presence.

"Thank you for loving me like that. I'll never deserve it, but I swear I'll never stop trying to."

"That isn't true," she informed him.

"I can turn the lights on if we're here too long." He ignored her argument because it was true. He'd never deserve her. He hopped out of the Hummer and then moved to help her out.

"I think I got a lot of stuff done that day I was here, but I don't remember. It's such a blur," Kaimi confessed as she leaned into his side as he wrapped his arm around her.

"Miss Walyuo, where have you been? I tried to call!" A rather short elderly woman with a heavily puckered mouth scolded Kaimi as soon as they entered the complex. Kaimi sighed.

"Sorry, Miss Poivous. I'm just here to get the rest of my things. Remember, I told you I wouldn't be renewing my lease."

"Yes, I know, but we have mail, so much mail, and the smell!" Miss Poivous was mutinous. "They turned off your power! Oh, the smell!"

Kaimi's brow furrowed, and she turned to unlock the door.

"I had to throw out all food! You're not getting your deposit back! Get rid of everything so I can air it out and show the apartment!!" Miss Poivous wagged her finger in Kaimi's face.

"We'll take care of it." Garrett stepped between his wife and her former landlord. "And she's no longer Miss Walyuo. She's Mrs. Haydenshire. My wife." The name certainly carried weight.

He did catch the pungent smell of something rancid that lingered in the air though. He tried not to scowl, as he kept up his disdainful glare.

"I don't care what her name is! Clean this out, so I can rent it!"

Miss Poivous threw her arms in the air and turned to stomp out of the apartment.

"Sorry. She's always been like that. She used to complain that Nana's oxygen tank was too loud when she rolled it on the little cart she had," Kaimi sighed.

"Nice." Garrett could not believe his eyes. He'd expected packed boxes and a few pieces of furniture that Kaimi wanted to move to their new home on the Ionas' farm. The apartment was still full of furniture and, from the smell of it, food and probably a dead mouse or two.

"I thought you packed everything." He tried not to sound as frustrated as he felt.

"I was only here one day. I tried to pack as much as I could. I don't know…. I guess I got kind of overwhelmed. All I knew was that I wanted you. So, I just got on the plane. I'm sorry. Obviously, that was a bad plan all the way around."

Her rhythms pulsed in anger, embarrassment, and fear. She cocked her jaw to the side and refused to look him in the eye, but he could see the makings of hot, angry tears that threatened imminent downpour.

"Hey." Garrett pulled her into his chest. *Auntie Kaimi loves you so much and she didn't mean to.* Aida's words rushed back to him. She'd sensed the potential for an argument, and truthfully, Garrett was rather irritated with the amount of work left to do. "Let's just get this done. You'd been halfway through hell when Nana died, and I dragged you the rest of the way. Let me help you. What do we want to do with all of the furniture?" He'd never been afraid of work, but having a few extra sets of muscles would've been nice.

"I thought I threw out all the food. We couldn't have had much. We never had much," she fretted as she eased into the tiny kitchen.

Garrett wondered how much he would be hated as second in command if he asked a few of his new coworkers to come help him move the furniture out of the apartment.

"Oh my gosh." Kaimi's voice shook, and Garrett jogged into the kitchen, wondering what she'd found. Tears were already pouring down her beautiful face when he reached her.

She was staring into a tiny bread box that had been placed in the corner of the countertop. There was a bag of what appeared to have been marshmallows suitable for roasting and several Hershey chocolate bars that had teeth marks in them. Ants were everywhere. Garrett tried not to shudder in disgust as he took in what appeared to have been a few sandwiches in chewed-through plastic baggies. Kaimi's hand trembled as she handed Garrett a sheet of folded notebook paper.

"My sweet Kaimi, I don't think I will be here with you much longer. Tutu Iona has told me that the boy you've had on your mind so much lately is the one my seeker has been seeking. Take these and take him camping. Let him see your beautiful soul in all of your favorite places. Share yourself with him now that I'll be out of your way. I love you so, Nana."

Garrett's eyes closed as he dammed back tears of his own. He wrapped his arms around her and swayed her softly.

"I didn't know they were there. We never kept anything in there." She tried to explain how food had been left in the apartment for weeks.

"It's okay, baby." He continued to soothe her. A moment later, his shield spun from his pores and encapsulated her in his own brand of tranquility.

She sobbed, and Garrett stood steadfast, letting her ruin his shirt as he tried desperately to help her bear the horror of death that takes everything not from its victim but from those left behind. When she'd cried herself out, Garrett tried to determine what to do next.

"Why don't you tell me what we want to move into our new house, and then if there's anything of Nana's you want to keep, we'll pack that. Whatever we can't use, we'll donate to one of the centers that helps people with cancer. I'll find one tomorrow and see if they can come take everything else." Kaimi nodded against him.

Garrett had never been so thankful for Aida in all his life, except for the fact that she'd quite literally led him to Kaimi.

If he'd gotten angry at her about the apartment and then she'd found that note, he couldn't imagine what that would have done to her delicate psyche. As he continued to cradle her tenderly to his chest, he let his mind recall chasing Aida along one of the many paths on the farm the day all of the hula instructors were coming to meet with Fionna and Malani.

"*Aida, baby, wait...*" he'd called as she'd raced headlong into her grandparents' home. She was supposed to play outside. Fionna's meeting wasn't over, but she must've known all along. Aida knew that Garrett would follow her anywhere, and she'd led him right into his life, right into the woman who was his other half. She'd led him all the way back home.

CHAPTER 19

IN THE EYE

Trying to get Kaimi to pack was a disaster. She got distracted so easily. There was no way she ever could have done this alone, and she shouldn't have had to. Her grandmother had just died. Garrett patiently tried to guide her.

"I just don't know if Nana would be upset if I don't keep all of this." Kaimi was going through her grandmother's jewelry. "None of it is worth anything monetarily, but she loved wearing it all."

Garrett drew a deep breath and instantly regretted it. As best he could determine, a mouse must've gotten in the apartment looking for food and had died in a wall somewhere. The smell was horrendous. They'd thrown open all the windows. It was improving, just not fast enough.

"Is there any you want to wear?"

Kaimi considered for a minute before shaking her head. "I don't think so, but I could make something out of it."

"Okay, then pick out a few things that remind you of Nana and whatever you want to craft into something else, and then donate the rest. Maybe someone else will like this." Garrett gave her his signature smirk as he lifted a gaudy orange-and-black beaded necklace complete with a hibiscus charm. Kaimi began giggling. It was the sweetest sound in his entire world. She laid her head against his chest.

"I'm sorry I didn't tell you how much was left. I just didn't want to think about it. I didn't really realize. I didn't mean to lie."

"Sweetheart, you didn't lie. This is part of what I was telling you a few days ago. I never let you deal with Nana's death, and I should have. I should have brought you back here weeks ago. Let's just get this done."

Kaimi nodded. She seemed to force herself to concentrate and selected a few trinkets from her grandmother's jewelry box. "There are all of those boxes of bills and paperwork and stuff. Nana never got rid of anything, but I don't know if there's anything important in them that I should keep. And just the quilts from in her closet, I think. Would you mind getting those?" Her voice shook as she made the timid request.

"Not at all. Why don't you go get the rest of your old room packed up? I'll get the quilts, and then I'll come help you in there."

"Thank you for being so sweet. You should have yelled at me." The regret in her tone wounded him.

"I wasn't gonna yell at you."

"You were biting a hole in your tongue." Her mood shifted yet again, and Garrett chuckled.

"I'm sure between now and the rest of forever we will get into an argument. Eventually, I'll let my asshole side show, and you're not gonna take my crap, which I really like about you, by the way. But it's not gonna be tonight on our honeymoon. Tonight, we're going to get ready to move in together because you're my wife, and I could never love anything more."

"Thank you." She squeezed her eyes shut tight to fight another onslaught of tears. Garrett kissed the top of her head as he cradled her to his chest.

"And if you hurry up, Mrs. Haydenshire, I think we could at least go see a shoreline before we go back to the farm for the night."

Kaimi pulled away from him and gave him her sweet, mischievous grin. "I'll hurry. I think it's just shoes and art supplies, and I need to clean up a little."

Garrett opened the louvered doors of what had been Nana's closet. He sighed. Clothes hung lifeless on the hangers. The smell of mothballs replaced the scent of dead rat that had thankfully dissipated as the evening breezes moved through the apartment.

He shuddered as the hangers gave a hair-raising screech when he slid them to the side. Garrett had always believed clothes were the worst possible things left behind. They held too many memories, too much life left in the designs, too much of the person residing in the empty shells.

He glanced upward and saw a half dozen Hawaiian quilts stacked on the upper closet shelf. He pulled down three and laid them on the bed carefully, keeping them folded. He returned and pulled the others down but was assaulted by several manilla envelopes that fell to his feet. They'd been dragged down by the quilts. He stacked the quilts and leaned to pick up the envelopes.

He gathered them up, and his brow furrowed. *Law Offices of Karen Kin* was stamped across one with matching letterhead that had edged out when the envelope had fallen. *Honolulu Testing Lab and Paternity Facilities* was written on the other. Garrett's heart thundered in his chest as he glanced toward Kaimi's room instinctively.

Even if he knows about her, she's an adult. He has no claim on her. He can't hurt her. He couldn't understand the terror that flooded his shield. It set of its own accord. He had no idea why his muscles flexed continuously. His blood ran hot and cold in the same moment. He had to know both what the paternity results said and what his shield sensed. He eased the paperwork out of the envelopes.

He studied a custody document. He allowed himself to breathe as he realized it was the document where Carlina had signed away all rights to Kaimi to her grandmother. They'd been signed two days after Kaimi's birth, but there it was. Garrett's mouth hung open as he stared at a second signature under her mother's name. The breath he'd drawn a moment before left his lungs in a gasp as he jerked open the other envelope.

The paternity results given in two sheets were on top, but underneath those… Garrett willed it to be anything other than what he was staring at. A dishonorable discharge command from the Gifted Branches of the United States Army was framed by numerous mug shots and a seven-page felony rap sheet. The last offense was dated three years before. Five counts of assault and battery, forgery, attempted murder, felony arson, and blackmail. Her father's life's work was written out before Garrett's eyes.

Akamai Halemano Wardlaw—there was a last known address given. It was somewhere on Kauai though Garrett didn't know the area well enough yet to be able to determine how far away he might be, and it was dated five years before.

Garrett memorized the name instantly. His mind was trained to master every detail of a rap sheet. He couldn't stop the process.

Her mother had lied to her. She'd known who her father was all along. Kaimi favored her mother more than her dad, but there in the mug shot photograph, Garrett saw the slight matching dimple on Kaimi's chin and the copper of her eyes that she'd inherited from her father—the felon.

CHAPTER 20

TOE SHOES AND UNTRUTHS

"Garrett?" Kaimi called. His heart thundered back to life as he tried to figure out how to hide the paperwork. "Are the quilts not up in the closet?" He haphazardly folded the documents and shoved them between the stack of quilts.

"I've got them." He carried the quilts with him as he rushed into Kaimi's room. Savage debate raged in his mind. He studied Kaimi. She was stacking up sketch pads on her old bed. The evening had nearly done her in. Her eyes were red-rimmed as she continually fought back tears and tried to forge onward toward their life together.

Her hands trembled as she stacked her beloved sketchbooks. The ones her mother made fun of and the ones Nana complained about her having. She thought they were a waste of Kaimi's time.

Garrett's Predilect took over his entire body. She didn't need to know her mother had lied or that her father was a criminal. Her mother had done nothing in Kaimi's life but hurt her, and her sperm donor didn't deserve to know her at all.

Garrett's jaw clenched in the determination of his decision. He set the quilts on a stack of boxes and moved to the bed. He opened the large sketch pad on top and smiled. They were fantastic images of women woven in and out of Hawaiian floral blooms. They were stunning in their detail.

"This is amazing, baby. Incredible." Kaimi blushed as she bit her lip and moved closer.

"Thank you. You're the only person who's ever seen those. I was on the flower ladies kick for a long while. I kept picking blooms from alongside the road and coming home and making them into women. It was stupid." She shook her head and rolled her eyes.

"No, it wasn't. These are amazing. Please stop downplaying them. You're an incredible artist."

She still didn't know how to believe him. Her mother had done a number on her, and Garrett was determined to prove her worth to her if it was the last thing he ever did.

"Thanks." She swallowed uncomfortably and moved to add a set of cheap, colored pencils to the stack.

"Hey, would you want to set up a studio in the house somewhere? I know it's kind of small but maybe out on that big screened-in porch or in the living room somewhere?"

"I don't need that. As soon as Maylea gets the hula studio opened, I'll be dancing all the time anyway." Garrett wondered if Tutu would mind him adding on to their free abode. They'd been pretty adamant that he and Kaimi live there, but he didn't want to impose.

"Anything else you want from in here besides these?" Garrett was eager to leave though he couldn't fathom why. The apartment was somehow tainted with memories of the father she didn't know she had.

"We don't have to take these. They'll take up too much room." The devastation was evident in her tone.

"Kaimi." Garrett lifted her chin with his hand. He stared deeply into the darkened copper of her downtrodden eyes. "We are taking these and all of your art supplies. And we're taking anything else that makes you *you*. I love you. Just tell me what makes you smile, and I'll pack it for you."

"Are you sure they won't be in the way?" she continued to fuss.

"No, I don't think *your* things will be in the way in *our* home." Deciding that he wanted to get out of there quickly and was tired of her downplaying her own abilities, Garrett moved to the closet. He picked up several plastic bins of art supplies and started a new box.

There was a large cardboard box in the bottom of the closet that contained dozens of pairs of toe shoes. Kaimi chuckled as she moved to help him.

"I always had to buy my own, and they're kind of expensive. Nana thought I would get better grades if she made me buy them if I didn't get Bs. But I couldn't ever get Bs, so I just started buying my own. I would clean up after class at the studio where I took dance in Honolulu, and my teachers would pay me more than they should have because they knew if I didn't have shoes I couldn't perform. I cried whenever I wore a pair out or they got too small because it took me so long to work to buy a new pair, so I just kept every pair I ever bought. I don't know why, but I just couldn't get rid of them."

"We can store them if you want, sweetheart." Garrett began planning to acquire a storage facility somewhere.

"No, I want to donate them. Maybe there are other little dancers out there that need some old shoes to practice in."

CHAPTER 21

THE SEEKER'S SHIELD

Two hours later, Garrett loaded the last box into the Hummer. He glanced at his watch. "Do you wanna head back home or go get lost somewhere?" All he knew in that moment was that he wanted to be alone with her. He didn't want anyone else to know where they were. He wanted to exist without the corrosive, intruding world. He had to keep her safe.

"Getting lost sounds really good," Kaimi whispered hopefully. Garrett drove until they came to a block of restaurants and food trucks.

"They make the best ono tacos on the whole island." Kaimi pointed to a small taco stand near the end of the market area. "We could take them out to the water."

"That sounds perfect." Garrett leapt from the Hummer and wrapped his arm around her as he helped her down. He kept Kaimi tucked close to his body and smiled as she seemed to revel being in his arms. They ordered a sack of tacos with guac.

"Turn here," Kaimi began guiding Garrett with excitement. "This is one of my favorite beaches. It's really calm. It's a little cove on Lawai Beach."

Garrett followed her directions as the folded papers that he'd shoved in the glove box on one of his trips to the Hummer ricocheted around in his mind. Five counts of assault. Attempted murder. Garrett's body gave a convulsive shudder.

"Park over there," Kaimi instructed.

He helped her out of the car and shifted the quilt he'd grabbed along with the bag containing their dinner so that he could pull her closer. They spread the quilt out just out of the water's reach and settled in. It was getting late, and not many people were out anymore.

"Are you okay?" Kaimi's timid question was almost lost in the sounds of the waves.

"As long as you're right here, I'm perfect."

She beamed, and as they finished up their picnic dinner, she crumpled up the taco wrappings and threw them away. She grinned as he reclined on his side and tucked her closely to his body.

"I'll always keep you safe. Always."

Her brow furrowed, and Garrett supposed, since she had no idea what he'd found, the statement was odd.

"I know," she assured him. "I never felt safe before I met you, and now, whenever you hold me or I lie on your chest and I can hear you breathe and your heartbeat, it's like I know I'm really safe, and that you'd never let anything else bad happen to me." Garrett squeezed her tighter. He cradled the back of her head in his hand and attempted futilely to hide her away in him. He shook his head and forced himself to think logically. His shield spilled from his pores and settled around them with fierce rigidity.

"Aida is so lucky to have you and Dan. It's so amazing to be in here with you and feel you like this. She must always feel so safe. I used to be scared all the time when I was a little girl. I always felt like someone was watching me. Nana thought I was crazy, but I swear a few times I saw this same guy outside my dance studio and one of the places where I went to school. It was weird. I probably just imagined it or whatever. I guess I've never been particularly self-assured."

"What did he look like?" Garrett demanded as he tried to keep himself calm. She was inside of his rhythms. She could feel his every emotion.

"Garrett," she scoffed. "He wasn't real. It was just one of those crazy kid things."

Kaimi turned until her back was to Garrett's chest so she could stare out at the darkened waters lit by the full moon. He squeezed his eyes closed and tried to will calm as he prayed for her protection.

CHAPTER 22
WISHES
~DAN VINDICO~

"Commander Vindico, are you bringing me coffee in bed this morning and taking me out to a swanky restaurant tonight because you're hoping to get lucky? Because you should know I'm in a very difficult place right now. I know we don't know each other very well yet, but I do have children." Fionna's broad grin through her flirtatious banter lit Dan's soul.

"Yeah, kids may be a deal-breaker for me," he teased just to hear her continued laughter.

"They are really cute kids."

"They're beautiful just like their mama."

Dan eased Fionna closer to him in their bed. She kept the heated mug cradled in her hands.

"And I know we're in a difficult place, baby. I was thinking maybe I could help you forget about all of that for a little while. Tomorrow's going to be big. Governor Haydenshire is starting the mandatory assembly at eight. I'm going to catch these fuckers, but I was hoping maybe we could spend the day together and the night together, have a little time just the two of us. I'm determined to prove to you that I can run Iodex and be there for you and the girls."

Fionna brushed a coffee-flavored kiss on his lips. "You're amazing, and you don't have to prove anything to me. I know we're going to catch these…people." She seemed to stumble over the wording. Dan had several suggestions of other verbiage she could've used for the perv that had stolen pictures from him, but he kept quiet. "But I would love to spend the day with you. We might want to pack a little more though." She wrinkled her nose, making him chuckle.

"I know, but tonight, let's just go out and pretend this whole thing isn't happening."

She nodded. "Did you look up that guy Garrett texted you about? I guess he forgot that it's six hours later here." She'd been more than a little annoyed when Dan's cell had begun chirping at four on Sunday morning.

"Yeah, I checked him out on the National Iodex register. Not a nice guy, but I can't figure Garrett on this. Is he already working? He's supposed to be on his honeymoon and keeping up with my kids, which I will always owe him for, I'm certain."

"Tutu said they went to move all of Kaimi's stuff out of her old apartment last night. She sounded worried about them."

"I texted him back everything I found out about this Wardlaw guy. Told him the guy's been living in LA since he was last released. He thanked me and then said he was gonna take Kaimi to bed. He added an extremely exaggerated typed symbol of his junk and then what I assume was a representation of her anatomy, so I'd say he's probably fine."

Fionna doubled over laughing. "He may have gotten married and grown up or whatever, but he's still Garrett Haydenshire."

"Our children's godfather," Dan added as they both cracked up.

～

Garrett Haydenshire

"When Mommy and Daddy get here, then I can go to hula class, and you can be my teacher," Aida informed Kaimi as she spun around Garrett and Kaimi's bedroom. Garrett was installing shelving in the closet, and Kaimi was trying to get Aida to talk about going to school the next morning.

"I can't wait to be your hula kumu," Kaimi assured her. "I think Tutu wanted me to help you pack your backpack for tomorrow. Remember, in just a little while we're going with Tutu and Papa to see your new school and meet your teacher."

Garrett halted the drill in time to hear, "Do you know how to make wishes?"

"Uh...wishes?" Kaimi seemed stumped.

Garrett set the drill on the dresser and joined them on the bed. "What are you wishing for, Aida Mae?"

"I'm not supposed to wish because I said that I wouldn't wish anymore because when Mommy and Daddy adopted me and I didn't have to live in the orphanage anymore and I got to live near you that was so many wishes. But now I wish I could have just one more wish. But I can't, so maybe you could wish for me." Aida began biting her lip as Garrett and Kaimi shared a heartbroken glance.

"What do you want us to wish for?" Kaimi took Aida's hands in her own. Garrett's heart swelled from the tender motion. *She would've made an amazing mom.* The thought occurred in his mind before he could stop it. He shook himself slightly.

"First, I would wish that Daddy and Mommy could come here now, and Halia and me could move into our new house with them. Mommy is so happy there. Did you ever feel her there?" Aida got distracted from her wishes.

"No." Kaimi shook her head. "I hadn't even seen your new house until you showed me yesterday."

Aida nodded and then drew a deep breath. "And if that wish is too big of a wish, then I would wish that you and Uncle Garrett wouldn't go back to Washington, DC, and that you would stay here with me and Halia because I think that we need you."

Before Garrett could formulate a response to that, there was a knock on the screened door.

"It's Papa!" Aida wriggled off the bed and flew to the door.

"How's Papa's girl?"

"I'm okay."

"Just okay? You know, Papa was thinking we probably could take the tractor up to the garden by your new house before we go meet your kumu, Ms. Claun." Aida's eyes lit as she nodded hopefully. "Well, come on then."

Garrett moved to the door and waved as Aida raced outside followed by her adoring great-grandfather.

"I don't know how Maylea ever tells her no. I would cry." Kaimi was distraught over Aida's wishes. "We have to tell her that she should never stop wishing for things. We have to show her that she's allowed to wish for as much as she wants."

"I'll tell her, and we're staying a few more days. I can at least make that wish come true, so I'm going to," Garrett informed his wife. She gave him a relieved grin.

Since finding out that Kaimi's biological father was living in LA and hadn't left the state of California for any reason in the last several years, Garrett allowed himself to relax and enjoy setting up house with his bride. He grabbed his cell from the bedside table and called Dan.

CHAPTER 23
STEADFAST
~DAN VINDICO~

"I'm not sure it will help, but if you think she needs you to stay, then I think we're okay here. I'll know more after tomorrow when we see who decides to come out of the woodwork."

"I feel like I should be there to help you with the sheer amount of evidence that's going to come in once Dad makes his bargain, but she's a mess, Dan."

Dan's heart sank. If he weren't absolutely certain that his baby girls were better off away from DC, he wouldn't have been able to stand the fact that his actions had inadvertently sent them away.

"I'm just not sure she'll be any better if you delay your return." He choked out his explanation.

"Yeah, but I kind of think we might hang another day or two and let her get used to school."

"Thank you. As soon as I make certain no one ever sees those pictures of Fi, we'll be out there. This is killing me."

"I know, man, and you need to be there. But I kind of wonder if we need to be here for Aida, and Kaimi's so much healthier here. It's crazy."

"Yeah. Fi and the girls are the same way. I should never have brought them back here after the summer. I don't know what the hell I was thinking."

"Dan, stop. We'll catch these douche-nozzles. You took that stupid, fucking job because Fionna freaked out about your being Chief of Elite. Just shut up and get it done. Kaimi and I will fly home Wednesday unless Dad's gonna actually hold me to my contract, which you know he won't. We'll figure this out."

"Yeah." Dan drew a deep, steadying breath.

Fionna headed down the stairs just then. "What's wrong with Aida?" She already knew.

"She wants Garrett to stay there."

"My poor baby."

"Let me talk to her," Garrett demanded.

Dan handed the phone over to his wife. To his relief, after a few minutes, Garrett had reassured her and she was even smiling.

～

Garrett Haydenshire

"You know, I always hated the first day of school," Garrett informed Aida as he walked beside her holding her hand the next morning. Her new elementary school was less than a mile from the farm. She'd requested very meekly that Garrett be the only one to take her to school that day. His shield was firmly set over her as they walked.

"You did?" Her brow furrowed. She'd been stocked full of stories from everyone who adored her on how much she was going to love school, but Garrett knew she wasn't really hearing any of the encouragement. Now, he had her attention.

"Yup." He nodded.

"Why?" She was intrigued. She needed to know it was okay if she didn't like school today as long as she really gave it a chance. He'd never understood why people didn't just shoot straight with kids. No amount of Malani telling Aida stories of her and Fionna's school days was going to make Aida less nervous about starting a new school in the middle of the year, when her mom and dad were almost five thousand miles away. Aida had enjoyed the stories, but she was still terrified.

116

"When I went to school, we didn't know who our teacher was gonna be until we got there that morning. I didn't know where to go or anything."

"But I met Ms. Claun yesterday, and she showed me my classroom and my desk and the library."

"Hey, yeah, you're right, and remember Auntie Kaimi said she taught Ms. Claun's little girls hula last year and that they were really nice."

"Yes, and I think Ms. Claun is very nice, and she knows Mommy."

"That's true. Hey, you know what else I used to hate about the first day of school?" Garrett continued as they walked. Aida shook her head. "I hated lunch the first day. You never knew what the cafeteria was serving."

"But Papa packed my lunch. He made me Mommy's chicken salad on Hawaiian rolls and Maui chips and a mango that I got to cut up, and Tutu packed me four Aida cookies like Mommy makes me, and she said I could have one and share the other ones with Sarah and Harper and one for the new friend she said I was going to make today, and Tutu is always right."

"Really?" Garrett feigned shock. Aida gave an excited nod. Her sweet smile played on her lips. They were nearing the school and were joined with other children along the path.

"And I never knew if my friends were gonna be in my class," Garrett continued.

"My friend Sarah is in my class. Remember you came to pick me up at her house when it stormed. Ms. Claun put my desk right beside Sarah's desk."

"Wow, she must be *really* nice."

"Aida!" Two little girls about Aida's height were waiting on her at the entrance to Koloa Elementary School just as their parents had promised Tutu they would be.

Garrett released his shield just in time for Aida to sprint toward her friends.

"Uncle Garrett, this is Sarah and Harper." She introduced them in her best grown-up voice.

"Well, hello there, ladies." Garrett grinned.

"My daddy says you and Aida's daddy are gonna clean up all of the crime on our island. People keep taking things at the hotel where he works, and he says you're like superheroes!" Harper announced dramatically.

Kauai is gonna work out just fine. Garrett chuckled.

"We'll try to take care of all of the bad guys so that you don't have to worry about them, okay?"

"Okay." Harper began scanning the large grass field in front of the school as if she were trying to locate future criminals in her midst. Garrett leaned down to kiss the top of Aida's head.

"Do you want me to walk you to your classroom, or do you want to go with Harper and Sarah?"

"Come with us, Aida. I'm gonna be your school helper. That means I get to stay with you all day and teach you everything about our school. And I told Ms. Claun to let me be that because you're already my hoaloha." Sarah couldn't get the plea out fast enough.

"Okay." Aida seemed very pleased that Sarah considered her such a good friend.

"And Papa's going to meet me right here and take me home." She bit her lip as she turned her huge brown eyes on Garrett.

"He'll be right here, baby girl. Auntie Kaimi and I are going camping tonight, but we'll be back on the farm tomorrow, remember?"

"I won't forget to remember." She leaned up on her tiptoes, and Garrett knelt down as she kissed his cheek.

"I love you, Aida Mae."

"I love you, Uncle Garrett." She squeezed her arms around his neck tight and then waved as Sarah dragged her away.

CHAPTER 24

FRICTION AND FORCE

~JEFF STRENTON~

"When Dad gets involved, shit starts to happen and heads generally roll," Logan assured Rainer and Jeff as they glared at students entering the building.

"Have you heard any more about Dan's dad?" Rainer seemed deeply concerned. Jeff supposed that came from having a father you really loved and then losing him. That certainly wasn't something Jeff had any experience with.

"He's doing okay. He's trying to govern from the hospital. Mrs. Vindico is driving everyone nuts though. Dad said when they were all in school together, she wasn't so crazy. Apparently, Lindley did her in."

Jeff and Rainer nodded their understanding.

"Em's on her way up here. She's gonna play Fionna's counterpart. That seemed to work for the Angels, so I'm sure things will start to happen."

"I still wonder if Portwood's not playing with fire. If Fionna or Emily figure out who these ballsacks are, they can't testify." Logan was in a fierce mood that morning. Jeff wondered what had him so on edge.

"Yeah, but because these crimes are data-linked, once we have the morons, we'll have all the evidence we'll need. The trace on the paychecks will tell us a lot," Jeff whispered.

No one was anywhere nearby, but he certainly didn't want any of the intricate plans to go awry because he had a big mouth.

"That's true," Rainer agreed. "We just need some kind of direction, then we can get this cleaned up, and Dan can take Fionna to Kauai. Emily says she's a disaster without the girls."

At that moment, Vindico escorted his wife in on his arm. Jeff smiled and waved as did Logan and Rainer. Fionna actually looked better. She seemed more relaxed than the last time Jeff had seen her. She was clinging tightly to Dan though.

"Look, there's Fionna Styler!"

Jeff turned to see two sophomore girls whispering and pointing. "She's so beautiful it's not even fair to the rest of us."

"I know, but I went to an Angels challenge a few years ago, and she was really sweet. She was the only Angel who stayed late just to make certain everyone who wanted her autograph got one. And then she adopted that little girl from Brazil. She's so cute."

Jeff chuckled as the girls passed, still staring with rapt adoration at Fionna.

Rainer shook his head. "I guess Dan's not the only person who gets tongue-tied when they see her."

"Dude, every one of my brothers except Garrett had a crush on her. The Angels programs didn't last long on the farm," Logan explained rather crudely.

"Thanks for that." Rainer scowled as Jeff cracked up.

"Hey, why is Mentor Vindico's wife here?" Ben Cobson seemed to appear from nowhere. Jeff spun, startled to see him.

Logan rolled his eyes. "I don't know. She's the strongest Receiver of our generation. Her husband works here. Dad asked her to be here. She can be wherever the hell she wants to be. Pick one," he snarled.

"Geez, you're in a mood this morning," Rainer challenged. Jeff was glad he wasn't the only one who'd noticed.

"Yeah, well, my father-in-law phoned to say he thought he'd holiday and come and see his lovely Adeline. He's decided he'll be in this weekend. The beginning of the only forty-eight hours that

Adeline doesn't have to work for the next three weeks," Logan huffed in his best Australian accent. Jeff and Rainer cracked up.

"No one's father-in-law could hate them as much as mine hates me. Every time he comes to the hospital, all he does is glare at me," Jeff informed them.

Rainer slapped Jeff on the back in a show of solidarity. Logan offered him a slight nod of agreement.

"I'm sorry I asked. I was just curious." Ben seemed just as shocked by Logan's response as Jeff and Rainer. He turned the eager questioning on Jeff. "Governor Haydenshire brought her in?"

"I can't discuss it, but I'd say she'll be up here a lot." Jeff still felt bad about brushing Ben off so many times lately.

"Shouldn't she be home taking care of his kids?"

Jeff had heard Ben make chauvinistic remarks before, but that was extreme even for him. Rainer and Logan looked disgusted.

Rainer's jaw cocked to the side. "They moved the girls to Kauai. They're moving soon. He's already turned in his resignation dated January 31st. Governor Vindico offered the position to Mentor Jackson. Why do you care so much?"

Ben shrugged, threw another glare toward Dan and Fionna, and then walked away. The Vindicos were talking with Portwood and Ericcson near Mentor Vindico's office. Emily rushed through the front doors.

"I'm sorry I'm late!" She raced to Rainer's side. He was beaming instantly.

"Hey there." He chuckled.

"I had to run by the arena, and I forgot how far away Venton is from our new house. I was used to coming from the farm."

Will Haydenshire and two of his employees from the Senate Bank made their entrance next.

CHAPTER 25
HALL OF LECTURES
~DAN VINDICO~

"Let's get this done." Governor Haydenshire did not appear to be in any mood for joking. Anger and gravity permeated his energies. Fionna stepped closer to Dan. The Crown Governor's fierce energy worried her. Dan wrapped his arm around his wife.

"Are you okay, baby?"

She nodded. Determination was armored in her quiet demeanor and her graceful stride. Emily and Rainer joined them, and Fionna moved to stand beside Emily.

"We're going to figure this out. No one's going to see any of that," Emily quietly reassured Fionna. "I promise." They hugged and held each other's hand.

Dan walked behind Governor Haydenshire and right beside Portwood as they marched into the auditorium. Emily and Fionna eased into the room after Iodex had made their bold showing.

Tension was palpable in the stagnant air. The auditorium wasn't used but a few times each year and hadn't been aired out. Governor Haydenshire moved to the podium. All of Elite Iodex lined up behind him. Dan and Portwood were front and center and were wearing matching, challenging glares as they stared out at the entire Venton student body.

"I'm not in a great mood this morning, so I think I'll just start our little meeting with sit down and keep your mouths shut." Governor Haydenshire began his lecture in the same outraged tone he used when he was lecturing one of his children or anyone he'd had a hand in raising. Dan, Logan, Rainer, Will, and Emily all gave the same slight shudder.

"I have quite a bit to say, so settle in and listen up. If any of you are actually taking advantage of the exorbitantly expensive education this Realm is providing you, then you've certainly heard of Edmund Burke. He was a Gifted Irish statesman, for those of you who've decided Gifted history isn't worth your time. Burke was known for several quotes that I feel apply here, so listen and you might learn something. The first quote would be, 'The greater the power, the more dangerous the abuse.'

"Those of you who've decided to purchase advanced copies of tests and then use them to gain yourselves better grades and have therefore been blackmailed by the sellers are just realizing what happens when good people decide to sell their power to gain themselves an advantage."

Nervous glances shot around the room.

"Another Burke quote that suits most everyone here would be, 'The only thing necessary for the triumph of evil is for good men to do nothing.' I'd say it's a safe bet to assume that most every one of you sitting here knows something about what's been going on all these many months.

"Either you, yourself, have purchased a copy of a test, or you know someone who has. You may even know the people selling them or the people threatening others. You may be being threatened. So, how do we go about restoring your own personal power and sanctity? How do we start afresh? How do we restore this academy back to what it once was—a powerhouse of learning and dignity? The most sought after, most competitive Gifted Academy in the American Realm.

"I stand before you, the Crown Governor of this Realm, and I'll tell you exactly how we're going to do good so that evil doesn't triumph, but I'll also give you a warning. If I do not get the answers that I want, if we do not restore the order of this school, I will shut Venton Academy down."

Gasped outrage lit through the student body.

"Your parents can find somewhere else for you to finish your Gifted education. I believe the closest Gifted Academy would be Easton in Baltimore, would it not, Chief Vindico?" Dan's newly acquired title quieted the students as their curiosity was piqued.

"Yes, sir. Fifty miles from here." Dan gave a nod to the governor.

"If you think you might like to continue your education here in Virginia, then this is how we will proceed. Iodex officers and other Senate officials will be stationed throughout the school today. If you know anything at all about either the stolen tests, or any other vile thing that might be going on here, come forward today. Do good.

"If you've purchased a test copy, whether you're currently being blackmailed or not, tell us and your record will be cleared. We will not report the incident to your parents. Your permanent record will not reflect your serious lack of judgment. You are essentially free. Your parents have all been alerted to our decision and have been asked to allow us to handle this. They've also been informed that cheating was widespread and that we would like to handle it without their involvement. Therefore, no one else holds power over you, and I strongly caution you to never sell your power again, no matter the price. Never sell yourself into bondage, which is essentially what anyone does when they break the law. You will forever be beholden to that moment in time.

"So, all you have to do is talk, and you walk free. If you've been involved in the blackmailing process in any capacity, come forward. You will not be expelled from school. If you've paid the twelve-hundred-dollar required price to have a drug test covered up for you, and you can go ahead and wipe the astonished looks off your faces— we know a great deal more than you're aware of—but if you've done this, come forward and let us help you. You will only be required to attend drug abuse sessions here with one of the Venton Auxiliary counselors. No punishment of any kind will be enacted, if you speak.

"I'm standing before you offering you a blank slate. I suggest you take it. Guilt is quite an anchor to try to outswim, so when someone throws you a life raft, you'd be smart to hang on tight and drop the anchor in the sea. Take your power and your dignity back. This will not be an opportunity you're given often in your adult lives, so live carefully.

"All that our Elite Officers want to know is what you've done and the process you went through. You never know if your story might help us put an end to this tyranny you've all been living with for far too long. I think those of you who have been bullied, frightened, and abused because one bad decision led to so many others are probably a little tired of living with the tyranny this academy has suffered.

"If I do not see most every one of you in one of the many offices set up here by the Senate, then tomorrow we'll begin calling you in individually. Decide you'll just stay home until this blows over—guess who'll be the first people whose homes we search. Ask any of my children who are here today, I do not joke around when people's livelihoods are at stake. I've had quite enough of you making decisions you cannot stand on. The foundation is crumbling rapidly, and it's time to abandon the path you've found yourselves on. Take today to build something better."

CHAPTER 26

EARNEST

~GARRETT HAYDENSHIRE~

Garrett drove toward Anini Beach with his right hand laced through Kaimi's left. She was beaming and singing along to the music from her phone. She was intoxicating. Her innocent beauty was so incredibly raw. The way she existed on the edge of an impulse drove Garrett wild. He'd always keep her safe but never try to restrain her. She was his tender, wild baby, and he wanted only to watch her fire burn brightly and to exist in its irresistible heat.

"Park there." She was bouncing in her seat.

"Excited, sweetheart?" he teased.

"Yes! Let's go!"

Garrett chuckled as he leapt from the Hummer and helped her to the ground. They grabbed all of their gear from the back and headed out toward the beach Kaimi preferred for camping. They picked a spot under a few palm trees that would be well out of the way when the tide came in.

"Wow." Kaimi stared at Garrett's tent with awe. "That's really nice."

Garrett nodded, though she was making him slightly uncomfortable.

"I've always liked to camp, so I never minded spending a little money on things for it. I used to work all the freaking time, so when I got to go out, I wanted to enjoy it."

127

"There's a great camping store down in Poipu. That's close to where we live. We should go sometime. I've...never really bought anything there, but I loved to look."

Garrett understood that she'd never had the money to purchase anything at the store. "Maybe we could go tomorrow while Aida's at school."

She helped him unfurl the large tent from his pack. He zipped off the top covering to allow them to stare up at the sky that evening. Then he opened several of the flaps so that the breeze could air the tent out as soon as it was staked. They worked quickly and soon had a campsite that was going to make for one hell of a romantic evening.

"Okay, perfect!" Kaimi exited the tent and set several large beach blankets nearby.

"Not yet." Garrett pulled her to him. He untied the top of the tiny bikini she was wearing. The beach was empty on a Monday morning in January, and he planned on taking advantage of their privacy. Kaimi giggled and then shook her head at him.

"Now, it's perfect," he informed her.

"This isn't a topless beach, Deputy Haydenshire, and I could get in trouble for this," she sassed. "And you should probably know that since you're an Iodex officer."

"Whoops." Garrett smirked as he tossed the top of the bikini deep within the tent. "Now bring me those titties, baby." He cradled her head and positioned her so he could devour her mouth with lush, hungry kisses as he groped her exposed breasts. She was gasping for breath when he finally released her.

"Camping with you is way better than with my friends," she informed him wryly.

"You did marry me, so I sure as hell hope you'd rather be with me." He reached back and pinched a handful of her luscious ass.

"Would you be good?"

"I'm always good, sweetheart. You know that."

She rolled her eyes and shook her head at him. "Will you behave, please?"

"I can't come up with a single reason why I would start that now?"

"Okay, fine. You can play, but let's go paddleboarding."

He laughed and helped her inflate the paddleboards they'd purchased the day before. He lathered his hands with sunscreen and proceeded to give her a massage.

"I don't want your nips to get burned, baby. What would I suck on?" he explained as he spent several long minutes rubbing down her breasts.

"I am wearing a rash guard to paddleboard," she informed him. "Sand hurts if you fall hard enough."

"All right, all right."

Thoughts of her father flew from his mind as they paddled out on the boards. They were carried away on the beach breeze as she reached and grasped Garrett's forearm. He was close enough to catch her as her board threatened to topple over in a slight wave.

"I've got you." He would always have her. He would never let her fall. He would never let anyone or anything hurt her. She wouldn't stay on Kauai without him, but he would get her back to her island as soon as he possibly could.

Those were the vows he made to himself as they began riding the waves. The vows somehow mended the deep scars on his heart and miraculously began to ease their painful strain. The healing was dramatic as they spent the morning laughing and playing in the gentle waters.

A little while later, they paddled in and jogged back to their campsite.

"I'm starving." Kaimi pulled out one of the coolers she'd packed that morning. Garrett lit a camp stove with his hand and helped her make her chicken phillies.

He was astonished as he watched her. She was so alive on Kauai. Her eyes were bright, and her cheeks held a rosy glow. Her shoulders were relaxed, and her body was lithe and flowing with boundless energy. She'd even been shocked at how well she'd recovered. She associated it with Tutu's teas and baths that she'd adhered to strictly, but Garrett was almost certain the island's volcanic energy rhythms had restored her own. They inhaled the sandwiches and several bottles of water. Kaimi snuggled close to Garrett the entire time they ate.

"How about a nap, Mrs. Haydenshire?" He was a little tired from playing in the water and his late-night Iodex searches for Wardlaw. Kaimi looked intrigued.

"Can we make out first?" she requested somewhat abashedly.

"Hell yeah, baby."

He leapt to his feet, threw their plates in a nearby recycling bin, and grabbed two blankets. Kaimi helped him spread one near the door to their tent, which was in the shade of a few palm trees. She bent over to enter the tent, and Garrett gave her a shuddered growl as he swatted her backside, which she'd effectively shoved in his face.

His pulse hungered for her. His body longed to be inside of hers. He wanted to spend the afternoon with her, but he yearned for nightfall when he could use the darkness to seclude her and take her all for himself. His shield all but demanded it.

They used the baby powder she'd packed to rid their feet and bodies of sand. Garrett settled on his side, and she curled into his muscular frame. He pulled the rash guard back off her. He was desperate to feel her rhythms beside his skin.

The magnetic pulls of their bodies had Garrett's cock vying for attention as soon as the spark ignited between them. He moaned as he gently brushed her cheek in the palm of his powerful hand. He leaned and dipped his tongue in her mouth as she let her hand explore the hardened length she felt press into her abdomen.

"That's it, sweet girl, grab me." He turned his head and crushed her mouth to his own. Her entire body gave an eager tremble as Garrett's hands sought her exposed breasts. "So damn beautiful. I ache for you." His vow had her panting and pulling his length with voracity through his swim trunks.

"Please tell me." Her insatiable plea was earnest in her intrigue. She was as fascinated by his body's responses to her as he was by the way her breasts swelled in his hands. The way her lips glistened with tender heat every time he touched her. The way she squeezed so tightly around him. It was the most heavenly thing he'd ever felt. The way her rhythms lit and fused with his as he made them one.

"You drive me wild, sweet girl. The sounds you make when I suck you here." He traced her breasts again and then teased her nipples until they were throbbing and in desperate need of being sucked until she felt relief from the fevered strain. "The way you taste when I bring you in my mouth. You make me so hard I ache to pound that sweet pussy, so damn tight it feels like heaven. That ass, baby, my god. So fucking gorgeous. You're so fucking perfect, I'll never get enough," he managed to elaborate before he laced his fingers in her hair and brought her in for more of his voracious kisses. A needy moan was her response as he wound his tongue in an erotic dance with hers and began to suck.

"Kaimi!"

Garrett's heart thundered as he jerked back. He grabbed a nearby quilt and threw it over them.

He blinked several times as he stared up at Shaun Westin, a supposed friend of Kaimi's that was good for just about nothing, and some girl Garrett recognized from a few of the pictures on Kaimi's phone.

CHAPTER 27

EXPECTATIONS

"Oh, hey, Starren." Kaimi's rhythms were vibrating from her erotic energy rolling into embarrassed pulses. "What are you doing out here?"

"We heard you were back in town. We went out to Tutu's farm, and she said you were camping. We figured you were here," Starren offered uncomfortably.

Thinking quickly, Garrett jerked his white undershirt over his head and pulled it over Kaimi. Shaun rolled his eyes. Garrett assumed he didn't like the display of ripped muscle and tattoos. Garrett shot him a challenging glare. Kaimi sat up.

"Thank you," she whispered. "Yeah, we're back for a few days. We cleaned out the apartment and moved to the farm. We're actually heading back to DC soon, but then we'll be back for good."

Garrett didn't like her having to explain their lives to friends who hadn't really shown themselves as being there for her.

Starren nodded uncomfortably. "So…you really married him?" she finally quizzed as if Garrett wasn't seated right there.

"Yeah." Kaimi held up her left hand to show off her large engagement ring and tattooed band.

"Are you wearing a ring too?" Shaun huffed incredulously.

"Yes. I am," Garrett snarled. He lifted his left hand and pointed to his ring with his right. "And what the fuck is that supposed to mean?"

"Nothing. Just surprised, I guess."

Garrett narrowed his eyes and offered no response. He felt no need to justify himself to the complete douchebag who stood before him. The one that had hounded Kaimi for months to go out with him and when she'd explained her health problems had practically climbed out a window to make his hasty retreat.

"We were just checking on you, Kaimi, and we wanted to say congratulations." Starren elbowed Shaun rather forcefully.

"Thanks." Kaimi sighed. "And I'm happier than I have ever been. Garrett is an amazing husband. You don't have to worry about me."

Shaun gave a slight eye roll, and Garrett's fists clenched of their own accord. His biceps gave an ominous flex. The deep desire to sink his fist into Shaun's indignant face was growing stronger with each passing moment. His shield sizzled around him.

"Well, thanks for the congrats. We were just really enjoying the beach until we were interrupted," Garrett informed them.

Kaimi tried to hide her grin but couldn't quite manage it.

"Oh, sorry." Starren stepped back toward the parking lot.

"If you need us, call us. Starren just moved into my apartment," Shaun informed Kaimi. It seemed apparent to Garrett that he was trying to make Kaimi jealous.

"Really?" Kaimi's shocked scowl had Garrett chuckling. She stared at Starren like she must've lost her mind in the last few weeks.

"Yeah." Starren bristled as she laced her hand through Shaun's. "Maybe you and I could hang out after you get back."

Garrett started to tell her no but didn't want to come off as a controlling asshole.

"Yeah. I'll call you," Kaimi lied.

"Bye." Starren waved as Shaun spun and led her back toward their car.

"I will find something to arrest that little shit for. Fair warning," Garrett defied.

Kaimi doubled over laughing. "Here, I'll make you feel better." She removed the T-shirt from her tiny frame. It was so large on her it hadn't obscured much anyway.

"Yum, I do feel better." Garrett reclined Kaimi under him and began another long, languid make-out session with his wife.

His hand had just made its way down Kaimi's slender waist and into her bikini bottom to gain himself a handful of that fan-freaking-tastic ass when another shadow obscured the sun.

"What the fuck?" Garrett covered them again and rolled. He was certain Shaun had come back to get another few quips in, but his eyes goggled as he took in Representative Kalakona. He tried to determine what to do. What the fuck was she doing out there? He stood and scooted Kaimi his shirt with his foot as he offered his hand to Victoria Kalakona.

"Aloha, Deputy Haydenshire. Tua Iona told me you two had come camping up here when I looked for you at the farm."

"We're honeymooning." Garrett wondered if having sex outdoors in Hawaii was illegal. He hadn't read up on the law books as of yet, and he certainly hadn't paid much attention to the laws people were rarely incarcerated for.

"Yes, congratulations. I saw that you'd married rather quickly."

Kaimi tried to discreetly ease into Garrett's T-shirt.

"Yeah, well, when you meet the right girl…" Garrett slid to the side two steps to try and give Kaimi a little more coverage.

"I was hoping you could give me a better estimation on when you and Commander Vindico will be able to move here permanently. When I offered Dan the job, I had no idea it would take him so long to get the problems at Venton taken care of." Annoyed challenge perforated every word of her complaint.

Garrett ground his teeth. He didn't care for being lied to, and Kalakona had just spewed out pure bullshit. She'd been kind and offered Dan all the time he needed just until she had his name on the dotted line.

"We're doing the best we can, Mrs. Kalakona. Believe me, Dan wants to be out here as much as you want us here. But he did agree to do a job, and neither of us will ever shirk our responsibilities."

"I am aware of that, Deputy Haydenshire. Are you aware that this beach and most of Kauai's beautiful shorelines require that women keep their breasts covered? As an officer of this state, I would expect you would not only enforce the law, but that you would also follow it. That goes for your wife as well." The unspoken reminder that the entire Realm had seen photographic evidence of his wife taking a drag rang loud and clear.

"I got it." Garrett narrowed his eyes. He did know that most of the island's more private beaches let topless women sunbathe. He knew that technically women never had to cover their breasts if they didn't want to. Breastfeeding was allowed everywhere. The beaches attached to the big resorts would not let tourists go topless, and Iodex would occasionally step in, but it wasn't an arrestable offense. Tourists were always scolded more harshly than locals.

"I'm running for reelection in September. I want to be known as the representative who cleaned up Hawaii's crime problems and their occasional lack of decorum," Representative Kalakona explained, almost as if she'd heard Garrett's thoughts.

"Dan and I will do everything we can to help you achieve those goals, Representative." He offered the only correct response. He had been raised among the Senate after all. He knew how to play the game even if he wasn't a fan of the representatives who were out for their own gain more than the people they represented.

"Thank you," she stated coolly. Kaimi stood beside Garrett.

"Mrs. Haydenshire." Mrs. Kalakona offered Kaimi her hand. "That's a big name to live up to. Are you certain you can handle that?"

Fury lit through Garrett. His shield flared. "She is an amazing woman, and I am incredibly proud to call her my wife. Are you certain you can handle *that*, Representative?"

"Certainly." Kalakona offered Garrett her hand. "I'm so pleased you've married someone from my islands. That looks good for me."

CHAPTER 28

EVIDENCE

Garrett was stunned. This wasn't at all the side of Kalakona he'd seen on the plane when he and Dan had flown in to take their oaths of office.

"Have a nice campout." Kalakona gave an overly critical look at their tent and campsite and then spun and stalked back to her awaiting driver.

"Damn, she's a bitch," Garrett spat when she was well out of earshot. Kaimi was still staring bewilderedly after Representative Kalakona.

She gave a slight nod. "Maylea keeps saying she's scared of something though, remember?"

"Scared of what?"

"I have no idea. She's been in Hawaiian government since we were babies."

"Yeah, well, if it walks like a bitch and talks like a bitch…"

"I've never heard of anyone getting onto locals for not having a top on," Kaimi fussed. "I've gone topless here before."

Garrett scowled. "In front of Shaun."

A broad grin spread rapidly across Kaimi's face. "Are you jealous?" she chanted just before she began giggling.

"Yeah, baby." Garrett wrapped his arms around her and brought her into his chest. "These are mine." He let his hands move down her sides, and his thumbs grazed the sides of her breasts. They were pert and eager for his caress.

"Right, because you've never looked at anyone else's." Her mood shifted slightly from thrilled that she'd made him jealous to huffy about the other women Garrett had been with. He chuckled and touched his forehead to hers.

"Mrs. Haydenshire, I believe you are the one wearing my ring and the one that has my heart, that I honestly didn't even know still worked until you informed me that I was hot while I was fixing your car battery." Kaimi buried her face in his chest. He could feel the heat of her embarrassment roll through her rhythms.

"I was mortified. I could not believe I actually said that."

"Would you hush and take that shirt off so we can go on with our honeymoon?"

"Noooo!" Kaimi shook her head adamantly. "You heard her. I'm not losing you your job or something."

"She's not gonna come back out here. She wanted to stroke her own ego. She wants to pretend she's calling the shots so she can delude herself into thinking she has me and Dan by a string. Trust me, she doesn't. All she's interested in is being reelected. She has to be in DC most of the year. As long as nothing gets fucked up too badly here, and we always make her look good, she doesn't really care."

"Still, I think I'll be a good girl." Kaimi was genuinely frightened of Victoria Kalakona. Garrett wouldn't have that. No one was going to scare his baby. He shook his head.

"I like it when you're a bad girl for me."

She gave him an adorable smirk and shook her head. "I'm keeping this shirt on. If a guy gives you his shirt, you get to keep it. That's the rule." She bit her lip and couldn't quite wiggle away from him.

"Is that so?"

"Yes."

"You can keep all of my shirts as long as I get to take them off you whenever I want."

∼

Jeff Strenton

"Write down everything you hear even if you don't believe it's pertinent information. You never know if what Johnny tells us might match up with what Susie says and then we have another puzzle piece in place." Portwood was elaborating on the orders Vindico had just given.

Jeff smiled. He'd always wanted to work for Dan Vindico, but he was rather fierce. His voice seemed to come out shouting without much effort. Fionna had lightly touched his forearm when he'd been barking relentlessly a few minutes before, and he'd quieted down some. "Officer Strenton, why don't you and Dan man an office. I'll work with Governor Willow. All other officers pair off with either one of the banking officials or one of the volunteering governors. Let's find something out today."

Jeff tried not to be disappointed. He knew he was the rookie and still had to prove his interrogation techniques. Obviously, what was at stake was quite serious, but he wished Portwood trusted him enough to let him help one of the other volunteers. Governor Sapman entered during Jeff's mental lamentations, and he quickly decided that working with Vindico, even in a bad mood, was vastly preferable to working with his father-in-law.

Three hours later, Jeff wanted to beat his head against the desk. Vindico was no longer even trying to hide his eye rolls as student after student came in to discuss what they knew about what had been going on for the past few months at Venton. Fionna was seated between Jeff and Dan. Even she appeared to be losing her patience.

"Yeah, man, I mean, I bought a few tests or whatever, but they were for a friend of mine. He needed help, and I didn't want to tell him no because he's a Receiver or something, and he gets real upset if people don't help him cause they're, like, weak and stuff," a sophomore Vis Virres Predilect droned on. Fionna gave an audible huff, and Dan patted her thigh.

"Let me see how you paid for the tests you bought for your friend."

The sophomore handed Dan a Visa. "I had to do a cash advance though. They didn't just take the numbers and the date and stuff. You know, like when you go online and talk to Vickie Vaj Vinson."

Vindico gave another distinct eye roll. He appeared sickened as he copied down the numbers on the credit card and asked what website the guy had visited to purchase the tests. It was a website they'd written down several times, one of a dozen or more.

Dan shook his head as the idiot left. "I miss interrogating real, actual felons. At least they knew when to shut the fuck up."

CHAPTER 29
THE HAYDENSHIRE BOYS
~RAINER LAWSON~

Rainer drew a deep breath and draped his arm around Emily. She was trying not to giggle. Governor Haydenshire was seated at the desk. He was rubbing his temples.

They were listening to yet another young woman explain that the reason she'd paid to have a drug test covered up was because she'd had a cold and had heard that cold medicine would show up as ecstasy on a drug test. Rainer's eyes narrowed. His training kicked in. He nodded and gave the girl a smile.

"Yeah, I had a cold a few weeks ago, and Em gave me something for my sinuses. But you know I'm Iodex, so I was worried about the Senate drug tests." He waited on a hopeful look to appear in the girl's eyes then he leaned in slightly. "Who did you say gave you the meds?"

"My boyfriend got it for us," she supplied readily. Her eyes goggled. "Uh…I mean…I think I got the cold from my boyfriend. My mom probably gave me the medicine."

"What did you say your boyfriend's name was, dear?" Governor Haydenshire's weary voice urged her onward.

"Uh…Craig…" the girl lied. Emily glanced from Rainer to her father and shook her head.

"Oh, Kelsey, did you and Greg Sanders break up?" She feigned concern. "You were such a cute couple."

"We didn't break up. We're gonna get married after school just like you and Rainer."

Emily smiled as Rainer tried to turn his chuckle into a cough.

"Well, Kelsey, congratulations on your pending engagement. Would you please tell Greg that I'd like to speak with him, just to check to make certain his test wasn't a false positive." Governor Haydenshire didn't appear to have the patience for this kind of evidence gathering.

"Yes, sir." Kelsey stood. "But you're not going to say anything to our parents, right?"

"I don't go back on my word. You will both need to speak with the Auxiliary drug counselors here about what happened with your tests but nothing more. I'll have the counselors reach out to you both."

"Great, thanks. Those guys kept calling me and saying they were gonna tell the school if I didn't pay them, but I was out of money."

"Who called you?" Rainer leapt just before Kelsey opened the office door.

She pulled her cell phone with a hot-pink, rhinestone-encrusted case out of her purse. "These are the numbers. It's always different." She handed Rainer her phone. He nodded and copied down the numbers.

"Have they ever left you a voicemail?" He asked the same question he'd asked the last ten students.

"Yeah. Those three on there are from them. It's like this creepy voice." Relief played in her eyes when Emily gave her a tender smile. Rainer knew Kelsey's fears were easing just a little.

"Would you mind if I casted your phone and copied off the messages? I promise you we would never copy anything else off here," Rainer made his fervent vow.

"I guess so." Rainer casted Kelsey's phone and moved her voicemail messages to one of the enhanced Iodex laptops they'd set up just for this scenario.

A few minutes later, Governor Haydenshire leaned back in the large desk chair and shook his head.

"Emily Anne, please, for the sake of my sanity, tell me neither of you nor any of your brothers did anything like this." He threw his hands out to the desk covered with numbers he'd written down and the laptop they were feeding the information into.

"I promise. Connor Saran-wrapping the Auxiliary building and the rest of us making out in the corridors with whoever we were dating is about the worst of it. Oh, and Will and Dan casting and moving all of those mentors' cars." Emily laughed at the memory of Will getting yelled at for a solid hour.

Governor Haydenshire chuckled and did look thoroughly relieved.

"We weren't stealing them, Dad. We were relocating them," the governor mocked Will's excuse as he rolled his eyes. "Those boys are lucky to still be alive, and now, they have kids of their own. They both deserve ones just like themselves. That's not really fair to Brooke and Fionna though." Emily and Rainer joined in the governor's laughter. "I do seem to recall Garrett tying and then shield casting rope between two classroom door handles that were across the hall from each other so that neither door could be opened when the bell rang and no one could touch the rope." He shook his head as Rainer and Emily laughed again.

Emily cringed. "Do you remember when Dan and Garrett taught Cal how to do that thing with his shield so that it pushes back against the gravitational waves, and then they all jumped off the cafeteria roof?"

Governor Haydenshire rolled his eyes. "Do I remember rushing from the Senate to Georgetown because Cal had two broken ribs and Garrett had a broken ankle? Trust me, I remember." He sighed. "As I recall, Dan sprained his wrist and elbow. And I can think of several other things Garrett and Cal did, but they would never have done this. Whoever is behind all of this is making more than I do."

Jeff Strenton

Fionna wilted on Dan's shoulder when he returned from telling the line of waiting students they were taking a quick break for lunch but that they would stay as late as needed to make certain everyone who wanted to talk got that opportunity. Jeff wondered if he should leave when Dan kissed the top of her head and cradled her closely.

"I feel like a freaking priest."

Jeff and Fionna both began laughing.

Jeff turned his attention to the sheer quantity of evidence they'd taken in just that morning. "Some of this stuff has been good though. With all of these credit card numbers, we can trace where the money is going. Even if we can't find a name on the account, we can shut it down. That should get some attention."

"Yeah, and I want to know where the money leaving the accounts is going. Speaking of money, the paychecks should be auto-depositing in a few hours. That means the traced paycheck will be deposited somewhere. By tonight, we should have learned something there as well."

Fionna looked completely exhausted and still hadn't lifted her head from her husband's broad shoulder.

"But this is a lot of guilt to sort through, isn't it?" he soothed as he kept her wrapped tightly in his arms.

"They do all feel really badly, and they're all so relieved Governor Haydenshire gave them a fresh start. Most of them are trying to help, but they don't understand how it works outside of the part they played. So, it's guilt and relief and confusion and frustration and a ton of fear because they broke their own trust. Now, they're struggling to trust that Governor Haydenshire won't go back on his word. Fear is really difficult for a Receiver because we have to take it on when they feel it. Every single bad thing people do comes from fear."

Dan nodded. "Once you start blackmailing people, you're creating masses of enemies all desperate for any opportunity to get you off their back. It's a house of cards. If you make one wrong move, it will come crashing down. These morons get paid and then come back for more. They don't know what they're doing. Eventually, the wells run dry, and you either have to up the ante or move on. Incessantly threatening people leads you nowhere when they have nothing left to give."

"That's why Aida's parents were killed, isn't it?" Emotion strangled in her throat.

Jeff's eyes closed. Part of him wished he wasn't in the room, but most of him wished he could've reassured Aida more about the move. God, that kid had been through hell.

"Kind of," Dan whispered. "Pravus was Wretchkinsides's top extortion man. Extortion is different from blackmail. He had the whole area paying him not to destroy their businesses and homes. And he never failed to make examples out of people who couldn't pay." Dan shook his head in disgust. "That's how he kept them paying."

Fionna's cell phone chirped, and she managed a smile as she read the text. "Emily wants to know if I want to go get some lunch. I think she'd like to get out of here for a little while too." There was a desperate plea that rang in her tone.

"Sure, baby, I'll just grab something here." Dan was trying not to sound disappointed, Jeff could tell. He wondered if even her own husband occasionally forgot how powerful she was.

"You and Rainer could come with us," Fionna eased.

"No, I'll miss you. That's what you're feeling from me, but we could eat and maybe talk to another few students while you're gone."

A sweet grin spread across Fionna's face. She leaned and kissed his cheek and then waved as she rushed out of the office.

Dan shook his head. "She won't ever just tell me, 'I can't take feeling what all of these kids are feeling anymore. They're driving me crazy. And I don't want to feel what you're feeling anymore either.'"

Jeff nodded his understanding. "That has to be rough. To feel all of the things she just listed out with them would be miserable. Bec's like that too, though. I know sitting up there in that hospital day in and day out has to be making her nuts, but she never complains. I'd go insane."

"Fi rarely complained when she was pregnant, and I know she was miserable there at the end. They're a lot tougher than we are."

A knock sounded on the door. With a sigh, Vindico stood to open it.

"Oh, hey Ben, are you here for confession as well?" Jeff was shocked. He couldn't fathom that Ben Cobson was cheating on tests. He'd always worked hard. He was the Head of Ioses Order.

"Of course not. I just thought I could help you." Ben sounded offended as he entered the office.

~

Garrett Haydenshire

"You suck so bad at this." Garrett continued to harass his wife as she tried to play Frisbee with him.

"Humph." Kaimi giggled and then aimed the frisbee at Garrett's head. He lifted it from the air with ease.

"I think we should start playing for clothes, baby." He waggled his eyebrows as he spun the Frisbee from behind his back to her slower this time.

"Would you shut up? You like how I suck." Kaimi stuck her tongue out as she finally caught the Frisbee. Garrett gave her an echoed growl.

"We could play for that."

With a broad mischievous grin, Kaimi narrowed her eyes and shot the Frisbee hard over Garrett's head. He leapt but couldn't quite catch it.

"Ha!" Kaimi began jumping up and down with delighted laughter as Garrett retrieved the Frisbee. He shook his head, tossed the Frisbee to the side, and ran headlong across the sand at his beautiful bride. He folded her up over his shoulder so her adorable ass was right beside his face. She squealed and kicked her legs, but Garrett just chuckled as he held her with ease. He headed toward the water. Kaimi was laughing hysterically. She stuck her right hand down the back of his swim trunks and pinched his ass.

"Hey, now." Garrett lifted his shoulders and leaned forward slightly. He caught Kaimi with his left arm and cradled her just over the warm lapping waters of the Pacific. "What do you think you're doing, Mrs. Haydenshire?"

"Pinching you," she sassed.

"That will only get you into trouble, baby." Challenge and intrigue lit in her eyes, and Garrett's heart begin to fly in the customary beat timed to just being in contact with her. He wasn't even certain it beat at all when her skin wasn't connected to his, when her volatile rhythms weren't there to rejuvenate and enliven his own. But suddenly her rhythms shifted again. Ease and relaxation broadcast from her beautiful copper eyes. Her body calmed, and with a replete grin, she let her eyes close.

"Do you feel that?"

"Feel what?" Garrett could feel the sand under his feet, the water that covered him to his waist, and a breeze as it whispered through the air, but he couldn't feel anything else.

"It's in the air. I'm home. I feel it. It's kind of like…" Kaimi's eyes opened and her brow furrowed.

"Like what?" Garrett was intrigued. Whatever she was feeling, her rhythms were suddenly running with more peace than he was accustomed to.

"When you hold me and I concentrate, I can feel how much you love me. Here in the water, I feel so happy. It's aloha, but that sounds stupid to you," she choked out her abashed explanation.

Garrett's frustration fed his stubbornness. He was upsetting her by not really accepting Tutu's ways of life or her own. He'd promised the people of Hawaii he'd learn their ways. He didn't give a damn what Kalakona thought, but the Hawaiian people deserved a well-run Iodex that did care about their lands and their ways of life.

"I want to feel it. Show me how," he begged.

Tears sprang to Kaimi's eyes as she nodded. "Okay, stand me up." Garrett stood her on the ocean floor. "Close your eyes and let the water run through your hands. Just kind of breathe in. First, you can only smell the salty air, but then keep breathing deeper each time." Garrett swallowed, and with a single nod he decided to trust his wife and the rhythms of the island. He knew they were there. He saw them in her. He just had to believe.

CHAPTER 30

HOUSE OF CARDS AND A HURRICANE

~DAN VINDICO~

"Jeff's graduated, so now I could try to get information for you like he was before." Ben had restated the same plea six times in a row. Weary irritation coiled in Dan's mind. He needed Fionna to come back. She was all that was keeping him calm as of late.

"I know you want to help, Ben. I appreciate that, but this has gotten more serious than I ever thought possible. This is a full Iodex investigation. My father is in the hospital in the Cardiac Intensive Care Unit. Wilshire is getting closer to losing his job and his pension with each passing day. I'm not involving any more students. Whoever is doing this has gone too far."

He wasn't pulling punches or trying to befriend any more kids. His wife and his family were somehow on the line once again. This time he was playing by the rules. Going rogue had lost him a child. Creating his own student police force stood to cost him his wife's dignity and things that belonged to them alone.

"But I could go back out there and get in line, listen in on what students are saying to corroborate what they tell you." Ben began cracking his knuckles one after the other in a nervous chain that seemed to have him bound.

"I appreciate the offer, but no."

"If you change your mind…" Ben stood dejectedly.

"I'll let you know." Another knock sounded on the door. Ben opened it to leave, and Chance and Arial rushed inside.

"Shit," Dan and Jeff both whimpered.

~

Rainer Lawson

Portwood and Logan joined Rainer and Emily as Governor Willow and Governor Haydenshire bid their farewell. Emily hugged her father. She'd just returned from her lunch with Fionna. She'd had a good time, but Rainer knew she was devastated Fionna was moving so far away.

"I'll be back after this trial, but with Arthur out, they need the rest of us there," Governor Haydenshire apologized.

"Sir, we understand. I really appreciate your help," Portwood vowed.

"We'll be back this evening, Landon. I want to know where we trace that paycheck to," Governor Willow reminded his officers that he was willing to help them as much as they needed.

"Thank you both. As soon as we get through these confessions, we'll dive into that," Portwood assured both governors.

He turned to Rainer and Logan as soon as the governors were out of earshot. "Is there any way we could divide this up, so I don't have to hear any more about how his girlfriend had just broken up with him because he *accidentally* slept with her best friend, and he was so distraught he had to buy the tests because he just couldn't study."

Logan and Rainer both laughed as Emily gave Portwood a sympathetic grin.

"Unfortunately, I don't really think we have the manpower for confession triaging, sir." Rainer sighed.

"We just need twelve teams of Jeff. Then they could read all the emails and figure this out before these sick bastards plaster the Internet with pictures they were never meant to see," Logan lamented.

"After everyone heads home, Jeff and Ramier can enter in all of the new information we've gathered and come up with new phrases to run through the casts on the servers," Portwood pointed out.

Rainer felt horrible for Dan and Fionna. He and Emily had fought the hounds of hell from the press for too long for him ever to make photographic evidence of their lovemaking. Hell, the press had done that for them on their honeymoon, but Dan had done nothing wrong when he'd taken those pictures. The fact that someone stole them with the intent to defraud one of the men Rainer most respected made him sick.

A hesitant knock sounded, and Portwood drew a deep breath. "Put your clerical collars back on, boys. Confession's open again." He flung open the door and Brodie Quentin entered. Rainer remembered him from school, but he didn't know him well.

Emily's eyes goggled. She grabbed his hand. Rainer felt her immediate draw of his protective energy. His head jerked upward to meet Portwood's stunned realization. Logan eased in front of Emily, always ready to protect his little sister.

"Come on in." Portwood gestured to the seat in front of the desk as they all understood that Brodie's energy strains were reading heavily with his guilt.

"So...I can just talk, and you won't arrest me or whatever?" Brodie's voice was strained and terror-ridden.

"That was the deal." Portwood gave nothing away. Logan and Rainer leaned in as Emily tried to steady her rhythms by making constant draws of Rainer's.

Brodie broke out in a sweat and glanced at the door. Logan slid in front of it. Backing out was not going to be an option. "I'm probably gonna end up getting killed for this or something."

"What's your name, son?" Portwood sounded genuinely concerned.

"Brodie Quentin, and I don't know who I've been working for, but I've made a shit ton of money. I know I shouldn't have, but I just did whatever he asked, and it didn't seem too bad."

"Why don't you start at the beginning? We'll work our way through everything that's happened," Portwood eased patiently. He seemed to realize that Brodie's psyche couldn't withstand much more.

"Okay, uh… I guess last year everybody knew Wilshire was boning Mentor Bryant or whatever, and we could all pretty much do whatever we wanted. So, a couple of brainiacs over in the computer lab had a bet going that they could get a few copies of the final exams out of the test vault just for kicks or whatever. They sure as hell didn't need the copies. They got straight As. They just wanted to prove they could do it and get away with it because no one cared what was going on anymore." Brodie shrugged.

"Okay." Portwood nodded. "Could you give me their names?"

"Yeah, but they graduated last year. It's gotten way, way bigger than that anyway." Brodie's body physically seemed to relax with every word that egressed his mouth. As he eased so did Emily.

"So, they stole a couple of first-semester final exams, then one of them sold a copy to a few guys who wouldn't have passed without them. It was just a stupid thing. After that, somebody figured out they could get the tests off the mentors' laptops if they casted the thumb drives. Did you already know about that?" Brodie quizzed confusedly.

"Yes. Just one moment, though. Haydenshire, go get Dan, now," Portwood commanded. Logan raced out the door. Brodie looked relieved to stop talking.

~

Dan Vindico

"…and then Stephanie Greenwood broke up with Conner Cannon and then he started going out with Karen. And Karen and I are like BFFs, but then he broke up with her after just a few dates. I'm not sure they were ever like girlfriend boyfriend or if they were just like, hey we aren't exclusive, but I think that means that Stephanie Greenwood was using drugs and so she probably paid to get a test changed or whatever. Then when Conner stopped going out with Karen he told his friend Gavin that Karen was really annoying, which is like crazy, right? So, now I think maybe Conner is on drugs too, because my friends are completely not annoying."

Dan stared at Chance and wondered how the hell he put up with

Arial. Yet, Chance stared at Arial like he'd never seen anything so incredible. Jeff's head was in his right hand propped on the desk.

"Dan!" Logan exploded through the door. Jeff's head shot upward in shock. "Come on. You need to hear this!"

Dan outpaced Logan and Jeff by several feet. Fionna was coming in the front doors as he raced past.

"Dan?" She panicked.

"Come on," he urged, and she joined the men racing to the office.

He was momentarily stunned to see Brodie Quentin seated across from Portwood. He had him in a loose, relatively friendly seating arrangement. He was getting information and wanted Brodie to keep talking. As Dan had been the one to teach Landon when to lean across the desk on your knuckles with an ominous scowl to intimidate the hell out of a criminal and when to sit relatively relaxed to make the informant think you were on their side and wanted to help, he recognized the arrangement instantly.

Fionna reached and touched Dan's forearm. Her frantic energy shook him from his interrogation mode. She was trembling but trying very hard not to look frightened.

Portwood and Dan began a silent conversation. Landon glanced back at the door and furrowed his brow. Dan gave a minute headshake. Fionna wouldn't want to leave the room. He was certain.

Portwood gave a single nod. He gestured his head to the side, and Dan eased Fionna toward the back corner of the room. Emily was pale and holding tightly to Rainer's hand.

Dan was torn. He wanted to be in Brodie's face. He wanted every piece of evidence the idiot was willing to give up, but whatever he'd done, it was bad enough to affect Receivers, and being Fionna's Shield would always come first. He was going to have to let Portwood man this one.

CHAPTER 31

BOILING POINT ELEVATION

"Go on, Brodie," Portwood eased. He was still playing nice. "Somehow, I guess these people casted all of those drives that came with the laptops when they handed out the supplies. I don't know who did it. Like I said, I don't know who I'm working for, but last night he called me and he was freaking out. He kept saying shit about how he knew where my kid brother goes to school and stuff. You gotta keep him safe. I mean, he's just a kid. The guy kept saying that he could get him anytime." Brodie sounded absolutely terrified.

"What's your brother's name and where does he go to school?" Portwood seemed to let the realization that they weren't dealing with out-of-control children settle on him harshly. This was a real case. These were adults, and whoever was running this had the makings of a criminal mastermind.

"Uh, Benjamin Stranos. We call him Benji. He's only five. He's my stepbrother. He goes to McCarron," Brodie explained.

At that moment, Dan knew his decision to send the girls on to Kauai had been the right move. He no longer held any doubt. This was escalating far too rapidly. He was also loath to admit that perhaps the two o'clock pickup rule wasn't all bad.

Still playing nice, Portwood pulled his phone from his pocket.

"Yeah, send two cars out to McCarron Elementary. Have them circle around and check the kindergarten hallway. Make certain Benji Stranos is in his classroom, and if anyone tries to access him, call me immediately. Then sit in the parking lot. Call me when you've made damn certain that every single kid goes home with the right person."

"Thank you." Relief played heavily in Brodie's weary eyes.

Portwood nodded. "All right, we'll keep Benji safe. You talk."

"I don't know that much, honest. We get these texts. It'll have the people's names and cell numbers. Then if they've been buying tests, it'll have this code. See." He showed Portwood his phone. "So, that's the guy's name." He pointed to the screen. "And then that's his school number. That's how we prove to them that we have the record of them buying. Then those are codes like if it says 04 that means he's a Sophomore and obviously Hum is Humanities and then the 6 means he's bought the last six tests or quizzes. So, I tell him we know all of that and then the 650 is how much he has to pay. I get to add on however much of a fee I want to. So, like, for that one I made it 800. I get to keep the $150 and then I get these big payouts once a month. They just show up in my checking account. Last month I earned $26,000. I don't know who's doing it, but that's a ton of money. I could never make that in one month working while I'm in school."

"Are you the guy who called me?" Dan tried to modulate the fury in his voice.

"No, sir." Brodie shook his head adamantly. "You're the biggest take yet. Whoever's running this called you."

"You sound pretty certain we're talking about one person. Are you sure there aren't several people running this?" Portwood edged closer to Brodie.

"I don't know. I've talked to him on the phone a few times, but mostly it's emails and texts."

"I need to see those emails." Jeff erupted from his seat. Brodie nodded uncomfortably.

"Okay, and I know you're like a genius or whatever, but honestly, I thought it *was* you for a long time. I couldn't figure you with the junk truck and secondhand clothes or whatever. I figured it was all a front. I mean, you're banging Becca Sapman, and she's crazy about you. I figured you needed some way to keep her happy. Not to be hating on you or anything. I'm just saying this guy's really smart too. He knows what he's doing. You're not gonna be able to trace those back or whatever it is you do." Jeff was visibly infuriated. He was vibrating in his chair, his shield reddened with rage. "Until Mac told me to find the guy from Tech to make it look like you, I thought it was you."

"Mac?" Portwood leapt back into the conversation.

"That's just what I call him. That's how all of the texts used to start. MAC—Make A Call. I guess in my mind I kind of named him Mac." Brodie looked slightly embarrassed to have admitted that.

"So, you found Christopher Reynolds to set me up," Jeff spat angrily. Portwood threw a glance Jeff's way that had him backing down.

"Yeah, I got six thousand dollars until you found him. Then I had to give the money back. Maybe you can trace this guy's emails, but I'm telling you he knows what he's doing." Brodie's forthright confession was infuriating Jeff, but Dan and Portwood knew they were quite literally holding gold.

"What about the numbers he's texting from?" Portwood continued.

"The first of every month, I get a box of dozens of burner phones. Somebody leaves them under my desk in my first period class. I call from those, so I guess he has a bunch. I don't know."

"But you always get the instructions on this phone." Portwood held up Brodie's iPhone, but something occurred to Dan.

"That's why you got in the fight back in the fall. The one in Mentor Bryant's classroom with Kellan Morris. Was he messing with the phones?" Dan demanded.

"Yeah, he's such a prick. He wanted a bigger take so he wanted more jobs, but he just kept screwing them up. He just up and decided he was going to take mine. After that fight, Mac stopped giving him phones at all. I don't know how he found out about it, but he knows everything all the time."

"She knew," Dan gasped. "She knew all along and wasn't going to tell me. She knew you were fighting about something having to do with the tests, and she got mad and never fucking told me!" He flung open the door.

"Where are you going?" Portwood demanded.

"To find Katherine Bryant!"

CHAPTER 32
HIGH-LEVEL VOLATILE INFORMANT

"Dan, I don't understand. Stop!" Fionna finally shouted her demand as she raced after him. He forced his muscles to halt their frantic race. He wasn't certain if he was running into abdication or censure. He spun and drew several breaths.

"I don't understand what's happening. Tell me where we're going," she demanded. She'd battled through the labyrinth of adolescent minds fraught with guilt and terror and confusion all their own. And at the first moment he'd realized there was a piece of evidence he'd not been missing but that had been knowingly kept from him, he'd threatened to shut her out all over again.

"I'm sorry," he apologized. "Uh…" He ran his hands through his hair and tried to navigate his own frantic thoughts and rhythms so he could explain them to her. "Brodie is what we call a high-level volatile informant. That means he has a great deal of information he can give us, but he's very likely to get spooked. Whoever is running this show is coming unglued.

"The email went out last night to all of the parents explaining what the assembly this morning was going to be about. Some of the students must've found out as well, and now, they're running scared. They freaked and called Brodie last night to threaten his family. So, they're worried Brodie might know enough to get them caught. Keeping Brodie safe and keeping him talking will be very difficult, but Portwood knows what he's doing."

Fionna nodded, but confusion was still flexing in her rhythms.

"Do you remember Vitrio in Vegas?" Dan tried to draw on her very limited interactions with law enforcement and criminal organizations.

"Yes, of course." She sounded horrified.

"Same deal here. Vitrio knew a great deal, and he was willing to tell me what he knew in exchange for going to jail where…uh…he thought no one could get to him." Dan choked over the explanation. He knew what the next words out of his wife's lips were going to be.

She shook her head. "But Vitrio didn't survive prison. How are you going to keep Brodie safe, and what does Katherine Bryant have to do with all of this? What fight were you talking about?"

Dan tried not to let his dogged determination take over. It was putting up a willful fight.

"At the beginning of the school year, when Dad took over, long before Halia was born, I was in Dad's office when a fight broke out in Katherine Bryant's classroom between Brodie and Kellan Morris. I broke it up. Dad suspended them for two weeks. But he suspended them before I got to interrogate them. I'd gone back to check on Bryant because she was hit during the fight. She was a total bitch. Remember, that's the day you came up here and we went to register for stuff for Halia."

Fionna's determination began to reform out of the waves of her confusion. "That was the day you told her off."

Dan nodded. "She asked me if I wanted to know what they'd been fighting about. I smarted off to her because she'd been a total bitch, like I said. So, she's known all along that they were fighting over that box of phones, and she decided to be a vindictive brat instead of putting Venton first. I plan to call her on it right now."

"Okay." Fionna seemed relieved she now understood and seemed to realize that Dan was going to make a conscious effort to include her in this every step of the way. "Let's go." They raced past the lines students eager to get their confessions in.

Dan halted just outside of Bryant's classroom. He kept Fionna from moving across the doorway. He heard Bryant talking, but it obviously wasn't to a student. He motioned for Fionna to be quiet. She moved against the wall just outside the door. They leaned in and listened.

CHAPTER 33
ASSAULT AND ASSUMPTIONS

"Why the hell are you even here, Terry, other than to keep rubbing it in my face?" Katherine's voice shook on the verge of tears. Fionna closed her eyes. She shuddered from the emotions rolling out of the room. Dan wrapped his arm around her.

"I thought you might need some money, Katie. Sorry. I was trying to help you." Terry Bryant's offer was full of derision and incredulity.

Fionna shook her head, but Dan didn't need anyone to tell him that Terry Bryant didn't want to help his wife. He was being an asshole. It was evident in his tone.

"Oh, you'd love that, wouldn't you? You'd love me coming to you asking for anything at all. And don't call me Katie! You know I hate that. I'm not your child. And I don't want anything from you. I won't live under your thumb anymore. The cost of favors from you is entirely too high," Katherine spat viciously. "I still can't figure out how we got to where we were. How could I have allowed you to control all the money *I* was making? You know what, you can have it all. Nothing is worth being married to someone who wants to reward me when I finally give in and try not to vomit while I force myself to have sex with you. Just stay the hell away from me. You can't control me anymore. I haven't loved you in a long time, and I never will again. In fact, I hate you."

Dan strengthened his hold on Fionna. His shield bled from his pores without him consciously having to summon it. The sick perversion the Bryants had created out of their marriage would never get anywhere near his baby. He wouldn't allow that kind of malignancy. It was despicable.

Katherine Bryant hadn't destroyed her marriage. Her husband had. Fionna convulsed from what she was hearing and had felt before Dan pushed it all away from her. He kept his shield expanding, distancing everything but his all-encompassing love.

"I've got you," he whispered in her ear. "I'm right here." But suddenly they heard a desk slide ominously across the lacquered floors. The squeal rang of warning.

"Let go of me," Katherine demanded.

"You never told Dean that, now did you, Katie?" Terry sneered.

"Get your disgusting hands off me!" The terror-filled demand echoed in the air. Fury leaked into Dan's shield. He couldn't block it out. It was coming from him. The sound of Katherine Bryant being backhanded had them moving.

"Dan, help her!" Fionna ordered, but he was already in the classroom.

In a quick move, he shoved Terry Bryant with all of his might. Terry stumbled backward and then tumbled over a student desk.

"What the fuck is wrong with you?" Dan snarled over Terry Bryant. He jerked him up off the ground and pulled the cuffs from his belt loop. "You're under arrest for domestic battery. That's an eighteen-month stint in Felsink, Mr. Bryant, and five years of counseling. I hope you enjoy that." He dragged Terry from the room and marched him down to one of the interrogation rooms. Tuttle and McCoy were hearing confessions. Both of their heads rose when Dan threw open the door. "Can one of you take Mr. Bryant to the Senate for me? Definitely domestic battery and I'm betting assault as well. See how much he likes the box."

"You got it, Dan." McCoy stood and narrowed his eyes in on Terry. "Before I moved to Vegas, I was putting away assholes like you in the great state of Texas. That's the thing I've missed most since I got to Elite."

Dan chuckled as he handed Terry over and headed back to Katherine's classroom.

Fionna had eased to her side. Dan saw his wife's soothing cast work over Katherine Bryant. Unlike an Ioses shield, a Receiver's cast could be entered from the outside without causing any harm. Dan moved closer to Fionna and Katherine.

"Are you all right?" He didn't know where to begin or if he should bring up the fight at all.

"I'm fine." Katherine stepped away from Fionna, and she dropped her cast. Katherine's hand sought her right cheek in an effort to somehow rid the pain that was inevitably etched in her soul.

"If he was abusive, why didn't your lawyer bring that up at the custody hearing?" Dan decided he was going to ask even if he didn't get an answer.

"He's gotten much worse, and why do you care?" Katherine defied.

"Katherine, Dan could ask his dad to go ahead and grant you a divorce if that's what you want. Terry is abusive even if it's only recently escalated to physical abuse," Fionna soothed.

"And why would you help me now?"

"Because sometimes it's hard to stand up for yourself, and because you need to be able to move on with your life." It seemed Fionna wasn't backing down no matter how hateful Katherine had behaved in the past. Dan knew Fionna could certainly feel the despair and the embarrassment that had to be quaking in Bryant's rhythms. He also now understood the claim that he was abusive. She'd projected her own pain onto the Vindicos' marriage in an effort to deal with the trauma.

"Well, thank you, Mrs. Vindico. I would love to move on with my life, but I feel certain that I deserve so much more hell to walk through. Everyone seems so sure I should be punished. It must be true," Katherine spat indignantly before she stomped out of the room.

Fionna shook her head. Tears welled in her huge sienna eyes. Dan wrapped her up in his arms as she began to cry. It had all been too much. She'd wanted so much to be a part of the investigation, but it was taking its toll.

"Just hold me, please." She knew he was deeply concerned and that he needed to know how to make her better. Dan locked his shield around her.

"Fi, baby, why don't you go on to Kauai."

"No, I talked to Tutu. She and Papa had gone to check on Aida at lunch, and she was having a good time. She loves her teacher, and she made a new friend named Kealia. Halia's okay. I'm supposed to be here with you. I can feel that."

Dan tried to refuse the doubt that took hold in his mind. "Are you sure? This is about to get even more intense. Even I can feel that." He may not be a Receiver, but he knew when a case was reaching a summit. It was who he was.

"I'm okay," she assured him. "Let's go back. Brodie knew more. He wasn't finished. His energy relaxed with each word he spoke. It broke my heart for him. I don't guess I'd make much of an officer."

"I think you're an incredible officer, and wife, and mother, and woman. I'm so sorry I somehow got you caught up in all of this again." He'd apologized a million times, but it brought no solace to his terror-filled soul.

"Stop." Fionna placed her index finger over his lips. He kissed it automatically.

"I love you so much." He choked over his vow. It formed on his lips from deep inside of him in a place that only she could ever access. She was the only person who'd ever held the key.

CHAPTER 34

STRATEGIC REFRACTION

They returned to the questioning room to find Brodie still talking. Jeff was typing rapidly on an Iodex laptop and casting it at the same moment.

"Anyone else?" Portwood encouraged.

"Mac doesn't tell us who else is doing this. That's the only other people I know about."

"If you're one of the top guys, why do you have mostly Cs?" Jeff retorted from behind the screen.

"I don't cheat," Brodie huffed.

Dan stifled a chuckle. Jeff still had a great deal to learn. There may not have been any honor among thieves, but they often had their own code they lived by. Dan had always considered it some kind of negotiation between a thief and his conscience. Brodie was perfectly willing to take other students' money, but he wouldn't use the test copies himself.

"What can you tell us about the covered drug tests?" Frustration etched Portwood's chiseled features.

"All I know is that the computer lab sent an email out to the students at the beginning of last year that said they could get a drug test covered for $1200. I don't know where that money goes, but as long as I keep passing the email around, I get part of the take."

"There are other kids wanting to make confessions." Rainer glanced at the door at the long line of impatient students.

"You're not gonna tell anyone everything I told you?" Brodie panicked.

"No, we'd never make you. We do need your help though," Portwood said. "Go out there, and if anyone asks, tell them you were buying tests or whatever."

"Everyone knows I only get Cs."

"Then tell them you're using. If Mac contacts you again, I want you to either call Dan or me immediately."

"Yeah, okay, but what if whoever is doing this is out there? I waited forever to come in here when I was sure no one was watching. I can't just walk out of here. I told you he's freaking out. He was seriously fucked last night." Dan and Rainer both scowled angrily.

"Watch your mouth. My wife is standing right here," Dan reminded Brodie.

"Sorry, Mrs. Vindico. I was trying to make them understand."

Fionna nodded. "It's okay. What if we all left Brodie in here like we'd been having a meeting or something? He just said he made certain no one saw him come in. We can all walk out and tell the kids in line that we're opening up more rooms so we could see more of them. He can stay here until everyone's gone home for the night. No one would ever know he'd even come in."

Portwood was visibly impressed. "Does that work for you, Brodie? I think I'm going to leave you in here with Officer Strenton. I'd like you to come up with anything we could run through the detection casts he's set on the servers."

Neither Jeff nor Brodie seemed thrilled with Portwood's plan, but neither of them argued.

~

Garrett Haydenshire

"This is really good." Kaimi was taking huge bites of the taro burger Garrett had just cooked over the nearby grills. She was leaning languidly against him with her back to his chest. The sun was dipping toward the ocean, but not fast enough. Garrett willed its rapid descent.

He was brushing tender kisses along Kaimi's neck as she finished eating.

"I'm hungry for something else," he informed her. His hot breath mingled with the humid air. His need danced all around her in his pulsing rhythms. She shivered and set the burger down. She turned around and stared up at him with that innocent fire lighting the copper in her eyes. It was the most erotic thing he'd ever seen.

"What?" she whispered furtively.

"You." He kept his hands tenderly exploring all of her slight curves. His body longed to be devoured by hers. "Too damn many interruptions today. I want you all to myself. I want to have my way with you, and I don't think I can wait much longer. I'm not that patient."

"There are people over there." She gestured several yards down the beach where a group of teenagers were coming in from paddleboarding.

"They need to leave. I'm tired of waiting. I want to own you."

Kaimi's eyes flashed in intrigue and desire. Hesitation played on the golden rims, but it was far outweighed by Garrett's hunger for her.

CHAPTER 35

SUPPORT

~DAN VINDICO~

Dan's heart sped and then tried unsuccessfully to find a steady cadence as Clarence Pendergrath entered the office where Dan and Fionna were seated. Fionna laced her hand in Dan's and, to his shock, offered Clarence a kind smile. He was gently guiding in a girl that Dan assumed was Kristen Cinders.

"Can we talk? I found out some other stuff, and she needs to tell you something." Clarence seemed ready to bolt at the slightest movement. Dan was torn between going ahead and throwing his shield over Fionna or allowing Clarence to prove he was going to be more than his father ever hoped to be.

"Of course. That's what we're here for today," Fionna assured him softly. She leaned toward Clarence, and Dan nearly had a heart attack. His shield pulsed furiously. She patted his arm and shook her head at him.

Relief echoed in Clarence's slight nod. He shared an uncomfortable glance with Kristen. She looked petrified.

"Uh...so, I was thinking..." Clarence grimaced. Kristen squeezed his hand while Dan and Fionna ignored her constant draws from him. "I mean, Dad and Uncle Nic looked for your house for all those years, right?"

Dan narrowed his eyes hatefully. Kristen gave Clarence a panicked headshake.

"All I meant was obviously your house isn't on Google or whatever. I figure it had to be one of those guys I was hanging out with that day who told people where you live. That's how your house got vandalized. It has to be." Dan was still trying not to think about Clarence's casual mention that his own father and Uncle Nic Wretchkinsides had relentlessly searched for Dan in order to kill him.

"Okay," Fionna answered for him. "Who were you with that day?"

"Of all the guys in that car, I think it was Liam Northrup. He's kind of a prick. All of a sudden, he's getting perfect grades, so he's probably buying or being given test copies. He was bad-mouthing you as soon as we saw you and your kid that day."

"Liam Northrup is an Ioses Pred," Dan disdained.

"So?" Clarence scoffed.

"Shields rarely attack other Shields."

"Rarely isn't never."

"Did you have anything else to tell us?" Dan urged. He was growing impatient with the entire process.

"Uh…yes, sir," Kristen managed in a timid whisper.

Fionna gently elbowed Dan. He needed to listen even if it was the last thing he wanted to do.

"Go ahead," Fionna soothed.

"I think I know who's been changing the drug tests." Kristen's delicate neck tensed as she swallowed. "And I know because I did a line with a few friends of mine a couple of times and then there was one of those surprise tests, and the girl that gave me the coke also told me that her dad could fix my test. I only had to pay half. I've never done it except those two times, I swear. I didn't like it, but they were all doing it. It made my rhythms really weird. I blacked out. Clarence saved me. He stayed with me to make sure I was okay, and he's been going with me to one of those anonymous drug counseling centers downtown on Tuesdays." She gave him a tender grin. Her continued draw of what appeared to be adoring love from Clarence astonished Dan as he realized that Clarence was the reason she was no longer using. He'd given her strength and support and an out. His father may have been a murderer who deserved his fate, but maybe Clarence was going to be more than his old man.

"Okay," Dan managed. "Who gave you the cocaine?"

"Libby Ellington, sir, but please don't tell her I told you. I think she really needs help. She's using even harder stuff now. She's a mess."

"Did you pay Medio Ellington directly, or did you use the email system?" Dan pressed harder.

"I gave the money to Libby and then my test came back negative." Kristen shrugged. "She really, really hates her mom. I kinda think she started buying to make her mom look bad, and then her dad made sure that wouldn't happen. I mean, that could be it, right?"

Clarence wrapped his arm around her, and her eyes lit as she turned to gaze up at him. Dan felt his mind and his soul begin a war. The sight before him made no sense to his shield. His rhythms ran disjointedly until Fionna sent her soothing pulse through his forearm.

"You're not going to arrest me or tell my parents?" Kristen begged.

"No, that was the deal. Governor Haydenshire is going to want you to see a drug counselor here at the school though."

"I'll go with you. I told you he always does what he says he's going to do." Clarence nodded toward Dan.

"Thank you, Mentor Vindico." The relief of the pressing guilt seemed to physically lighten Kristen.

"No problem. Thank you for telling me all of that." Dan was still studying Clarence's interactions with Kristen. It was like looking in a microscope at some kind of foreign substance.

CHAPTER 36
ALIAS

"Sir, look what I just found." Jeff leapt as soon as Dan reentered the office where Jeff had been hiding out with Brodie. The last students had finally been sent home by Portwood with the promise that if they didn't get to give their confession today that Iodex would return to Venton the next day.

"What?" Dan sighed. Will and Natalie Gorham from the Senate Bank were setting up everything to read where the traced checks had ended up.

"Your house was a job. I found the emails."

"With my help," Brodie reminded him.

Jeff gave a less than discreet eye roll as he showed Dan and Fionna the emails he'd located.

"Each of the guys were paid. LN 4249 and PS 2247." Jeff pointed to the student numbers of the email recipients. "Uh, that's..." He spun his chair and typed the numbers in the student database on another laptop.

"Preston Steimer and..."

"Liam Northrup," Dan concluded for him. Fionna and Dan shared a knowing gaze. Clarence was telling the truth.

Will Haydenshire came in the room. "We're ready. We're set up in the lunchroom."

Dan drew a deep breath and tried to discern what to do with the fact that he now had the names of the children who'd attacked his home. Everyone made their way to the cafeteria as Brodie headed out to the student parking lot.

"Before we dive into that, did either Liam or Preston come talk to anyone today?" Dan demanded from the assembled grouping of officers and the returning governors along with Fionna and Emily.

"Uh…" Tuttle flipped through a folder. "Yeah, I talked to Liam Northrup. He started off scheming. 'I'll give you everyone I know that's buying tests if you swear you won't arrest me.' I told him that he only needed to tell me what he'd done to keep from being arrested. He balked and then bolted."

Dan nodded. "Okay, but no one talked to Preston Steimer?" All of his officers began flipping through the detailed notes of their day.

"How about this?" Portwood urged. "Let's trace this check. See where that takes us. We might be able to follow the payout on your house, which is more than we have now. All we have from these emails is conspiracy. If we don't get what we want, you and I can take a drive in a squad car out to Steimer's house and put them him in the tank. I imagine he'll talk."

Dan was struck at that moment by a number of raw emotions. How much he was going to miss Portwood and his original team. How much he missed Garrett. He and Garrett had been working over criminals together off and on for a decade. Their routine had drummed confessions out of the tightest mouths of the Interfeci. How much he wanted this over with coupled with how he never wanted it to end. The dichotomy of his ever changing life cleaved his already fractured soul. He didn't understand what he was allowed to hold on to and what he had to let go.

Suddenly, Fionna was by his side. Her fingers laced through his. Her beautiful eyes locked on Dan's. She encompassed all that ever was and all that ever would be. She sealed him tightly inside of their impenetrable bond. She was all that would ever matter. He just had to hold on to her.

"Yeah," Dan choked out his agreement. Portwood offered him a nod. The memories between the eight men who had been the Elite

Squadron for so long, the ones that had stood steadfast beside Dan to take down one of the most vile, corrupt criminal organizations in the world, formed in their eyes.

"Will." Portwood turned with an audible breath. "Let's let Officer Strenton man that trace, okay?"

"You're the boss." Will gestured Jeff to the chair in front of four Senate banking laptops. Fear and determination formed on Jeff's features as he seated himself in front of the computers. He casted two of them and leaned in. Every governor save Dan's father stood in wait, along with most of Iodex and several high-level officials from the Senate Bank. The pressure was certainly on.

He swallowed, and with a nod he began. "Okay, here's the initial draw. The Venton payroll account was queried, and then the money was disbursed to all of the employees' accounts. Obviously, most of them were direct deposited and then confirmations were sent back through the Senate servers. Here are a few that were divided and sent to multiple accounts—if they have their paycheck split into a checking account and then a savings account or something like that." Jeff drew another restorative breath and continued. "Uh, here you have a few that were automatically debited, like a wage garnish or child support payment or something that comes out every paycheck." He was pointing to dozens of account numbers. The Venton payroll servers had been repeatedly casted with high-level technology casts, so every action was lit in a kind of linear drawn map. Most Venton employees banked at the Senate bank, so the lines were fairly mundane. The divided lines were more intriguing, but Jeff was losing some of the governors. He needed to speed it up.

"This is the tagged paycheck." He hit a few keys, and with another cast of his hand, the monitor showed one lit line. Everyone leaned in. "It followed the same protocol. That's why it was so difficult to discover where all of the extra money was going, I assume." Jeff gestured to Will who nodded his agreement. He gave Jeff an encouraging smile that reminded Dan of Governor Haydenshire.

"So, let's see where it was deposited." Jeff hit several keys rapidly. "It went to a Senate Bank account 002189754-2012," Jeff read off the account number. Will typed the numbers in another banking laptop and his eyes goggled momentarily.

"That's Katherine Bryant's account." He shook his head.

"No." Fionna's still small voice shook in its adamance. "Dan, it isn't her. I would've felt that. Make it do something else, because it isn't her," she urged Jeff.

He nodded and studied the screen for a long moment. Then realization formed on his features. "Look, it's moving. It looks like it was programmed to stay in her account for five minutes and then it was moved." Jeff was typing again rapidly.

"This is ridiculous. Obviously, it is her," Governor Sapman retorted. "Stephen divided her pay. She clearly had ins with the staff here. Dean set that up for her. Are we really going to listen to a Receiver saying that she knows because she can 'feel' it?" His finger quotes around the word "feel" had fury igniting deep inside of Dan. He narrowed his eyes, but it wasn't Dan that spat out a retort.

"Excuse me, Governor Sapman, but I take great offense to that!" Governor Eleanor leapt in to defend Fionna.

"It isn't her," Dan vowed adamantly.

Jeff seemed relieved that other people were backing Fionna. "It was moved to an offshore account in New Zealand. I can't get any more information, but I can tell you that the money is still in the account. It hasn't been accessed… Wait!" Jeff gasped. "A five-thousand-dollar transfer was just made. It's moving now!"

"Well, where is it going?" Governor Sapman ordered. Jeff shot his father-in-law an annoyed glance as everyone watched the highlighted transaction work its way across the world.

"It just hit Sydney, Australia, then two bounces in China," Jeff read out what he was watching. "Portugal and now Switzerland." The beacon homed in for a few seconds.

"Maybe there's another unnamed account there," Portwood suggested hopefully.

"No, it's moving again." Dan pointed to the lighted path on the map display on Jeff's laptop.

"Toronto, and now it's back in the US." Jeff casted and enlarged the map. "LA, Vegas, Denver, Dallas..." The dot halted and pulsed over Dallas, Texas.

"Dallas?" Portwood's brow furrowed. Dan shook his head. How could every single discovery in this investigation end with more questions?

"Could this have anything to do with Hubbert, Landon?" Governor Haydenshire stepped in. "Don't we have a few transfers from Hubbert Academy to Venton?"

"I can get that for you, sir. It's here on the Venton roll logs," Jeff supplied humbly as he typed into yet another laptop. "No transfers, sir. I can run anyone in the school that ever resided near Dallas if you'd like."

"Yes," Portwood ordered.

"Dean's from the Dallas area, isn't he?" Governor Willow eased. He'd positioned himself between Dan and Governor Sapman. Governor Willow was one of a very few men who could somewhat contain Dan's wrath and his temper. "Waxahachie or something like that?"

"Yes, he is." Fury tensed in Governor Haydenshire's reply.

"Tuttle!" Portwood commanded.

"I'm on the phone with them now." Tuttle waited on an answer from the Realm Bank in Dallas. "Elite Iodex Officer Ryan Tuttle from the DC office. I have an account I need a name on now," he demanded.

Jeff handed Tuttle a slip of paper containing the account number. Tuttle slowly read it off to the bank manager. With a nod, he grew quiet. "I'm here. Go ahead," he assured a moment later. His eyes goggled. "Are you certain that's the name?" Tuttle shook his head. "Okay, thank you." He turned to Dan. Shock rang in his shield. "It's registered to an Alex Mueller."

Fionna gasped. "Are you serious?!"

"I've got the account here, Landon." Will gestured back to his laptop.

"Shut it down. Seize everything in the account as evidence," Portwood gave the fierce order. He didn't appear to be willing to mess around anymore. Everyone seemed to agree this had gone on long enough.

With one nod, Will locked down the account and transferred the money to a holding account owned by Iodex. "Dan, there's over a half million dollars in this account."

"Then we just found something, didn't we?" Dan tried to discern what to do next. "Get me every transaction made out of that account since its inception." Will casted the computer, and banking documents began shooting out of the nearby printer.

In the pause, Jeff turned from the computer to Tuttle. "Wasn't Alexander Mueller a physicist? Didn't he give the Non-Gifted superconductivity? He's dead, so obviously he isn't using this account. Why were you all so shocked?"

Tuttle nodded. "Yeah, that's him. It's also one of Dan's most common aliases whenever he was in a situation where it was unlikely that anything would go wrong. It would've been his most-known alias."

Dan's jaw clenched. He shook his head. "Every email you've traced has come in and out of Venton servers. Whoever is doing all of this had access to the thumb drives, or they wouldn't have been able to cast them. The ground wire to the test vault on campus grounds was blown. So, who the hell has that much access to this campus that also knows about my aliases? I doubt my own father even knew that was my most-used alias. And why would they have set up an account in Dallas?"

Portwood drew an audible breath. "That's what we have to figure out. It's going to be a long night. Every piece of evidence needs to be gone over with a fine-tooth comb. Go get some dinner, kiss your kids, and apologize to your spouses for me. Meet us back here in two hours," Portwood commanded all of Iodex. He turned to Dan. "Let's go see what we can drum out of Preston Steimer. This Liam kid did come in to see us, but Preston didn't. That tells me he's the one with the most to lose."

"Yeah, just let me get Fi home," Dan agreed with a slight sigh. Jeff stood and shrugged into his jacket.

"Let me go check on Becca for a little while. She's so sick of eating hospital food. Let me just take her some dinner, and I'll come right back."

"Yeah, I'll run Em home and be back," Rainer agreed.

"No, let me stay and help," Emily insisted.

Fionna was still fuming over Governor Sapman's disdain. "Me too!"

"Hey, I'll take all the Receivers I can get." Portwood shot his decree directly at Governor Sapman.

"Smart man," Governor Haydenshire huffed.

CHAPTER 37

TIPPING POINT

~JEFF STRENTON~

"I'm here, baby. I'm coming in," Jeff assured Becca as he entered the hospital.

"Oh my gosh, I'm so excited!" Becca sounded exhausted. The juxtaposition between her words and her tone concerned him.

"Are you excited to see me or because I have pizza and fudge ripple ice cream?" he teased her. He casted his phone as he stepped on the elevator.

"Can't it be both?"

Jeff chuckled as he opened the door to Becca's room and ended the call.

"Hey." Becca lifted her hands up from her seated position on the bed. "I'm not supposed to get up," she explained as Jeff stowed her requested dinner on the table and leaned down to squeeze her tightly.

"What happened?" He wondered why she wasn't supposed to get out of the bed. She looked pale and more exhausted than usual. Her eyes were dark and swollen.

"There was protein in my urine, and I was bleeding again earlier. They did some more scans of Aaron. She said they may have to take him at the end of the week if I don't improve."

Becca was trying desperately to sound excited and reassuring, but Jeff picked up on her terrorizing fears.

183

"Baby, I'm sorry. I should've been here. I didn't know they were doing all of that today. It's going to be fine. Adeline's great. We're gonna get through this."

Becca gave him a timid nod. "I'm just glad you're here now." Her voice shook as the fear began to take hold. She must've fought it all day. She'd wanted him, and he hadn't been there. Guilt took up residence in his shield as he wrapped her up in him. She began sobbing in earnest as his shield encapsulated her.

"I'm scared," she finally admitted. Jeff nodded. He cradled her on his shoulder and rubbed her back. He wished more than anything that he could take away all of the fear and all of her pain.

"I know, but it's going to be okay. I swear. I've got you. I'm right here."

Becca nodded against him. She clung to him with force.

She shook herself a moment later and wiped away her own tears. "I'm sorry. I didn't mean to freak out." She tried to force away her terror through sheer strength of will.

"Baby, it's fine. I just don't want you to be scared. I don't ever want to let anything scare you or upset you. I'm your Shield." He tried to explain what that meant, but he was sure she already knew.

He forced a smile and tried to decide the best way to tell her he couldn't stay with her all night. "Hey, how about some pizza or ice cream or pizza with ice cream on it?" He tried to tease her and earned himself a slight giggle. She nodded and drew a deep breath.

Jeff left the bed just long enough to retrieve the food. He wondered if somehow he could get her to eat and then hold her until she fell asleep in the next hour. He found the irritation that he couldn't stay with his wife and baby driving him. The sooner they figured out this case, the sooner he could be the husband and father he needed to be.

"Tell me what happened today?" Becca urged. She seemed desperate for something else to think about.

"Governor Haydenshire scared everybody to death, and then everyone started coming in to confess." Jeff inhaled a piece of pizza in a few bites before he went on.

"I bet Arial was all over that." Becca giggled. Jeff laughed as he recalled Arial tattling.

"Chance is a moron." He shook his head and watched over Becca as she picked at her pizza. She'd never been able to eat when she was nervous. His heart ached.

"Who else came in? Did anyone say anything about the pictures of Fionna?" She began pulling the pepperoni off and eating those. Jeff decided that was something, so he continued talking.

"No, but Brodie Quentin confessed, and he's apparently a major player in all of this. I figured out who vandalized the Vindicos' house. Dan and Portwood are headed to pick them up now."

"Wow!" The more interested in the story she became the more she ate. Jeff tried to think of what else he could tell her. "What about Medio Ellington?" she whispered though no one else was in the room.

"I'm not sure what they're gonna do about him. We've got him with tons of evidence. I'm sure Portwood is a little hesitant to arrest him because of his wife and everything. I don't know if Libby came in today. I have to go back in a little while so we can go over all the evidence."

Becca's face fell as she gave a disappointed nod. Jeff was trying to keep her distracted while he considered actually having Aaron outside of her body in just a few days. He would have to remain in the hospital for several weeks if she delivered him this early, even with the energy casts that had sped his development.

"Ben Cobson came in and was begging Dan to let him help." Jeff rolled his eyes. His annoyance with Ben had grown dramatically as of late.

"I'm still angry about what he said about Fionna." Jeff had told her when he called her earlier in the day about Ben's quip that Fionna should have been home taking care of Dan's kids. "He's always been kind of a prick though. He thinks he's so smart. He's just jealous that you always beat him out, and you got appointed to Iodex." Becca had always been protective of Jeff, but the long day and her nerves appeared to be getting the better of her.

Jeff leaned and kissed her cheek. "Dan told him no."

She worked her way slowly through one piece of pizza. Jeff took a spoon and began feeding her the ice cream. She giggled and let him spoil her. He was thrilled she was eating.

CHAPTER 38

THE VENGEFUL KING

They continued talking. Jeff relaxed a little as Becca's smile returned when she tucked into him. She was finished with the ice cream, and he threw out the container and eased back beside her. He didn't have much longer, and he wanted to spend a little time with Aaron before he had to return to Venton. He eased her shirt up and let his soothing rhythms move through her womb to his son. They both beamed as Aaron nudged Jeff's hand with his tiny foot.

"Hey, little guy." Jeff leaned and spoke into Becca's stomach. Aaron moved closer to the sound of Jeff's voice. Becca laughed and teared up at the same moment.

"He always moves when he hears you. I get so scared when I don't feel him for a while."

"He's probably sleeping or something." Jeff prayed he was right and that nothing was actually wrong with their little boy. Becca nodded as Aaron continued to respond to Jeff's voice and his love as he kept a steady stream of his energy flowing through to his son. A slight knock sounded on the door, and Jeff started to pull Becca's shirt back down, but she stopped him.

"I'm sure it's just Adeline. Aaron's missed you." Jeff kept his cast moving to Aaron who did seem to be reveling in his father's rhythms. He was kicking up a storm.

Adeline entered, but she was followed by a crowd. Jeff jerked Becca's shirt down as Rainer, Logan, Governor Willow, and Governor Sapman entered the hospital room.

"What is going on?" Jeff demanded. He'd been rather enjoying spending a little time with his wife and his son.

"I thought I might visit my daughter," Governor Sapman spat.

"I'm really sorry, man. We didn't mean to interrupt." Logan looked truly sorry. Rainer nodded his agreement. "Portwood called. They decided we're shutting down every angle we have tonight. We're here to arrest Ellington," he explained in a barely audible whisper.

"Dad just signed the warrant, but you're assigned as one of the arresting officers." Logan held up the paperwork for Medio Ellington's arrest.

Becca looked terrified. She reached for Jeff's hand. Her other hand flew to her stomach. Jeff could see Aaron's foot prod her bump. He was searching for Jeff. He'd become rather accustomed to feeling Jeff cast him at night.

"Uh, okay, fine, I guess." Jeff wasn't certain what else to do. He slid his hand back over Becca's swollen belly, trying to soothe Aaron. "Could we have a minute?" He finally decided that he needed to at least reassure her as best he was able before he went back to work.

"I'm sorry. We can't really be seen hanging out in the halls. We're a little concerned Ellington's gonna freak and bolt," Logan explained.

Governor Willow nodded his agreement. "I am sorry, Jeff. I commend you on all of your hard work and for being a tremendous husband and father. George, your son-in-law is quite a young man. This whole thing is just more than either Stephen or I ever imagined."

Governor Sapman looked begrudged to agree.

"It's okay," Becca whispered. "I'll take care of Aaron. You go work." She rubbed everywhere Aaron kicked his disapproval.

Drawing a deep breath, Jeff tried to remember all of the arrest procedures. He usually sat behind a computer and located criminals. He hadn't ever actually been out on an arrest.

"When you're ready, I'm going to run another stress test, then I'll give Becca something to help her rest since you won't be here tonight," Adeline explained discreetly.

Jeff leaned and kissed his wife. He tried to forget the sheer number of people staring at him.

"You're sure you're okay?"

Becca gave a nod though she was most certainly lying.

"I'll stay with her," Governor Sapman assured.

"Yeah, that's sure to make her feel better," Logan spoke under his breath.

Dan Vindico

"I hope Strenton doesn't choke," Portwood commented as he and Dan climbed into the SUV.

"He won't. You have to let him do this on his own. Ellington's not dangerous. He's not going to fire at them or even run. Let Jeff get this one under his belt, and he'll be able to handle the next on his own. You have to let him develop that ego he needs."

Portwood smiled and seemed to accept the advice. "All right, you're sure this is how you want to play this? Guns blazing. Take in everyone we have?"

Portwood navigated one of the Iodex Expeditions through the DC gridlocked traffic headed out to Kensington.

Dan considered the question. He would typically let Interfeci members walk free until he had enough evidence on them to keep them in prison for the rest of their lives.

This was different. None of the people involved, save the moron who had stolen pictures of his wife, did Dan want imprisoned at all. They were children caught up in an adult game. They couldn't see their way out because they were all pawns serving a vengeful king.

He'd tried not to go in guns blazing to save his father's reputation, and that had only alanded the governor in the hospital suffering a heart attack. This had to end. He needed to take Fionna home. He needed his baby girls. He missed them more and more each moment he went without them.

Garrett had admitted over the phone that Halia was getting more disgruntled with each passing day. She needed her parents, and they needed her. He couldn't keep dragging this out to play politics for his father any more than he could for Representative Ellington. Her daughter had a problem, and she needed help. Ignoring her drug use to save her mother's image wasn't serving anyone. Medio Ellington had done nothing but make his daughter think she wasn't as important as his wife's career. This had to end.

"Yeah, I'm sure. I've got to get Fi out of here. Dad's got to stop trying to work two jobs. Somebody has got to actually care about these kids more than the reputation of that school or their political careers." His vow gained fervency as they drove. "Someone inside that building knows entirely too much about me. I can't continue to let them have access to Fionna."

"Agreed. But I'm not sure whoever is running this is just a misguided kid. He sounds more like a criminal mastermind. I guess we can either arrest him now and put him in Felsink to try to reform him, or I can put him away in Coriolis for life in another few years."

"I'm still in shock at the way this was all set up. I'm pretty sure whoever it is, they're already a criminal mastermind." Dan let his classes run through his mind. He tried to see each face on the cover of a mug shot. It just didn't seem to fit.

"Hey, if you want to take Fionna home for a little while and let her sleep, you can. She seemed pretty worn out in there," Portwood eased. He seemed to be trying to make his offer without engaging Dan's temper.

"She is exhausted," Dan agreed. "And Governor Sapman spewing shit like that isn't helping, but some fucking moron has pictures of her that no one else was meant to see. So, to me, letting her help means we get this solved in a few days and not a few weeks. After that, I'll take her to Kauai and let her recover from this shit that I somehow got her involved in yet again."

Garrett was five thousand miles away, but Dan needed to talk to someone. Landon knew the risks and the rewards of being in law enforcement. He had a woman who meant the world to him and a baby on the way. He knew what Dan was experiencing and had enough life under his belt to be able to offer him something worth listening to.

Portwood seemed to consider. "I wish I knew what to tell you. I'm just as lost as you are. I knew you'd hate teaching there, but I thought Fionna and the girls would be safe. It doesn't seem to matter. And I'm not buying that you somehow got careless and loaded those pictures on your Venton laptop or that you somehow stuck one of those casted drives in your personal one. You're Dan Vindico. I know Fionna chilled you out or whatever, but your very being is here to keep her safe. You're *her* Shield. I don't think you're capable of a slipup like that. It just isn't in you." That was the very thing that had been plaguing Dan since the night he'd gotten the phone call. "I think someone, somehow, stole those pictures from your phone. That's what you took them with, right?"

Dan clenched his jaw for a moment. He didn't want to share this with anyone at all, but maybe they could figure it out together. He drew a deep breath and prayed Fionna wouldn't shoot him for having this conversation.

"Yeah...and she texted a few to me." Portwood nodded his understanding. "But I never cast my phone. You know that. It wasn't cloned that way, and I can't think of anytime I've left it unattended."

"Someone stole those pictures from you. You didn't screw up and give them away."

Dan considered that. "I usually leave my phone out on the desk when I teach in case Fionna needs me. I don't see how it's possible someone could've gotten their hands on it long enough to copy it." He began treating himself as the victim though he was loath to admit that was true. Portwood seemed impressed with his willingness to consider other options. It certainly wasn't something he would have done a year before.

"Did you ever get called out of the classroom for anything or leave it in your office? Loan it to a kid?"

"Yeah, occasionally, I guess. It's possible, but of the handful of kids I let use it, I was standing right there. I would've known if they were fucking with it. I teach mostly Ioses kids. Just seems far-fetched."

"We're going to arrest a Shield right now, aren't we?" Portwood exited off the interstate and picked up the pace. They flashed their badges and were allowed through the gates of the massive neighborhood. The blue lights started flashing. The pulsing fire gathered in Dan's veins.

There was an older Aston Martin Vantage sitting in the driveway. In all of Fred Scheckles's incessant, irritating meddling, he had been right about one thing.

CHAPTER 39

CELESTIAL EVIDENCE

~GARRETT HAYDENSHIRE~

"Are you cold, sweetheart?" Garrett turned on his side to cradle Kaimi under the sheets and sleeping bags he'd zipped together. She shook her head and traced her finger timidly down Garrett's bare chest.

"I'm perfect," she whispered as their bodies remained intertwined in each other. The salty air held their erotic energy, rolling and dancing together from the passionate love they'd just made. Garrett inhaled deeply of the salt and sand, the brine and dew rolling off the ocean, and that heavenly scent of her when he stoked the fire in her soul and allowed himself to be engulfed in her heat.

Her body was languid, and his love wound around her in his rhythms. They were all alone in that space and in that time. With every shallow breath she drew, her body swayed against his. He tucked her hair behind her ear and gave a gentle caress to her cheek as her blinks grew heavier. Her face gave a healthy glow from being on her island and being in his arms. His heart timed its rhythmic beats to her pulse. It was absolute perfection. It was far too early for them to go to sleep though.

"Garrett, look!" She pointed out the open mesh top of the tent. The evening sky had been putting on a stunning display all for them as the sun set and left the moon to shine in its absence. The moon now lit

193

the indigo sky and the swirling Pacific, but then Garrett saw something he'd never seen before. He saw the band of colors that faintly spanned the distant horizon.

"What is that?"

"It's called a moonbow." Kaimi eased herself upright, and Garrett joined her. The sheets and sleeping bags shifted slightly as they moved. "It's made when the water in the air reflects off the light of the moon at night instead of the sun. There aren't many places in the world where you can see them. They're pretty rare." She stared up at the celestial gift they'd been given. It was as if the night sky and the heavens themselves knew that they were always meant to be.

"I've been camping out here for years, and this is the first time I've ever seen one!" She was thrilled. Garrett tried to study the phenomenon, but his eyes kept drifting to her. His own shooting star who he'd somehow managed to find and catch. She was his own lightning in a bottle. He just had to keep her glowing. Keep her fire stoked so she could share her beautiful light.

"I love you." The fervent vow erupted from the recesses of his heart. She grinned as her eyes moved from the heavens back to his.

"I love you too."

∾

Dan Vindico

"Iodex. Open the door!" Portwood demanded as he pounded on the Steimers' front door.

It flung open.

"What on earth?" a woman gasped. Dan assumed she was Preston's mother.

"Mrs. Steimer?" Portwood quizzed.

Her husband joined her at the door. "Why are you here?"

"We're here to speak with Preston," Dan demanded. Suddenly, there was a rustle in the bushes. Dan spun just in time to see Preston rush out the side door of the house.

"Landon!" Dan shouted as he leapt over the porch railing. Two seconds later, he had Preston on the ground. He was mildly impressed that he hadn't lost his skill in his time off.

"Not bad, Danny." Portwood chuckled as he slapped cuffs on Preston's wrists as Dan jerked him upward by the scruff of his neck.

"What's going on?" Mr. Steimer demanded.

"Sir, if we could go inside for just a minute, we'd be happy to explain." Portwood had always been more polite than Dan. Mrs. Steimer appeared willing to do most anything to get everyone back inside and out of view of their neighbors.

As they entered the mansion, Dan noted a large flat-screen television mounted over the stacked stone fireplace.

Representative Ellington's husband has been arrested at Georgetown Hospital for alleged tampering with Venton drug tests, was scrolling along the bottom of the screen. Jeff, Rainer, Logan, and Governor Willow were leading Medio Winston Ellington out of the hospital and into a squad car. They panned to a stock shot of the Pentagon.

"Representative Ellington's office has been unavailable for comment thus far. We will bring you details on this situation as we get them," an unseen reporter vowed just as Mr. Steimer switched off the feed.

"What is going on, *Commander* Vindico?" he sneered pompously. Clearly Dan's reputation preceded him. The Steimers appeared to be in the camp that believed Dan should either have been arrested for killing Dominic Wretchkinsides or at the very least should never have been employed in law enforcement ever again.

"Who owns the Vantage in the driveway?" Dan asked.

"That's mine." Mr. Steimer turned concerned in an instant.

"It was identified at my home the night it was vandalized."

"You want to tell them, Preston, or shall I?" Portwood challenged.

"Dad, I swear. I didn't do anything."

"Oh now, Mr. Steimer, I have a great deal of evidence that says otherwise. Why don't you tell your folks what you did to the Vindicos' home? As it stands, you're looking at conspiracy, bribery, blackmail, and felony vandalism, just to start with."

"It was just a stupid prank, I swear."

CHAPTER 40

ENDS OF THE EARTH

~GARRETT HAYDENSHIRE~

"Come on!" Kaimi slid from the sleeping bag and tugged on her bikini bottom. Beaming at her, Garrett slipped into a pair of jeans and followed her out of the tent. She took off toward the moonbow, and Garrett was woefully unable not to follow her.

To the ends of the earth and back, Haydenshire. He recalled Dan's adamant vow, only now he understood it. Kaimi reached her hand back as she ran, and Garrett caught it. He let her lead him onward, watching her head fall back in delighted laughter as he allowed her to slightly outpace him.

The heavenly scent of her reached his nostrils on the sea breeze. Her body was lithe in her excitement. Her breasts bounced enticingly as she ran, and the copper in her eyes held its hypnotic fire. Garrett was done for. There was no turning back. The life behind him wasn't worth having anyway. His life's blood resided on the tiny island.

To the ends of the earth and back, he would follow his soul's mate.

~

Dan Vindico

"One of the governors will have to set his bail, sir. He's just given a full confession. They will take that into account, but it will be tomorrow morning before you can pick him up." Portwood explained the procedures to the Steimers.

"Please, Chief Portwood, you're not going to take him to Felsink tonight," Mrs. Steimer begged.

"No, ma'am. I'm not, but his cooperation will be the best way to keep him out of there for good."

"Preston, son, you tell them whatever they want to know. Tell them everything. Do you understand me? We'll deal with this, but I will not have you going to prison," Mr. Steimer ordered his son who was handcuffed in the back of the SUV.

Preston was biting back tears as he nodded his understanding. With that, Dan slammed the door, and Mrs. Steimer fell into her husband's arms.

"I'll let you know when he's set to go before the board," Portwood assured them.

Preston called Dan's name but it was muffled by the glass between the front seats and the back. Dan summoned and turned on the microphone in the SUV.

"What?" he spat.

"Aren't you gonna get Liam and Seth too?" Preston pled.

"Sit back and shut up, Mr. Steimer. I'm running this show, and I'll let you know when we need something from you."

Portwood pulled his cell from his pocket.

"Lawson," rang from the casted phone.

"Hey, are you still at the office?"

"Yeah, we just put Ellington in a cell. I was just about to call you," Rainer explained.

"I think I'm gonna move everyone there. I have a feeling we're going to be doing a lot of interrogations tonight. Would you see if one of the guys would give Fionna and Emily a ride in?"

"Governor Haydenshire will bring them. I'll call everyone, sir."

∼

"I really needed some money. My dad said I had to start paying my car insurance when I got that other ticket. So, I was complaining about it to some friends at school, and they told me to text this number and see if I could make some extra cash." Preston couldn't get his confession to fall from his lips fast enough. "So I did, and I had to, like, call and text people before he'd let me have some real money. Whoever he is, he hates you," he informed Dan. "He talks about you all the time on our calls. He was pissed you got hired on. He's always telling us that you're only there to catch Wilshire, and you didn't seem like you cared at all. It was better when Sullivan was there. You treated us all like we were already working for you in Iodex. I don't even want to work for Iodex. It's my senior year and your shit hard assignments dropped my GPA. All you care about is your wife and kids. That much was pretty freaking obvious." Preston's indignation seemed to ease his guilty conscience.

"So, you did ten thousand dollars' worth of property damage to my home and my cars because your GPA fell? If you don't want to go to Felsink for several felony counts of vandalism, I suggest you become very forthcoming with every single thing you know about who's running this very quickly," Dan menaced.

"I don't know who he is. He put out an all call asking if anyone knew where you lived. Liam said he saw you standing on your street that weekend it snowed. It wasn't that hard for a couple of us to follow your kid home from the bus one day." Dan's shield flared around the room in abject fury. Logan and Portwood both cringed.

Preston seemed to see that as a sign that he should talk faster. "That was a huge payout. I just got paid for that and then I stopped answering the texts. It was stupid. I got the money I needed, and that was all I wanted." Preston gestured to his cell phone. Logan was leaning on the desk going through everything on the phone. He gave a nod that there did not appear to be much communication to or from Preston and the unknown guy calling the shots.

"What about the morons you decided to pull this little stunt with? Did they keep working, or were they out as well?" Logan demanded.

Dan was shocked at how much he sounded like Garrett.

Preston considered momentarily.

"You're looking at three years minimum in Felsink if they try you as an adult, and that's just for conspiracy and felony vandalism. We have you on several other charges including child endangerment that you just admitted to. I see here that you turned twenty-one a month ago, Mr. Steimer," Portwood sniped.

"Yeah, Seth Carver does a bunch. He's one of the guys that picks up the money," erupted from Preston's mouth. "Liam started after the test vault thing. I'm not sure he even knew about it before then. I don't know if he's still working for whoever this is though."

"Smart man," Dan sneered as he left the room and let the door slam on his way out. "Anyone talk to Seth Carver today?" he quizzed the officers seated around the room going through the vast amount of evidence they'd collected. Fionna and Emily were working with Rainer and Jeff. They were going over banking documents on the computer.

"Hey, Dan, are you sure you want to leave this account seized?" Jeff quizzed. "This seems to be the only one. I could spoof it and then we could see where the payouts are going."

"No." Dan shook his head as his officers began flipping through folders and searching documents on computers to see if they could locate Seth. "I want him scared, and I want to force him out from under his rock. We're shutting down every angle we have. I'm choking him out. In fact, Officer Strenton, why don't you get Lawson to show you how to set up the call tracer. Maybe we'll luck up and get a phone call tonight. Has anyone talked to Ellington yet?"

"No, he's still in there, but his wife's office is calling constantly. He says he doesn't want a lawyer." Ericcson shrugged.

"I don't see a Seth Carver in anything that's been entered, Dan," McCoy volunteered.

"Get his address, take a few guys with you, and bring him in for me," Dan ordered.

"Yes, sir." McCoy grinned. "I know it's temporary, man, but I missed you. Hawaii's lucky they got you." He shrugged into his heat-synced jacket and strapped on his holster. Fionna was beaming over the assessment.

"Let's see if I can't get to Hawaii. Then we'll find out how lucky they are. I can't keep putting my girls through this."

"We'll get them, Dan. They're coming out of the woodwork." Tuttle pointed to the vast entrance to Iodex. Two security guards were escorting in Dedric Monahan and Claire Fitzgivens.

"We, uh…didn't get to talk to you before you sent everyone home, but we decided we probably should now," Claire's voice shook as she explained. "We heard you arrested Preston."

"Come with me." Tuttle pointed to another interrogation room. Ericcson stood to join him.

"I'm gonna go talk to Ellington." Dan sighed. This endless night seemed to just be beginning.

"I'll come with you." Fionna stood. "His energy is terrified, and he feels really guilty about all of this." Dan smiled at her tenderly. He used what was left of his resolve to force away the thoughts of what would happen if he didn't dismantle this spider's web that seemed to have caught an endless number of flies. He reached his hand out and grabbed hers.

"Come on, baby."

"Man, he never called any of us baby," Logan scoffed as he exited the room with Preston and Portwood. "I'm jealous." Everyone laughed and seemed appreciative of the slight lift in spirit as Dan kissed Fionna's hand.

"Sorry, Haydenshire. I have a thing for island girls," Dan teased just to keep the laughter going as he headed into the interrogation room.

"Medio Ellington." Dan offered as a greeting. He felt genuinely sorry for the crumpled man seated before him. Fionna gave Ellington a weak smile, but his energy seemed to overwhelm her.

"Are you Commander, Officer, Chief, or Mentor Vindico now?" Ellington half-heartedly retorted.

"Right now, I'm the guy you need to talk to if you have any hope of saving either your career or your wife's."

Medio Ellington gave a weak nod and drew an audible breath. He seemed uncertain where to begin.

CHAPTER 41

PERSPECTIVE AND PRIORITIES

~GARRETT HAYDENSHIRE~

"Oh, I see. You run me all the way out here chasing a rainbow, and now I get to carry you back. Is that how it works, Mrs. Haydenshire?" Garrett chanted as Kaimi leapt on his back and he folded her legs around him so he could give her a piggyback ride back to their tent.

"Yes, and it's a moonbow. They're way more special than a rainbow." Garrett was delighted to have her on his back. To feel her bare skin pressed against the chiseled muscle and her sweet breath on his neck.

Her rhythms were running in trilling excitement, but they were ebbing as she grew tired, despite the early hour, from all their playing during the day and their amorous lovemaking just a little while before she'd spotted the phenomenon in the sky.

"Hold on tight, baby. I'm gonna take you for a ride."

She squealed as he bounded across the sand, holding her tightly to him as he charged into the life ahead of them. She was laughing by the time they reached their campsite. She eased off his back with a great deal of grace.

"Most perfect honeymoon campout ever," she declared.

With a heavy smirk, Garrett spun and lifted her back up. Her legs wound around his waist this time, and he kissed her heatedly.

When they finally broke apart to gasp for breath, he nodded as he kept her cradled to his chest with ease. She laid her head on his shoulder and wrapped herself around him tighter.

"Perfect," he agreed. "Now, I think it's time to put my baby to bed." He carried her in the tent and set her on her feet. He kicked off his jeans, and after ridding himself of as much sand as he was able, he climbed back in the sleeping bag. She started to crawl in after him, but he halted her progress.

"Only naked girls in the bag, sweetheart."

"I'm going to pretend I'm the only girl you've ever said that to."

Garrett thought for a moment. "You don't have to pretend. You are the only girl I've ever said that to, but the rule still applies."

Kaimi didn't look like she really believed that, but she did shimmy out of her bikini bottom. Garrett gave her a shuddered growl as he tucked her in beside him. They lay there for a moment in peaceful tranquility, staring up at the stars as the ocean's constant kiss of the shore began to lull them to sleep.

"You never took any other woman camping?" she finally whispered her disbelief.

Garrett tried not to chuckle. He was growing used to her body giving willful resistance to sleep. Her mind wouldn't let her rest. He'd found that setting his shield around her and tucking her close to him seemed to bring her peace that allowed her to sleep.

He suspected that part of her rapid healing had been because she'd really been sleeping fully while they'd been on Kauai. He eased her closer to him and kissed her cheek.

"Only you. When you go camping with someone, you have to really spend time with them. I never wanted to do that. I only want to spend time with you." He began caressing her body with his hands, trying to soothe her to sleep. "Dan tried to sneak Amelia out with Will and me one time when we were camping at Great Falls, but that was an epic failure." He wasn't certain why the story had come so vividly to the forefront of his mind.

"What happened?" Kaimi was intrigued, and Garrett realized he was doing nothing to lull her to sleep.

"It was odd to have her along. Will and I didn't know how to act.

Dan just wanted to sleep with her which was why he'd begged her to sneak out and come along. But since we were only eighteen and nineteen and he couldn't really think with the head above his beltline, he never considered how that would take place. She certainly wasn't going to agree to fuck him with Will and me anywhere in the general vicinity. She was miserable, and the whole thing was awkward. The sun went down, and she freaked. She was freezing and mad that he thought she would have gone for his plan. Owls started hooting and she saw a spider. The next thing I knew, Dan was apologizing and taking her home. She was mad at him for a week."

Kaimi nodded. He felt her slight smile and wondered what she was really thinking.

"I don't think Maylea would like camping much either."

"Definitely not, but Dan's not big on it anymore. He's good with the big bed and Fionna on his chest. Fionna requires air conditioning, coffeemakers, and curling irons at her disposal. I, however, love that you're here with me. I love being all alone out here with you. I love seeing you here with paradise around us, and that you love this as much as I do." His voice snagged on the emotion in his throat.

"I *do* love being out here with you. It's perfect. Thank you for coming here with me." She nuzzled her head into his chest, making him smile. "I think you're the only person who'll ever understand me."

"That's how it's supposed to work, isn't it?" His cast formed around her, filled with his adoring love and his ultimate acceptance.

Kaimi gave a slight nod. "I think so."

"Go to sleep, sweetheart. I'm right here." Garrett kept her cradled tenderly in his protective embrace.

Dan Vindico

"I knew Libby was using as soon as she started, and I knew she was doing it to get back at us." Medio Ellington continued his gut-wrenching confession. "Sandra decided she was going to run as the antidrug Senteon representative for her reelection. She won by a landslide. She loves her job, and truthfully, she doesn't have a great deal of time for Libby. She's not home very often, and when she is, they end up in a shouting match. I realize now that I shouldn't have done this, but I'd accepted one of the four positions as lead medio in the lab at Georgetown.

"I had to increase my hours. Life went on like that for a while. Sandra and I weren't home, which seemed to make Libby happy, but I got emails last year from a few of Libby's mentors saying she was skipping class and being disrespectful. I didn't say anything. I blamed myself. Then the first drug tests from fall semester came in. I ran the samples, and right there before my eyes, my suspicions were confirmed. My baby girl with marijuana, psilocybin, ecstasy, cocaine, nitrites, fentanyl. I was sick. Two of her friends tested positive as well —little girls I'd helped raise. They'd been in school together since kindergarten." He shook his head in disbelief.

"I locked up the files and went home. I confronted Libby. She swore she would stop if I would cover the test for her, but she never stopped. When I threatened to kick her out, she swore she'd go to the press with the fact that she was using because Sandra was a terrible mother. She's held that threat over our heads for almost a year and a half now. Then it got worse—much, much worse.

"I started getting emails saying if I didn't want my wife's career ruined along with my own for what I'd done, I had to cover any positive Venton test and that I would be paid for it. I refused the money, but I did cover the tests. I thought I was doing it for my wife and my little girl, and it just kept getting worse. There are more every test. I'm so sorry. Is there any way you could just arrest me and let me do my time or whatever without the press having to nail this to Sandra?"

Silent tears were leaking down Fionna's beautiful face. The despair and desperation flowing out of Ellington's energy was overwhelming. For a moment, Dan tried to force himself to think like a Receiver. What wouldn't he do for one of his girls? *I wouldn't have done that.*

His job, Fionna's job, nothing was worth covering up a serious problem with one of your kids because of your reputation.

"I'm sorry, Medio Ellington. I can't guarantee you that, but I am trying to put a stop to all of the insanity going on at Venton. Covering up the problem didn't help. So maybe it's time to bring them out in the light to heal them. Libby needs help. You know that, and I know that, and I think it's time we worry more about Libby than Representative Ellington. I will talk with Medio Sawyer and tell him that you never accepted any money for covering the tests, but I doubt that he will allow you to remain employed. I'm very sorry for that as well," Dan vowed.

"Let's be real, I don't deserve to be employed by one of the finest hospitals in this country. What happens now? I've never been arrested before."

Fionna's body gave a slight shudder, and Dan grasped her hand. He pushed his soothing strength to her and nearly lost his breath as she drew from him deeply.

"You'll be moved to the holding cells here in the Senate for the rest of the night. The governors will be in tomorrow morning and will start the arraignments for everyone we've taken in. You can use the phone if you'd like. Call your wife and let her know where you are."

Dan opened the office door and directed Ellington to one of the phones along the back walls used by prisoners.

When he returned from the phone, he looked bereaved. "I couldn't get Libby or my wife. Is there any way you could let Libby know where I am?"

"I'll take care of it."

CHAPTER 42
HIDDEN DANGER
~GARRETT HAYDENSHIRE~

Garrett gasped for breath. His heart hammered as he jerked himself upright. He rubbed his eyes and tried to remember where he was. Kaimi and Cal and the phone ringing and sirens and gunshots all ricocheted in his mind.

The past and the present swirled in a bewildering mass. He couldn't make sense of anything. He reached across the sleeping bag, and his body calmed as soon as he felt her soft, smooth skin. She was curled up in a ball, buried under the covers.

After trying to steady his frantic breaths, he reached tenderly to her sleeping form and slid her back beside him. She gave a contented sigh as she felt his body surround hers completely.

"I love you," Garrett whispered into the salt-soaked air. He brushed a kiss against her damp forehead. "God, I just love you so much. I'll keep you safe. I swear."

He clung to her and tried to will his body back into fitful sleep.

He awoke again sometime later. He heard something. Kaimi was still tucked safely in his arms. Garrett's heart thundered as he eased himself upright. The ocean's steady roll hadn't quite masked the metallic crash and then someone cursing.

Garrett eased his arm out from under his wife and slipped his Glock from the bag stowed in the back corner of the tent. Working silently, he slipped on a pair of jeans and crawled out of the tent. He led with his pistol and worked from the tent outward.

Three trash cans were on their sides several feet away, but no one was in sight. He kept a constant scan on the beach as he set his shield firmly around their tent.

The ocean breeze whispered through the foliage, and Garrett heard another noise. He spun and saw a feathered tail dashing away. *Roosters don't generally cuss.* His breaths frantically pumped through his lungs.

"Garrett?" Kaimi's panicked plea rang from the tent.

With another frenetic sweep of the shoreline, Garrett rushed back to her.

"I'm right here." He caught her as she raced into his arms.

"Don't leave. Just don't. Please!" She tugged at his back in an effort to burrow into his chest.

"Baby, it's okay. What's wrong? I just heard something. Some roosters got in the trash cans," he lied. He didn't want to scare her.

Her heart pounded against his chest. "I would never leave you, baby." She nodded against him but refused to loosen her grip. Garrett cradled her head with his hand and set his shield over the two of them this time. "I'm right here."

"I'm sorry. I didn't mean to freak out," she managed. Shame drowned her rhythms.

"It's okay. I'm right here. I'll never ever leave you."

If her own mother would abandon her, he supposed she had every right to doubt that anyone would stay with her forever, but he would reassure her until the end of time. He would prove himself above all others. He would never leave her or forsake her, just as he'd vowed.

"I've heard the roosters here before. It scared me, and I was all alone. I'm just so glad I don't have to be alone anymore."

"Never ever, I'll always be here. Let's go back to sleep, sweetheart." He would be her Shield through the night and through their entire life.

Kaimi begrudgingly released him and crawled back under the covers, while Garrett kicked off his jeans. He tried to discreetly hide the pistol nearby.

"You don't think it was only roosters." Kaimi shivered in her proclamation.

"I don't know what it was, but I will keep you safe."

"Sometimes there are local kids who come out here and take stuff from campers because they think they're tourists," she offered hopefully.

Garrett's eyes closed as he felt her heat and her energy slip through the pores of his skin.

His breaths came faster. His heart hammered as Kaimi languidly slipped her hand to his cock and then continued downward to his sac. She stared at him with expectant curiosity. The copper of her eyes glowed enticingly in the light of the full moon. The dust of her sleep still rested in them as she gave a heated moan as his hands sought her breasts.

This time was different, without pretense or voracity. Garrett wanted to take his time and make love to his wife slowly and thoroughly. He wanted to occupy her fully, to make her body fit to his own as he eased himself inside of her perfection and formed her around his hardened length.

He dipped his head to hers in a slow, lush kiss as their lips melded together and the heat from their bodies pulsed with their all-encompassing love. His tongue sought hers in slow syncopation. His hand glided down her body over the curves that needed his tender care and his fierce protection.

Her body seemed to understand his own without ever sharing words. There was a sweet tranquility about her this time. A need to be worshipped and cared for, to be tended entirely by his hands and his soft, hungry lips and by the throbbing steel length of him that her hands sought and caressed so gently the feeling was ethereal and exquisite.

Garrett let his thumb gently touch her lips, the color of strawberry wine. He wanted to indulge until he was drunk on her. He stared into the depths of her eyes. The questioning need that resided there could only be answered with his body. It swirled there in the copper fire. She wanted him to make her better, to starve out the fear and the rejection that so quickly set its restrictive coil around her heart. She needed to feel his love and let it permeate the very marrow of her bones as much as he needed to feel that from her.

The hollow spaces of her luscious body starved for his fullness as he ached to penetrate her and bring them both relief. What she couldn't seem to believe from his words he would prove with his body.

He leaned and kissed her again. He never wanted to stop. He wanted to devour her slowly and drive her out of her mind. He would fight the vicious monsters in her head just as he would end any physical foe that set to do her harm. He was never complete unless he was wound up deeply inside of her.

He kept his kisses drowning and lush. They had all night, and nothing else mattered but the way she felt in his arms and the hungry grasp of that virgin sweet pussy wrapped tightly around his cock.

Garrett couldn't recall any other time that he'd wanted to draw sex out even with her. With all of the other women he'd been with, it had been in an effort to have release and then escape. With Kaimi, it was a desperate hunger to permeate her. But here in the light of the full moon on the Kauaian shoreline, he finally let the island's rhythms guide his own. Slow and steady with the pulse of her need and the tremble of her body, he slipped his hand from her breasts down to the heart of her.

The dirty banter he normally whispered in her ear or that growled from his lungs seemed unnecessary. Their quiet moans and breathy gasps mixed with the rhythmic waves of the Pacific and made a melody all their own. Her body gave soft, needy writhes inside his overmuscled embrace.

"I want to touch you, baby." His passionate plea came between his gasped breaths and hungry kisses. Kaimi gave a languid nod as her body trembled from his tender caress of her mound.

He felt her temperature rise. Her breath caught deliciously as he slipped his fingers inside the slick heat that begged for his care.

Kaimi's body gave a timid tremble. The wet heat began its ravenous drip as she kept her eyes locked on his.

"I love to touch you. I love to feel you and to take all of you. I love that I know how to make you wet for me. You feel incredible." He panted as she writhed against him. "I love that your entire body belongs to me." His plea wasn't meant to dominate her though she seemed to like that on occasion.

It was the truth, raw and aching, just like he felt whenever his body longed to be one with hers. Her eyes closed in the ecstasy of his all-encompassing love flowing through his hands into her body. He pulled his hands away and sought her breasts, letting it build as he slowly ignited the fire within her. He painted her nipples with the wetness he'd coaxed from her.

With a hungry groan, Garrett brought his hands to her hips and leaned her back, granting his eager tongue access to the swollen tips of her fevered breasts. He sucked the luscious candy in rhythm, soothing and tending her every need.

As his desire gained intensity, Garrett could think of nothing but permeating her. With precise gentility, he began rubbing her slit with the lube Tutu had given them with one hand and the lush cheeks of her backside with the other.

"Turn over for me, baby." He eased as he helped her form her back to his chest so they were both on their sides. "Let me have you."

Still moving with delicate precision, Garrett kept Kaimi's body tucked right beside his own. He allowed no space between them. He spread her legs with his right thigh and gently prodded her lips with the fevered steel length between his legs. A fire burned relentlessly in his groin that night. He needed her to drown his need in her quenching depths. He kept her cradled closely to him, holding her breasts with his left hand and forearm as he kept his right sending soothing pulses through her mound as he eased inside her.

A low, needy gasp escaped her mouth as he began to thrust gently. He filled her with his own erotic energy flowing constantly from his member and through his hands into her skin.

No words needed to be uttered. He knew how to make her feel incredibly sexy and wildly turned on. He just had to prove to her how much she was desired.

"Yes," moaned from her as he drowned her body with his own desperate hunger. It pulsed from every fiber of him and wound around her as he made her all his own. Their rhythms fused together in ecstasy. Her swollen lips throbbed constantly around his strain. It was utter bliss.

She was his in entirety. It was absolute perfection. Her body contracted, and he was done for. He spilled out inside of her as an intense orgasm finally claimed victory over her. She trembled as he exploded with a thundered groan of ecstasy.

"You okay, sweetheart?" Garrett managed as he eased from her and cradled her tightly to his chest.

"Perfect," she whispered as she curled up in his protective embrace. He kissed the top of her head and let everything they'd just shared run through his mind. She was absolute perfection, more than he could ever have dreamed of, and by the grace of God, she was his.

CHAPTER 43

ALWAYS LISTEN, ALWAYS BELIEVE

~DAN VINDICO~

"Dan, we have the triangulator set up," Jeff explained.

"Good. Can I get a low-level team to go out to the Ellingtons' and let Libby know where her dad is?" Dan directed his question to Portwood.

"Sure thing. Temps, would you and Bo head out to the Ellingtons' and let Libby and anyone else there know that Medio Ellington is in custody?"

"Yes, sir." Temps stood and shrugged on his Iodex jacket.

Dan returned to another desk and began going over confessions heard by other officers throughout the day.

A half hour later, Fionna's mouth fell open as Temps led Libby Ellington and Kenya Keaton in wearing cuffs.

"What the hell?" Portwood asked.

"Sir, they were on her front porch with meth pipes. There was a pile of poppers right there. I couldn't see that and not arrest them. They didn't even put it away when we asked." Temps shook his head. Libby was too high to really be aware of where she was.

Portwood shook his head. "Take her down there and put her beside her dad. Get them both some water and some food. Let's try to sober them up."

Dan wondered if Medio Ellington had ever seen his daughter high with his own eyes. He wondered if perhaps the problem hadn't been real enough, so they were able to pretend it away, but that opportunity had rapidly past.

～

Long after the sun illuminated the DC skyline, Dan's cell rang. He tried to shake off a deep yawn as he glanced at the number. His heart raced as he read the word "blocked."

"Jeff," he shouted, shaking everyone from their fatigue. "Now!" He directed Rainer and Logan to the call tracer and triangulator. Everyone moved into position, as Dan immediately answered and casted his phone. Jeff picked up Dan's rhythms off the phone and directed them into the triangulator. Logan, Rainer, and Tuttle forced the signal through to the enhanced map. Ericcson and McCoy kept the machine from overheating.

"Mentor Vindico," came a male voice through a voice disguiser. Jeff's cast grew in intensity. Dan could feel him working his shield through the energy inside the cell and through the towers.

"The enhancer is on the phone. It's an app," Jeff mouthed.

Portwood nodded his encouragement.

"You really think you're going to scare me? I know you're tracing my call. I know you're shutting down everything you have on me, but I still have those pictures of your precious wife. She likes it dirty, doesn't she?"

Fury erupted in Dan's soul as Fionna's eyes squeezed closed. Emily shook her head in defiant anger and immediately embraced Fionna.

"I think I'm gonna add a little more fun to our game. Since you seem to be enjoying getting people to talk, send the money to the address I gave you. You have twenty-four hours or the whole world will get to see what sweet Fionna Styler, innocent Arlington Angel, really likes."

"The call is coming from Venton's campus!" McCoy worked the triangulation as the line went dead. The signal dropped and everyone's cast faded away.

"I'm sorry, Dan, that's as far as we got. Definitely on the campus, but I can't tell you from where exactly."

Dan couldn't quite make out what McCoy was saying. Horrified tears were beading down his wife's beautiful face.

"We have to find him!" Dan demanded.

"Now we know where to look. Classes don't start for another hour. He lives on campus." Portwood reminded Dan that they had figured out a few things. The value of that information was not worth his wife being humiliated in front of all of Iodex, however.

Dan shook himself and pulled Fionna out of Emily's arms. If she wanted to hide, he would be her Shield.

She buried her face in his chest as he tried to soothe and calm her with every officer in Iodex giving him sympathetic gazes. "Shh, baby. I'm going to find this prick and end him." He kissed the top of her head and wrapped her up in a fierce embrace.

"Let's get to Venton," Portwood commanded in an effort to give Dan and Fionna a little privacy.

Garrett Haydenshire

Just before he fell back asleep, Garrett bolted upright again. He rubbed his eyes as Kaimi whimpered. He summoned a light cast in his hand and threw the sleeping bag back until he located his ringing cell phone.

"Haydenshire." He finally managed the customary response when he received a phone call in the dead of night.

"Garrett, I'm so sorry to awaken you. It's Tutu…uh, Aida insisted that we call you. I can't calm her down. I think you better come back to the farm."

"What's wrong with Aida?" Garrett tried to determine what to pack up first or if they should just leave and come back for the tent later.

"Aida is all right, but she's having a rather strong premonition. Maylea only had one or two like this when she was growing up. But it involves you and Dan. I'll explain everything when you and Kaimi arrive. Papa is trying to calm her down now, but she needs you."

"I'm on my way." Garrett had no idea what Tutu was talking about. Millions of thoughts fought for attention in his mind. Kaimi was already dressed and throwing things in bags, having only heard his half of the conversation.

Forty-five minutes later, Garrett slammed the Hummer into Park and leapt out. Kaimi didn't await his assistance as they raced into the small farmhouse in the middle of Fionna's family's property.

"Aida!" Garrett shouted as he flung open the front door.

"Uncle Garrett!" She flew into his arms, sobbing convulsively.

"What's wrong? Tell me. I'll fix it!" Garrett cradled her inside of his arms and inside of his shield.

"Daddy needs you right now. You have to go back home. Now!" she pled.

"I can't tell you what's happened. She has these from time to time. They're much stronger here, just like Maylea's. I've called Dan, but they aren't answering. I have a very difficult time reading Dan when he isn't here in contact with me. His shield is too strong for me to work through. She's able to feel him because he's casted her so many times and because they're so close. Either that or she's feeling Dan through Maylea's rhythms. She's terrified. I don't know what's happening with Dan, but clearly he needs you."

Aida's telling him not to be angry at Kaimi swam back through his mind. He shared a quick glance with Kaimi. She nodded, and Garrett lowered his shield. She began rubbing Aida's back tenderly.

She soothed, "We'll go back home right now. Okay? We'll help your Mommy and Daddy. I promise."

A half hour later, Garrett was helping Kaimi up onto his father's jet. Papa had assured Garrett that he and Kai would unpack the Hummer of all of their camping gear and stow it in one of the barns, and that they would take care of Garrett and Kaimi's new hale.

"Fi!" he shouted when she finally answered her phone.

"What? Is something else wrong?" Fionna had been very recently sobbing. It broke Garrett's heart.

"No, baby. What the hell's going on there? Aida woke up freaking out. Tutu called me, and now we're flying home. What's wrong with Dan?" Garrett tried to sound soothing, but panic was his predominant energy strain.

CHAPTER 44

RAMIFICATIONS

"They can't just do that." Kaimi was pacing in the center aisle as the plane climbed steadily into the sky. "He was supposed to have until the end of the month. This isn't fair." The injustice of it all seemed to be more than she could stand.

"I know, sweetheart, but when you have the pictures, you make the rules." Bone-tired exhaustion had taken up residence in Garrett's entire body. He wished Kaimi would just come sit beside him. Something in the ragged anticipation of what was to come had him restless and needing to feel her rhythms beside his own.

She was too distraught, her rhythms too erratic for her to rest or even sit. She ran her fingers through her hair constantly and bit her lip.

"Come here, baby, please." He held his hand out to her, not certain how she would respond. She moved to him and even cuddled into his hesitant embrace.

"I've never done that," she admitted in a fretful whisper with her face pressed against his hardened chest. Garrett's mind was moving through scenarios on how to catch this fucker rapidly. When he reached one dead end, he would move to another potential possibility. It took him a moment to realize she'd spoken.

"Never done what?" He shook himself slightly.

"Never taken pictures while having sex. I guess I never had a lot of sex at all until I fell in love with you." She shrugged.

Garrett kissed the top of her head. "I told you we'll try out anything you want, but I'm thinking right now Fi's wishing she and Dan had never done that either." Kaimi gave a regretful nod before a deep yawn overtook her.

"I'm so worried about her. This is awful. No one was ever meant to see that. And she's Fionna Styler. The whole country has her cast as a sweetheart, and she is that, but she's allowed to have other sides too. They just aren't allowed to see her other sides."

Garrett was struck by the fact that Kaimi seemed to consider Fionna to actually be two different people. She was Maylea to the Hawaiian people, and she was the famed Arlington Angel, America's sweetheart, to the rest of the world. For a moment, Garrett allowed himself to wonder who she was to him.

He nodded. "She should be allowed to have other sides that she doesn't have to share, but we're not dealing with respectful, law-abiding people."

~

Jeff Strenton

"All right, the server casts are picking up messages. I'll have to trace each one down, but maybe we'll figure out where he is," Jeff offered Dan and Fionna hopefully.

"Can we help?" Fionna asked.

"I'll help," Ramier soothed. He and Jeff were certainly the only people who knew how to run the kinds of traces that were needed to catch the prick that was torturing the Vindicos.

"Wow! They're coming in fast." Jeff's mind and body moved into overdrive. The messages were flashing furiously across his screen.

"Of course they are. He knows he's beaten. He's getting out. Calling in every penny he has coming his way, and then getting the hell out of town," Dan stated knowingly.

"No." Jeff shook his head as he studied the floods of emails.

Ramier stepped in. "These can't all be real, Dan. He's trying to get something through, but he knows we're onto him."

"These headers are complete crap. Does he think we're idiots?" Jeff scoffed. He was genuinely insulted. Tagging emails with lines like, "Make certain the money goes into the account," was going to lead them nowhere fast.

"We have to trace these. Start with the first fifty…" Ramier began his command.

"And work from the middle out," Jeff concluded for him.

"Yeah, Strenton. You're gonna do just fine."

Portwood sighed. "Fine, trace them. Just try to figure something out quickly. I want every other available Iodex officer going dorm room to dorm room. Do quick searches. Anyone gets antsy, bring them to me. Start with the Vis Virres dorms."

Vindico nodded his agreement.

Jeff set to work, though he wondered if Chief Portwood was aware that his order to begin with Vis Virres was every bit as prejudiced as Governor Sapman's declaring that Fionna's astounding powers were pointless.

Ramier seemed to have had the same thought as he and Jeff shared a quick knowing glance.

Garrett Haydenshire

Kaimi shifted. Her body gave a distressing shudder against Garrett's.

"Kaimi." Garrett cleared his throat as his eyes blinked open. They'd given up an hour in and decided to make use of the bedroom on the Crown Governor's jet but not for reasons Garrett would've preferred under any other circumstances.

Exhaustion and Kaimi pointing out that Garrett would need to be in top form to catch these morons had driven them to sleep. But Kaimi's rhythms were frantic in her slumber.

"Kaimi," Garrett urged with more force as he tried to awaken her from her nightmare. "Sweetheart, shh. It's okay." He cradled her closer. A frantic gasp lit through her lungs as her eyes flew open. Her heart thundered against Garrett's side.

"Bad dream?" Garrett was certainly no stranger to nightmares, but he couldn't recall Kaimi having one the entire time they'd been sharing a bed.

She sat up and rubbed her eyes. "Yeah, I think so. My body's just confused."

"You want some coffee or something? I think we'll be landing soon." Time seemed baffling and variable as they flew toward the sun and rapidly lost hours.

Kaimi nodded and eased out from under the covers. They'd slept in their clothes, so she tried to smooth her shirt and jeans.

Garrett kept an eye on his wife as he moved to the kitchen area of his father's jet and prepared a pot of coffee. She hugged her knees to her chest and stared out into the endless sky, watching it turn a distressing purple as the black night faded into the new day. Garrett handed her a warm mug of her favorite beverage and seated himself beside her. She seemed to want her own space, so he tried not to lament not being able to wrap her up in his arms.

"What happens when we get there? How are you going to stop this person from doing this to Maylea? Can we go get Duke?" Garrett found it odd that her jumbled mass of thoughts brought him peace. He considered how he could make her feel more secure.

"Dan's the best damn cop in the world." He began speaking without much thought. If he and Dan were going to run Hawaii, she would need to know what to expect from his job. "But I swear, it's like Fi is his saving grace and his fatal flaw. If it involves her, he goes to complete shit. He doesn't think. He stops being a cop and just becomes this massive Shield for her. I need to make certain he's not missing anything because of what's at stake."

Kaimi nodded thoughtfully, so Garrett continued. "I think it would be better if we left Duke at the farm and went straight to Venton. We need to find this guy before he decides to go ahead and launch that video. No one has wanted to say this out loud or even think about it, but if those pictures or the video leak, it's more than Fionna's reputation on the line. Dan's job in Hawaii and most definitely her running a dance studio where tons of little girls learn to hula could all be at stake."

"I wondered about that, but I just kept thinking it would be so awful because she would be so embarrassed, and that was bad enough."

"We need to get this shit taken care of. Clearly, Kalakona isn't interested in waiting on us much longer, and she doesn't even know about this picture thing."

CHAPTER 45

PREPARE FOR BATTLE
RAINER LAWSON

"I could obviously kick down one of these doors," Logan scoffed as they exited the elevator on the third floor of the Vis Virres dorms. Rainer shook his head as he banged on the next dorm door with his clenched fist. Students were beginning to leave the dorms and head to the Venton buildings for their classes.

"Iodex. Open up!" Rainer commanded.

"Or we'll kick it down!" Logan added.

"My God, Logan, would you shut up? What is wrong with you?" Rainer banged again just as Logan's boot reared back. Thankfully, the door swung open before he made contact.

"What the hell? Hey, look, while you're here, I was supposed to get paid this morning, and there's no money in my account!" a guy Rainer recognized huffed indignantly. All sense of sleepless, punch-drunk banter bled from both Rainer and Logan as they exchanged a quick glance.

"We need to come inside," Logan demanded. He shoved the door the guy was partially blocking open.

"Uh…" The guy seemed to realize that having Iodex officers in a dorm room that was bursting with what were most certainly stolen electronics might not have been the best idea.

"What's your name?" Rainer took in ten Xboxes, several PlayStations, dozens of iPhones, a stack of laptops, and two flat-screen televisions stowed around the relatively small room.

"Do…I need a lawyer or something?"

"Even with a lawyer, you'll have to tell us your name." Rainer edged closer to the desk. He was certain there was something there that would ID the moron that stood before them.

"Matt Bowers. We had combined Phys Ed. together, remember?"

"Oh…yeah." Rainer nodded his lie. Being the son of the most famous Crown Governor of all time meant that a lot of people were certain that they knew Rainer and were equally offended that Rainer didn't know them.

"My dad was up here yesterday. Did you miss that meeting or something?" Logan discreetly eased himself toward the stack of Xboxes on Matt's bed as he offered Matt a lifeline.

Relief played heavily in Matt's eyes. "Right, I was actually just coming to find you."

Rainer rolled his eyes.

"I can tell you where all of this stuff came from and not go to jail, right?"

"That was the deal," Logan agreed.

"I think you might want to come with us now though," Rainer urged.

Logan pulled a set of cuffs from his belt, and Matt's eyes goggled.

"I thought you just said I wasn't gonna get arrested!"

"I'm not arresting you," Logan assured him. "Let's look at this as more of a precaution."

"A precaution against what?" Matt did willingly place his hands behind his back as Logan cuffed him.

"You've got several felony counts of possession of stolen goods, so this is to keep me from having to shoot you, if you should decide to run."

"What?!" Matt was on the verge of panic as Rainer shoved him forward and led him toward the Admin building.

∼

Jeff Strenton

"This is insane. We'll never get through all of these. Whoever this is, he knows how to distract us with this nonsense. He obviously knows we've got all of the Venton servers casted," Jeff complained again. They needed to do something different, anything different. They were getting nowhere quickly, and they were burning hours with virtually no hope of getting any clues.

"He knows we're closing in. He's going to call in every bit of money coming his way, so I'd bet my badge at least some of those emails are going to take you somewhere on this campus and then we're gonna have our guy, Strenton. I know it's shit work, but right now I need you to pipe down and get it done," Portwood reprimanded.

Jeff's jaw clenched as he nodded. "I'll keep going. I'll do whatever you want, but I think I could cast the electric grids to the school, sir. Sending emails at this rate has to be a major draw. He's got to be using dozens of computers. We could locate the dorm room in minutes."

Jeff watched hopefully as Dan and Portwood had a silent conversation.

"How dangerous is that?" Dan edged between Jeff and Ramier to force Ramier to look him in the eye.

"I know what I'm doing," Jeff huffed to Dan's broad, muscular back.

"He can do it, Dan. He's not a kid anymore. He's a hell of an officer. You picked him out for us. Now trust your gut," Ramier vowed adamantly.

"Just please let me try," Jeff begged. He would do anything to catch this moron.

"All right, Strenton. Get it set up, and tell us what you need. We'll do whatever you tell us," Portwood allowed.

Determination and drive fought for dominance in Jeff's shield as he set to work.

One of the coolant officers made his way to the back of the Crown Governor's jet.

"We'll be landing in just a moment, Deputy Haydenshire. Your father said to tell you he's on his way to Venton. He left your Highlander in the Iodex lot."

"Thanks." Garrett nodded his understanding and offered the man a kind smile. He regretted not knowing his name, but he didn't know several newer members of his father's staff. Kaimi gave him a kind smile as well. Her rhythms were tensed with worry as they rolled in their customary erratic patterns.

"It's gonna be okay, baby," Garrett tried to soothe her.

"I know." Kaimi sighed as she finally let Garrett embrace her. "I just had that weird dream, and I think my rhythms are all off." He was shocked to hear her admit that. He suspected the island had soothed her enough to allow her some insight into her own psyche.

"Tell me what you dreamed about." He had no idea why he wanted to know, but his shield was flexing in an effort to leave his own body and cover hers. It was an odd sensation.

"It was stupid." Kaimi's body gave a harrowing tremble as she tried to lie to herself.

"I still want to know. I can't let anything scare my baby." He felt her timid smile against his chest.

"It was about Representative Kalakona. It was weird. Things kept happening that I didn't understand. I kept screaming, but you couldn't hear me. So, I screamed louder, but you couldn't get to me. I was trying to keep someone safe, and I needed help but you couldn't help me. Then I woke up." Garrett's shield continued its disconcerting pulse. He considered her dream.

"I know Kalakona freaked you out, and it's been a hell of an endless day. I'd never let her or anyone else hurt you...or us," he concluded, as he suspected that at the heart of her terror-filled nightmare had been that something was tearing at the two of them.

He heard the landing gear descend. With a quick draw of breath, he had to think about what needed to happen in the next few hours. Kaimi nodded her understanding of his vow and seemed to sense his need to prepare for battle.

CHAPTER 46
TRADITIONS
~JEFF STRENTON~

"All I can tell you is whoever this is, he's got it out for both of you." Ramier continued to shake his head as he rapidly clicked through email after email while Jeff worked over the power grid for all of Venton. "Every email leads me straight back to either strenton.jeffrey@venton.edu or vindico.dan@ventonmentors.edu.

"Okay, but where are they saying they're coming from initially? You're not getting to our emails until you dig further, right?" Dan leaned in. His entire body seemed braced for war. Fury lit his words, and indignation thrummed in his rhythms. Jeff could feel them from across the room. Double-Predilected energies pulling in synchronization were incredibly powerful.

"Yeah, from what I can tell, he's basically pulled every Venton address he had access to. They're all from here." Ramier sighed. "Sends me all over the freaking globe and lands me back here."

Jeff's cell phone rang from his pocket. He fought back a whimper as he tried to keep his cast intensifying on the power grid and answer his phone. He panicked when he saw who was calling.

"What's wrong?" he demanded of Adeline.

"Jeff, Becca's blood pressure skyrocketed, and she's bleeding again. I've got her sedated for now, so you can't talk to her. I just wanted to let you know if we can't keep her blood pressure down, the baby is going to have to be delivered today." Adeline sounded morose. Vile terror and heartsickness washed through Jeff with a jarring wave.

"Okay, do I need to come now? Is Bec okay? Did she ask for me or anything?" he managed in a horrified choke. He felt the tension in the room amplify as concerned glances were shared all around him.

"I sedated her almost immediately. We're keeping her Gifted energies drained. That lowered her blood pressure but also means that Aaron might not be getting the amount of Gifted energies he needs, so I can't leave her like this long. She said to tell you she's fine and not to worry, actually."

Jeff was certain those had been Becca's precise words as they sounded exactly like what she would say.

"I'll call you if anything changes. Right now, keeping her under is working, so let's see where that leads us. I'm monitoring both of them constantly."

"Call me if I need to come or anything." He tried to swallow the panic that had cinched around his throat.

"I will," Adeline assured him.

"Is everything okay, Strenton?" Portwood eased. His tone was much kinder than it had been a few moments before.

"Dan!" Rainer's voice shook Jeff from his shock. He and Logan were leading in a student in cuffs.

Dan Vindico

"I don't guess you're about to tell me he's our guy, and we can all go home?" Dan was certain Rainer and Logan had just uncovered yet another piece of an endlessly complicated puzzle.

"No, but he was hoping if he talked, we'd lose the cuffs," Logan supplied.

"That depends on what he has to say." Portwood appeared to be losing patience almost as rapidly as Dan.

"Uh…" The guy stared bewilderedly at Dan. "I need to not go to jail, so just ask me anything. I'll tell you what I know. I mostly just parked my new truck in the senior lot and let people put money in and stuff."

"Matt's dorm room is loaded with thousands of dollars' worth of stolen electronics," Rainer explained.

"They weren't stolen!" Matt vowed adamantly. "They owed the money. If they didn't have my cut, I'd offer to let them pay me that way. Then I sold the stuff to make my cut, so they didn't have to front the cash. I was being nice."

"How admirable." Portwood gave a dramatic eye roll. "Here, in the big-boy world, we call that blackmail, and it'll have you sitting in your very own room at Felsink Reformatory for a minimum of seven years."

Something occurred to Dan. "When you paid whoever it is that's calling the shots, did you always send the money to the PO Box, or did you ever pay him in merchandise?"

"Mostly, I just sent the money to whatever address they sent me. They used to let people pay them like with phones and stuff, but that was when they were making most of the calls, and we were just picking stuff up." Matt couldn't get the information out of his mouth fast enough.

Dan heard the electromagnetic meter boxes from the large server room give a slight hum as Jeff began his intricate casts. Dan glanced back, still concerned Jeff was going to injure himself to catch a criminal.

Messing with power grids and meters could be extremely dangerous. If a Gifted person handled that level of electric energy incorrectly, it could be deadly. From the sound of the phone call he'd just received, it seemed Jeff was going to be a father much sooner than later. With a slight prayer, Dan continued, "Did you ever see this person when you delivered the phones? Can you give us a description? Tell us anything you know."

"I never saw them, but I always had to put the stuff in that big courtyard between Ioses house and the old library. You know, they have that, like, big statue thing in the center by that fire pit."

"You mean the statue of my father." Rainer was obviously irked.

Dan offered him a sorrowful glance, but hope began to pulse in his rhythms. Fionna's smile soothed his heart. She felt his reserved optimism.

"Oh yeah, I guess so." Matt nodded. Dan allowed himself a moment to ponder Matt's relative IQ.

"You put it in the stones near the fire pit?!" Jeff gasped.

Rainer and Logan looked equally as shocked.

"Yeah, a bunch of times. Always behind the one with your name on it." He gestured to Dan. "Then all of a sudden they called me up one day freaking out. They said someone almost saw me, so it could only be cash from then on." Matt shrugged. "So, I started taking my cut in electronics 'cause you can sell them super easy on the Internet."

"Nobody but Ioses knows about the stones." Jeff still appeared to be in utter shock. Dan rolled his eyes. He resisted the urge to beat his head against the painted brick walls of the building they were working in. An outdoor drop-off could be accessed by absolutely anyone.

"He's right. That thing is seriously sacred," Logan agreed.

Dan certainly knew about the large stone fire pit beside Ioses Order. The statue of Governor Lawson had been built the year following his death several years after Dan had graduated. They'd built the foundation out of stones which held the name of every head of Ioses Order for the past fifty years. The statue was attached to the fire which remained burning under a constant shield cast to symbolize the light Governor Lawson offered the Gifted people and that he expected Ioses to protect. It was certainly sacred to every person who called themselves a Shield, but the entire school was well aware of the Ioses courtyard. Obviously, Matt had accessed it many times, and he was a Vis Virres Predilect.

"Yeah, I saw all your names and initials and shit carved in the stones. I never told anybody. I just stuck the stuff in there and left. Then I'd get paid."

"Whoever this is…" Jeff could hardly seem to formulate the words.

"He's in Ioses," Rainer concluded for him in a heartbroken sigh.

"No, he isn't. Everyone knows about the fire pit. I don't know what initials you're talking about, but obviously people who aren't in Ioses know about them as well," Dan pointed out.

"I never knew about them until MAC told me to put the stuff there," Matt stated thoughtfully.

"I assume MAC is for Make A Call," Portwood asked.

Matt nodded. "Yeah, see,"—he pulled out his phone and started scrolling—"here's the ones where he said to put them behind the stones in the courtyard."

"All right, show me these damn stones," Dan huffed. "Jeff, are you good or do you need to leave?"

"I'm okay for now. I think. They've sedated Bec. She's been getting worse. They may deliver her today, but they're going to leave her sedated for a while." He tried to explain what was going on at the hospital to people who hadn't been living his own personal hell for the last several months.

Fionna rushed toward Jeff, but his shield had set firmly around him and nothing was going to get through. She was crushed though she certainly understood. If an Ioses shield set of its own accord, it was impenetrable even to a Receiver. It set in times of fear, weakness, sickness, or injury.

"All right, Strenton, she's got the best medios in the world. You know that, but you're sure as hell not missing your son's birth. If they call again, I'm ordering you to leave immediately and go to Georgetown. I don't care what you're in the middle of doing. You get there and you be there. No matter what happens, she needs you to be her Shield. You got that?" Portwood's fierce command reverberated in the murmured nods around the room.

"Yes, sir." Jeff nodded.

"Let's go. Leave him here." Dan directed Matt to a nearby chair. "You watch him," he ordered Rainer.

Matt's disdain broadcast from his features, but he didn't object as he fell into the chair awkwardly without the use of his arms.

Dan, Fionna, and Portwood followed Logan toward the Ioses courtyard.

"It really is a big deal," Logan explained again as they marched toward the west end of the vast campus. The bitter cold burned Dan's nostrils as he inhaled. He slid out of his leather jacket and wrapped it around Fionna. The icy pain drove him. His muscles armored themselves against the odds.

"What's a big deal?" Portwood's order danced like smoke before his mouth.

"It started the year we started school. I'm pretty sure the heads of Ioses then did it because they knew Rainer was coming," Logan explained. "But no one but Ioses knows about it. They told us that we couldn't even tell Garrett and Cal."

"Okay, I'll bite. We used to use the benches in the courtyard to study, have bonfires, and to make out. What does any of that have to do with the shit this university seems to literally be buried in?" Dan's patience was dying a rapid death.

"That was way before the statue was built. Just come on. I'll show you." Logan began jogging so everyone joined in.

CHAPTER 47

CARVED IN STONE

~GARRETT HAYDENSHIRE~

With his jaw clenched in determination, Garrett narrowed his eyes and wrapped Kaimi under his arm. He glared at Clarence Pendergrath who was running into the same building that Garrett was currently leading his wife toward.

"Where's the fire, Pendergrath? The one you undoubtedly set." Garrett joined Clarence on the stairwell. He kept Kaimi back. She wasn't going to get anywhere near anyone with the last name Pendergrath.

"Fuck off, man. I just solved the whole damn case for you. And just for the record, I'm not my dad," Clarence huffed.

"Watch your mouth in front of my wife!" Garrett ordered, not certain why he was suddenly so furious. Kaimi's brow furrowed in confusion. Garrett certainly never refrained from cursing in front of her.

She shook her head at Garrett. "I'm guessing you two know each other?"

"Garrett!" The reprimand pierced through Garrett's fury as his father's voice rang in his ear.

"Oh, hey, Dad," he managed. "I thought you were already here?"

"I had a meeting with George Sapman before coming over.

Portwood brought something to my attention that I thought perhaps he might like to help with. I should have known better."

They all kept moving at a steady pace. "Clarence, what were you saying about solving the case?" His father's inquiry was heard by everyone in the main server rooms of Venton.

"Where's Dan?" Garrett demanded of Rainer who was watching some kid he had cuffed in a chair.

"Logan took him out to the Ioses courtyard. Matt here says he used to make drop-offs there."

"Did you ever see the guy? Do you think you could ID him?" Garrett edged closer to Matt.

"Son, he is standing in a room full of Iodex officers. Do you really believe no one has asked him that yet?" Governor Haydenshire appeared to be in a vicious mood and not willing to take any of Garrett's crap.

"It doesn't matter. I know who's running this whole thing," Clarence vowed again. "He just called me."

"Right, you know, and we don't," Ericcson scoffed and then went back to helping Jeff set some kind of cast on what appeared to be the entire electrical gridwork for the campus.

"Well, I mean, he should be good at recognizing douch... criminals." Rainer joined in everyone's disdain though he'd corrected quickly in front of his father-in-law. All of those who'd fought the battle that horrible afternoon the year before, the officers they'd lost, the blood that had been shed—it had changed them all.

"Do you ever get tired of people expecting you to be your old man? Ever get sick of people thinking that just 'cause you're his kid you must be just like him?" Clarence seethed.

Rainer was visibly shocked. His brow furrowed, and his shield stuttered for a moment.

"Yes, he does, and Rainer isn't Joseph, and you aren't Candor, Clarence. You're both your own men, and you can both decide what kind of mark you want to leave on this world." Governor Haydenshire's words fissured the shields that surrounded him.

Garrett's brow furrowed as he tried to figure out which would be harder—to live in the shadow of a man who could do no wrong, in the eyes of the Realm, or one who could do no right.

Dan Vindico

"The first meeting of Ioses Order each year, every new member makes his mark on one of the stones. Whoever is head of the order that year tells them to pick the stone with the name of the Shield who we think has made the most difference in the world," Logan explained as he jostled the large stone with Dan's name on it away from the structure.

With a grunt, he pulled it forward and revealed the back of the smooth stone. He pointed to his initials. "And here's Rainer's." On the bottom of the stone was a large cross mark with RL and EH inside of it. Fionna grinned. Dan was extremely humbled by the sheer number of initials on his stone, but that wasn't the most intriguing thing by far.

"What the hell?" he gasped.

"Yeah, that wasn't there when Rainer and I were running Ioses."

There, across the middle of the stone, was a quote by Sun Tzu. "Opportunities multiply as they are seized."

Fionna leaned down to study it. "Isn't that quote from *The Art of War*?"

"Yeah, honey." Dan nodded. "It was also a favorite quote of Candor Pendergrath."

Portwood rubbed his temples. "Okay, so there is plenty of room to stuff electronics there, but I still don't see how this makes it a Shield running this."

"Whoever this moron is, they've clearly been studying Pendergrath," Logan pointed out.

"Or they're related to him," Dan challenged.

Fionna shook her head. "Dan, you promised to believe me if you were going to go back into law enforcement, and I'm telling you it isn't Clarence. He was telling you the truth yesterday. He's been telling you the truth the whole time. He told you about Brodie."

"Logan, how are all of these carved?" Dan quizzed.

"We had to do it ourselves. Friction and heat with our fingers, which if you think about it is probably a really bad idea since the people doing the carving are sub-freshmen and have no idea what they're doing."

Dan hoped against hope.

"Do you really think we could get a handwriting analysis off that?" Portwood clearly had the same thought.

"I think I'm not willing to leave one proverbial stone unturned with everything we stand to lose. This wasn't carved when the whole order was watching. Whoever did this came back later." Dan gestured to Logan. "We already have all of the students' handwriting in a database."

With a nod, Portwood called in the handwriting experts from Iodex who said they would be there quickly.

CHAPTER 48

FATHERS

~GARRETT HAYDENSHIRE~

"Does the name Alex Mueller mean anything to you?" Rainer asked the kid in cuffs instead of listening to Pendergrath's spawn.

Confusion furrowed Matt's brow. "Yeah, Alexa Miller's in my Occamy lab class. What does she have to do with anything?"

"I am standing here telling you who did this. Why are you asking him stuff?" Clarence roared.

"Man, you're crazy. He's like Mr. Ioses Order. He's a total kiss up. He'd never pull something like this. He's already gotten an appointment to New York. He wouldn't throw that all away." Jeff rolled his eyes as he worked his intricate casting on the electric meters that were fed through several grids on the Venton campus.

Garrett had stepped in to help. After Jeff had explained what needed to happen, Garrett was able to hold and shield Jeff's casts so he could work faster.

"Why did you ask him about Alex Mueller?" Clarence demanded of Rainer. His smirk said he already knew the answer.

Rainer rolled his eyes. "Why don't you tell me since you have this all figured out?"

"Because he used his name to do something, right? He used it because it's one of Vindico's aliases, one my dad knew about! I'm telling you he's obsessed with my dad."

Kaimi studied all of the officers in the room. "What if this kid is a kiss up *because* he's been hiding all of this? I mean, that happens, right?" She shrunk back and moved closer to Governor Haydenshire, since Garrett was currently holding two very powerful electric shield casts with both of his hands.

"That certainly seems possible to me, sweetheart." Governor Haydenshire offered Kaimi his kindest smile.

"These emails are just coming faster. He must be using three dozen machines!" Ramier finally spoke up in an effort to keep from drowning. "And they all lead nowhere. If he's calling in debts, he's getting it done because I'm not."

Portwood raced back into the room.

"Dan and Logan are working with James and Indite. We may have a handwriting sample of sorts."

"I'm almost done," Jeff assured everyone. "Just keep feeding me that stream," he directed Garrett. Suddenly, he froze. All of the color drained from his face as he halted the flow of electricity. Garrett stepped in so that he wouldn't lose his work.

Jeff stared down at his pocket in terror. His hand shook violently as he answered the ringing cell phone.

"Please tell me she's okay," he begged.

Garrett's brow furrowed as he glanced from Ramier to his father. Ramier's head fell into his hands.

"It's Becca," Rainer mouthed.

"You're taking her now?" Jeff choked out. "I'm on my way. I'll be there as fast as I can." He swallowed down what appeared to be acrid fear and nausea. He shook his head. "I don't care if she knows I'm there. I want to be there. Don't take her back until I'm with her. She'll be scared if I'm not there." His command seemed to surface from a deep well within his soul. With a determined huff, he ended the call and turned to Ramier.

"They're gonna deliver her now. She's…she's really, really bad." Jeff was well on his way to tears.

Ramier gave him a reassuring smile. "Adeline is the best. Just ask

Logan. She'll take care of Becca, but you go on. You heard Portwood. We'll figure this out and then we're all gonna come to Georgetown to meet your son."

With a slight nod, Jeff turned to Garrett. "Can you just keep that stream running to the discs there? You'll be able to see the eddy currents light up. That will show you where all of the electricity is heading. You should be able to see a massive draw."

"I'm on it. You go be a dad," Garrett urged him onward.

With that, Jeff sprinted out the door.

"Landon." Governor Haydenshire leapt as soon as Jeff disappeared.

"Yeah, I've got it, sir." He pulled a folded piece of paper from his pocket. "Took a while. Called in lots of favors. He lives in a duplex out in Elkridge."

Ramier turned from the computer monitors. "From what we can tell, he's kept tabs on Jeff since he was born. I did a whole lot of digging and even found several chat rooms where Jeff's dad actually taught him to program. He's better than his old man now, but his father was very instrumental, and obviously, Jeff's dad is one hell of a hacker."

"Jeff doesn't know who his father is?" Kaimi wondered out loud. Garrett swallowed as Ericcson stepped in to help him complete Jeff's intricate casts on the meters.

"His father has been helping him quite a bit as of late, and I think it might be time for them to at least see each other. Jeff isn't far from becoming a father himself. If you don't need me here, I think I might take a drive out to Elkridge," Governor Haydenshire explained.

"Sir, let me send a few officers with you. I'm not sure how his dad might react," Portwood urged.

"The man's a hacker, Landon. I can't imagine me showing up with flashing blue lights and sirens would get me anywhere at all."

"Governor Haydenshire, sir?" Kaimi gave Garrett's father her pleading gaze with that light of hope that ignited the copper in her eyes. Garrett stared at her for one long, drawn-out moment wondering what she was going to say.

"Do you need something before I go, sweetheart?"

"Oh, no, sir. I was just wondering if maybe I could come with you.

Uh…" she hemmed uncomfortably as she glanced Garrett's way. "I might could help. I want to do something, and I don't know my dad either. My mom doesn't even know him, but if someone knew where he was, sometimes I think maybe I'd like to talk to him. Maybe. I don't know. But, probably I would like that. And I could probably explain to Jeff's dad that it might mean a lot to Jeff if he reached out."

The mug shots and rap sheets clawed at Garrett's shield. They seared like damning fire in the recesses of his mind. Nausea swirled in his gut as he considered what he was keeping from her or what he was keeping her from.

"I would really appreciate your help, but we need to go now. Are you ready?"

"Yes, sir. Thank you!" She threw her arms around the governor's neck, making him grin as he embraced her sweetly. She moved to Garrett and carefully kissed his cheek, trying not to interrupt the delicate cast work.

"I love you, baby. Please be careful. Stay with Dad, okay?" Garrett knew everyone in the relatively small room could hear him, but he had to make his plea.

"I will. Promise. I'll be fine." Kaimi was elated to be doing this. Garrett nodded and tried to bury her father on the other side of the country. He couldn't negotiate his way through that right now. Later, after they moved, then maybe he'd tell her. He threw himself into finding whoever was threatening his best friends.

CHAPTER 49

TURN OF THE TIDES

~JEFF STRENTON~

Jeff floored the truck and immediately decided he was buying himself a new car as soon as he made sure Becca and Aaron were okay. That thought led him to another. He picked up his cell phone and dialed into the main Iodex precinct line.

"This is Elite Iodex Technology Specialist, Jeff Strenton." He tried not to stammer and to sound commanding.

"Uh, okay, I don't believe I know you yet, but go ahead." The dispatcher chuckled. Jeff clenched his jaw in fury.

"My wife is at Georgetown about to undergo major surgery to give birth to my son. Wanted to let you know that I plan on getting there quickly."

"Yes, sir." The dispatcher's tone changed in an instant. "Just give me the make and model of your car and your tag number. Would you like an escort?"

"Nope, just don't want to stop."

"Yes, sir. Be careful, and congratulations." All Jeff could pray in that moment was that congratulations would be in order and that this wouldn't be the worst day of his and Becca's life.

"Thanks." Jeff swallowed down his terror and refused to believe that anything at all would be wrong with either his beautiful wife or their precious little boy.

Suddenly, his phone vibrated in his hand. He furrowed his brow and eased off the gas as he read the odd text.

~

Crown Governor Stephen Haydenshire

The lengthy hours weighed on Stephen as he opened the van door for his newest daughter-in-law. She was chewing on her lip just like Emily. Stephen smiled and wondered how long it would take for Kaimi to be comfortable around him. *Garrett's moving her five thousand miles away, so it could be awhile.* He tried not to regret his son's upcoming move.

"Did you and Garrett have a nice time in Kauai?" He cranked the van and tried to get to know the woman who'd somehow turned it all around for his wayward son. Her deep crimson blush was not what he'd been expecting. He tried to turn his chuckle into a cough.

"Yes, sir. We had so much fun. It was amazing. Garrett's always amazing." Just the thought of his son had her beaming.

"I'm certainly glad you think so," Stephen teased her.

"He is. I mean, you must know that, because you're you. But I can't believe how lucky I am. I can't believe I'm married to him." She seemed to settle into the seat beside him.

"I get the impression Garrett feels the same way about you." That elicited another broad grin.

"We went camping last night. But last night kind of went on a long time even though we left Kauai in the middle of it. We had fun though." Kaimi seemed to want to talk, so Stephen nodded. He glanced at his phone to make certain he was heading toward Randall Strenton's apartment. "There for a while, I thought when Garrett finally moved out, he was going to build himself a tree house. He's always loved to camp."

"Do you know Representative Kalakona?" Kaimi asked abruptly.

"Uh…" Stephen tried to navigate the subject change as he wondered what had brought about the question.

"Not very well, but I've spoken with her more since she decided to try to get Dan and Garrett to move out to Hawaii than I had before."

Kaimi nodded, but she seemed suddenly distracted by interstate signs blurring by the windshield.

~

Jeff Strenton

"This is Ramier," sounded in Jeff's phone as he continued to fly toward Georgetown.

"Hey, it's me." Jeff swallowed. "I'm about to send you an email with an attachment. I have no idea what it is or where it came from, but it's signed 46339 again so it's from our hacker friend."

Ramier was silent for a moment. "I'll take any help we can get right now. Have you heard anything else about Becca?"

Jeff found it odd that Ramier changed the subject. "I'm pulling into the hospital now."

"Give her our best."

Before Ramier ended the call, Jeff heard, "Why don't you believe me? That moron has been asking me shit about my dad constantly since I got here. Seriously, he'd been, like, studying him and Uncle Nic. Even I was never that interested in my dad."

"Is he still saying it's Ben?" Jeff scoffed.

"Yeah, he's pretty adamant."

"He's a moron. I'm going in. Good luck." Jeff ended the call without a response.

Georgetown was covered in press. Several whispered curse words exited his mouth as he finally managed to locate a parking place. He leapt from the truck and raced toward the entrance.

He grabbed a guy standing on the sidelines who wasn't carrying a microphone. "What the hell is going on?"

"Governor Vindico's being released in a few minutes, and someone said Governor Sapman's daughter has gone into labor." Jeff drew a deep breath as he managed a spite-filled nod. He continued to push through the crowds and shoved open the doors, flashing his badge to gain entry to his own son's birth.

CHAPTER 50
SOAP

"Jeff!" Adeline's command rang out as soon Jeff raced off the elevator. "Come on!"

"Becca!" Jeff's voice shook as he sprinted to her side. She was pale and drawn and completely unconscious.

"We're going to leave her out for the cesarean. You'll have to take care of the baby until she wakes up, okay?" Adeline soothed. "With the extra castings, we feel like we have him developed to around thirty-three weeks. We'll give him a steroid shot and leave him on oxygen until his lungs finish developing, but he's almost four pounds. He would have been pretty big if she'd gone full term. Right in here." Adeline directed the surgical team into an operating room.

"I'll do anything either of them need," Jeff vowed. Mrs. Sapman was blinking back tears as she offered Jeff a kind smile. Governor Sapman was pacing and refused to meet Jeff's eye. Ms. Harrickson had promised to come as soon as she got off work.

Jeff clung to Becca's hand. He pushed his energy through her and into Aaron. She might not know he was there, but he wanted Aaron to know he would always be there. He would never leave either of them. He would be the dad he'd never had. He would be there for every second of everything. He would never let them down.

"Please say they're going to be okay," he finally begged Adeline.

All she offered him was a reassuring smile, which did nothing to reassure him.

Becca's body shifted slightly. Her face turned toward Jeff.

"I thought you said she was completely out." He brushed her hair away from her face and squeezed her hand again. He willed away his own tears as he tried to imagine what the next hour would bring. Becca was freezing, and her face still held the terror Jeff hadn't been there to see. It eased slightly with every caress of his hand.

"She is, but she feels you and so does Aaron. Look." Adeline pointed to the monitors. Aaron's feed had begun to pace more rhythmically as had Becca's.

"I'm here, Bec. I'm right here," he soothed as he was directed to a rolling stool at Becca's head and a curtain was erected over her bump.

∼

Crown Governor Stephen Haydenshire

"Representative Kalakona came out to your campsite?" Stephen tried desperately to make sense of the conversation he'd been having with Kaimi. Nothing seemed to hold her attention for any length of time. He couldn't fathom Victoria Kalakona interrupting their honeymoon.

"Yes, sir. Sorry I got distracted again. I'm really, really tired." Kaimi hung her head in shame.

"No, no, it's fine. I was just surprised to hear that. What did she say when she was out there?"

"She got kind of…mad…uh…about Dan and Garrett not moving out there yet…and some other stuff."

"That's certainly not what she said when she was pleading with them to accept the positions," Stephen huffed.

"Yeah, that's what Garrett said too." A deep yawn overtook her. "I can't wait for you and Mrs. Haydenshire to come out and see us there. I love our house. Garrett hung some shelves for me in our closet." This conversation was giving Stephen slight whiplash. "For my art supplies. It was so sweet. He even hung up the curtains over the sink

I'd been sewing. He somehow found a place for everything in our new house. It's kind of tiny, but I think it's perfect. I love it."

Stephen sighed audibly as he nodded his complete lack of understanding. He decided to try once more.

"I'm so pleased. Now, what exactly did Representative Kalakona say?"

～

Rainer Lawson

"Just shut up, okay. We're working on it!" Rainer bellowed as Clarence Pendergrath started in yet again.

"It's spiking again!" Garrett shouted as he managed to both cast the electric feed lines and read them.

"Same place?" Portwood edged closer.

"Yeah." Garrett nodded and allowed Ericcson to push his sunglasses over his eyes so they could continue to stare at the glowing lines.

"These are class lists!" Ramier gasped. "He knew the servers were casted and locked. He only had access to emails he'd been given before. If this email Jeff just sent over is his, and I can narrow down some kind of schedule from these email addresses, we might just have our guy!"

"Do it! I'm calling Dan!" Portwood urged frantically.

"That's definitely Ioses dorms. Senior floor," Tuttle confirmed. Rainer's heart raced in volatile anger. How could a Shield have done this? How could a Shield be doing this to one of their own?

"I told you!" Clarence erupted again.

"All right, fine! What the hell has Ben Cobson been saying to you?" Rainer demanded.

"He knows way too much. I swear to you he's been studying my dad and Uncle Nic or something. He knew shit he should not know. He called me a little while ago and asked me about those custody documents. The ones they did for your uncle." Clarence edged closer to Rainer as he hissed his explanation. "He kept asking me how Iodex found out about them."

"What!?" Rainer was stunned.

"Yeah, and it was weird. He wanted to know how you found out. He kept asking me who your inside guy was. The weirdest part about that is every single time I got a letter from Dad when I was in that hellhole in New Mexico, that's all he talked about too. All he cared about was how Vindico had figured out about the custody documents. He was fucked-up, and Coriolis didn't help."

"What did you tell Ben when he asked?" Rainer couldn't believe what he was hearing.

"I kept telling him it was Vindico, and that he always found everything out. I told him Vindico was the only guy my old man was afraid of. Ben was obsessed with how they got caught, and then he told *me* how Uncle Nic stole the original custody documents from Jack Stariff's office. He said they paid off one of the Visium Predilect legal interns from Venton. How the hell would he know that? I didn't know that. I didn't even know they'd forged custody documents or whatever. I told him you guys figured out a bunch of stuff, and Dad never knew how."

Rainer's eyes met Portwood's in a horrified stare. Portwood spoke what they were beginning to understand. "Are you thinking that maybe someone heavily suggested that the Georgetown interns were swapping the drug tests to set them up?"

"Ben convinced them to go to Dan and tell on their fellow interns." Rainer was stunned.

"That sounds a *lot* like something my dad used to do with a mind cast," Pendergrath pointed out.

Portwood casted his phone so everyone could hear him.

"Coriolis Prison," a voice answered.

"This is Chief of Elite Landon Portwood badge number 18647. I need the visitor log for Candor Pendergrath from March of last year through his death."

"Yes, sir." They all heard a keyboard clicking. "Emailing it to you now."

Ramier was frantic. "I'm running a complier cast on these emails.

It looks like there are only seven students that were in all of these classes."

"How did you know about Brodie?" Portwood demanded of Clarence.

"I didn't just come in here accusing people randomly. I've been talking to people. They're not gonna tell you everything. They're just saying enough to keep themselves out of trouble. I wondered if it was Ben a few weeks ago when he got more and more relentless asking me stuff, but I had to have hardcore proof. I knew you'd never believe it. I knew you'd protect your own. I'm not a moron! For fuck's sake, I'm Candor Pendergrath's son. He was a lot of things, but stupid was not one of them."

"Here's the email." Portwood started scrolling on his phone. "Anastasia Maric was in several times." He raised his eyebrows to Clarence.

"Girlfriend." Clarence rolled his eyes. "Wanted money."

"Sasha Broz?"

"Same."

"I don't see anything in any way indicating Mr. Cobson in this list." Portwood was still studying his phone.

"And you think that someone smart enough to pull off all of this"— Clarence gestured around to the school at large—"used his real name to check into Coriolis Prison."

Portwood seemed to allow that as he scrolled again. "Holy shit," he gasped a second later.

"What?" Rainer demanded.

"Someone by the name of Joseph Lister was in to see Candor"—he paused and counted on his phone—"forty-seven times since last March."

"Fuck. It is him." Garrett shook his head.

"Wait. Who is Joseph Lister?" Rainer asked.

"The name Vindico used to leave with hotel clerks in Moscow whenever he was in the country and found more evidence on my dad. He loved to keep Dad on edge," Clarence explained.

Portwood nodded. "Dan used to constantly make fun of Candor's self-assigned nickname—soap. Joseph Lister is who came up with carbolic acid. It's used to sterilize things for surgery, including surgeon's hands."

"A more powerful soap," Rainer spoke almost to himself.

Portwood and Garrett both nodded.

"Did your dad tell you about that?" Rainer demanded of Clarence.

"If you mean did my dad lose his shit every single time Vindico was in and out of the country keeping track of Uncle Nic when they didn't know about it then yes. That would be how I knew the name. I don't typically make it a habit of knowing bullshit about who invented soap."

Portwood was already back on the phone. He repeated his name and badge number and then commanded. "Send me the digital photo scan from when Joseph Lister visited the prison. Now!"

CHAPTER 51
FAMILY

~DAN VINDICO~

"Okay, Dan, I've gotten it as close as I can. Let's feed it in and see what we find." Letisha Indite fed a scanned photo of the carved rock into a specially casted laptop. It was rapidly comparing and scanning handwriting samples from the Venton students' registration forms for the school year. "This probably won't be a perfect match because of the stone surface as compared to the paper, but it should be able to narrow it down to just a few students."

"I'll take anything you can give me," Dan assured her.

Crown Governor Stephen Haydenshire

From what Stephen was able to determine from Kaimi's rather disjointed conversations, there was something she didn't want to tell him about what had been going on when Representative Kalakona had interrupted their campout. As it was their honeymoon, Stephen only found fault with Victoria for rudely interrupting, but he wasn't certain how to communicate that to Kaimi without making her more uncomfortable.

"This is it." He pulled into a tiny, poured cement parking lot outside of a slight row of four duplexes. Kaimi gave a determined nod as she studied the aging decor.

"Do we have some kind of plan, or are we just gonna go, 'hey, you have this totally great kid who's about to be a dad and if you could maybe stop not being in his life that'd be great'?" Kaimi asked with a hopeful twinkle in her eye.

Stephen found it odd to be laughing at a time like this. He suspected he knew what his son had fallen in love with first.

"Truthfully, I'm not certain how this might go. I doubt he's expecting me. He has no idea Ramier figured out who he is. To our knowledge, he's never even seen Jeff, but obviously, he knows about him. I'm no good at speechwriting. I usually just try to get to the heart of the matter unless I'm yelling at one of the kids, and then I figure they deserve to listen to me ramble."

Kaimi laughed as she leapt out of the van and followed him to the door.

With a quick and fervent prayer, Stephen let his fist tap out his hopes.

~

Jeff Strenton

The precision of Adeline and the obstetrics nurses and neonatal medios drove Jeff to distraction. He wanted Becca to be awake, so he knew that she wasn't in pain. His shield protested by way of sizzling against his skin. Adeline worked methodically but was carrying on a conversation with the anesthesiologist.

"She's doing great, Jeff. Just watch her rhythms on the monitors," Adeline soothed. But Jeff was tired of staring at the monitors. He could hear the swoosh of Aaron's echoed heartbeat, but in that moment Jeff wanted to hold his son in his hands. He needed his family to be whole and complete and together.

"Okay, here we go." Adeline gave him a nod. Jeff had made certain to stay north of the blue curtain. He had no desire to see his wife cut open. He wasn't certain he could stomach it, and that his shield wouldn't react violently. He felt Becca's body jostle and jerk back and forth on the table, as Adeline tugged with a fair amount of force.

Jeff's eyes goggled, and he forced himself to stand so he could see what was happening. With a final pull, Jeff gasped as his son was removed from Becca. They quickly wiped his face, and a gurgled scream filled the air.

"He looks good," one of the neonatal nurses commented as she cut the cord, took Aaron, put him under a light, and began scrubbing him off. Jeff didn't know which way to look. Adeline was healing Becca's abdomen from the inside linings out, and Aaron's oxygen tubes were being taped on his tiny face which he didn't seem to like.

"Three pounds, fourteen ounces," rang from another nurse. "He's going to be just fine, Medio Haydenshire." The proclamation from the neonatal pediatric medio brought air back to Jeff's lungs. Emotion Jeff couldn't contain leaked steadily from his eyes as he willed Becca to awaken so she could see him. Suddenly, Aaron was being placed in his extremely inexperienced hands.

Jeff shook his head, but to his shock, Aaron stopped screaming as soon as he cradled him awkwardly. "I, uh…I don't know what to do with him."

"Just hold him, Mr. Strenton. He needs to feel your energy. He recognizes it. We're going to give him the steroid shots now."

Aaron's body tensed violently when the needle entered his leg, and Jeff fought the urge to screech at the nurse to get away from his baby. His shield pulsed angrily in an effort to surround his son. With another quick shot, the nurse stepped away and smiled.

"You can cast him, Mr. Strenton. It would be good for him." Jeff wasn't certain if he was relieved that the nurse picked up on his anger or if he cared at all. His green orb surrounded his tiny baby boy, and Jeff's body eased as Aaron immediately stopped crying.

"If you'd like to use a pacifier, I'll place a few here in his cradle. He can stay with you. We'll check him every half hour or so for the next few days. Becca should awaken in an hour or two. If you'd like, we can put him in the incubator so the governor can see him," the medio that had been assigned to Aaron explained.

"No." Jeff shook his head. Something about Aaron meeting anyone else was horribly wrong. "No one should meet him before Bec."

Adeline's broad grin gave strength to Jeff's decree. "I'm almost done here. Let's turn off that drip. We'll be in to cast her every few hours to get rid of the rest of the birthing fluid and to contract her uterus back to size."

Jeff nodded, but he couldn't keep his eyes off his little boy sleeping soundly in the casted light blanket. He was so small it terrified Jeff. How was he supposed to keep him safe?

"Okay." Adeline began healing the puckered scar left from the scalpel. Jeff's body relaxed slightly when Becca's abdomen no longer held any sign that she'd been cut open.

"We'll leave him in an incubator when other people want to see him to keep him from any germs and to keep his temperature steady when you're not casting him. We'll watch his oxygen reads for the next few weeks. If they develop as I feel they will, you can take him home in ten to fourteen days hopefully, but it could be three to four weeks. He'll need to be in the casted blanket twenty hours a day. That will improve his jaundice."

Jeff nodded again. His mind couldn't seem to make sense of how abruptly his world had changed.

The medio who'd sped up Aaron's development via his Gifted energies was sporting quite a pompous smirk. Jeff recalled the fact that he stood to receive quite a grant if his experimentation on Aaron proved to work.

"Becca should be able to go home in three to four days. Her blood pressure has already stabilized just from no longer being pregnant. She's going to be sore for a week or more. We'll do several intensive casts throughout the day and night," Adeline explained. Jeff tried desperately to remember everything he was being told.

"He's going to need a bottle." A nurse moved closer, careful not to intercept his fierce shield.

"Bec wants to nurse him." He had no idea how he'd remembered that Becca hadn't wanted Aaron to have bottles, but it pulsed in his mind at that moment.

"We can either hook him up to an IV, or he can have a few before her milk comes in." Certain that he did not want any more needles near his child, Jeff dropped his shield and accepted the bottle filled with enhanced formula.

"We'll get him latched on when she's awake," another nurse soothed. Deciding to just attempt it and praying that Becca wouldn't be upset, Jeff placed the tiny nipple of the bottle to Aaron's lips and was astonished when Aaron immediately began suckling. Jeff smiled through his tears. He was unable to believe the miracle he was somehow holding in his own hands. Becca was the most incredible woman on the face of the earth. He was certain.

"Just keep him in your arms against you, skin to skin, and keep these blankets casted so he stays warm. Hold him in your shield as much as you're able, soothing energy and warmth inside it. We'll leave you here with your wife and your son. Touch the button here if you need anything," was the final instruction before Adeline lowered the lights in the room and left Jeff with his family.

CHAPTER 52

A SHIELD

~CROWN GOVERNOR STEPHEN HAYDENSHIRE~

"'Bout damn…" Randall Strenton's face held his stunned disbelief as he swung the door open with a twenty crunched in his hand and stared at the Crown Governor.

"I'm not delivering pizza," Stephen quipped.

Randall gave a slight nod as he seemed to debate what to do. "It was Chinese actually," he finally stammered

Stephen nodded his understanding. "I'd like to speak with you briefly about your son, Mr. Strenton, and if I know my daughter-in-law,"—he glanced at his watch with a nod—"your grandson."

"I don't really think Jeff wants me to have anything to do with all of that, but he really needs to catch this guy at Venton. I've been feeding him information, but he isn't responding."

"No, I imagine he isn't, since he's in an operating room with his lovely wife, helping her have their baby."

"Oh." Randall seemed momentarily incapable of processing that information.

"Maybe instead of texting him all of the clues and stuff you've been finding, you could text him congratulations." Kaimi held up her own phone displaying a text from Garrett stating that they'd heard from Governor Sapman and that Becca and the baby were both doing well.

"Who're you?" Randall asked rather rudely.

"That is another one of my incredibly talented daughters-in-law, and I'm going to ask you to improve your tone."

Kaimi looked stunned by Stephen's scolding, but she forced a slight smile.

"Mr. Strenton, sir, I don't have any idea who my father is. I was just hoping maybe you'd at least try to let Jeff know that you're here and that you've been helping him. He's such a great guy, and you have a grandson. Don't you want to meet them?"

Confusion and anger broadcast from Randall's face as he shook his head.

"Look, I don't know why you're here, but if Jeff's not gonna get the job done, someone needs to. Whoever is doing this bought plane tickets to Aruba yesterday."

Stephen's jaw clenched before he willed his own restraint. "Do you want to help Jeff catch this kid for your own glory or so you'll feel a little less guilty for abandoning your son before he ever even arrived? Let me assure you no amount of computer help is going to make up for your not being a father. He needs more than cryptic text messages and emails to help him with his work. He's your son, and he needs a father. So, why don't you stop hiding behind your own guilt and your own ego and come out from behind your many computer screens and be a man, Mr. Strenton."

Kaimi's eyes goggled, and Stephen was reassured that he'd gotten his message across.

~

Dan Vindico

Fionna was shivering, and Dan wrapped his shield around his wife and filled it with what heat he could summon from himself and the air around them, which wasn't much.

"We can go back inside, but I have to set it up all over again," Indite offered apologetically.

"No. I'm okay," Fionna assured through her chattering teeth.

"It's slowing down, sir." James and Indite both leaned in.

"Looks like you've got an eighty percent possible match on six students." She handed the laptop to Dan to read the names.

～

Garrett Haydenshire

"All right, there were only seven students who were in every one of these classes." Ramier read the monitor to his right. "Cobson's name is on the list."

Garrett was still trying to shake off the sheer amount of electricity he'd pushed through his shield. He blinked his eyes repeatedly but couldn't quite read the screen yet himself. Ericcson had taken over when Garrett's shield had visibly weakened, and he'd collapsed on the ground. McCoy was shoving protein bars and enhanced water down him.

"This is the photo ID Joseph Lister used each time he was at the prison. Is this Cobson?" Portwood held up his phone to show Rainer.

He gave a morose nod.

"You're certain?" Landon demanded again.

Garrett stood and willed his energy to come back to him in full force. "Landon, man, you're a great chief, but you and I both know a Shield did this. You gotta come to terms with it. Candor would've loved that as his final act he could use this kid to stick it to Dan."

He sprinted out the door with Rainer on his heels headed for the Ioses dorms.

～

Crown Governor Stephen Haydenshire

In the space of the standoff between Stephen and Randall, several alarms sounded from inside the duplex.

"Shit!" Randall left the door standing open and raced back into the living room. "You've scared him, but you haven't caught him!"

"What is happening?" Stephen demanded.

"Jeff?" Becca's eyes blinked open hesitantly.

"Thank God you're awake." He moved to the bed, still carefully holding Aaron to his chest.

"What happened?" She shuddered and began to sob. She couldn't remember. Jeff tried to wipe away her tears while keeping Aaron safely in his embrace.

"It's okay, baby. He's here, and he's fine."

Becca cried harder as she reached for the baby. Jeff eased Aaron into his mother's arms, certain he would be safer and happier there. "See, he's perfect, just like you." Jeff kissed her forehead and reheated both of their blankets.

"I don't understand." Becca was frantic, and Aaron was beginning to fuss. "Why is this blanket glowing?"

"It's casted. It's supposed to help his jaundice." Jeff pushed soothing energy to Aaron and was astonished that he quieted down. "Your blood pressure spiked, and they sedated you. Then it spiked again while you were out, so they did the C-section, and he's here. I've been calling him Aaron in my head for a while now, but if you don't want to name him that, I told them I wasn't filling out the papers until you were awake. I had to give him two bottles because they were gonna put an IV in his foot. He has to eat a lot because he's so tiny. I don't know. I just didn't want them to do that. I'm sorry."

Becca smiled though her tears were still flowing. "It's okay. I just can't believe he's here." She stared down at their little boy, and tears of overwhelming joy replaced those of fear and confusion.

"Hey there, little guy. I'm your mommy. I'm sorry I missed you getting here," she whispered as Jeff eased beside her to hold both his wife and their tiny, precious, little boy.

Adeline tapped on the door. "Jeff, Dan needs to talk to you if you can spare a minute to call him. He sounded pretty frantic." With a confused nod, Jeff glanced at Becca.

"It's okay. You've been taking care of him for a while. I can do it now." She grinned as Aaron grasped her finger tightly in his tiny fist.

A woman followed Adeline in. She smiled. "I'm Marcia Royson. I'm a lactation specialist. Why don't you handle that call, and I'll see if we can get Aaron latched on."

Jeff managed to stand and grab his phone. His own exhaustion and euphoria made him slightly dizzy.

"Jeff!" Dan sounded infuriated.

"Yes, sir."

"I know this is a hell of a bad time and that you have much better things to be doing, but did Ben Cobson ever say anything at all that would've made you think he could be doing this? Anything?" Dan demanded.

"Uh…" Jeff tried to think. His head ached with all that had happened. "He's always worked in the laptop lab, oh…" A thought formulated slowly in Jeff's memory. He tried to recall all of the conversations he'd had with Ben in the last six months. He was distracted momentarily as he watched his son begin to suckle from Becca's right breast. The nurse had a mermaid tattoo on her forearm.

"Oh my God!" Jeff was stunned by his own realization. "It was him. He knew about your tattoos! He knew Fionna and you have matching tats. I didn't know that. Does anyone else know that? How would he have seen her tattoos unless he'd seen her…you know…without her clothes on? Remember that day he asked you about them? How did I not realize that?"

"I will kill him," was the last thing Jeff heard before the line went dead.

CHAPTER 53

THE ART OF WAR

~CROWN GOVERNOR STEPHEN HAYDENSHIRE~

"Here! Give Jeff this." Randall thrust an external hard drive into Stephen's hand as he tried to shut down the alarm system sounding from one of his many computers.

"What is going on?" Stephen demanded again.

"He's erasing everything! You spooked him, and now, you're not going to be able to convict him. All of Jeff's work will be lost."

Stephen shook his head as the absence of the alarm throbbed in his mind. "And that's the evidence we need?"

"Yes, obviously!"

"If you want Jeff to have that, Mr. Strenton, you need to drive down to Georgetown and give it to him yourself."

Kaimi nodded thoughtfully. "Because he deserves to know you've been helping him. He deserves to know his father. Even if you're ashamed of what you did and of the past twenty years, you can't keep hiding from this and hiding from life. It isn't always easy. Believe me, I know, but sometimes you have to make the jump and learn to fly."

"So, if your dad just showed up and wanted to talk to you...?" Randall studied Kaimi intently.

"I'd talk to him," Kaimi vowed.

~

Dan Vindico

Dan sprinted to the top floor of the Ioses dorm. The door to Ben's room was shield casted. Dan ground his teeth, summoned, and drew the energy out of the cast in an instant. The door shuddered violently as he booted it open. The knob lodged into the sheetrock behind it. Seven computers were still running. The screens were entirely blank. Logan moved to them and casted one.

"He wiped everything. The hard drives are blank."

"Where is he?!" Dan demanded. They both turned to stare out the open window onto the green glow from the fire escape. It was casted as well. Frustration surged through him as Dan summoned again.

~

Garrett Haydenshire

"Holy shit!" Rainer pointed to a descending shield orb in the distance.

Cobson had casted the gravitational energy around him, curved his own shield, and was using it to slow his descent to the ground. He'd jumped off the roof of the Ioses Dorm.

McCoy reached them just then. "Who the hell taught him to do that?"

"Dan," Garrett fumed. "Dan's been teaching him to fight all year."

Rainer summoned, but Garrett shook his head. "Don't drain it. The fall might kill him. We're going to have to take him once he lands."

They took off but halted abruptly and stared in shock as Cobson suddenly dropped his own cast.

"Fuck, is he suicidal?" McCoy sounded horrified.

"No. Dan taught him that too." Garrett shook his head. "Come on."

When Ben was still twenty feet from the ground, he casted again. The force of his shield against the gravity caused him to suspend in air for a moment. In the slight bounce of his body, he threw himself hard to the side and got a few feet farther away from them.

Dan and Logan reached them. "Come on!" Dan raced toward Ben.

"Dammit, Dan, wait! He's at a distinct advantage from up there, and he's got a pistol." Garrett pointed to Ben's right hand.

"How the hell did he get that on campus?" Logan demanded.

"I'm sure that's something Pendergrath could've taught him too," Rainer reminded them.

Cobson dropped the shield cast again.

"Get down!" Dan demanded as they all hit the ground at the same moment that Ben fired.

Garrett's shield deflected the bullet.

It would've hit Dan if he'd been a split second later hitting the grass.

"Did you teach him that too?" McCoy gasped.

"Yes." Dan summoned with both of his energy streams. He spun in thermal energy, slowed the particles in it so it would cool even more mixed in with his shield, and they raced toward Ben.

He hit the ground on his ass but scrambled up and raced toward the parking lot.

Dan threw. Getting hit with a frozen shield cast was going to hurt like hell.

But Ben managed to leap behind a parked car. He summoned from the battery and threw heat toward Dan's cast.

"Dammit, Dan, you are never fucking allowed to teach ever again!" Garrett shouted.

Portwood, Ramier, Ericcson, Tuttle, and Barron all located them.

Garrett made use of the distraction they provided. Keeping his shield up, he raced away from Ben by twenty feet, sank low between two parked SUVs, and watched once he'd reached the bumper.

Elite was racing toward him and had all of his attention as Ben tried to dodge in and out from between parked cars while firing randomly. His bullets were deflected readily.

Dan summoned and threw again. His shield hit this time. Garrett chuckled when Cobson was knocked flat on his back and slid fifteen feet across the concrete, screeching out curse words the entire time. He released the pistol when he rolled to the side in agony.

Garrett sprinted to him and kicked the 357 Magnum away. He

shook his head. "Got Daddy Pendergrath's favorite pistol as well," he chanted.

Ben leapt up. He tried to cast again, but Garrett swung. Ben stumbled backward and dropped his cast. "You really think you're gonna win, fucker? Against me?" Garrett laughed derisively.

Ben threw a rage-fueled fist toward him, but Garrett caught it, lifted his arm until his shoulder was almost out of its socket, and swung his right leg out, knocking Ben to the side and then to the ground. He landed his boot in his back. "Who the hell do you think taught Danny to fight?"

Portwood and Dan made it to them. "Unbelievable! I hope the governors bury you alive." Portwood's disgust rang in his voice and broadcast from his scowling face as he made it to them. He slapped cuffs on Ben's wrists.

CHAPTER 54

WHAT VENGEANCE WROUGHT

~DAN VINDICO~

When Garrett stepped back to catch his breath, Dan summoned and held Ben on the ground with his shield. Panic shattered through it though, as he felt spite-filled glee form in Ben's energy and then heard the deafening explosion from the parking lot.

"What the hell?" Garrett gasped as they saw the fire.

"McCoy, stay with him!" Dan released his shield as McCoy stepped in to keep Ben from summoning. They sprinted toward the fire as students began running the other way.

"Oh my God!" Dan panicked and set his shield firmly over himself as he, Rainer, Portwood, and Garrett followed Logan and Ericcson straight into the fire. Dan drew the heat out and released it into the air. Garrett and Rainer followed suit. When Logan diminished more of the heat from the fire, Dan raced in and pulled Brodie Quentin from his brand-new Corvette completely engulfed in flames.

Dan hoisted him to the ground. The smoke was too heavy. Garrett shook his head and pushed Dan farther away while he administered mouth-to-mouth. Brodie woke a full minute later, vomiting smoke and ash while Garrett gasped for breath.

Gifted ambulances arrived moments later, and gurneys were set up in the parking lot. Dan and Garrett were both strapped with oxygen masks. Fionna made it to him with tears streaking down her face.

Dan finally jerked the oxygen mask off and held her tightly, constantly assuring her that he was fine.

"You put that back on right now!" she demanded and he obeyed.

She broke down completely when Logan writhed on a gurney while they healed a third-degree burn he'd received on his arm when his own shield had weakened slightly so he could help Dan shield Brodie as he'd pulled him from the car.

"I just can't believe this." Fionna shook her head.

"Is Brodie okay?" Dan pulled the mask away again to ask the medio who was measuring his oxygen intake levels.

"Smoke inhalation and oxygen deprivation just like you all. We're healing the burns on his left calf now, but it might scar. It's a bad burn. We'll get you all to the hospital and heal your lungs and nasal passages."

"Oh my gosh!" Kaimi was sobbing as she raced to the gurney Garrett was on. He ripped off his own mask and clung to her tightly.

"What happened?" Governor Haydenshire's eyes closed in momentary horror as he tried to help Logan sit up after his leg was bandaged and cool casted. He steadied a cup of enhanced water offered to Logan as his son downed the drink in a few sips. He then rushed to Garrett to check on him as well.

Dan's head jerked to the side when he heard another rasping cough. Portwood's face was covered in smoke. There was an oxygen mask outline etched in the black powder.

"Are you okay?" he managed in a slight gasp.

Fionna pulled the oxygen mask back over Dan's face.

Dan nodded. "Yeah, are you?"

"Just smoke inhalation," Portwood assured him as if that weren't a relatively serious condition.

Garrett still hadn't released Kaimi. His face was buried in her shoulder, and she was clinging to him with force.

"Let me send for Adeline, son." Governor Haydenshire seemed to finally be able to formulate thought.

"No, Dad. I'm all right. She'll freak. I'm sure I'll see her at the hospital in a minute anyway." Logan's voice was graveled and weak.

"More water," Governor Haydenshire ordered the medios.

"Yes, sir." They handed out more bottles to everyone being treated.

The weight of everything that had happened coupled with the fact that he hadn't slept in well over twenty-four hours had Dan slumping against his wife. He was shaken awake when a microphone was thrust in his face.

"Commander Vindico, can you give us some idea what happened here this morning and the student's name who's been apprehended?"

"I can't comment on an open case." Dan coughed, shook his head, and shoved the mic away.

"Get the press away from these ambulances right now!" Fionna demanded as she stood and directed the reporters away from Dan and Garrett.

Two hours later, they were released from Georgetown into the care of their loving wives. Adeline was not allowing Logan to be released until he endured an entire IV bag of fluids, and she personally healed his arm and checked his cool casted bandages.

"Let's go home," Fionna urged.

"Baby, I can't. We can only hold Ben for twenty-four hours on suspicion. We have to find some evidence." Dan was still coughing though he tried to quell it for Fionna's sake.

Kaimi panicked every time Garrett coughed or cleared his throat. Dan assumed the sheer amount of time she'd inevitably spent in the waiting rooms of hospitals had led her to her frantic terror over Garrett.

"Sweetheart, I'm fine. I swear." Garrett was trying not to lose his patience, but it seemed to be a mighty task at the moment. The pain in Kaimi's eyes had him softening as he pulled her into his arms and began whispering in her ear as they headed toward the Senate.

"Dammit!" was the first thing they heard when they made their way into the Iodex offices. Ramier was shaking his head as Portwood paced.

"Every one of them is completely blank. The only good thing I can tell you is that whatever pictures of Fionna he had were deleted along with everything else." Ramier jerked his hand toward the dozens of apprehended laptop and desktop machines.

"What about the car?" Dan turned hopefully to Tuttle who was wiping his hands on a rag.

"I've been all over it. He turned off the rev limiter and heat casted the engine. If the kid hadn't lived so close to Venton, it would have blown on the road somewhere. Thank God it happened where we could get to him, but any prints were burned up instantly." Tuttle sounded as simultaneously disgusted and thankful as Dan felt.

"Could someone please explain to me how this happened?" It seemed Fionna wanted answers, and as Dan hadn't yet been able to provide her with them, she was taking them to Ioses Predilects as a whole. "How did a Shield do this? You're so good. Your shields are the only things that block out emotions for Receivers. I don't understand."

Emily had been called from practice when Logan had been burned. She was sitting by Rainer's desk nodding adamantly.

Relative discomfort worked through the men listening to her pleas as they all shifted their gaze to Dan, not certain how to answer her honestly. Dan eased her body into his with a gentle caress.

"It was several things. One of them was that he thought I should've gone to prison for what I did. He wanted to punish me himself. He sought retribution, and I'm sure Pendergrath fed that beast every single time he went to see him. Eventually, Ben let his shield take over everything else. He sought only to protect himself, and that's always a recipe for disaster."

"Yeah, and I have absolutely nothing to keep him in that cell or to even bring him in front of the governors with," Portwood huffed indignantly. "Going to see Pendergrath in prison is sketch as hell but not illegal."

Governor Haydenshire came in at that moment as Kaimi turned to him with pleading eyes.

"You're going to be able to bring him up on charges, Landon. Be patient. Jeff's father is going to come through, but we have to give him time to swallow his pride. That can be quite a bitter pill to get down."

"Jeff's dad has everything on an external computer drive," Kaimi explained.

Garrett turned to his father. "Where the hell is this drive, Dad?"

"It's on its way to Georgetown. Ultimately, it will be given to Officer Strenton who, as you all know, is the man who will have the most difficult time with all of this. In this one day, he's not only brought a baby into the world who is going to be in the hospital for quite a while and require close care after that, he's realized that people aren't always what they appear. Even men you trusted and counted as friends can turn around and stab you in the back. A classmate of his was almost killed, and he's about to meet the man who didn't even stick around for his own birth, so I'd say let's let Jeff have this one. He'll be here with that drive. I'd bet my title on it."

CHAPTER 55

APOLOGIES IN ACTION

~JEFF STRENTON~

"Here, I'll take him. Why don't you try to sleep some?" Jeff lifted Aaron from Becca's arms. He'd fallen asleep nursing again. Becca's sweet, contented smile soothed Jeff's horrifying day. She nodded and handed him a burp cloth.

They'd been instructed to nurse Aaron every two hours and then when he finished to give him a tiny bottle of enhanced formula until Becca's milk came in. He'd passed every checkup given in the last three hours with flying colors and had been allowed to stay in the room with them.

"Are you okay?" Becca asked as Jeff settled in the rocking chair by the bed to give Aaron his bottle.

"Bec, you're here and he's here. You're both completely perfect, so everything else doesn't even matter. That's all I care about."

She grinned. The tender healthy glow of her cheeks, that Jeff hadn't seen in so many weeks, had returned, and he was overwhelmed by everything that perfect moment held. Aaron grasped his finger and latched on to the bottle Jeff placed to his lips.

Aaron couldn't seem to stay awake for any length of time. His eyes were hardly ever open, but in that moment, he stared up at Jeff with his eyes just as crystal blue as Becca's and gave a contented sigh.

Jeff cradled him closer and kissed his fuzzy hairline, unable to believe he was safe in his arms. He knew he'd never deserve something so astoundingly perfect as his wife and his precious little boy. Aaron drank half of the bottle and then was sleeping too soundly to consume anymore.

"Do you want to talk about everything that happened?" Becca offered again.

Jeff shook his head. "No, I want you to rest, and I want to be in here with you. That's all I want."

Becca nodded, but worry plagued her features. "You're so good with him." Her eyes fell to their baby boy.

Jeff chuckled and shook his head though he was pleased with the assessment.

There was a timid knock on the door just before Adeline eased inside. She looked stunned momentarily. "Uh, Jeff…" She swallowed. "Your mom would like to come in and see you for a minute. She has something she needs to tell you. We'll just need to put Aaron back in his incubator." She pointed to the enclosed cradle Aaron had to stay in if anyone but Becca and Jeff was in the room.

Jeff's brow furrowed. His mom and the Sapmans had been in an hour before. The governor had even been civil and had congratulated Jeff and praised Aaron heartily.

Becca had explained that the baby would have to stay in the incubator if anyone else was in the room and kindly requested that they have him out for a few hours. It was weird that his mom would go against Becca's wishes.

Jeff watched Adeline give Aaron another quick check and then lay him in the incubator. She rechecked his oxygen tubes and then sealed the see-through cradle.

"Is Logan okay?" Becca asked though she was studying Jeff.

Adeline nodded. "Yeah, I finally let him go back to work. He was losing patience with me. They're in a mess. They have no evidence, but you already knew that. His arm is fine. I just…completely freaked out."

"I would've too," Becca assured her.

Adeline smiled. "I'll send your mom in."

"Wonder what's up with Mom?" Jeff laced his fingers in Becca's and seated himself beside her.

"Maybe she wants to see him one more time before she has to go back to work or something."

Jeff doubted that since she'd just gotten off a few hours before, but he certainly didn't have any ideas himself. "I love you." He couldn't remember if he'd told her that in the last few minutes, and he just always needed her to know.

"I know. I love you too." She eased herself to the side and lay on his chest. Jeff kissed the top of her head and gave a fervent prayer of thankfulness for all he'd been given in this endless day.

"I'm so sorry." Ms. Harrickson kept the door pressed to her body so no one else could see in the room. She sealed it back quickly and began rubbing her hands together. She seemed frightened to speak.

"What's wrong, Mom?" Jeff sat up. His shield was giving disconcerting whirs, but he had no idea what had brought that on.

"Oh...uh, well..." Ms. Harrickson's eyes fell to Aaron sleeping soundly in his incubator and tears welled in them. "He's just so precious. He looks so much like you."

Becca beamed at her. "I think so too."

"You can hold him in a few days, Mom," Jeff assured her, wondering if she was just desperate to see Aaron again.

"I know, sweetheart. I want him to be healthy. I'll wait as long as I need to." She drew a deep, steadying breath and swallowed down what Jeff assumed must've been fear. "I don't really know the right way to tell you this. I don't know if there is a right way. You've had quite a day or two, but it seems you're running out of time. I knew you wouldn't want him in here."

"Wouldn't want who in here?" His mother's obvious discomfort had Jeff's shield tensing in more violent twists.

"Your father is in the waiting room. He needs to speak with you. I told him I'd ask you for him."

"What?!" Jeff gasped. His mouth hung open in shock as fury and rejection swirled violently in his stomach.

"He has something to give you. He says it's the evidence you need to convict the young man Rainer and Logan arrested this morning." His mother's pleading words pulsed furiously against his skull.

"Jeff." Becca reached for his hand, and he supplied it out of habit more than anything else. He could think of nothing but the fact that his father had shown up at the hospital the day of his son's birth when he should have been there twenty years before. "Maybe you should go talk to him. I wish I could go with you. Maybe you could let him come in here so I can be there with you."

"No." Jeff shook his head. "No, he's not seeing you, and he's not seeing Aaron. I'll be back." He tried to steady his thundering heartbeat and the nausea that washed over him in waves of hot anger and cold disgust. His shield set against his own muscles. It was agony, but at that moment, Jeff appreciated it.

He stomped out of the room, leaving his mother and his wife in his wake. His eyes scanned the faces sitting in the maternity waiting room. Jeff was shocked to meet his father-in-law's face. Governor Sapman offered him a kind smile and stood as he neared.

"Are you okay, son?"

"I guess." Jeff wasn't certain his heart could withstand much more. There'd been too many shocking things to have experienced in one day's time.

"Look, I know I've been hard on you since you and Bec announced to me that she was pregnant, and I know you've done nothing but be a great husband to her. I may be stubborn, but I will eventually admit when I'm wrong. I've been an ass ever since the first night you showed up in that half-running truck to take my baby girl to a dance. I am sorry—very, very sorry. My wife was right. I never gave you the credit you deserved. No one makes my baby girl's face light up like you do. I don't expect you to ever accept my apology. I don't deserve that, but I want you to know that I really am sorry. You're a fine man, and I know it's been your incredibly hard work that's gotten you where you are. It's a long way from where you could have been." Governor Sapman gestured to a man leaning by the Coke machines in the back corner of the large room.

Jeff wasn't certain how to respond. He couldn't take his eyes off his own father long enough to look at the governor.

He continued, "I'm very thankful for who you are, the man you became, and for all that you are for my daughter. I want you to know that." The governor squeezed Jeff's shoulder in an effort to bolster him. "I think he has what you need to keep this kid behind bars. Do you want me to come with you to talk to him?" Jeff was absolutely astonished at Governor Sapman's kindness and concern. "I'd be happy to, or I can talk to him for you. I know out here is not where you want to be when your wife and little boy are in there." He pointed back to Becca's hospital room.

"I'm fine, sir. I do need to get back to Bec and the baby, but I'll see what he wants."

The governor slapped him on the back as Jeff forced his feet to move in the general direction of his sperm donor.

He tried not to feel the anger, tried not to remember the times he'd been hungry, the sheer number of times they'd had to move because rent was raised and his mother could no longer afford it. The hours he'd worked and then come home to study before falling asleep in his books just to start over again the next day haunted his weary bones.

The whispered disdain from other students over Jeff's lack of new clothes and new school supplies hissed in his ear. Everything people said to Becca about dating him. The governor's scowl when Jeff would open the door to his beaten-up truck and help Becca climb in formed in his mind. He clenched his jaw as he met the man's eyes. They matched his own with haunting accuracy.

"What do you want?" he choked out.

"Uh...Jeff," his father managed. He ran his hands through his thinning hair and couldn't hold Jeff's eye for any length of time.

"Yeah?"

"I'm...sorry." He nodded as if waiting on a line to appear on a teleprompter. "I'm sorry this is the first time we're meeting."

Jeff considered that. "Okay."

"I heard you'd married one of the governor's daughters. Her dad's not giving you a hard time or anything, is he?"

Jeff rolled his eyes. "I'm fine."

His father nodded again. "I'm the one who's been helping you figure out this guy at Venton. I'm 46339, or I became that."

"Iodex," Jeff quipped. He'd figured out the relatively easy code numbers quickly.

"Yeah." His father nodded. "Listen, I had a feeling your guy was gonna start erasing everything when it came out in the press that Governor Haydenshire had threatened to shut down Venton, so I casted this drive and copied off all of his hard drives. It should have everything you need including the pictures and the video of Vindico's wife. She's quite a looker," he commented, and Jeff scowled furiously. His father seemed to have realized his mistake. "Uh…not that I looked at them or anything." He didn't lie well.

"But anyway…your father-in-law says Iodex only has today to come up with enough evidence to convict this kid, and that should be everything they need." He hesitantly held out an enhanced external hard drive. Jeff took it without ever coming in contact with his father's hand.

"Thank you." He tried to feel relief that Ben would remain behind bars and that maybe they could make sense of everything that had plagued the academy for the past year, but in that moment, all Jeff could feel was anger and hurt. His father gave another nervous nod.

"Is the baby okay and everything? I heard he was early," he broached. "The news said your wife was having a hard time. Is she good now?"

"Yeah." Jeff nodded. "They're both fine. Great actually."

His father looked genuinely relieved to hear that. "That's good. I'm glad." The awkward silence seemed to bother both of them.

"Thanks," Jeff offered again and glanced back toward Becca's room. "I really need to get back to them. They may need me, and I want to be there." He couldn't stop the defiant challenge from taking flight from his tongue.

His father's eyes closed for a moment as he nodded his defeat. "Yeah, you don't want to miss that. They need you, and you should be there always. I'm sorry I wasn't." His mumbled regret cut like a dagger. Jeff tried to fight the pity he felt. He tried desperately not to feel forgiveness becoming an option in his mind.

"Maybe we'll see you around," he offered as he tried not to feel any hope at all.

284

"I'd really like that." His father's eyes held a desperation that wounded Jeff.

"You have my cell," he reminded him.

His father smiled. "Yeah, maybe when you get settled, we could go out for a bite or something. I know you're an Ioses through and through though, so whenever you think you might be ready, I'd really like to meet your family." His hand shook as he hesitantly offered it to his son.

Jeff recoiled slightly but forced himself to shake his father's hand before he rushed back to his wife and his little boy.

CHAPTER 56

WHO YOU AREN'T

"What did he say?" Becca was frantic but was still catheterized and unable to get out of the bed.

Jeff's eyes flitted to Aaron's incubator. He hated him being in there. He needed to be out and in his arms so Jeff knew he was safe. "He gave me a casted drive he says has everything we'll need to convict Ben."

Becca's mother had joined Ms. Harrickson in the room in Jeff's absence. They'd been gathered near the enclosed cradle, gazing at their grandson, but upon Jeff's return, they were both staring at him.

"Well, that was nice…kind of," Becca tried. Her hand moved to her mouth, and she began chewing on her nails. Jeff couldn't halt his grin. He loved her so much. His heart ached for all she'd been through. "Shouldn't you take it to Mentor Vindico or Chief Portwood or something?"

Jeff hadn't considered leaving the hospital until Becca was released. "No." He shook his head. "I'll just call and get someone to come get it. I'm not leaving you here."

Becca's brow furrowed. She transitioned her gaze to their mothers. "I'm sorry, but could I talk to Jeff alone for a minute, please?"

"Of course." Mrs. Sapman moved to the bed and kissed Becca's cheek. She patted Jeff's bicep and gave him a quick hug. Ms. Harrickson waved and followed Mrs. Sapman out into the hallway.

Jeff could hear them discussing Aaron as the door closed. He moved to the cradle, assuming Becca wanted their little guy out as much as he did.

"You can leave him in there. He's sleeping so well, and I want to talk to you." Jeff seated himself near her thighs. He laced his fingers through hers. He just needed a moment to feel her energy healthy and vital again. It had been so long, and the intoxicating strums of her rhythms took his breath away every time he felt them.

"I know you don't want to leave me and Aaron here, and I know seeing your dad must've been really, really hard. But I need you not to just shield out everything you're feeling because of me and Aaron. I'm okay now. Honestly, I feel better than I have in months," she explained. "We're a family now, and I wish you would talk to me about Ben or Brodie or your dad or anything. I want to be there for you. But most importantly, right now, I think you should be the one to take that over to the Senate. You should be the one to figure all of this out. It should be you. It means so much to you, and I think you need that after all of this time.

"Aaron and I will be okay here for a little while. He'll just sleep and eat until his daddy gets back from work." Jeff smiled instantly. *Daddy.* The word warmed the recesses of his weary soul and lit through his heart as fresh air entered his lungs.

"I need to be here. You can't even get up yet. I want to help you with him and with nursing him and everything. I mean, not that I do the hard work or anything." Jeff chuckled as Becca beamed up at him. "Mostly, I just keep thinking how freaking lucky our little guy is. I'm a little jealous." He winked at her. They laughed together, and Becca's giggles soothed the rest of the pain and the terror the day had brought.

"You've helped me all day long. You help me do everything. You were there despite everything going on, and I know you'll always be here when we need you. Go to work for a little while. Help your real friends figure this all out. Aaron and I will be right here when you get back. The lactation specialist will help me nurse him or with whatever he needs." The fervency of Becca's vow was the only thing that had Jeff considering leaving for a little while.

"Are you sure, because I can just get Rainer to come pick it up, and I can stay right here with you?"

"I'm sure I'll be okay, and I'm sure you need to be the one to figure this out. I know you. This has been haunting you for months. You need to know you've done everything you can to keep him in jail. Honestly, I think you need to talk to Ben before he heads to Coriolis." There was a raw pain in her whisper.

She'd had Ben Cobson pegged from the beginning. She would often roll her eyes and scowl whenever Ben would come around. She'd never liked him though she'd never really been able to figure out why. Her pain was for Jeff who felt he'd let all of Iodex down for a traitor. One of his own kind had broken the very structure of what it meant to be a Shield.

Jeff nodded his agreement. He couldn't speak. The pain he'd shut up tightly all day wound around his throat like a jagged noose.

"I don't want to leave you," he finally choked out, feeling weak and childlike himself. His head jerked to the side. Aaron was grunting sweetly in his sleep. He stretched slightly and then settled back into the warmth of his incubator. Jeff and Becca shared a tender, intimate grin.

Becca squeezed Jeff's hands. "I know, and I think you don't want to leave because you'll miss us and because some part of you is terrified that you'll somehow not be there like your father wasn't there. That will never happen. You aren't him. You are the most amazing man in the world, and you're going to be there for Aaron and for me forever. I know you will." Jeff allowed her words to wash over him like a warm, healing balm. He knew she was right. She was always right. As he allowed himself to consider actually going into work and hammering out the inflicting details of all that had been done, he felt a deep desire begin to burn low in his gut.

"You're sure?" He had to ask again.

Becca gave him her sweet grin and nodded. "Just bring me my little boy. He can keep me company while you're gone, and if I already have him, I can just nurse him whenever he wants."

"Okay." Jeff rushed to the enclosed cradle. "I want to hold him again before I go." He scooped Aaron up rather expertly he thought and heat casted his blankets again. He whispered to his son that he would return as quick as he could and then settled Aaron against Becca's chest. Aaron nuzzled his face against Becca's right breast as she tucked her bedding around him. A deep yawn contorted his tiny features, and he curled into his mother's tender embrace.

"Seriously, he's the luckiest guy on the planet, and he doesn't even really appreciate what he has." Jeff laughed with his wife as purpose coursed through his veins. He set the numerous chill-casted bottles on the rolling table and moved them to Becca.

His strength returned. He was overjoyed with the ability to tease and joke with his wife and to care for their little boy. His body needed to find the justice in the tedium of the day.

Jeff kissed the top of her head and then touched her chin and guided her face upward until their lips met. The kiss lasted longer than he had really intended, but as Becca drew from his mouth into her beautiful lips, he knew everything was going to be okay.

That kiss held every single thing he would ever need to go on.

CHAPTER 57

QUESTIONS AND ANSWERS

A few minutes later, Jeff raced into Iodex with the drive clutched tight in his fist. Suddenly, he was being heartily congratulated on becoming a dad.

To his shock, Governor Sapman was already there making apologies. He apologized to Emily and Fionna for his comments about Receivers and even made another public apology to Jeff.

"My little girl being in the hospital was more than I could stand. I'm sorry for everything I said. It's been a hell of a few months, not that that's any excuse. I am sorry, Stephen, for everything I said or did," he offered the Crown Governor very humbly. Governor Haydenshire chuckled and tucked Emily into his embrace.

"I suppose I could see where your little girl being in the hospital might make things rather difficult to endure, George. I'm just glad you're back and that Becca and your grandson are doing so well."

Things quieted down as Jeff passed around his phone with pictures of Aaron. Emily and Fionna swooned over the shots of his tiny little boy.

"You know you're not going to be getting that phone back for a little while," Dan teased as Fionna squealed over a picture of Aaron sleeping in Becca's arms. His face fell in that moment, and Jeff knew precisely what thought had crossed his mind.

"The lab class when you couldn't find your phone. The day you taught us to fight against multiple opponents!" Jeff gasped. "I beat him because you were my coach." His eyes closed in defeat as he shook his head.

"Which would've pissed him off even more," Garrett sighed.

Jeff didn't know how to handle the bitter reality of being so wrong. "I can't believe I thought he was a good guy."

Dan shook his head. "I wrote him a glowing recommendation to the New York precinct. Stop beating yourself up. Now let's finish this. Let's get the evidence together to present it to the governors."

"Yeah, let's see what's on that drive, Officer Strenton, and then let's get you back to your wife and baby," Portwood soothed.

Visible relief formed on Jeff's features, and it seemed to make Dan and Portwood smile.

Fionna returned Jeff's phone to him. "He's beautiful," she assured Jeff as she laid her head against her husband's chest. He wrapped her up in his arms.

Jeff and Portwood both turned away as tears began leaking down her face.

～

Dan Vindico

"I've got you." Her tears tugged at the scars in his heart left so long ago. "Let's get this all pieced together, and then I will put you on a plane and get you to our baby girls, okay?" he soothed in her ear as he cradled her in his tender embrace. Fionna nodded against him.

"I know. I'm just tired." She tried to convince herself that was it. He nodded his acceptance of the lie, but it was so much more than that.

She'd been without her island for too long. She'd been without her grandmother's guidance, been without their precious baby girls, and had lived the emotions of every student on campus that morning when a car had exploded in an attempted murder.

Her dignity and their privacy had been taken from them. And then she'd watched her husband—the only shield on earth strong enough to withhold her powerful rhythms—rush into a blazing fire to save a child.

"I want to hold Halia, and I want to listen to Aida talk to me. I don't care about what, just anything," she finally admitted as her fists knotted Dan's T-shirt as she clung to the only thing that could save her.

Every Iodex officer in the room gave Dan a sorrowful look as they tried to find something else to do. Garrett looked morose as Kaimi teared up as well. If Fionna was crying, then Emily was going to automatically. Rainer seemed to realize this and had her head tucked to his neck before she gave in to the tears.

Governor Haydenshire shook his head and sighed. "As horrible as this day was, I think you'll all feel better if we get this puzzle solved."

Fionna pulled away from Dan's chest and managed a slight smile as she wiped away her tears.

"Here." Jeff laid the casted drive on his desk and then raced to the storage closet and returned with a dozen blank drives. A moment later, he'd casted and duplicated the drive provided by his father and handed them out.

"Come on, sweetheart. Let's see what we can find." Dan guided Fionna into a chair beside him while Garrett eased Kaimi into his lap as he booted another Iodex enhanced laptop.

Governor Haydenshire and Governor Sapman began making coffee and ordering in food in a true show of humility and of belief in Governor Lawson's decree that one job should never be held higher than another, and that every Predilect was needed for the Realm to function as it was meant to.

"All right, here are the emails from Wilshire and Bryant." Dan pointed to his screen. He'd decided to work from the earliest time stamps and move forward. Garrett spun in his chair, and Kaimi giggled as he'd effectively swung her with him though he'd grasped her waist to keep her from falling off his right thigh. Jeff, Rainer, Emily, and Logan, who'd been going over emails sent out to students demanding money, leaned closer as well.

"Right, but we've already seen those." Fionna's brow furrowed.

"Right, but this means Ben had them as well," Dan explained as he flipped through the emails he'd gone through so many months before. "Right here!" His voice rose as he found precisely what he was looking for. He began reading and shaking his head in shocked disbelief.

"Because if students from Mentor Bryant's classes were given the casted drives, and she was plugging them in to her laptop then everything on there was being copied, right?" Kaimi's intrigue lit as she watched the officers make sense of each piece of the intricate puzzle.

"Right, sweetheart." Garrett grinned and kissed her cheek.

"And she used her Venton laptop to email him because then her husband wouldn't see them," Kaimi continued.

Every married officer in the room including Ryan Tuttle shuddered in disgust. But they hadn't heard the half of it. Dan was staring at the answers he'd been after for so long it infuriated him. He narrowed his eyes and went forward with his decrees.

"Jeff, I'm sorry, but I'm putting out a warrant for your father's arrest and one for Ron Clover, the head of Venton accounting." Dan waved over two of the Iodex record keepers and instructed the warrants to be printed and acted upon immediately.

Confusion furrowed Jeff's brow though he didn't argue. "Okay, but why?" he finally asked.

"If he knew all of this, he's going to have to do some pretty big talking to convince me he didn't know who was doing this. That's obstruction of justice. In all of his help, if he knew more, he should have come forward."

Portwood, who'd joined the grouping a moment later, nodded his agreement.

"Okay, but maybe he was trying to let *us* figure it out." Garrett tried to discreetly gesture his head to Jeff. Dan shook his head and spun the laptop he was working on so that Garrett could read the emails he'd just discovered.

"Are you fucking kidding me?" Garrett gasped. Portwood's eyes goggled as the governors moved in.

Jeff shrugged. "It's fine with me. If he knew, he should have crawled out from under his rock. Don't *not* arrest him because of me." Jeff's disgust with his father concerned Dan, but he saw no other way to handle the situation. Suddenly, Dan's own father entered Iodex.

"Dad!" Dan gasped. "You're supposed to be home resting."

Fionna hugged the governor fiercely. "Are you sure you're okay?" She sounded as panicked as Dan felt. Governor Vindico chuckled as he embraced his daughter-in-law sweetly.

"I'm fine, you two. I'd kind of like to hear what we've found, and I'm sick to death of lying around. Your mother's driving me to distraction. I'll ease up, but I don't think a few hours at work will finish me off."

Governor Haydenshire grinned as he gestured to a nearby chair. "Sit, and we'll let our children regale us with their knowledge, only this time they do actually know what they're talking about unlike, say, fifteen years ago."

Governor Vindico laughed heartily as he nodded his agreement. "My favorite was, 'we weren't stealing them, Dad, we were relocating them.'" Governor Vindico and Governor Haydenshire both laughed over the memory as Dan cringed as the story was told yet again. Fionna began giggling, which brought a smile back to Dan's face.

"We do actually need to figure this out." Garrett rolled his eyes.

"Go ahead, Garrett." Governor Haydenshire lost all sense of playful banter. But Garrett shook his head and opened another few emails. His eyes narrowed as he read.

"Governor Vindico, I don't think you're going to have any trouble letting Wilshire fall now."

Kaimi's mouth hung open, "Wow," she gasped.

"Okay, someone talk," Portwood ordered.

Dan turned the laptop back to read Garrett's latest discovery. He drew a deep, steadying breath. "It seems Mr. Cobson became wise to Wilshire and Bryant's affair via their email from her laptop. He threatened to go public with the affair if Wilshire didn't cough up several thousand dollars every paycheck. Obviously, not wanting his wife to wonder where a quarter of his paychecks were going, it seems Wilshire talked Ron Clover into forwarding the required money to Ben from the Venton accounts. That's why he's been putting so much money back in the academy. He was probably able to add it in more discreetly that way. But it looks like Clover wanted more. So, either Wilshire allowed this or Clover did it on his own, but he set up both Chase Satzman and Katherine Bryant. Honestly, Fi, if you hadn't vouched for her, I would be arresting Bryant right now. This was done well."

"Wait, so Mr. Clover set up an entire mentor's paycheck, but you don't know if Wilshire knew about it or not?" Fionna asked. She seemed thirsty for justice as well. "And why couldn't we see those emails when Jeff cloned Wilshire's laptop?"

"Because he'd deleted them," Jeff, Dan, and Garrett all answered.

Portwood nodded. "He was trying to cover up every crime he was attached to. He paid back what he took out, and he failed to understand that removing an email from his laptop doesn't remove every copy of it everywhere it's ever existed."

"Let's go get the good chancellor for me, would you?" Governor Vindico ordered two of the low-level officers.

"Yes, sir."

Dan thought back to the morning in his father's office when he'd found out about the donations. He wondered just how much Katherine Bryant was aware of. His shield gave its customary shift. Not something most Ioses Predilects ever felt, but Dan closed his eyes to allow his other Predilect to formulate in his mind.

His eyes flashed open. He had no way of proving his theory if he couldn't get the Bryants to talk. *Fionna.* He did have a way to know if anyone was lying to him. She didn't have to testify if he could simply convince the Bryants that they wouldn't be able to lie.

"Reynolds," he commanded.

"Sir?"

"Pick up Katherine Bryant for me while you're getting Wilshire," Dan barked. "Terry's already in lock up."

Reynolds nodded his understanding as he and his partner shrugged on their coats and headed out to the squad car.

"Jeff, can you and Ramier find me everything you can about the account we shut down? I need to know who all was being paid out of that extra paycheck."

"Sure, sir," Jeff agreed.

Dan was rather impressed with Jeff's clarity of thought given that in the last twenty-four hours he'd become a father, met his own father for the first time, seen an arrest warrant signed for the man, one of his classmates had nearly been murdered, and a guy he'd counted as a friend turned out to be a criminal of epic proportion.

CHAPTER 58

SAFE AND SOUND

~JEFF STRENTON~

J eff tried to be completely silent as he eased back into Becca's room. He was beyond exhausted. His eyes blinked rapidly as they fought to stay open. A contented grin spread across his face as he took in Becca sound asleep in the bed and Aaron tucked safely in the incubator, also sound asleep. He moved to her bed and pulled the covers over her. He wondered how long they'd been out.

He brushed tender kisses on Becca's cheek and then scrubbed his hands before he lifted the incubator top to kiss Aaron. He gave another fervent prayer of overwhelming gratitude. After everything he'd seen and discovered that day, having his wife and his little boy there with him in all of their sweet, uncorrupted transparency was more than he could even comprehend at the late hour.

Glancing around the room, Jeff was too tired to begrudge sleeping in the slight leatherette recliner that accompanied the birthing suite at Georgetown. He settled in and was sound asleep a moment later.

～

The first vestiges of sunlight appeared over the skyline when Jeff awoke to the sounds of Aaron's rhythmic sucks and contented sighs as he nursed. Scrubbing his hands over his face, Jeff shook himself awake. He was going to need an entire pot of coffee if he was going to get through this day without falling asleep standing in the Senate Chamber.

"Sorry. I was trying to let you sleep." Becca stared down at Aaron who was consuming the beginnings of her milk with rabidity.

"How'd you get him out of the cradle?"

"They removed the catheter last night, so I can stand and even pee all by myself." Becca giggled.

Jeff slid out of the chair and joined his family on the bed.

Adeline peaked in with a broad grin. "I was in here an hour ago, and none of you woke up. Aaron looked so content in the cradle I didn't really check him well, but it looks like he's gotten the hang of nursing." She hooked a heart rate measuring device to Aaron's foot. Jeff was impressed at how Adeline was able to check him thoroughly while he nursed.

"Logan tried to tell me everything you found out yesterday. He was so tired when he got home last night I'm not sure I understood everything, but good grief." Adeline shook her head as she checked Aaron's mouth when Becca switched him to her left breast to continue nursing.

Jeff chuckled as Aaron's face scowled. He didn't seem to appreciate the pause in his breakfast and was contemplating wailing out his disapproval. Becca swooned and helped him continue his meal.

"The whole thing is insane," Jeff agreed.

Intrigue lit Becca's beautiful face. She wanted to ask but seemed to decide to wait until Adeline left them alone.

"He's eating well. He still needs to be nursed every two hours, and still give him a bottle afterward. Colostrum is great for him but until your milk is fully in, I still want him to have the formula. He may not want it, and that's okay, but the more weight the better for right now. I'd say he's going to be just fine." Adeline's assurances washed over Jeff. They restored his waning energies.

"What time do you have to go before the governors?" Adeline asked as she took Becca's blood pressure.

Jeff drew a deep breath. "I'm going into work at eight. The

arraignments begin at ten." He was shocked he'd recalled that so easily. His brain was sluggish and confused.

"There's more than one?" Becca's curiosity got to her, and she went ahead with her question.

Jeff chuckled at her intrigue. He tried to envision coming home from work every day to their home just a few miles away and taking care of their little guy together.

He allowed himself a moment to envision telling her about his day and the cases they were working, helping her make dinner, playing with Aaron, and then… He swallowed as he went on with the fantasy of getting her back in bed with him, under him, in his shield, the delicate tremble and the hungry gasp as he made them one. He wanted all of it so badly he could taste it.

"Yeah." Jeff drew a deep breath and tried to regulate his thoughts. "I'll tell you everything, but the entire thing is completely insane."

Adeline nodded her agreement as she made a few notes on Becca's chart.

Jeff continued, "They arrested my dad, but they let him go. It turns out he knew all the stuff, but he hadn't been able to pin it to a student directly. He hadn't even figured out he was in Ioses, but after they let him go, he just kept apologizing. It was weird." Jeff's chest began to unfetter as he began the long, sordid tale.

CHAPTER 59

FEAR

~DAN VINDICO~

"I still cannot believe this." Fionna was trying desperately to finish packing, but she was so tired it seemed to be more than she was capable of completing. Dan tenderly grabbed her shoulders.

"Come to bed with me for a couple of hours before we have to go back. We need some sleep."

Everything they'd discovered weighed heavily in his mind. Vile revulsion over the corruptness of the world weighted his shield. She felt it as well. She wanted so badly to get to the girls, but they had to sleep even if it delayed their move another day. "Please." Dan strengthened his plea.

With a nod, she set the hair product bottles she'd been arranging in a bag down on the counter and let him lead her to their bed. He gazed into her beautiful sienna eyes and then slowly began undressing her. He wanted her beautiful body bare and intertwined in his own.

He needed to reclaim what had been taken from him. He needed to restore the intimacy between them.

They'd weeded through hours upon hours of lies, and she'd methodically climbed through the guilt and the anger, the indiscretions that led to more lies that ultimately led to attempted murder. She'd gone with him to visit Brodie in the hospital. The world had taken its toll, and Dan sought only to restore her. He was whole only when she was fulfilled.

Her breaths came rhythmically as she watched him slip her bra from her arms. Her eyes were heavy in their exhaustion. Dan allowed himself but one kiss as he lifted her into his arms and laid her in their bed. He stripped off his clothes, hoping futilely that the emotions of their endless days might fall with his clothing to the floor and give his weary soul peace. He smiled as Fionna curled up safely on his chest. He cradled her body to his own.

"I'm right here. I've got you, and I'll always have you," he assured her.

She clung to him fiercely. "I know, and I know that I have to let you be you. I have to let you be an Iodex officer because that's who you are, and I love you so much. It scares me how much I love you. When you ran into that fire…" She pricked the tightly knitted cap of her emotions, and Dan tried to reassure her.

~

Garrett Haydenshire

"Welcome home, buddy. For a little while anyway." Garrett sighed as he set Duke down, after they'd rescued him from the farm. Their puppy circled around them in the apartment entryway, afraid they were going to leave him yet again.

"Poor baby." Kaimi seated herself on the floor in front of the couch, and Duke leapt into her lap and licked her face enthusiastically. She'd been yawning for the past several hours, but it seemed Duke was going to be loved before she would allow herself sleep.

When their retriever seemed assured they were staying put, he made his way to the bedroom. Garrett lifted him up into the bed just as he attempted the jump himself. Kaimi pulled on one of Garrett's clean T-shirts as he stripped down to boxers and climbed into their bed.

He was shocked at how much he missed the island and their home on the farm. They'd only been there a few short days, but his center seemed to have set there. He was going to miss DC though, which was not something he'd thought would ever happen.

"Want to talk?" he asked as Kaimi lay on his chest and began nervously tugging at the ends of her hair. She didn't respond which was answer enough. Garrett let his eyes close for a split second as he tried to figure out what to say. "Hey." He turned so he could look into that copper fire that ignited his soul. "Just tell me, sweetheart. You're scared. You're furious with me because you're scared. You're confused. You're disgusted. I'm good with it all. I just want you to talk to me."

"I don't understand everything," she finally confessed.

Garrett brushed her hair behind her right ear. "I've been working this case since before I met you, and I'm not sure I understand everything we found out today."

She offered him a weak smile and then pulled her body even closer to his. "I don't understand how everything spun so out of control. Everyone we talked to kept saying they thought he was a good kid. Dan wrote him a recommendation. I don't understand." She repeated her plea. "How could so many people have done so many bad things?"

Garrett sighed. "Fear, greed, lust, all of the big ones. They all got in over their heads, and there were so many pieces to that shit house of cards, no one knew how to end it until it blew up in a car fire on campus this morning."

"That really scared me." Pain and terror perforated her weary whisper.

"I know, baby. I'm sorry. I didn't mean to scare you, but I had to help him. That's who I am." He tried to explain to her what being a Shield was supposed to mean. Ben Cobson had perverted the true definition so badly no one seemed able to understand it.

"I know." She nestled her head under his chin, making him smile as he wrapped his arms around her.

Being married to a Shield wasn't an easy job. Until that moment, it wasn't something Garrett thought would ever apply to him, but here he was holding his beautiful, ethereal, magical wife in his arms and trying to somehow make it okay that he was more than willing to put his life on the line to save others.

CHAPTER 60
TRIALS
~DAN VINDICO~

"Dad, just don't do this today," Dan begged his father yet again as he and Fionna stood in Iodex awaiting the arraignments. "Give it some time. Give yourself some time to heal."

"Daniel, please. Go do your job, and let me do mine," Governor Vindico commanded angrily. Fionna touched Dan's arm and gave a minute headshake. With a sigh of abject frustration, Dan clenched his jaw shut.

"Hey, Danny, why don't you and Officer Strenton take Mr. Cobson down?" Portwood urged.

The nerves in the room were palpable. They quaked in the Gifted energies that surrounded him. Dan followed Jeff toward the holding cells while everyone else headed to the chamber room.

"Did you get to see Becca and Aaron before you had to come back?" Dan noticed Jeff slowed his pace the closer they came to the hall of holding cells.

"Yeah, for a little while. She was nursing him again when I left. Her milk came in so he's pretty happy about that, I guess." Jeff's brow furrowed, and blood flooded his cheeks. "That's probably not something I should say to people. I'm sorry. I'm just stupid tired."

Dan chuckled. "I wouldn't volunteer that around too much, but I just had a baby so I'm good with it. And that stupid tired thing won't really get any better until he's sleeping through the night."

"Great," Jeff sighed. "Are you still good with us signing the papers tonight at the hospital?" He seemed to suddenly remember.

"Yeah, Fi's thrilled to get to see Becca and Aaron."

Jeff halted abruptly at the entryway door that led to the now full set of holding cells.

"I don't know what to say to him, sir." His exhaustion and the sheer emotion of the last two days seemed to finally be threatening to pull Jeff Strenton under.

"You don't have to say anything to him. I'm planning on letting my mouth run. I'm so disgusted with him I may hit him. We'll see. Garrett always says never to plan anything, to just go with it because it's less liability that way." Dan grinned.

He and Garrett had been doing this for the past decade, and he couldn't wait to command Iodex in the great state of Hawaii with his best friend by his side. Jeff nodded and seemed to swallow down bile as Dan shoved the door open with a bang and stalked to Ben's cell.

"Let's go, Mr. Cobson. The governors are anxiously awaiting your arrival," Dan sneered as he unlocked the cell and jerked Ben Cobson out. He slammed him up against the wall as Jeff snapped cuffs back on him. "Boot him up," Dan ordered. With a slight nod, Jeff attached shackles around Ben's ankles.

Ben was scowling viciously as Dan shoved him forward.

"Enjoy the walk, Mr. Cobson. It'll be the last one you're taking for a while. They bring you your meals in Coriolis."

"You still think he's the shit?" Ben spat at Jeff as he directed his head back to Dan. Jeff's brow furrowed in confusion. "You were such a moron. Worshipped the ground he walked on. He doesn't give a shit about you. All he cares about is exactly what he told us the first fucking day of school. His Angel who'll be a whore for him whenever he wants and the fuck trophies she made him."

Jeff's mouth hung open in a gasped shock as he slid out of the way just as Dan's fist landed squarely in Ben's face, bringing him to the ground.

"Got anything else to say, Cobson?" Dan snarled in his face.

He pulled Ben up and then shoved him into the chamber room. His father's eyes closed in defeat as Ben spit out several teeth. Blood seeped from his nose and lips. Fionna's hand flew to her own mouth as her eyes goggled.

"Could I get a medio to heal Mr. Cobson? He fell," Dan menaced.

Two Senate medios rushed forward to fix Ben's jaw so he was able to speak on his own behalf.

"Daniel." Governor Haydenshire motioned him forward to the bench. "Considering everything you've been dealing with and what he took from you, I'm not going to ask you what really happened to Mr. Cobson, but I am going to remind you that you need to run Hawaii by the books. Hang up the cowboy hat here, please."

Dan nodded his agreement as he moved to the witness benches. He was called to the stand first.

"I want to hear this from the beginning, Commander Vindico. Every gory detail, I suppose," Governor Haydenshire urged.

"Yes, sir. I'll tell you what we've learned from the evidence provided us yesterday from the crime scene and from copies of Mr. Benjamin Cobson's computers. I apologize for this not being linear, but I'll do the best I can. A great deal of it was happening at the same time."

Governor Eleanor nodded. "That's fine, Commander Vindico. Just start from as close to the beginning as you can get us and walk us through it."

With a nod, Dan began, "Last year two students, both seniors who worked in the computer lab, broke into the Venton test vault. They successfully stole three final exams, copied them, and passed them out to their friends. They also sold a few copies to some students who likely wouldn't have passed without them. Ben Cobson, a junior at Venton at the time, learned of this, and instead of turning the men in, he decided he could do it better.

"But he wanted to do some research on the best way to set up something like this. He'd studied the work of the Interfeci at school and knew of Candor Pendergrath's arrest last year. It seems Ben created a fake ID using his real photo and a fake name to visit

Pendergrath forty-seven times before Candor's death. Per testimony given by Candor Pendergrath's son, Clarence, after Candor's death, Ben turned his questions on Clarence. He is willing to go under oath at Mr. Cobson's trial to discuss the questions Ben asked him."

The governors all nodded but didn't hide their shock well. Only Governor Haydenshire smiled.

"Keep going, Dan," Governor Vindico urged.

"Ben worked at the Venton computer lab all six years that he was a student at Venton. The academy decided to try to lessen paper waste. In order to do that, they had the students use thumb drives to turn in most of their work. Ben casted the thumb drives with what Elite Technology Specialist Officer Jeff Strenton calls a worm type virus. It would embed itself in all of the Venton mentors' laptops and feed him back information from their computers. His plan was to profit off copies of the tests, quizzes, exams, and the answer keys that he could sell.

"Around the same time the test vault was being broken into, Chancellor of Venton Academy, Dean Wilshire, began having an illicit extramarital affair with Mentor Katherine Bryant. Mr. Cobson learned of this affair by means of the thumb drives he'd casted that Mentor Bryant was plugging into her laptop."

"We'll get to the affair in just a minute, Dan. Right now tell me more about the tests that were being copied," Governor Haydenshire requested.

"Yes, sir. Officer Strenton estimates that well over a thousand tests were copied and sold to nearly seventy-five percent of the student population at Venton. This was corroborated by confessions from most of the student body." Dan drew a breath as the governors all nodded their morose understanding.

"There were websites that hosted old copies of exams given with permission by the mentors to be used for studying. Mr. Cobson frequented those sites and ultimately hacked his way into their email databases. He would then email out the offers of copies of upcoming tests in an effort to gain himself customers."

Dan shook his head as he tried to remember which came first, the chicken or the egg. "When that money didn't seem enough, Ben began blackmailing the students who had purchased the tests. He employed several other students as his debt collectors. I have their names here." Dan handed a sheet of paper to the court clerk. "If I may, I'd like to remind the board that blackmail was Candor Pendergrath's specialty. It would not tax my imagination to believe that Ben was being heavily influenced by Candor.

"None of the students being blackmailed knew who was running the show. He was rather methodical in his planning. The bribery aspect brings me back to the affair between Dean Wilshire and Katherine Bryant."

"All right, go on with that," Governor Eleanor urged.

"As I stated, Ben found out about the affair through emails from Wilshire to Bryant and vice versa. He phoned the chancellor and informed him that he would go public with their affair if he wasn't paid each and every month for his silence. Wilshire was obviously in a bind. I myself read the emails between him and Katherine Bryant, and I can tell you there was a great deal of fiery passion between them. The kind that will always leave you burned.

"Wilshire would not have wanted the Internet flooded with the copies of those emails, but he also couldn't pay out the kind of money Ben was requiring without his wife becoming aware of his affair. He paid off the head of accounting at Venton Academy, Mr. Ron Clover, to make the payout to Cobson each month from the Venton accounts. Former Chancellor Wilshire is in the holding cells with the charges of felony embezzlement. However, in order to rectify the books, Chancellor Wilshire made donations back to the school's primary account in smaller increments than the single payout going to Cobson. This, presumably, was so that his wife would not wonder about the money coming out in monthly withdrawals of the same amounts.

"It seems Katherine Bryant knew nothing of this. Ron Clover, however, didn't feel he was being paid quite enough for keeping his services silent, so he used a former mentor from the study abroad program's name to set up a full mentor's paycheck. He hid it well. The paycheck would bounce into Katherine Bryant's checking account for a very few minutes before it was moved out to an account set up by Clover.

"Chancellor Wilshire didn't know how Ben found out about his affair, and he proceeded to hammer out the details of his embezzlement with Clover via email. Ben had access to them all. When Clover set up the additional paycheck for himself, Ben moved in and let him know that if he didn't share the funds, he would go to Iodex with everything, so the paycheck was moved to an account set up by Mr. Cobson using one of my old aliases from my days on the Elite Squadron. It was then split three ways." Dan shook his head. "Mr. Cobson is of the opinion that I was not punished enough for what happened at the takedown of the Interfeci last spring."

Governor Haydenshire turned and glared at Cobson. "Ever heard the quote, 'Justice without mercy is tyranny,' Mr. Cobson? I highly doubt that's something Candor Pendergrath would've taught you when you decided to become his protégé, because that might've been worth knowing. I'm going to implore you to think about where you're sitting today. Would you prefer this court show you no mercy in the same way that you decided Commander Vindico deserved none when you had no firsthand knowledge of what occurred at that takedown or what brought it on?" He turned back to Dan without awaiting any response from Ben. "Go on, Dan."

With a nod, Dan continued. "When I was given access to copies of Wilshire's laptop at the beginning of this school year, the incriminating emails had been deleted, or obviously, I would have been sitting here months ago with this evidence."

Governor Vindico's brow furrowed. "You said the additional paycheck was split three ways. Who else was getting part of the paycheck?"

"Yes, sir." Dan sighed. "It seems Terry Bryant, Katherine's husband, became suspicious of his wife's extra hours and did a little hacking of his own via his wife's Venton laptop. Instead of confronting his wife about her affair, he decided he'd rather make a financial gain. He went to Wilshire and volunteered to be paid to keep his mouth shut. The entire Facebook snow job he put on just before his children's custody hearing was a sham.

"He'd known all along but wanted to come off as the victim. Wilshire went to Clover in a panic, and Clover cut him a deal. He'd share one-third of the extra paycheck each month as long as Wilshire never spoke of his embezzlement. I would also like to point out that Terry Bryant is both physically and emotionally abusive to his wife, Katherine, as was witnessed by myself and my wife."

Governor Haydenshire looked sick as Fionna nodded from the seats. "Continue and please arrange another trial between Katherine and Terry Bryant, clerk. I have a few things I'd like to amend."

"When Wilshire was relieved of his duties, Clover was concerned Governor Vindico might stumble upon his doctoring of the books. It seems Wilshire let them slide for many years, making the ability to embezzle hundreds of thousands of dollars easier. Clover became frantic when the teams from the Senate Bank were brought in to go over the books with a fine-tooth comb, and all of the Venton accountants were given mandatory vacation for three weeks. Terry Bryant decided he needed to be on campus every day to make certain his extra paycheck remained intact.

"He pushed for a job in the Duco department after three Duco mentors quit rather abruptly in the middle of the year. After a little more digging, Senate Banking Vice President William Haydenshire discovered that though the mentors were full-time and had worked over five years apiece, their paychecks were abruptly lowered. It seems Clover cut their pay in an effort to open a spot up for Terry Bryant. So, they quit and sought employment elsewhere.

"This brings me to another problem Mr. Cobson decided he could profit off of."

Governor Sapman held up his hand. "Before you continue, have the Duco mentors who quit corroborated this?"

"Yes, sir, and they are willing to testify. Iodex has also provided you copies of the Venton books, and William Haydenshire has highlighted where and when their paychecks were abruptly lowered. He is also willing to testify."

"Excellent work, Commander. Please continue."

"Mr. Cobson realized that Representative Sandra Ellington's daughter, Libby Ellington, was using drugs on a regular basis. Ben assumed Libby's father, Medio Winston Ellington, had been changing her tests for her, so that she was not removed from Venton to attend rehab. He contacted Medio Ellington and arranged for money to be paid to have any and all positive tests changed to negative.

"Medio Ellington accepted no money for doing this, but he did change approximately fifty-seven drug tests in the last two years. Mr. Cobson charged twelve hundred dollars apiece for each changed test, and then would go back and blackmail the students who had paid him for additional money later on. Libby, of course, knew what was happening, and Ben did share some of his funding with her to keep her quiet, which she presumably used to support her habit.

"She was, however, unaware of who was running the show. She contacted him via email, and we have confiscated her laptop as well. As of yesterday, when Mr. Cobson realized we were closing in and that one of his former employees had come forward and helped us, he wanted revenge. Evidence suggests that he removed the rev limiter from Brodie Quentin's Corvette and heat casted the engine. This resulted in the car bursting into flames on campus yesterday morning.

"Mr. Quentin is currently in Georgetown hospital recovering from burns to his legs and feet. We have no physical evidence relating Cobson to the car explosion, but I can tell you that he did a great deal of research on Gifted websites on how to cause the very engine of the car in question to explode forty-eight hours ago."

"That'll be circumstantial, Dan—you and I both know that—but I'd say that's one hell of a coincidence, Mr. Cobson," Governor Haydenshire snarled angrily. "Do you have anything to say on your behalf before I give my many decrees, or shall I proceed?"

"Doesn't really matter what I say, does it? Whatever he says you're just gonna buy like you always have. Doesn't matter what he does or how many laws he breaks. If Dan Vindico's talking, everyone's buying his bullshit," Ben huffed indignantly.

"You can change both your tone and your verbiage or I'll hold you in contempt. I have a question I'd like you to answer whether or not you speak on your own defense today or not. Why do you think we believe Commander Vindico when he presents evidence, Mr. Cobson?" He waited to see if Ben would answer, but he didn't. "I'm not certain what it is you resent most from your mentor. Is it his tireless work ethic? His adoration of his wife and family, or the fact that he worked and earned his status in this Realm and in this courtroom, so that we do believe what he says because he's never given us reason not to?"

"He didn't earn anything," Ben snarled. "His daddy's a governor and his best friend's daddy is the Crown. Same way Strenton is wearing a badge now because of who he knocked up."

Governor Haydenshire halted Governor Sapman's retort with a headshake. "Yes, Commander Vindico was born into privilege as were all of my children. But the distinctive line you are refusing to see, because it serves your purposes, is what those of us in power choose to do with our privilege. We cannot change our names or our birthright. But we can choose each and every day to use what we've been given to try to level the playing field for everyone else.

"Dan, and all of my sons who are in this courtroom today, have never rested on their laurels or on my paycheck. They have worked day in and day out to make this Realm a better place. Mr. Strenton was not born into privilege. In fact, he had much the same beginnings as you. The distinctive difference there is that he did take the opportunities provided to him and he worked day in and day out to try to better himself and the world around him. Becca's love and his badge were not handed to him, Mr. Cobson. He worked to earn them.

"So, while you will never be a governor's son or son-in-law, you could have had the same accolades all of the men you're so angry at have. Instead of using the opportunities and smarts you've been given, you decided to let the unfair circumstances your life handed you rule your shield.

"I know about your mother deciding she'd rather you no longer be in her life, and about your father agreeing to pay for your education as long as he didn't have to have any further involvement with you. And I'm certain those were crushing things to have endured, but instead of reaching out to people who would have been more than happy to help you and to have been there for you, Mentor Vindico included, you decided to prove to the world that you didn't need anyone at all. You sought out a vile criminal to continue to feed your vengeance. Candor

Pendergrath was many things, but he was an opportunist above everything else. He saw you as a way to have one last say, and he used you to his ends, I have no doubt. But Candor did not make you come to him. You went of your own volition.

"You let your shield push out the rest of the world. An Ioses Shield is to do just that. It is to protect, to harbor those you love and those you serve, and yes, certainly yourself, but you allowed your greed and your defiance to corrupt your shield. Now, we sit here in a shielded tangle of lies you created.

"Instead of the protector you were born to be, you became the very thing you should have sought to protect others from. You've thrown away numerous opportunities at a very, very young age, and you're more than welcome to be angry. You can be angry at Commander Vindico, or at me, or my sons, or at your parents, or at anyone at all, but I can tell you this—your anger will only serve to make you its master. As you can certainly see, if you'll allow yourself half a breath to admit your own guilt, you'll realize that everything you've done, all of the anger and vengeance toward other people, has only burned you.

"Actions born out of anger never ride alone. They are inevitably and unequivocally accompanied by regret. You almost murdered one of your classmates. Let that sink in with you for a moment. Really consider the consequences of this very slippery slope you knowingly threw yourself down, because as we've all seen here, one lie begets another and then another. Very soon, you're no longer even capable of recognizing the truth. You allowed yourself to exist in a shield of lies, Mr. Cobson, and now you've ensnared yourself with your own shield."

Governor Haydenshire turned to Portwood. "Mr. Cobson will be held in Coriolis prison until the time of his trial." Speaking again to Cobson, he continued, "After that, we'll see if perhaps you've learned something and we can make Felsink your new abode. But attempted murder is not something this court will ever take lightly. Your intentions were quite clear, whether they worked out how you intended or not."

"Yes, sir." Portwood jerked Cobson off the bench and dragged him back toward the Iodex offices.

Governor Haydenshire continued. "I'm in the mood to put an end to this disaster for good. If I could have the Elite Squadron please bring in the following people—Katherine Bryant, Terry Bryant, Dean Wilshire, Ron Clover, and Medio Winston Ellington. We'll adjourn for a few moments."

CHAPTER 61
TRIBULATIONS

Dan and Garrett shared an expression that said it was odd to remain seated, but that it was time to turn the page. Dan had handed in his newly acquired Elite badge that morning. Bringing Ben Cobson into the courtroom had been his last act as an Elite officer.

They both had their Hawaiian Iodex badges strung proudly on their belts, and the next morning they were flying out to their new homes and their new lives.

Emily had decided to throw the Thrilling Romance party that night at her home. It was to be a going-away party for Fionna. Since Kaimi was attending, Chloe was not. While their wives were indulging in libations and purchasing sex products, Dan and Garrett were going out to Big Mickey's subs with the Elite Squadron one last time.

Dan swallowed down his pride and his sorrow as he watched Jeff stand and follow Rainer and Logan out of the courtroom to acquire the rest of the prisoners.

Jeff Strenton deserved better, but he always gave so much more than was required. He was a Shield through and through, not one that could be corrupted because he'd lived the cold, cruel reality of the world, and he'd never let his ego keep him from asking for help when he needed it. Dan's eyes closed in a quick prayer that Jeff and Becca could find happiness together with their son, and that Jeff would get a few breaks in the coming years.

Having a time and a date when her girls would be back in her arms seemed to have soothed Fionna's frantic rhythms. That and knowing no one had photographs of her naked and a video of her begging for more.

Dan himself had deleted them from the drives Jeff's father had turned over. Governor Haydenshire had endured a very brief glimpse to corroborate another charge against Ben.

Dan drew a deep breath and gazed at his wife. There would never be photos made of the two of them making love ever again because privilege was a two-sided coin. It never came without expectations. He couldn't be proud of his work, and his father's work, and his wife's hard work, and then begrudge the people they'd worked for simply because they had expectations. He was a governor's son, and that meant he would always be known for his last name more than any title he himself ever earned.

She would always be America's Summation Sweetheart, and that meant other people had expectations of her. She didn't have to shoulder that responsibility if she didn't want to, but every action has a consequence. It wasn't fair, but it was the way the world worked. Governor Haydenshire was correct. To those who much was given much was expected, too much sometimes, but that wasn't going to change.

Fionna was smiling with tender pride as she watched Jeff step into his adult life as he paraded the long line of detainees back into the courtroom.

They assembled in front of the long bench of governors who'd returned at the same moment. Dan watched his father narrow his eyes with disgust and bitter regret.

He's still going through with this. Dan knew in that moment, and he was overwhelmed with the sickening loss.

Governor Haydenshire nodded his appreciation to Elite as they returned to their seats on the witness benches.

"Where shall I start?" He shook his head. "Medio Winston Ellington, please step forward."

Ellington looked shocked to have been called upon first. He padded forward.

"Yes, sir." He cleared his throat and stared up at Governor Haydenshire with a great deal of both respect and regret etching the lines of his face.

"I'd like to hear your plan going forward. Let's assume you aren't imprisoned for your part in this debacle, and the Senteon allows the punishment that you will never work in the medical field in this Realm be the only one. Where will we be seeing you?"

Ellington swallowed harshly and appeared afraid to hope. "My daughter needs a great deal of help. I'd like to see that she gets that help and to be there to see her through rehab. That's an extremely difficult process, which will ultimately have to go on the rest of her life." Bitter tears leaked down the man's face in the fervency of his plea. "I don't know where it will put my wife and her career, but we both allowed our priorities to get completely out of balance. We placed importance on the wrong things, and Libby was ultimately who suffered for our mistakes," he managed in a choked whisper.

Governor Haydenshire was visibly impressed. "You will still have to stand trial, Mr. Ellington, but for now, I'm sending you home. Be with your wife and your daughter. Try to put the shattered remains of this back into a life you can be proud of. Perhaps you should discuss Representative Ellington's stance on addiction with her. Perspective is a powerful teacher. Your daughter will be sent to the Virginia State Auxiliary drug rehab facility for the next four months. It is not a closed facility, so I expect both you and your wife to be there any day the program allows."

"We will. Thank you, sir," Ellington gushed.

"Would the Bryants step forward, please?" Governor Haydenshire demanded. "In light of newly presented evidence, I'd like to call to a vote redacting the decisions voted upon at the Bryants' custody hearing. All in favor say aye."

Ayes rang out from every member of the governing board. Dan was impressed.

"The board nominates Crown Governor Stephen Haydenshire to set and establish the ruling involving both Terry and Katherine Bryant," Governor Vindico decreed.

Governor Haydenshire nodded his understanding. "First of all, Mr. Bryant, let me say that I will never allow anyone to make a mockery of my courtroom and to knowingly lie under oath. Now, as for the den of vipers you and your wife leapt into, I suppose my position here is to weigh one sin against another, when I firmly believe one led *to* the other. With every harsh word or criticism, every single time you raise your hand to your wife, you dismantle your own already broken life stone by bitter stone. And as you learned, houses don't burn down slowly. Think about the example you're leaving for your children. Would you want someone treating your son or daughter the way you've treated your wife?"

Terry Bryant fought the shame but offered no response.

"I asked you a question, Mr. Bryant, and I want an answer." Governor Haydenshire's infuriated command shook through the room.

"No," Bryant choked. "No, sir. I wouldn't."

"Katherine, you have petitioned for divorce four times since your custody hearing. Would this be due to what you would consider an escalation of physical violence against you or the children?" The difference in tone the governor used between Terry Bryant and Katherine spoke volumes. He may not outwardly comment, but it was clear in his voice that abuse was going to far outweigh adultery.

"Yes, sir, but only toward me. I've never seen him hit one of our children." The sheer weight of everything Katherine Bryant had gone through, whether of her own making or not, seemed to collapse around her pleading vow.

"I am going to grant you your divorce, Katherine, and as I do not believe that someone who will stand before me and my colleagues and knowingly lie and then turn around and either physically or emotionally injure the woman he vowed to love and protect, after stealing money from the very academy where his wife works, is the kind of example that your children need, I am giving full custody of both children to you along with your current residence. Terry, you may see your children every other weekend after you've served your time in Felsink Reformatory, given that an Auxiliary counselor feels you are mentally and emotionally stable enough to be around them."

There was an audible gasp as Katherine Bryant broke down in convulsive sobs of relief on Dean Wilshire's shoulder. Fionna seemed to have to formulate how to force her bottom jaw to meet her upper. Dan wasn't certain how to react, but that certainly hadn't been what he'd expected.

Wilshire seemed as stunned as everyone else in the room, but he did embrace her tenderly and tried to wipe away her tears of relief. Governor Vindico cleared his throat and the room quieted.

"Terry Bryant, you and Mr. Clover, along with both Governor Sherman and Governor Hutchison, are hereby relieved of your positions at Venton Academy. Mr. Bryant, the savings shared between you and Katherine will still be split, so perhaps after your time in Felsink is over— and that will be up to the Senteon to decide—you can access the money to acquire yourself a new home. Do not approach either your wife or your children without an Iodex officer present until you have come back before this court. Prove to us while you're in prison that you'd like to turn your life around."

Dan watched his father's eyes move to Dean Wilshire who was still lovingly embracing his mistress in an open courtroom.

"Dean." Governor Vindico shook his head. "Tell me the truth, and right about now I don't really give a damn whether or not this is admissible as this does not pertain to your punishment, but my daughter-in-law is seated not ten feet away from you and believe me, she will know and she will tell me if you are lying."

Wilshire shook his head though he was still clinging to Katherine Bryant as if she held his next breath. "I'll tell you the truth, Arthur. I certainly owe you that much."

"Yes, you certainly do."

"Did you go along with the blackmail and the money off the top of the Venton books to save your wife embarrassment or to save your job?"

"I told Ellen I wanted a divorce four years ago, but she refused. She couldn't bear the acrimony of the Realm. We've continued to share our home as separately as we were able. I never meant for any of this to happen, Arthur. It is entirely my fault, and I will take whatever sentence I have coming, but please know that I was always trying to save my family from embarrassment and disdain of this Realm. As it turns out, I've only created more for them."

Fionna gave Governor Vindico a solemn nod. Governor Vindico winked at her before he proceeded.

"And what was all of that with the press conference?"

Wilshire's eyes closed in an extended blink. He opened them and stared at Dan's father. "I didn't know who was doing this. I had no idea. But I knew they were brazen and dangerous and willing to go to extreme lengths to get the money they wanted. I was…terrified." He grimaced. "I was terrified you were going to end up being his next victim. I thought if I could somehow make him understand that I would keep paying him, that might keep him from going after you. I tried calling and texting the numbers he'd used to contact me, but they never reached anyone. I used the only way I could think of to contact him—the press. I just needed to know where to send the money to keep him from doing anything to you. Given what happened on campus yesterday morning, I don't believe my fears were unfounded."

Fionna gave the governor another solemn nod. Wilshire was finally telling the truth.

Governor Vindico nodded his acceptance of that. "I suppose on some level I appreciate your effort, but you are hereby fired from Venton Academy. Your savings accounts will be divided between you and Ellen, and your vast retirement funds will go to rectify the Venton books and to cover everything that was stolen from the school that wasn't covered by your donations. Since you received no money from the embezzling and there is enough in your retirement accounts to repay the academy, we have decided that you can return home until your trial. The Senteon will decide if you'll serve time."

Wilshire nodded as he closed his eyes against tears of his own.

"As for you, Mr. Clover, we have decided that you will be held in

Felsink Reformatory pending your trial. The Senteon will also decide your fate," Governor Vindico decreed. "While you are there, I deeply encourage you to talk with the counselors and do the work. Don't continue to make decisions that will land you back in there."

With the slam of the gavel from Governor Haydenshire, it was finally over.

Dan gave his father pleading looks, but the governor was determined. The loss crushed Dan. He couldn't stand it.

Governor Vindico stood before everyone was dismissed. "I have an announcement to make, and as it does result from everything we've discovered in the last few days in regard to this case, I've decided that this is probably the only place to say such a thing." He cleared the emotion from his throat and drew a deep breath.

Dan heard Kara sniffling and saw Fionna wrap her arms around her. They were seated beside Zach, Meredith, Tim, Lindley, and Dan's mother, who was stoic in her gaze at her husband. Dan knew she was furious about his decision, but she was going to stand by him through thick and thin.

"In a school that fell under my care, I allowed an affair between the chancellor and a mentor, a student to become so utterly misguided that he now stands charges of attempted murder among a dozen other things that will inevitably land him in prison for many years to come, drug test swaps to occur, tests to be stolen and sold for profit, and hundreds of thousands of dollars to go missing.

"Although I certainly had no direct hand in any of that, I firmly believe that the buck stops here. Therefore it is with great regret that I am stepping down as a governor of this Realm as of the upcoming election season in September. It has been an honor to serve this Realm for the past thirty years, but this Realm deserves better than I have obviously given."

Dan's head fell in overwhelming regret. The very thing he'd been trying to save for the past five months had been his father's job, and it was the one thing he'd lost.

Fionna's soothing energy moved toward him. She slid onto the bench beside him and laced her fingers through his. His saving grace. His conquering angel. She lifted him once again from the depths. She stepped in and solidly stood beside him in his harrowing regret.

She continued to keep his hand firmly in hers as they stood outside of the Senate behind his parents and with his sisters and their husbands as a solid unit, listening to Governor Vindico repeat his speech to the press.

CHAPTER 62
TO THE FUTURE

Dan signed his name for what felt like the hundredth time that afternoon seated in Becca Strenton's hospital room. Aaron had been taken to the NICU nursery for a thorough checkup, while Patrick Haydenshire passed documents from Dan and Fionna to Jeff and Becca, making the Vindicos' old home the Strentons' new one. Becca looked better than either Dan or Fionna had seen her in months.

The healthy glow of her cheeks and the clarity of the light in her eyes seemed to elate her adoring husband.

An hour later, Dan was heartily shaking Jeff's hand, pleased with the entire transaction.

"Thank you so much!" Becca repeated yet again as she and Fionna hugged.

"You're sure you don't mind if I go tonight?" Jeff asked his wife again as Aaron's incubator was wheeled back into the room so Dan and Fionna could see him.

"No, you should go. We'll be here nursing and sleeping," Becca assured him.

"Oh, that reminds me!" Fionna rushed to her purse and extracted a catalog and order form of products that were going to be displayed at the party at Emily's that evening.

"You can just order anything you want, and it goes through Emily's party hostess. I highly, highly recommend the shaving cream and lotion," she explained as Becca turned the shade of the hot pink vibrator display that was on the cover of the catalog.

Her abashed giggle had Jeff grinning ear to ear.

~

Garrett Haydenshire

"You're sure you want to go to this thing at Em's?" Garrett quizzed Kaimi as he helped Will and Levi shove some of the furniture from his apartment into his parents' barn.

"I'm sure. It'll be fun. I'm excited. I'm kind of glad your mom isn't going to be there. Not that I don't love your mom," she whispered.

Garrett pulled her into his arms for a kiss. They were spending one last night on the farm before they flew to Kauai to make it their permanent residence the next day. This seemed to delight both of his parents.

Will and Levi headed into the house for some water after helping Garrett.

"If I order something that I think looks fun, will you use it with me?" Kaimi was bouncing in her excitement as Garrett shoved another chair into the barn loft.

"Hell yeah, baby." He turned and motioned for her to hop on his back as he made his way into the house that had raised him carrying the girl who had saved him. The one who had brought him back home.

~

Two hours later, Garrett, Rainer, and Logan all fell into seats at the long table set aside for Iodex at Big Mickey's. Dan was already there talking to Jeff and Landon.

Beer glasses were raised at Ramier's urging. "To two of the greatest Iodex officers ever to wear the badge, two of the finest Shields we could ever have served with, who are leaving us for a life of endless sunshine, bikini-clad women, and surf swells, we wish you well, gentlemen. We totally think you sold us out, but what can we say? We'd trade you two in for that package as well."

Everyone laughed as Tuttle stepped in. "To Dan and Garrett. It's been an honor to serve with you," he vowed adamantly.

Dan and Garrett both shook their heads.

Dan stood. "Thank you all for that, but we're also raising a glass to John tonight. I know Elite will miss you. In my time as chief, we couldn't have accomplished much of anything without you. You're one hell of a Shield. Boston is lucky to have you."

Ramier grinned. "I'll miss all of you more than I can ever say, but I won't miss the hours." He laughed. "How about to the future and to better things on the horizon for all of us."

Dan allowed that and drank a long sip from his freezing cold mug. Mickey brought around huge platters of subs and everyone dug in.

Dan reseated himself, and Garrett edged closer to Logan. "Hey, can I ask you something? I need your advice."

"You want my advice?" Logan asked. He appeared dumbfounded.

Garrett chuckled. "Yeah, is that okay?"

"Sure."

"Don't let this go beyond the people sitting right here." He gestured to Dan and Rainer who were the only people within earshot. Logan nodded his understanding. "If you hadn't needed Adeline's dad to testify at her trial, would you have helped her find him?" Garrett's heart thundered in his chest as Logan considered the question.

"If she'd really wanted to, I would have, but I probably would have tried to talk her out of it. As awful as that sounds, her mom was so horrible to her I was a disaster when we went to meet Lucas, because I couldn't stand to think that someone else might hurt her or reject her, you know?"

Garrett nodded adamantly. "Believe me. I know."

"I'm a Shield. I'm *her* Shield. She's more important to me than anything or anyone else, so I went against everything inside of me to find him and introduce them. It was too risky, but I didn't have a choice."

"What's going on?" Dan knew Garrett far too well to have allowed a question of that magnitude to pass at a party without question.

Garrett swallowed down another sip of beer. "You know that Wardlaw guy I had you check on?"

"The guy who's living in LA? The five assaults, armed robberies, two incidents of arson, endless counts of theft, drug and weapon sales, and openly threatening four Iodex officers and two state Senteon representatives guy?"

"Yeah, him." Garrett tossed down the Philly cheesesteak he'd been consuming a moment before.

"He's on numerous watchlists," Dan reminded as Garrett forced a slight nod.

"He's Kaimi's dad." Stunned disbelief rocketed around the table. "She doesn't know. I found some papers when we were cleaning out her grandmother's apartment. I don't know what to do."

"Damn," Logan gasped.

"She's going to be mad if she finds out you knew all of that and never told her," Rainer warned.

"Yeah, but she'll also be alive," Garrett vowed.

~

Dan Vindico

Dan was still reeling from Garrett's confession about Kaimi's father when Jeff took the vacant seat across from him.

"Hey, listen, I just wanted to say thank you again for everything you did for me. I could never have done half of this without you. I'll never be able to repay you, sir, but I wanted to thank you again."

Dan smiled and shook his head. "You earned everything you have, Officer Strenton, by the grit of your teeth. And you listen to me, always go with your gut just like you did yesterday. You're one hell of an officer and a hell of a guy. I'm very proud of you."

"Thanks," Jeff managed in a slightly abashed choke. "We'll send you pictures of Aaron and everything."

"You better, and remember, you're technically over me now. I'll be talking to national pretty often."

"Oh my God, my baby brothers are my bosses. How the hell did that happen?" Garrett feigned disgust as Rainer and Logan laughed.

"Hey, if you and Becca and Aaron might like an island vacation and you can talk Portwood into a little time off, you can come stay on the farm anytime," Dan assured Jeff as everyone quieted down.

"Thank you." Jeff sounded shocked at the invitation.

"Nope, he's never allowed to have vacation," Portwood harassed as he joined the conversation.

CHAPTER 63

HOMESICK

~GARRETT HAYDENSHIRE~

Raw emotion clogged Garrett's throat as he paused to take a moment to run his hand over the cool quilt that hung on the back of the porch swing. He remembered to feel the weight and texture of the kitchen doorknob that he'd turned thousands of times in his life. He remembered to breathe in the scent of his mother's kitchen as he stepped inside—notes of cinnamon, vanilla, rosemary, and a few other herbs Garrett couldn't quite distinguish, mixed with citrus and the faint, familiar scent of Tide laundry detergent. The comforting smell of home filled his lungs, all while strangling his vocal cords with the longing he knew would not only accompany him to Kauai but wouldn't leave him for a long while.

There were a few of his mom's brownies on the cake plate that resided permanently on the corner of the huge island. Garrett was certain his younger siblings had polished off the others. He helped himself to one of the remaining ones and then moved to the fridge to pour himself a glass of milk from the gallon container that was always on the third shelf down right in front. He felt and then forced himself not to consciously acknowledge the need to physically fill himself with his mother's steadfast love as his teeth sank into the walnuts, chocolate chips, cocoa, and tender care.

He doubted everything. For a few selfish moments, he doubted ever agreeing to move to Kauai. He could've talked Kaimi into moving to DC. He could've flown out to see Aida one weekend a month. Recollections of how sick Kaimi was when she was off the island for any length of time took a harsh swipe at his chest.

He shook himself and pacified his mind with lies. He could fly to DC once a month instead. His logical mind told him that wouldn't ever work, but in that moment of weakness he needed desperately to believe that it might.

A million potent memories of Sunday dinners, football games, homemade ice cream, and harassing his brothers flooded his mind and then his shield. It set of its own accord, trying to save him from the emotion he didn't want to feel.

His father entered the kitchen just then. He took in Garrett standing with half a brownie in his mouth, his shield set inside of his own muscles, and red-rimmed eyes both from emotion and exhaustion.

A concerned but knowing frown formed on his features. "Kaimi's not back from your sister's yet. How about after you finish that brownie, we take a walk around the lake for old times' sake?"

Garrett devoured the rest of the delectable confection in one bite and washed it down with the milk. "Thanks, Dad."

"Anytime."

They bundled up, and Garrett followed the governor out the back door. The freezing cold air cleansed a little of the fear and sorrow from his lungs. He tried to feel and remember the dry grass as it compacted under his boots, the sleepy gardens put to bed for the winter, and the sounds of the lake water rippling against the gravel and rocks that surrounded it.

"You know, you're not the only one who's going to be homesick tomorrow," the governor soothed. Garrett's brow furrowed. "It's just not ever quite home unless all of our kids are inside of it."

"We'll come back to visit a lot, I swear." Garrett tried to console his father and himself.

"Phones and planes work both ways. Until you decided to move to Kauai, I couldn't quite rectify this Realm paying for me to have a plane at my disposal. Now, I'm so thankful for it I can't quite believe I was so opposed before. So, we'll come out to visit you a lot, I swear," he quoted.

"Good. I want that." That fact still surprised Garrett, but the longing was as palpable as it was undeniable.

Governor Haydenshire gently placed his hand on Garrett's shoulder, just the way he used to do when Garrett was young and needed a little guidance on which direction to go. He gave him a reassuring squeeze and then released him. "Kaimi told me that Representative Kalakona came out to your honeymoon campsite."

"Yeah." Garrett nodded. "Not sure what was up with that other than her selling Dan and me a bill of goods she's not going to deliver on."

Concern tensed the governor's features. "I'll admit that it struck me as odd that she sought out Daniel the way she did, after what *he* did."

Garrett didn't know what to say to that. He was suddenly desperate for his father to pour out his wisdom on an entirely different topic. "Hey, Dad, can I ask you something?"

"The answer to that question is always yes. You know that."

"When I was helping Kaimi clean out her grandmother's apartment, I found the custody documents where her parents signed over rights to her grandmother. But that wasn't all I found. Her father has a seven-page felony rap sheet. He's violent and...basically a terrible human. Kaimi doesn't know I found any of that. I don't know if I should ever tell her."

"Keeping things from your wife is a recipe for disaster, Garrett."

"I know, but you told me I had to build her a firm foundation. I swear that's all I can even think of. I keep trying to figure out how to do that. It seems to me that showing her all of that, after everything that's happened to her in the last couple of months, isn't going to do anything but hurt her more."

"That won't hurt her as much as it inevitably will when she finds out that you knew and didn't speak up, and she will find that out. You can do both, son. You can use this to prove to her that you'll be there with her no matter what life throws your way."

Garrett nodded his acceptance of that fact. "Just wish I knew *how* to prove that."

The governor nodded. "You don't build a foundation for a relationship the same way you build one for a house." He gestured back to the large farmhouse glowing in the distance. "It's not done in a few days with a couple of concrete trucks. You have to build it brick by brick, working every day. Some of the bricks won't be perfectly shaped either. So you have to work them into something usable before you mortar around them and move on to the next. Do a little each and every day, and sooner than you think you'll have it standing firm. But lying to her, even by omission, isn't going to form anything into a functional shape."

"Okay," Garrett sighed. "I'll tell her after we're in Kauai. I'll show her the papers."

"Good. You can do this, son. I know you can, and if you need any help, your mother and I are only a phone call away." He smiled. "You know, I married an Occamist too, so I might can help you even more than I'm able to help your brothers."

Garrett grinned and nodded. "She's so fucking amazing."

The governor laughed. "Yeah, that's always what I say about your mom, not in those terms per se, but that's always what I mean."

Deciding to take his dad up on some advice while he had the chance and not wanting this walk to be over with maybe ever, he went on with his question. "Okay, what do Occamists need that I haven't thought of yet?"

Governor Haydenshire stared out at the water as they passed the dock. "Room and time to create. But maybe even more than that, room to be able to create and it not turn out quite the way they hoped, and for you to cheer every bit as loud when it doesn't quite turn out as you do when it does." He gave Garrett a soothing grin. "Let her help you with the foundation you need to build, and make sure she knows that you don't want to build anything without her."

CHAPTER 64

THE CALLING OF THE SHIELDS

~DAN VINDICO~

The next afternoon, Dan's world fell back into perfect accord as Aida raced from Malani's hands into his arms at the airport. He lifted her up in the exuberance of his embrace. Fionna cried as Halia reached for her and clung to her mother with ferocity.

Dan could draw breath again. He could plan and make decisions. All of his beautiful girls were in his arms. They were safe and that is all that would ever matter.

That evening, he lay on a quilt on Poipu Beach with Fionna dressed in a bikini top and a sarong. He was feeding her pieces of fruit from the picnic Tutu had packed for everyone. Aida was sticking close by and would only go in the water if Dan or Fionna went with her. She'd been without her parents long enough, and she seemed to require their constant presence. Dan and Fionna tried not to fight over holding Halia who was thoroughly enjoying all of the attention.

She fell asleep, and Fionna reclined in a lounge chair, letting her sleep soundly on her chest as Aida worked on a sandcastle nearby with Kai and Garrett.

Garrett and Dan stood when they heard the specialized tone their phones gave when a low-level alert was issued. Dan brushed the sand from his hands and read the shocking words— Akamai Halemano Wardlaw has purchased a one-way plane ticket via Gifted Air Services Flight 3227 leaving LAX at 10:04 tomorrow morning PST and arriving at Honolulu International Airport at 11:34 AM HST.

"What was that?" Kaimi asked Garrett. She seemed fascinated with whatever his new job was going to require of him.

"Oh, uh,"—he shook his head—"nothing really. We get alerts whenever anyone on any criminal watchlists flies in or out of Hawaii."

Fionna instantly knew he was lying, but Dan gave her a very slight headshake.

He decided to let Garrett Haydenshire call the shots this time.

ABOUT THE AUTHOR

J.E. Neal (aka Jillian) vastly prefers coffee to tea, guac to salsa, the beach over anywhere else, and the world inside her head over the one outside her front door. She also loves not having to choose.

Driven by the question 'what if,' J.E. Neal's world began to manifest. What if there were people with powers the rest of us couldn't see? What if the energy of our world could be summoned and used at their will? Characters with these amazing abilities took shape in her mind. She created—and continues to create—an endless number of stories full of delicious escape from our reality where emotions are visible, desire is palpable, and danger is universal.

Learn more about J.E. Neal at JillianNeal.com

facebook.com/jilliannealauthor
twitter.com/JillianNeal_
instagram.com/jilliannealauthor

ALSO BY J.E. NEAL

TANGLE OF MAGIC

Tangle of Magic Boxed Set (Books 1-6)

Tangle of Lies (Book 1)

Tangle of Chaos (Book 2)

Tangle of Desires (Book 3)

Tangle of Fates (Book 4)

Tangle of Trust (Book 5)

Tangle of Ruin (Book 6)

ENERGY OF MAGIC

Shield and Shattered Cages (Book 1)

Shield and Faltered Steps (Book 2)

Shield and Splintered Oaths (Book 3)

Shield and Humbled Crown (Book 4)

Shield and Vile Serpents (Book 5)

Shield and Coveted Splendor (Book 6)

Shield and Guarded Shadow (Book 7)

Shield and Worthy Sinner (Book 8)

Shield and Sacrificial Heirs (Book 9)